The Truth Commissioner

The Truth Commissioner

DAVID PARK

BLOOMSBURY

First published in Great Britain in 2008

Copyright © 2008 by David Park

The moral right of the author has been asserted

Bloomsbury Publishing Plc,
36 Soho Square,
London W1D 3QY

www.bloomsbury.com

A CIP catalogue record for this book is available from the British Library

ISBN 978 0 7475 9129 0

10 9 8 7 6 5 4 3 2 1

Typeset by Hewer Text UK Ltd, Edinburgh
Printed in Great Britain by Clays Ltd, St Ives plc

The paper this book is printed on is certified by the © 1996 Forest Stewardship
Council A.C. (FSC). It is ancient-forest friendly. The printer holds
FSC chain of custody SGS-COC-2061

FSC
Mixed Sources
Product group from well-managed
forests and other controlled sources

Cert no. SGS-COC-2061
www.fsc.org
© 1996 Forest Stewardship Council

For Alberta, James and Sophie

Now there is at Jerusalem by the sheep market a pool, which is called in the Hebrew tongue Bethesda having five porches.

In these lay a great multitude of impotent folk, of blind, halt, withered, waiting for the moving of the water.

For an angel went down at a certain season into the pool, and troubled the water: whosoever then first after the troubling of the water stepped in was made whole of whatsoever disease he had.

St John 5, 2–4

Beginnings

H E'S NEVER BEEN ANYWHERE he's never been. Apart from the time Fenton took him to see the sea and a couple of other places he can hardly remember, he's only ever been where he's been before. The familiar is what he knows and never willingly strays from, so all his life has been a slow trawl through the safety of his own area where the boundaries are fixed and mind-narrowed into a meshed grid of streets and a couple of roads that only rarely has he followed into the city's centre. When there's a catch it's never spectacular – loose change lifted from a kitchen board or bill money nestling on a mantelpiece behind some brass ornament, once even an old run-around that he kept until the petrol ran out and then torched. Not spectacular but enough to sustain and even nurture a greater ambition. The desire to be someone. That's all he really wants.

So now the journey he's being taken on feels as if he's travelling to the end of the world and he's frightened that he could fall off its unknown, unchartered edge. In the car, wedged tightly between the hard rods of the two men's shoulders and legs, he tries at first to look out of the window, thinking that he needs to memorise it so that he can make his way back the first chance he gets, but as the minutes turn into hours, he gives up and knows that there's no way he can unravel the endless tangle of roads back to their origin. He's more frightened of the distance that he's travelling than the three men in the car even though he knows them to see and what they're part of. He feels like he's drifting slowly out of the world to which he belongs and he thinks of an astronaut he once saw on television doing some repair outside the craft while attached to it by a cable. What happens if the cable snaps? And in the car he feels suddenly weightless, carried away from home and safety by currents he can't resist or even see. He shivers suddenly and one of the men squirms away from him as if frightened of contracting some contagious disease.

They pick up a fourth man who gets into the front seat and stares at him then turns away again. It's a look he's seen before. He knows what it says but this time he doesn't give back defiance and instead drops his eyes to the floor. If someone in the car spoke he might be able to tell what they're thinking and what's going to happen to him, but the only voice belongs to the man who sits in the front passenger seat and gives directions to the driver without moving his head or gesturing, so he's not even sure that the words actually belong to him. When the man on his right takes out a packet of cigarettes and offers them to the others, only the driver, the youngest of the four men, asks for one and it's lit for him and passed into the front. He wants one, too, and he turns his head sideways to look at their owner but he's answered with a mouthful of smoke in his face.

He wants to go home but is scared now to say anything. He tries to think about it. If he says it, he will sound like a child and they'll have no respect for him, but maybe a child is what he needs to be. Maybe that's what will be best for him so if he's young enough they'll take him home where he belongs, deliver him back to his own street like a package in the post. The hazy smoke from the two cigarettes drifts lazily past him and he really wants one. He thinks of asking but doesn't because children don't smoke and then the silence starts to press against him and it feels as if he's drifting in the vastness of space, as if he's been cut off from the mother ship. He has to find something to hold on to so as his fear slimes in his throat and raises the pitch of his voice he says, 'I want to go home.'

The man in the front half turns in his seat and points his finger at him. 'Don't speak,' he says. 'Don't speak until you're told to.' He goes instinctively to answer him, to say something in reply, but the man to his left presses his elbow into his side and it's not done to hurt but to warn him and feeling the fear in that touch, someone else's fear, he falls silent.

They're in the country now and the fields on either side of the car roll in like green waves. It's getting darker and there are no street lights. This is the worst place he's ever been and then the car bounces along a narrow lane where trees lean forward and almost brush the sides with their branches. When they stop in front of a house he's signalled out of the car – he sees already that no one wants to touch him – and when he gets out he looks up at the sky and feels the terror of its arching blackness, its multitude of stars. He's almost glad to be inside the house and then he's sitting in a room with the reassurance of old furniture and, even while his eyes scrutinise it professionally before dismissing it as offering slim pickings, the questions start.

'Why did you do it?'

'I don't know,' he says. 'Honest to God, I don't know.'

His first answer results in a back-handed blow to his face and the slow soft plop of blood from his nose that drips hotly on to his lips but the pain itself is almost cauterised by the sudden shock. Soon after there's a blow to the side of his head that also catches the corner of his eye and ignites a sharp flare of pain. Now he's crying.

'Stop that before you get something to cry about,' the man says and he does what he's told because this man sitting in front of him frightens him more than anyone he's ever known. And it's not because of the sudden, unpredictable flurry of his fists, which is something he understands, but because his eyes say it's personal and he doesn't know how it can be when they've never seen each other before.

'When were you first approached? What did they say to you? How much were you paid? What did you tell them?' It's the same questions, over and over again.

'They said they'd have me killed. That they knew my family and they'd have them done as well,' he says, pretending to cry. 'I hardly told them nothing – I didn't know nothing. I just made up stuff because I was scared. Swear to God I didn't know anything about anything. How could I know anything?'

The questions seem to go on for ever and he answers them all with what they already know and what he thinks they want to hear. He gives them any good reason under the sun and he pleads with practised sincerity so that they might believe him. But he lies to them because he knows it's not the right answer and how can he tell himself, or them, the truth that he did it because just for a while it made him someone? That he liked the meetings with Fenton, that out of nothing, out of nowhere, he found an importance that he savoured as much as anything that had ever happened to him. He thinks of the day Fenton told him they were letting him go, that he was no use any more, of how it was a waste of time and money. Its memory still tastes sour. But he never did it for the money. Honest to God, he never did it for the money.

Sometimes he thinks he never did anything for the money. Even the breaking into houses, even the thieving. Not really for the money. There was something he liked about being in other people's houses, about stepping into someone else's world, touching their things, seeing what they had, how they lived. Sometimes taking things was only his way of justifying to himself what he was doing and the risks he was running. Sometimes, too, he took things that had no value and couldn't be sold, took them just because he liked them and wanted to have them for a while before he threw them away again.

He has to tell everything for the tape recorder and sometimes he gets it wrong and they have to start all over again so it takes a long time. After he thinks it's over he asks, 'Can I go home now?' but there's no answer and he's left alone in the room until someone who wasn't in the car comes and looks at him. The man doesn't speak but puts his fingers under his chin and angles his face as if inspecting it. Then there's shouting from outside, voices arguing, but although he knows it's to do with him he can't hear the words through the locked door. The silence that follows frightens him more than the shouting. He touches his eye socket tenderly with the tips of his fingers – the skin feels swollen and softly misshapen like the burst remnant of a balloon and when he puddles it with his finger it moves and stretches.

As he delicately presses his nose with the back of his hand dark spots of hardened blood the colour of rust drop on to his skin and he quivers them to the floor. He tries to look through the lock of the door but the key on the other side blocks his view. Going to the window he opens the curtains and tries to peer out but all he sees is his own reflection and even though he knows he could switch off the light his fear of the dark prevents him. It's a large, solid window but on top it has two tiny fanlights each not much bigger than a shoe box. It doesn't look possible but the memory of the shouting voices and the silence drives him on so he picks up the chair he's been sitting on and positions it against the glass. It takes him a few seconds to understand how to angle his head but when he's worked it out he knows he can do it. He hesitates, suddenly more frightened of what's outside than what's in the house, then shivering like a swimmer just emerged from the coldness of the sea he slips his head sideways through the narrow space and as his feet squeak the glass he contracts his shoulders and squirms into the opening. It's too small, too tight, but he sleeks and slithers his body like an eel and bit by bit trembles himself through until his head and upper body are outside, and as he lowers his hands to reach the sill, his legs come finally free and without their anchorage he tumbles to the ground.

The world is strange, stranger than he's ever known, and it takes his breath away. He hears his own whimper as he looks up at the white fullness of the moon and the air is scented with smells he doesn't recognise. There's the distant wail of some animal and he presses his back into the comforting solidity of the brickwork but there's no respite because almost immediately he hears a voice shouting in the room behind him and he's no choice but to get to his feet and hurtle further into the unknown. Round the side of the house and across the yard – he suddenly freezes unsure of where to run. There's the grey blur of metal sheds but the terror that they might hold animals propels him forward again down the side of the house and into a field that's full of trees. He knows it's not a forest – the trees are all in straight rows – but doesn't know what its name is. As he runs he hears the voices shouting and the banging of doors. The voices are angry and it makes him run faster, stooping down under the canopy of branches, and sometimes he almost trips as he stumbles over uneven ground and his feet press against hard objects that feel like stones buried in the grass.

He can't run any more – he's never been a good runner – and his chest is swelling with fire so he cuts across the rows and hunkers down behind a tree. There's a smell he thinks he recognises – it's like the brown sweetness of the empty beer bottles stacked at the back of the club – and as his hands pluck nervously at the grass he finds an apple but its flesh is pulpy and rotten and he throws it away in disgust. They have torches, their fuzzy yellow rosettes of light turning this way and that, but one is starting to shine a path steadily towards him.

'I want to go home,' he says as his hand grips the bark of the tree that's unlike anything he has ever touched before. It's uneven and furred and gnarled and feels so alive in his hand that he wants the dead touch of brick, of concrete, of the streets where he belongs, and he says again, 'I want to go home,' and he's never meant anything as much as he means this. He looks at the light getting ever nearer in its swinging arcs and shuts his eyes for a second as if that might make it go away but when he opens them he sees the white-faced plate of a moon set amongst a cold rack of stars and the shadowy shape of his pursuer slowly closing in the dusk.

Henry Stanfield

E VEN NOW, IF SHE were to ask him personally and stand so close that he could drink from the brown depths of her eyes, he might just say yes. But she is already in her diving suit, standing stiffly with the others on the far side of the boat like an Antony Gormley figure cast in black metal. Even in a profession that continues to cling quaintly to the dress of a bygone era, these young men and women look curiously separated from any recognisable reflection of themselves and although he stares at her, the dark brown eyes he savours so much are blanched by the light that falls on her ridiculously enormous goggles. A taste of sickness lingers in his mouth and as each moment goes by Henry Stanfield feels a little more of his dignity being slowly shredded. Hopefully he had found a shielded spot to empty the contents of his stomach as the boat entered a particularly choppy channel just after they had made their way across False Bay. Somehow he had expected the Indian Ocean to be glass smooth and appro-priately perfumed with mystery, but this far out, the incred-ible blue of the water is relentlessly chopped by sizzling, spitting, ridged frets of white and to add to his ever-increas-ing sense of the expedition's inherent ludicrousness, and indeed vulgarity, comes the unwelcome affliction of splayed feet and drunken lurching. To move anywhere takes on the challenge of a steeplechase as he tries to step over the boat's detritus that layers the deck in a mess of buckets, ropes, bits of indeterminate machinery and clothing.

At the end of a three-week fact-finding trip to South Africa, to see what lessons could be gleaned from their experience of a Truth and Reconciliation process, this is not the perfect climax he had envisaged. He had eagerly anticipated, had even started to arrange, an end-of-trip dinner in one of Cape Town's most celebrated east-coast restaurants where they would sit on the edge of what he previously assumed to be an inordinately elegant ocean, eat exotic seafood and he could deliver humorous stories about the workings of the law. Presiding at a long table, cigar and glass of wine in hand, entertaining his newly formed secretariat with a final night of the best of his old favourites, his tried and true repertoire guaranteed to generate laughter. Holding court – that was what he had imagined, not holding on to the side of a rickety old boat captained by someone who looks as if he has modelled himself on Robert Shaw's Quint. The old salt has already rolled up a trouser leg to reveal a white-seamed, sickle-shaped scar that he claims was inflicted by a shark. More likely to have been a drunken late-night tumble from a motor bike or a dockside tangle with fishing gear but amazingly when he invited them to touch it, to trace the supposed teeth marks, Laura had been the first to take up the offer, like some doubting disciple nervously reaching out her hand to feel the stigmata. Then one by one they had all followed suit as this Captain Ahab bristled with pride and the bravado that inflates every one of his barked commands and his barrel-chested rollicking gait as he scuttles from one end of the boat to the other like some scabbed and crusted crab.

The one pleasure he has found in the whole sorry business was momentarily wiping the smug grin off the old sea dog's face when he had presented them with his indemnity forms that supposedly absolved him of any responsibility if anyone was eaten by a shark.

'Thank you, Captain,' he had announced, 'but I think it only fair to inform you that this crew you propose to take out on the high seas is in fact a collection of lawyers, of the finest legal minds. So if you could just give us a chance to peruse this document for a second?' He enjoyed the muffled sniggers of his team, the sudden look of discomfort on Ahab's face, and felt particular pleasure in the laughter he saw crinkling her eyes. 'So the organisers accept no liability for personal injury, loss to property or limbs, accidental bodily damage accruing from intimate contact with any predatory sea creature and in particular a shark.' Then they had read the long list of waivers in a parody of studious legal expertise, each one finding a line to expose to communal laughter until they had milked it dry and agreed that when they got back home they would have one of the documents framed and hung in their offices.

However, the fun of that moment now seemed poor compensation for the realities of the experience unfolding before him. They had always decided that the trip would end in Cape Town where the final three days were to be personal time and in truth it was a suggestion that originated with him. After three weeks of the suffocating, endless meetings with the smugly condescending ANC and their carefully chosen supporters; detailed study of legal documentation and lengthy reports; long pointless journeys on dusty roads to the townships to talk to those who had participated in the Truth and Reconciliation process and the interminable lectures on the need for *ubantu*, the African philosophy of humanism – it had seemed a pleasant prospect to finish with the cooler air of the coast and some well-earned relaxation. Days when he thought there might be opportunities, possibilities of development and even, in his most optimistic and private imaginings, consummation. But things had gone wrong from almost the first day when, as white-bellied and bloated clouds blotched the deep blue of the sky and vanquished the top of the mountain, he found himself no longer leading a team of previously industrious and sober members but a group of high-spirited youngsters let loose on the first day of the summer holidays and suddenly and bitterly he had been confronted with the realities of their age difference and his hopelessly out-of-touch concept of what constituted a good time.

It had begun good-humouredly enough with a competition in the sea-front shops to buy the tackiest shark souvenir and even he had participated, purchasing a bottle opener shaped like open jaws, and close to the beach they had bunkered up at a little bar with a veranda under a makeshift canopy of tarpaulin to compare their purchases. It was a no contest in the end when Simon produced a little plastic toilet from which a shark's head appeared as it was flushed. They had drunk beer from bottles and he felt comfortable enough, still able to enjoy the prospect of shaping the rest of the time available. He had started to imagine that there might be dancing after the meal, started to consider how she might feel in his arms, but the intense pleasure of that was broken when they were approached by a couple of white kids distributing fliers and selling the prospect of cage-diving. If they had been pushing the finest cocaine, or free sex, Stanfield could not have imagined it inducing a more excited reaction and despite his attempted dismissal of the idea, with what he seemingly alone considered a series of witty ripostes about having met enough sharks in court over the years, within a few moments the whole group was entirely sold on the excursion. And then all at once the tables were turned and for the first time he found himself on the receiving end of their collective kickback. So as he listened intently, his smile growing a little thinner by the minute, he heard them tell him that it would be 'the experience of a lifetime', that it was 'the very latest and very best thing', that it was totally safe and there was 'nothing to be frightened of'. This imputation of fear sees the final trace of his smile fade and forces him into some heavy-handed and embarrassingly pathetic references to his responsibility for collective safety, and a series of rhetorical questions about how it would look if he were to lose one of the working party to a shark. As his words tumble inelegantly out he knows he sounds like a parent of unruly children, or a teacher admonishing his wayward charges, and in desperation he tries to save the day by conjuring facetious newspaper headlines that announce something about a shark eating a shark, but he can't quite find the killer one he's looking for and so in full retreat he holds his hands in the air and surrenders.

There are times like this when the sad reality that he is of a different generation impinges sharply on his consciousness, reminding him that he is in fact more than old enough to be the father of most of them. It's not just in their clothes and in particular their predisposition to wear multi-pocketed trousers with more zips and buttons than a mechanic's boiler suit; their incessant texting on mobile phones that are also constantly brandished in the air like badges of honour to take some photograph; it's not even their laptops and iPods and their curiously innocent embrace of technology like children who have found Hornby train sets under the Christmas tree. It's in their use of language that he feels it most, the way when they are excited they revert to a minimalist vocabulary that spins on a few self-consciously faux and wearisomely trite examples of adjectival slang, the way they never speak in complete sentences but use a kind of shorthand that appears to serve them admirably in the delivery of both facts and emotions. Every utterance seems to take a short cut, to be bereft of pleasure or style, and he supposes that is why they prefer to get in a steel-framed cage and be lowered in the ocean to get a close-up view of a shark than engage in the more civilised and demanding art of conversation over a meal. He feels a sense of superior sympathy for them as he considers their insatiable need for thrill, thrills of the most base and vulgar types that speak only of an absence of human intelligence and appreciation of life. It's the genera-tion of the bungee jump, bouncing feverishly up and down on an ever-diminishing return, the generation of ecstasy tablets, of the binge. If he were truly their teacher he would gather them round and try to explain that all his days he has known what it is to be thrilled, show them how to find pleasure in the warmth of that sun-ripened grape that stirs the wine into life – the slow sweet burst of the cluster on the tongue; the aria, the requiem that takes you to the very edge of your own mortality; and above all, far beyond everything else, the thrill of a woman's body you touch for the first time. Nothing is better than that first moment and so it fills him with regret that in relation to Laura this pleasure is, even superficially, the prerogative of someone else. She wears his engagement ring on her finger and every time it sparkles in the light it sends a shard to his heart that she has given herself to a rugby-playing buffoon in property development who knows the cost of everything and the value of nothing, someone who splashes his money on fripperies, each more vulgar than the next, and who seems to spend so much of his life on a sports field or golf course that he wonders what time is left him to give his adoration to the woman of whom he is clearly unworthy. Stanfield wonders if he has ever seen the beauty of her eyes with the same clarity of vision that transfigures him every time he meets their gaze.

There is still time to change his mind and clamber into one of the suits, ignoring the fact that it will parade his paunch, that he will feel reduced to a common level, but if she were to make her way towards him and lead him by the hand he would undoubtedly follow. However, he knows that it's already too late – he isn't sure if it's to save face or lose it – because she stands with her back to him, one of the group of tar babies who melt seamlessly into each other and whose excited preoccupation acts as a barrier to any interloper. The boat's engines are cut and the vessel rocks gently in the shifting cradle of the waves but sometimes, as if at the receiving end of a more forceful hand, it dips deeper before rising again. He assumes that they are anchored in the preposterously named Shark Alley and that soon it will be time for the charade to commence. Two of Ahab's crew carry a sawn-off oil drum and tip its contents over the side. His stomach churns again as he watches a crimson mix of gore and blood stream into the sea, its stain steaming through the water. Without knowing why he thinks of Macbeth's bloody hands and his words about turning the ocean incarnadine. He feels that there is something intensely primitive about what he's watching, something redolent of the amphitheatre and barbarous games. At least the modern hunt wraps itself in some aesthetically pleasing rituals and Stanfield feels a surge of resentment against her for her participation, for a second wills her to have too close an encounter, be confronted by the vulgar recklessness of it all. Let her be shaken. Let her need something solid to lean against. Let her have the humility to acknowledge that he was right and then lift her tear-stained eyes towards him for the comfort he will know how to give.

But his reverie is shattered by the high cries of excitement as they catch the first sighting. They're pointing, squealing, cameras held aloft like silver-headed flowers seeding light, and despite himself he crosses to where they've seen it, rubbing the back of his hand across his mouth in an attempt to erase the sourness. There are two: a kind of galvanised blue-grey colour, smooth stretched skin like wet plastic, bigger than he had anticipated and sleek in the water as if moving in the slipstream of their own silent arrogance. One comes close, a sudden disdainful shadow, perhaps a metre under the surface and then for a second brindled and striped by parabolas of light. The other has gore in its mouth as with a quiver of its tail it shakes blood through the water like exploding dye, its jaws shaking the find the way a terrier might shake a rat. He feels his own heart beat a little faster and directs scorn at himself before shouting a quip to the spectators, but it gets lost in the breaking wave of hysteria and then as cylinders are strapped to backs and the steel cage is hoisted into place, he finds himself in the way and so he makes his unsteady path to a new vantage point.

Afterwards he is struck most by how their paucity of language leaves them unable to communicate what they have seen. The words tumble out in broken, incoherent fragments until eventually they are reduced to single words and the air quivers like a single plucked string with shouts of 'unbelievable', 'wow', 'cool' and, perhaps the most popular, 'wicked'. There is a great deal of hugging and high-fiving to which he is not party and when Laura has changed and rushes up to tell him what it was like he avoids looking into her eyes and listens with as much indifference as her excitement will fail to register. When she has finished he nods and smiles, asks her if she likes dancing, but in all the rush of noise she doesn't hear his question and turns her head away before he can repeat it. Then she pats him on the arm and once again he has to endure the skirmish of light in the rosette of her ring. He watches her return to the backslapping crew of her colleagues whose friendship, now strengthened by shared experience, constructs an exclusion zone round them and feeling his new isolation more keenly than ever he takes himself to the stern of the boat and hunkers down on an upturned crate. The rising spray-ladened wind moistens his face and, as the engine starts up, he watches the sea churn and choke itself on funnels of white foam. He wonders how the sharks feel having had a close experience with the human representatives of the law, of truth and reconciliation. Do they now share their excitement and describe it as 'wicked' or 'cool'? Do they even possess the curse of memory at all? He tries to contain his spreading anger by telling himself that with a little creativity it will shape itself into a good story, that he will be able to mine a rich vein of laughter. Already he constructs a comic portrait of Captain Ahab, searches for a punchline that will send the story spinning into folklore. Of course he will have to reinvent his own role, airbrush the inconvenient parts that go against the flow, but it's what artists do and above all he is an artist. The screeches and laughter of his team rise up unabated: he cringes as he thinks how often he will have to endure a full-bodied reprise of it all on the homeward journey but then as the boat veers slowly to shore, he comforts himself with the warming thought that he might be able to work the return flight so that she sits beside him. Then the salted bitterness of the air is rendered a little sweeter by the conjured image of her resting her head on his shoulder and as she slips into sleep he imagines the warmth of her breath on his cheek, the way her mouth will be opened slightly and raised towards him like a child's.

And more than anything they are children, bright-eyed with idealism and the belief that the report they will present in a month's time will illuminate the way forward, that they will have played an important part in constructing the way out of the morass, in building a new bridge to healing and forgiveness. So how would they feel if he were to tell them now that it's all been for the optics, that what will happen and how it will happen has already been agreed, mapped out, and the fixity of the main boundaries established like every continent after every war? A few small disputed areas still exist that might be left as neutral or placed under joint administration but by and large it's a done deal. So perhaps it was not such a bad thing that they have had their compensatory fun, their day in the sun, even the obligatory ritual of a visit to Robben Island where they were given a tour guided by an ex-prisoner. Afterwards they had a group photograph taken in the entrance to the prison, under the sign which reads: 'We serve with pride.'

A snow cloud of petrels flakes thickly around the boat, hovering as if frozen on the layered air before free-falling. He watches and envies the effortless grace of their flight, their balletic eloquence, and then his eye catches something further off. Too big to be anything else. He doesn't want to admit it at first and then he starts to laugh. He looks around for someone to share the joke with but there's no one close enough to hear his voice, so when he speaks, the words are for himself:

> ' "God save thee, ancient Mariner!
> From the fiends that plague thee thus! –
> Why look'st thou so?" – With my cross-bow
> I shot the Albatross.'

It can't be anything else. Nothing has that wingspan. The joke is delicious and he feels a rich syrupy laughter lace and warm his throat like the sweet burn of whiskey. It's an albatross – unbelievably it's an albatross! He suddenly shivers. Who is he? The Ancient Mariner? A bleached-boned and weary Poseidon? Samson with his locks shorn? He savours the self-mockery and each one fixes the bitterness of his smile deeper in the frozen mask of his face. An albatross! He holds his face up to the white-mottled wrap of sky as a ragged laugh breaks free and he shouts the word 'Wicked!' to the falling flakes of petrels that spangle the salted air.

If he is honest with himself, and there are occasions when he admits the painful benefits of such moments, then he has to admit that it was the job's title that first prompted his acceptance. 'Truth Commissioner' has a nice ring to it and its accompanying salary is almost as generous in its scope. Also in momentary truth, his career in recent years has stalled a little, diverted into the dull-as-dishwater and hopelessly technical sidings of railway-disaster inquiries, or arcane and never-ending reviews of contentious anti-terror legislation. Having moved from what he found to be an increasingly moribund and emotionally stultifying stint at the Bar, to do some work at the International Court and experience the pleasures of a cultured European city, he has continued to live comfortably off his two books on human rights and the law. A couple of years' lecturing proved rather intoxicating – all those beautiful young women diving for the showered pearls of his words – but rather like an alcoholic working in a liquor store, he knew it was not the most prudent of places to see out his days and so when the opportunity came to be involved in investigations into human-rights abuses in various parts of the world's cesspits, he grabbed it with both hands. The Balkan business secured his international reputation and no doubt placed him on the short list for similar job offers. However, he was genuinely surprised to be invited personally by the Prime Minister to this present post, one of six on offer, and despite his best cynicism found himself unexpectedly susceptible to that chummy telephone flattery. An Irish Catholic mother and an English Protestant father allow him to straddle both tribes and, despite spending the first twelve years of his life in a leafy suburb of Belfast, he has no personal or political baggage to be unpacked by either side. Not even any meaningful or sharp memories to prick him towards anything as strong as a prejudice.

The job title has a magisterial ring to it but also a rather totalitarian, industrial edge and he enjoys this juxtaposition of ideas. But what he enjoys most is thinking of the book that will surely come out of it and already he's batting ideas around for the title – *The Whole Truth . . . Nothing but the Truth . . .* perhaps even *The Freedom of Truth.* He dismisses them all as too hackneyed and obvious, like Perry Mason potboilers. As yet he is undecided on the book's genre and it's possible that he might include autobiographical material, give accounts of some of the phases of his career including the most dramatic parts of his human-rights work. He toys with the idea of eschewing a dry academic work and writing for a more populist market, imagines readings at literary festivals in sleepy English towns in marquees garlanded by delicate braids of sunlight.

There is another reason, of course, that prompted his acceptance but there's a limit to how far truth can be allowed to journey so he's not quite prepared to admit, even to himself, that having a daughter living in the North might also have been a significant factor. A daughter called Emma whom he hasn't seen for five years. A curious coincidence, he tells himself instead, the type of coincidence that life inevitably throws up. That's all.

The one thing, however, he knows is that whatever rewards accrue as a result of his acceptance, he will have earned them, not least the fact that he will spend the next two years living in a city that he considers much the same way as he might think of a piece of dirt that he hoped he had shaken off his shoe. It's true that they've given him a rather luxurious apartment overlooking the river and sought to accommodate every possible requirement, and it's also true that he's only an hour's flight away from his London home and Hampstead Heath, but the thought of the actual job precludes any wild surge of pleasure. Still, there is the young team that has been assembled to service the process and of course, and not least, the lovely brown-eyed Laura whose faltering interview required a rather large helping hand before the post was hers. Still, in comparison to the demands of some of his fellow commissioners, it was a small price for them to pay. He thinks with disdain of the Finnish commissioner, the squat little barrel of a woman with truncated legs whose two preposterous poodles have been allowed to sidestep the laws of quarantine; of the obligatory South African judge who seems to have ensconced a veritable tribe of relations in a most desirable residence in the very heart of Hillsborough.

He wishes it were Laura who stood beside him now and not Beckett who stands his customary ten feet away, the nothing-to-say, red-haired Beckett who has been appointed by the PSNI as his protection officer and driver. Beckett in his grey Marks and Spencer's suit and shiny shoes, who is silent as a Trappist monk. The early-morning air is cold and edged by a razor wind that cuts at the cheekbones and pinches the eyes into narrow slits. It's always good to show willing but he wonders why his presence was deemed necessary – something no doubt to do with the constantly reiterated and linchpin word 'transparency'. It's impossible to speak to those in authority without hearing it drip from their tongues like honey, usually coupled with some vacuous statement about the 'integrity of the process'. Transparency and integrity – words no doubt that help the user feel ennobled and elevated to a higher plane than his listeners.

So what he is now watching is supposed to be the practical implementation of these concepts and as the first security vans and police vehicles begin to wind their way through the harbour estate he pulls up the collar of his overcoat. Elliot, Simon and Matteo stand at the door of the shipyard's old and long-defunct drawing office ready to receive the first delivery, the identification badges in their lapels and the metal clips on their boards blinking weakly with reflected winter light. Behind them stands a phalanx of clerical assistants and members of the private security firm who have won the public tender for the work. He has already been given an inspection tour of the building's restoration and refurbishment, observed the high-tech security system – clearly not the one used by the Northern Bank – with the infra-red scans and bar codes, the palm-print identification, the heating and humidity controls, the computer terminals and the internal and external security cameras. He has seen the certificate from the pest-control company stating that the final rodent has been irrevocably exterminated from the environs. So here, where in a former age under the vaulted ceiling the plans of great White Star ocean liners were drawn, stretch rows of metal tables, partitioned and numbered, and above and around them purrs the steady hum of electricity and an expectant readiness.

On his own he has already toured the area and found it freakishly attractive, a bit like visiting some windswept tundra of history where each year leeches off another little bit of what must have been, leaving only the silted dry docks and the swathes of cracked concrete from which sprouts every type of wild flower. Leaving, above all, the infinite desolate sense of space emptied of whatever begat it. A few of the flowers he looked at bore no resemblance to any that he had ever seen, as if they were phantom mutations of raw metal, sparked into life by some long-dead welder's fiery fantail, their filaments as if iron: their stamens the shred of steel. When he arrived there had been no sunlight and the waters of Belfast Lough and the sky had met in a seamless meld of grey. Now the river has weakened and the sky lifts itself a little higher and tries to imprint the water's surface with a new pattern but it resists and seems to hug its own coldness. The lurid yellow of the enormous cranes strikes an attempt at defiance but they look like nothing so much as giant hurdles waiting for a Finn McCool to jump them.

And already they are talking of restoring this place in the city's favourite passion of self-consoling mythology. It will, no doubt, be a giant theme park where they will build a facsimile of the great ship, construct hotels and exhibitions, hope to bring in the tourists from Japan, from America, from everywhere, for an exclusively virtual experience. It saddens Stanfield to think of the vulgarity that will be unleashed, the way he imagines this place will become the equivalent of some casino town in the Nevada desert. There is one memory from his childhood that he suddenly recalls and it's being in his father's car on the other side of the river and following an open grain lorry, pigeons swooping on it. The sour sweet smell of the grain. Swinging around across the bridge and more birds. Great shifting parabolas of starlings shading the

22

sky in charcoal. It must have been at the end of the afternoon for suddenly the bridge itself is black with the released shipyard workers, lunch boxes in their hands, heels clacking, voices calling like the boys selling newspapers on street corners.

The curse of memory. Scabs on the soul. Even with most of his life behind him he thinks only of the future, of what can still be savoured. Of what experiences still await. He looks across the water and smiles. Nothing amuses him quite so much as the city's gauche attempts to reinvent itself as a cosmopolis, nothing makes him smile more genuinely than to see its newest makeover. So on the other side of the river, in front of the wasteland of book depositories, tyre depots and warehouses, and on the water's edge, sit some of the city's more recent buildings, styled with features that echo Venetian palazzos but look as if they have been constructed out of a child's building set. Behind him Beckett coughs and he remembers his driver doesn't have the benefit of a coat as he turns to look at him. Beckett's face has reddened in the wind as if worn raw and his hair is a sudden flash of colour as if a match has been struck in the greyness of the morning.

'It's cold,' Stanfield says, 'we'll drive back round and watch the arrivals.' Beckett doesn't answer but simply nods and holds the door open for him to get into the back of the car. Stanfield notices the broad wedding ring on his finger but in the car he can't be bothered to attempt further conversation.

The arrivals are in full flow now with the files and papers being carried into the building where they will be catalogued and stamped with their delivery date. Some come in file boxes but most are in manila or green folders tied with string. A few have clearly been rehoused inside new covers but most wear the marks of their age and use and are badged with grubbiness – the circles of cups, the scribble of ballpoint, the greased or sweated fingerprints of those who perused them. Some of them bulge at the seams and corners of papers loll like tongues out of mouths. Some are carried inside plastic bags – the type used to remove evidence from crime scenes. He feels a desultory randomness about it all, a sense of fragmentation that bodes badly for those charged with putting it all together, for those whose job is supposed to be to shape it into meaning.

One of the policemen stumbles and a file is spilt to the ground. There is a communal gasp as if they are watching an urn spill its ashes and, as the first pages flutter into the air, rushing hands grasp for the escaping paper. One evades the frantic clutches and mischievously scampers momentarily above head height before wallowing slowly to earth and grateful capture. 'Gentlemen, careful please!' Matteo's authoritative voice rings out as he steps forward with his arms outstretched, shepherding the deliveries to the door. Stanfield silently congratulates him – it's always good to see someone exercise authority and he believes that it's what marks the led from the leader. There are always those who despite their abilities don't have what it takes when the testing moment comes, who, in the mysterious vocabulary of the young, don't have 'bottle'. He commends himself for the leadership he has already shown in demanding, upon the entirely genuine threat of resignation, that all files and case notes be removed from their diverse locations and centrally stored under the Commission's independent protection. After a third file mysteriously, and no doubt conveniently for those charged with its protection, went missing, it was obvious that immediate action had to be taken. Faced with the full welter of reluctance and obstruction from the local apparatchiks, he led the entire team of commissioners to the

Prime Minister's door and, with the prospect of an international embarrassment, the demand was finally granted.

So now on a grey Belfast morning they are gathered in, brought to this place in guarded convoy from secret prearranged rendezvous. All of them, dating from over three decades, even including those whose families have declined to take part in the process. Over a quarter fall into this category, some because they have already buried the past and choose not to relive it, some because they prefer not to have made public aspects of their particular case, and inevitably others from both sides who denounce it as a whitewash, a conspiracy. He has even met a few individuals already who have clearly become emotionally dependent on their grief, who have jerry-built a kind of lop-sided, self-pitying life out of it and are unwilling to risk having even that taken from them, in exchange for their day in the sun. Good on them, he thinks, because he has no wish to extend his tenure any further than necessary.

He looks at the faces of those standing outside the drawing office. The wind has whipped their cheeks so that they look as if they bear thin tribal incisions cut in their flesh. And after all, what was it really, except some rather pathetic and primitive tribal war where only the replacement of traditional weapons by Semtex and the rest succeeded in bringing it to temporary attention on a bigger stage? Now the world doesn't care any more because there are bigger wars and better terrors and all that remains is this final tidying up, this drawing a line, this putting to bed – the euphemisms he has had to endure are potentially endless – but as he takes one final look at the sealed tightness of the sky and then tells Beckett to drive him to the office, there is only one image that he nurtures and it's of an old manged, flea-infested dog returning to inspect its own sick.

*   *   *

'Everything go OK?' Laura asks him as he removes his coat.

'Everything went fine apart from one of the files being dropped and almost blowing into the Lough.' She isn't sure whether it's appropriate to laugh until she sees him smiling. 'Matteo's keeping a good watch on things. Another hour or so and everything should be in place. Any chance of a coffee? It was very cold down there.'

'Sure,' she says.

'And, Laura, get one for yourself and then we'll go through today's meetings.' He watches her leave the room. She's wearing a blue trouser suit with a short bolero-type jacket and a pink silk scarf at her neck. He wonders if her Neanderthal fiancé has been biting it. For the first time he notices the slight swell of her hips. Hips that will shell children like peas. He looks again at his mobile but as always there's no call from Emma and he's a little cross with himself that he continues to divert valuable emotional energy from his own needs, that he continues with this charade of unacknowledged birthday and Christmas cards. If she doesn't want to be his daughter, he should accept that, respect her decision. He tells himself that life goes on, that perhaps it's better in the long run to live unencumbered, that travelling lightly gives him the freedom he needs.

He would rather Laura could find a cup and saucer to serve his coffee in, instead of a mug with a ridiculous slogan, but accepts it politely. She sits on the other side of his desk and when she takes her first sip from her mug leaves a little smudge of lipstick on the rim. There's something already about her that begins to disappoint him a little.

'So who's first up?' he asks, already knowing the answer.

'It's Connor Walshe's mother and sister.'

'Right, and you'll take notes?'

'Yes. Do you want tea and biscuits?'

'No, I think we'll forgo that, so many to get through today. We don't want anyone to stay longer than they need to or we'll end up with a backlog.' He watches her nod and studies her face as she tilts it upwards. She's wearing a little too much make-up and it puddles on her cheekbones but her eyes are bright and – he can think of no other word than sparkly. Sparkly like the ring on her finger. But he is always the optimist and he has not quite yet given up all hope. Who knows what working closely together in emotionally intense circumstances for an extended period might bring?

'So you've read the file?' he asks her.

'Yes, and I think it was the right decision to deal with the disappeared first of all. They've had to wait so long for answers.'

'Yes, I'm sure it was,' he says, savouring her approbation. 'Only right, only right. But of course we have no absolute guarantees that the necessary answers will be forthcoming.'

'What can be gained now by withholding the truth?'

For a second he thinks of trying to explain that the truth is rarely a case of what will be gained, so much as a case of what might be lost, but the phone rings and a secretary tells him that the Walshes have arrived.

'They're early but that's no matter. Will you meet them and bring them to the chamber?' He watches her leave before turning his eyes to the file on his desk. Its contents make him nervous because the possibilities are so starkly flagged and coming so early in the process it has the potential to be portrayed as a symbolic success or a failure that will throw a long shadow over the Commission's credibility. He needs a body. Simple as that. Other types of cases can be fudged, blurred at the edges, but this one, like all those of the disappeared, requires an entirely tangible outcome and he's not convinced as yet that he can pull it off. Still, if he succeeds it will be a real feather in the cap and preclude any of the other commissioners stealing an early advantage. It's a risk he has no choice but to take.

With the file under his arm, he walks down the long corridor of the city-centre building that was formerly Church property, past the leaded windows and into the large chamber room which at its far end also contains two large windows. The stained-glass portrayals of Christ walking across the storm-tossed sea towards the terrified disciples and healing the blind man are abstract enough to be considered art rather than religious proselytising. They were also protected by a preservation order so they had to stay but everything else in the room has been neutralised with walls and ceiling painted in creams and whites and a new concealed lighting system introduced. The specially commissioned desks and chairs are made from a light-coloured ash and there's a new sound system and facilities for translation into Irish and Ulster Scots if required.

He sits at one of the smaller side tables and opens the file. Its grubbiness contrasts with the pristine surroundings. Part of him feels repelled by what he has to touch, worried by what viral strains and spores might linger in the bruised patina of the pages, and he wonders, in private at least, if he should wear gloves. He tells himself that it could be seen as the reverence that scholars display when they study venerable and valuable manuscripts in museums but, as he ponders this, the door opens and Laura leads two women into the room. It's clearly mother and daughter, the mother holding nervously to the younger woman's elbow. He welcomes nervousness, finds it so much more malleable than anger or aggression. The size of the room alone will intimidate them and as he stands to greet them, he launches into the agreed protocol, but allowing himself to show his disregard for templates by embellishing the given one with his own personal style.

'I'm very pleased to meet you,' he says. 'It's very good of you to come. Please take a seat.' The older woman reciprocates by nodding her head but the younger one sits impassively, staring intently at his face. He senses something in her unrelenting gaze that makes him a little uneasy but she says nothing as he launches into his explanation of the process, then outlines the people who will be called and how they will be questioned, about their entitlement to free legal advice, about their right to counselling, about whether to have the press present or exclude them. As he talks, Stanfield looks at the younger woman who he already gauges is the dominant of the two and tries to weigh her up. She is about forty, not unattractive in a plain sort of way, with narrowed blue eyes that seem fastened on his face and thick black hair pulled back too severely in a clasp. He glances at the mother occasionally as a kind of relief but when he looks back, her daughter's gaze is unwavering and gradually his words fade into an inconclusive silence. It's as if she knows him from somewhere else, that she's met him before. He looks at Laura and she smiles reassuringly back but before he can continue, Mrs Walshe speaks.

'All we want is Connor back so we can bury him,' she says and her voice is a deferential whisper. She clutches her daughter's hand and doesn't look at him as she speaks. 'We just want him home so we can put him to rest. That's all we want. We don't want any trouble; we just want him home where he belongs.'

'Of course, of course,' he says. 'It's been a terrible experience for you.'

'They told us that he was gone away, that he was living in Dublin or England, but we don't believe it. Connor didn't know how to live anywhere other than here and if he was alive he would've got in touch with us. A phone call or a letter – he would've sent us something.'

'And you've heard nothing in all this time?'

'Nothing: not a single word.' She dabs at her eyes with a paper handkerchief and then stares at her hands. They are thin-fingered and blue veins already push against the shiny tightness of the skin. Prematurely old hands. The rings look as if they've been bolted on. She looks much older than her age. He thinks that perhaps the tea would have been a useful distraction, a counterbalance to the unsettling pull of grief.

'And you're happy with the list of people we've called?' he asks, studying the list of names drawn up by the secretariat.

'No, we're not.'

The voice is strong, sure, and when he looks at her she meets his eyes defiantly. She has let go of her mother's hand and sits straight on the chair.

'You're not happy, Miss . . .' He searches for her name in his papers.

'Mrs Harper,' Laura tells him.

'Please, Maria – we don't want any trouble. We just want Connor back, we're not looking for trouble.' Then turning to him the mother says, 'The rest of the family don't want us to go through with this – the oldest boys especially. They say we're just stirring up more trouble for ourselves.'

'Why are you stirring up trouble?' he asks.

'Because of what they said about Connor. They don't want it all brought up again in public.'

'It would be best if all the family were of a single purpose in this. Experience elsewhere tells us this. But you want to go ahead?'

'What other way are we going to get the truth? What other

way are we going to get him back? But I don't want any trouble.'

'Mum, this is the only way to get him back. I've explained it all before. We've been through it a dozen times.' Her voice is edged with frustration and when Stanfield looks at her he sees her blue eyes are fired with an intensity that makes him nervous. It's something he's seen at different times in women's eyes and never has it been the harbinger of anything that was good for him. It's the fire that burns when they have fled like refugees into some different country, a landscape contoured mostly by bitter anger and loathing as they finally realise whatever they have decided is the truth of him. In this limbo world he knows they have journeyed beyond the reach of any enticement, that they have had a surfeit of whatever future it was they thought he could give them. He saw it in Martine's eyes in the moments after she had received the final diagnosis and the unbearably young doctor's awkward benediction of sympathy. In the car afterwards as she sat in unbreachable silence, he felt it was him, rather than her illness, that she reserved most hatred for. And what was the cause? That he should carry on living when she was going to die, that she deserved life more than him? That for all his infidelities, his selfish trespasses of the flesh, she was going to be the one to be punished? That must have been the moment when the seed was sown and afterwards behind the closed bedroom door when she and Emma shut him out to share their private grief, the moment when their daughter came to the belief that somehow his sins had the miraculous power to grow an insatiable malignant tumour.

'So, Mrs . . .'

'Mrs Harper,' Laura tells him.

'So, Mrs Harper, you're not happy with the list of people called?'

'Maria, please,' Mrs Walshe says.

'There's no other way – I've explained it. You know there's no other way.'

'We just want him back. We don't want any trouble.'

'I know your daughter, Mr Stanfield,' she says, not looking at her mother.

Stanfield stares at her but her face betrays no clue as to the import of her words. He searches her unbroken expression but beyond the intensity of her eyes is unable to distinguish what she hopes to achieve if anything. Is it a threat, or some kind of leverage? Is it an indication that she knows from her what sort of person she claims he is?

'Emma?' he says, unsure of where he's heading.

'I work in the same school.'

'You teach with her?'

'I'm her classroom assistant.'

'Right . . .'

'But as you know she's off now – on maternity leave.'

He doesn't know but acts as if he does, staring at the papers in front of him, trying to keep his focus and not betray any of the confusions that spring around his head.

'A terrible thing to lose your child,' Mrs Walshe says and her words make him physically start. 'No one knows the pain but those who've been through it.' He looks at her daughter but there's no change in her expression or any sign of connection with the words.

'It must be very painful,' he says, lifting his eyes to the back of the room. 'Listen, why don't you go home and talk to your family, think it over, decide if you want to go ahead?'

'We want to go ahead. We want the truth,' the daughter says, opening her handbag and taking out a letter.

'OK, if that's what you want. But you said you weren't happy with the list of those to be called . . .'

'I've written it down, explained it all. The name's here.' But she makes no effort to hand over the letter, the envelope whiter against the blackness of her coat.

'Are you sure, Maria?' her mother asks and in wordless answer the younger woman stretches out her hand towards him offering the letter.

As he takes it, just for a second, it feels like the letter from his daughter that five years' separation has failed to bring and in his hand it feels suddenly fragile. He sets it on top of the folder, holding its ends with both hands. His name is on the front. He can't remember how his daughter's handwriting looks.

'We'll not take any more of your time,' the daughter says as she stands and signals to her mother. 'I want you to read the letter. Everything we have to say is written there.'

'We'll be in touch very shortly,' he says but staying in his seat. 'Laura, could you show Mrs Walshe and Mrs Harper out?' He watches them make their way to the doors, the sound of their feet echoing in the vaulted silence of the room, then stares at the envelope. What is it he would like it to say? That she doesn't hate him, that she understands he loved Martine in his own way, his own imperfect way, but he never sought to hurt or humiliate her? That she wishes things had been different? He tries again to remember what her handwriting looks like but it blurs into uncertainty. Could he ever persuade her that to love many – and he tries to convince himself that it was love he always felt – doesn't mean that he had less love for them both? It's important for him to think of it as love because otherwise they were only the sordid satisfactions of the self and he can't bring himself to believe that. True, there was always desire, the stirrings of the flesh, but he tells himself its origins were always in his head, in his capacity for the adoration and worship of beauty.

33

His daughter is going to have a child of her own. He is uncharacteristically confused about what it is he feels. Holding the unopened envelope in his hands he feels first a perverse pleasure that some day she, too, will feel what it is to be judged and found wanting. It is the prerogative of all children to turn the coldness of their critical gaze on the flaws of their parents. No one can survive it unscathed, he tells himself. But then the momentary pleasure is replaced by a sense of how much further she has travelled beyond him. A child will take her to a different place, perhaps carry her irrevocably beyond his reach or any future need of it. And a child, too, that he might never see. He doesn't know how he feels about the unborn child but as Laura returns to the room he doesn't turn his gaze towards her walking towards him because he is suddenly frightened that what she will see looking at her is an old man.

'Interesting,' she says, standing on the other side of the desk. 'You haven't opened the letter yet?'

'No,' he says, 'not yet.'

'Congratulations.'

'Congratulations?'

'You're going to be a grandfather.'

He looks up at her and for the first time takes no pleasure in her smile then slowly opens the envelope.

He is unsure if he should say anything to Beckett or not. It's none of his business and he doesn't give Stanfield the impression that he'd thank him for sharing anything remotely personal, so at first he just gives him the address and asks him to drive him there. It's about twenty-five minutes outside Belfast in a tidy town where the rural indigenous population and middle-class commuters cosily coalesce. When Beckett asks him if he knows where the address is exactly, he has to say that he doesn't and so they have to stop and enquire in a garage. It's a five-minute drive from the town's main street and as he feels a rising flush of nervousness he tries to distract himself with conversation.

'Do you have children?' he asks.

'Two,' Beckett says. 'Two girls.'

'What age?'

'The oldest is nine, the other six.'

Stanfield feels as if he is cross-examining a defendant determined not to give anything away. On either side of the road are developments of new houses, all depressingly similar. 'What are their names?'

'Flora and Fiona. Their mother's Scottish.'

He searches the houses in the Close looking for clues that might distinguish his daughter's home but then realises that he has no idea what he's looking for and his nervousness is beginning to rattle against the hollow opening inside him. A terrible thing to be frightened about seeing your own child. It'll be the first time in five years, five years in which she has acquired a husband whom he has never met, a teaching job he knows nothing about and now a baby about to be born. A stubborn child always and his frequent absences during her adolescence helped separate them from whatever intimacy is supposed to exist between father and daughter and forged the bond tighter with her mother.

Beckett glances at him in his mirror looking to see where he wants him to stop. It's difficult to see the numbers in the dark. Will she even see him, let him through the door? He catches a number and then works out that it's two houses along. 'Just here,' he says as if he always knew it. It's a small, detached bungalow with white walls and a tiny square of front lawn open to the road. In the driveway sits a grey Volkswagen Golf – he forgets how to tell how old it is from the registration. The front room's lights are on but the curtains are pulled and it's possible to see a little of the hall through the glass panels on other side of the door. He doesn't want to get out of the car. The hall is painted a cream colour and it looks like there is a wooden or laminate floor through to the kitchen. It's completely ordinary, devoid of any feature or design that would allow him to glean something of the life inside. Beckett is looking at him again in the mirror and just when he knows he's about to get out and open the door for him Stanfield leans forward and stops him with a tap on the shoulder.

'I'm sorry,' he says, 'I've just remembered something important. I need to go back to the apartment.' He slumps back in the seat and avoids catching Beckett's eyes in the mirror as the car is turned and heads back to the city.

When they're almost at the apartment he feels a reluctance to return to its emptiness and he's almost on the point of asking Beckett if he wants to go somewhere for a drink but knows that it's a no-hoper and inappropriate to ask someone who is both on duty and driving. As the car pulls up outside the apartment block Beckett gets out and opens his door.

'Sorry for the wasted journey,' Stanfield says, conscious of how much simpler it would be with Beckett if gratitude for service could be demonstrated by a discreet monetary recompense. He stands watching the car disappear, the lingering gaze of its tail lights a slowly fading blink of indifference. He wonders if Beckett will see his two daughters when he gets home or if they'll be asleep. Maybe he'll be lucky and catch them before they drift off and he'll sit on the edge of their beds and ask them about their day. He keys his security number into the communal doorway and then takes the lift to his top floor trying to remember such moments with his own daughter but although he's sure they existed, the memories are vague and blurred by the passage of time. He stares at himself in the lift's mirrored panel. Did he ever love her as he was supposed to do? His face is sharpening, the lines more pronounced at the sides of his eyes and across his forehead. He needs a drink to smooth things over, a drink to flush away some of this unfamiliar and unwanted seep of sentimentality. A child is a responsibility. Easy for a responsibility to become a burdensome thing. Now she has chosen to relieve him of it why should he feel any guilt? Let him embrace the lightness of it, let him stretch his wings. He blinks, as if the reflex will enable him to see this more clearly, but in the glass it is his slowly receding hairline on which he focuses. He has started to look like his father did in those black-and-white family snapshots.

When he enters the apartment he doesn't switch on the main lights and, without taking his coat off, pours himself a drink and carries it over to the seat by the window. Down below, trembling razor shells of light fan across the blackness of the river. The unlit swathes of water look so dark and thick that it feels as if he could scoop up a handful and hold it in his palm without a drop being spilled. The wine tastes sour and he knows no matter how much of it he drinks it will not dissipate the growing sense of solitariness the apartment spreads over him. Further down to his right blooms the soft white haze of the floodlit tennis courts and the private club to which he has been given membership. He tries to lift himself with the thought of a tennis game with Laura and afterwards she comes back to his conveniently close apartment for a drink and well one thing leads to another but it feels hopelessly and desperately adolescent in its fantasy. However, the sparked consciousness of her confirms what he already knows, that there is only one salve for the spreading loneliness at his core and it doesn't come out of a bottle.

He hesitates and tries one last glass of wine but knows it's futile so he goes to the bathroom and splashes his face, then pats it delicately with a thick white towel, as if offering it gentle commiseration for the shock of the water. He looks at the bottles of fragrance, runs his index finger along them like a man about to select a book from a shelf, and pauses at the Guerlain. The words he likes as much as the scent – citrus, lapsang, hibiscus seeds and patchouli flower. As he spreads a little across his cheekbones and on his throat he feels a renewed flare of vigour and blames the stinking cesspit of the country he's temporarily found himself domiciled in for his momentary fall from grace. Hard to lift your head above it in a godforsaken land, he tells himself, where a ship that sank and an alcoholic footballer are considered holy icons.

He straightens his tie and runs a hand through his hair, confident there's still a decade before recession slips into a dignified, only partial baldness. The number is exactly where he remembers noting it and he smiles as he sees it listed in his address book under Emergencies. Supplied by a former civil servant who described his term in the North as his exile to the Gulag and recommended as high class and discreet in all aspects, he blocks his own number and dials. It's a woman's voice, polite, business-like, with no extremities of accent and mercifully free of coy, knowing intimacies. Yes, he's happy to pay by cash. Personal preferences? He can hardly tell her that a connoisseur has no particular favourites or that part of the pleasure is in the surprise, the fascinating uniqueness of each one, so he chooses at random from the menu with which she prompts him. He likes her adjectives, the terribly polite and pleasantly old-fashioned words such as 'elegant' and 'educated', but balks a little at 'warm-hearted'. He doesn't need to be reminded that it's purely a commercial operation but nor does he need to think that it's some act of charity. No, not in his own home – he'll meet her in a city-centre hotel and is happy to take her recommendation. Yes, she can prearrange and prepay the room – simply add the additional cost to the girl's payment. She needs a name, any name will do, and for a second when faced with the magnitude of that choice he is temporarily thrown. She's been here before and suggests names that sound in his ears like former footballers or travelling salesmen so as his eyes scan the stack of CDs sitting close to the phone he tells her his name will be John Tavener.

As he sits in the back of the taxi he feels a little nervous. It's not a new experience but nor is it a particularly frequent one. Desperate days. Needs must. He tries to remind himself of the formalities, runs through a mental checklist, confirming that he has left his wallet in the apartment, that he has the necessary cash, that he has no personal documentation on his person. He has one credit card carefully stashed for unforeseen emergencies.

The city looks unfamiliar, divested of its daytime features and dressed now in a hard neon sheen that lets it assume the anonymity of all cities at night. Yet as they get closer to the centre Stanfield tells himself it retains a distinctive tawdriness, the same working-class stigmata borne by cities such as Glasgow and Liverpool, and if it is superficially softened by new construction and the flattering glaze of glass and light, then he senses something primitive that still lurks just below the surface. Is it pure imagination, the fact that he has money in his pocket or simply that he is a stranger in a city at night creating the feeling of menace? His eyes follow a phalanx of arm-linked, bare-fleshed girls seemingly immune from the cold, only their raw sexuality worn as a coat as their high heels tap dance the pavement like a chorus line. A shifting, amorphous drift of young men in open-necked shirts thickens with undefined purpose. One of them holds a glass of beer in the air as a salute to female passers-by. Nestling on the railings of the City Hall huddles a ragged flock of Goths, black like crows. It feels like everywhere and nowhere but he tells himself that if he were to lower his window he would catch the sulphurous smell that curdles the air, as if a match has just been struck, part of the latent sense of friction, the hard edge against which unexpectedly and unpredictably life might at any moment be struck in this city.

The taxi driver's lascivious eyes fasten on each group of young women he passes and when he clocks a particularly scantily clad girl he blows a little stream of breath that Stanfield is unsure whether registers pleasure or a type of excited disgust.

'Some rare sights,' the taxi driver says. 'More in than out some of them.'

'A bit cold for it,' Stanfield says.

'Some of the goose bumps have goose bumps. Look at yon! What do they think they look like? You want to come back when it's getting-out time. You wouldn't believe what you see. If it was my daughter . . .'

Stanfield doesn't want to hear any more and he interrupts by asking if they're nearly there but the question is rendered redundant as the taxi pulls in at the front doors of the hotel. He pays while declining the opportunity to book a return journey then hurries out of the cold. He's been here once before when speaking at a conference and even though the foyer looks as if it's been refurbished he knows the layout and heads immediately for the bar. He buys a drink and then takes it back out to one of the leather sofas that litter the ground floor. He is a little early and so he sits back and observes the clientele. There aren't many people about and all of them seem preoccupied with their own conversation. A group of four businessmen stare at a laptop, pour each other cups of tea and eat sandwiches. Their accents are English and in between the tea and sandwiches there are bursts of mobile phone calls. He tries to remember what people did before their technological toys arrived to make them feel important, to advertise their membership of some exclusive club. He supposes it all came down to clothes and accent so he takes pleasure in registering their scuffed and chain-store shoes, the cheap functionality of their briefcases and hand luggage, their estuary accents.

Beyond them sit two couples, perhaps a set of parents and their son- or daughter-in-law. He wonders who is trying hardest to impress and then he remembers that he has never met the man Emma married. What did she tell his parents was the reason for his absence from the wedding? Has she persuaded her new husband of his culpability, his supposedly deeply engrained corruption? Who gave his daughter away or did they have a registry office ceremony laughing off all the moribund church traditions? Perhaps he had already given her away a long time before. He sips his whisky – tonight he feels the need for something stronger than wine, something to light a fire where only smoulders a grey bed of ashes. He has come early deliberately because the anticipation is part of the pleasure and it allows him to subsume each single woman he sees into the unfolding arms of his desire. So for a few seconds it might be the woman with the long black hair and the equally dark eyes, or the young woman in the red coat whose shorter hair accentuates her cheekbones and gives her face an attractive sense of innocence. But each walks past him oblivious, or indifferent, to his admiring gaze. For a brief moment one returns his gaze but before he can reach out to her with a smile she has fallen into the arms of the man waiting for her. And then just as he lowers his eyes to glance at his watch as if from nowhere she is standing in front of him.

'Hello, John.' Her accent and her face tell him that she is probably of Eastern European origin and as he stands to greet her he realises that she is about an inch taller than him. As she sits down opposite him he summons a waiter with the raise of a hand and asks her if she would like a drink. She orders vodka and Coke and smiles at him. He is glad she is from somewhere far away. He is glad about everything he sees – the blueness of her eyes, the pale unblemished skin, the light skim of pink lipstick and the blondeness of her shoulder-length hair that has an expensive cut. She is about thirty, perhaps a few years older, and when he looks at her he thinks of snow – cold and beautiful snow bereft of footprints, seemingly untrammelled or untainted.

'Hello,' he says, and then in the second of silence, 'You look good.'

'Thank you,' she says, moving her head slightly but in a way that seems to set her hair in temporary motion.

'It's cold tonight,' he says, still thinking of snow and then embarrassed by the banality of what he's just said.

She nods but says nothing as the waiter arrives with her drink and he is disappointed to see her thank him with the same smile she gave him a few moments earlier but he tells himself it's the currency she uses and that she will grant him exclusive trading rights in exchange for his. Before she can sip the drink her phone rings and she apologises before answering it and the conversation lasts no longer than the time it takes her to say 'yes' and 'everything's OK'. He looks at her clothes and they, too, please him. Nothing vulgar or loud, just a simple well-cut black suit that shows her skin and hair to advantage. At her neck is a single string of pearls – one of the few things he has never mastered the skill of evaluating. She turns off the phone and apologises again, saying, 'Just checking everything's OK. No more disturbance.'

'And everything's OK?' he asks.

'I think so,' she says, smiling at him and moving her hair again. It looks like a little flurry of snow. Everything about her is calm and confident and as she sips her drink she never takes her eyes from his and he knows that whatever disappointment or indifference she might feel he will be shown no trace of it.

'And what do I call you?' He knows immediately that it's a question that invites the stock response, 'Anything you like,' but she apologises again and formally offers her hand and tells him her name is Kristal. It feels slight and cold to the touch, the nails painted the same colour as her lips. He would like to put it to his lips but after holding it slightly longer than a normal handshake he lets it go. It slips slowly away, her fingers lingering against his. He wants to ask where she comes from, runs possible origins across his brain, but he knows it would be impolite and that the answer would be no more truthful than her name. What he is sure of is that she is in the country illegally, part of the economic diaspora that has started to play the Irish at their age-old game. Now some call them an economic necessity – 'they do the jobs that no one wants' – so here she is this young woman from somewhere far away who drifts across his senses like the first snow of winter. He hopes they take good care of her, that they treat her well, that she makes her money quickly and gets out. And as he drinks in the cold beauty of her he tells himself that it's not about economics but a spiritual necessity. That he will treat her well. That he will pay her well. And that will make it all right for both of them.

One of the businessmen is looking at her, looking at him.

43

He starts to feel uncomfortable. The place is too public. She glances to where his gaze strayed and reads his thoughts immediately. 'We should go,' she says. 'I'll go first.' Then she pushes a small square of paper towards him with a room number on it. 'Give me ten minutes. Third floor. Take the number. Sometimes someone forgets, spends whole night looking for the right room.'

He watches her leave and then tries to turn casually to his drink. It's the first thing that she's said or done wrong in reminding him that there have been others. Better to have allowed him to console himself with the illusion that he was the only one.

He finishes his drink with what he believes is appropriate nonchalance, then glances at his watch. The group of businessmen are refocused on the computer screen – one of them points things out to the others with the tip of his pen – so he stands up slowly and buttons his overcoat. Perhaps it is the drink, perhaps the heat of the building, but he has started to feel too warm and he reopens the buttons, takes off his coat and drapes it casually over his arm. Once again he finds himself in a lift but this time is glad there is no mirror. Things are slipping away from him. Something has been lost. He understands now that it was a mistake to take this job and come to this city. He doesn't believe in ghosts but there is something spectral about the thoughts that have started to haunt his consciousness. He tries to fasten on the memory of how blue her eyes were but the growing awareness of a deepening desperation begins to blunt the edge of his desire. How would he look if he were to see himself now? What did he look like in her eyes? He smiles as he remembers the light-washed greyness of the sharks then shivers a little. Does she see beyond his money and his expensive suit to something predatory? For a second he slips into the self-pity he abhors so much but then he remembers the apartment's spreading net of emptiness that threatened to trap him in its mesh, the black sheen of the river below, and when the lift door pings open, he steps into the corridor with a renewed conviction of his need and his entitlement to have it met.

She opens the door almost immediately, takes his coat from his arm and hangs it on the rail inside the door. He sees her hand instinctively brush away a little speck of fluff from the lapel – she is obviously a woman for whom detail is important. She has softened the lighting and on a bedside table sit two drinks. Everything is ready. But he needs to talk and he wants to hear her talk, wants to show her something more than she expects. He knows it is a vanity but he hopes to make her understand that he is different from what has gone before and that despite the exchange of money that she quickly and discreetly slipped into her handbag, despite the anonymity of the room, he has the capacity to give as much as take. So when she sits on the edge of the bed and starts to remove the jacket of her suit he stops her and taking her hand presses its white coldness to his cheek. More than anything he wants to give her tenderness, to have the same from her. If he can only have that, he will pay all the money in the world. Something is breaking in him and he drops to his knees at her feet and places his head in her lap. He doesn't care about dignity, doesn't care about anything, and for a second there is nothing and then he feels her hand gently stroking his hair and she's telling him that everything is all right.

Afterwards she talks a little but always carefully about herself. She's Polish and she hopes to earn enough money to pay her way through university. He smiles involuntarily when she tells him she wants to be a lawyer. He tries to ask if he can contact her independently of her employers but she shakes her head, continuing to say it isn't possible even when he tries to persuade her and is forced to use the vulgarity of the word 'arrangement'. Her hair is splayed across the whiteness of the pillow, the blueness of her eyes the only strength of colour, and when they close in sleep he knows he has lost her. He has paid for the night but as he lies perfectly still beside her listening to her breathing, he knows, too, that he wants to leave her now and not in the harsh and awkward light of the morning, so he quietly gets out of bed and going to the bathroom closes the door behind him. He showers as quickly as he can but doesn't allow himself to catch his reflection, then going back into the room he dresses, watching her all the time. The room is lit only by the city's neon and he goes to the window and stares out at the streets below. Of course there should be snow but instead there is only the fading wail of a far-off siren and occasional voices that fritter skywards in sharp-edged fragments. He looks at her one last time and then leaves.

Outside as he waits for the taxi he turns up his collar against the bitterness of the night. The cold and damp seep into the marrow of his bones. He imagines himself as the spilt file, his secret pages caught and scattered by the wind, then shivers as he thinks again of snow and how already the silent fall is covering the print he tried to tenderly lay down and feels the sadness of knowing that by morning it will have vanished without trace.

Matteo is adamant. The file has been doctored. His face is animated and for a moment he reminds Stanfield of a bloodhound straining at the leash, desperate to sniff out the renegade.

'It's an amateur job. A pathetically amateur job!' he says and it's obvious his anger is laced with excitement. He drops the file theatrically on Stanfield's desk then pushes his hand through his hair awaiting his master's approval for his perceptive diligence. Stanfield looks at Laura who has stood up and come closer to the desk to stare at the file as if it is some alien creature. He is suddenly conscious that they both know that he has perused the file without apparently detecting what supposedly is an amateurish job. Connor Walshe. He wonders why the file doesn't have a photograph of the boy.

'The whole thing is a sloppy mess,' he says neutrally. 'It's just like a drain that they've poured everything in.'

'It's what's been taken out,' he hears Matteo say and he's conscious that Laura is looking at Matteo and not him. She puts her fingers on the file.

'Perhaps it got spilt like the file the other day,' he says, attempting a joke. She has small, thin fingers. The ring is vulgarly ostentatious and out of scale with the size of her hand. As Matteo suddenly lifts the file she pulls her hand away as if shocked by the energy of his movement.

'The index has been altered and some of the pages have been added afterwards. It's not even the same bloody paper. What do they think we are – complete fools?' He splays pages across the desk then jabs his finger in relevant places. 'You see?' he asks and Laura nods her head. 'You see?' he asks again, looking at Stanfield. But Stanfield has already seen and has already understood. He thinks of the envelope Maria Harper handed to him but chooses to say nothing of its contents because already he is conscious of standing at the edge of a brackenish bog, a shifting swamp of a landscape where an ill-judged step might see him sucked into the morass. He has to be careful, perhaps more self-protective than he has ever had to be, as he increasingly glimpses a bottomless mire that waits for the foolhardy. So to think he shuts his ears to Matteo's self-righteous screech of the idealist and the simpering support he gets from Laura and stares at the grubby manila folder with its finger bruises and scribble where it looks as if someone tried to get their pen to work. He wonders with what other prints this soiled and sullen coloured folder are indelibly and invisibly marked. But his thoughts are called back to the moment as he looks up again to register the burn of anger in Matteo's eyes and hear him ask, 'So what are we going to do about it?'

In time, Stanfield thinks, when Matteo sits on his side of the desk, as he surely will, he will come to understand the recklessness of such a question, that by then to have got where he is, he will understand that only the young believe that management is about doing things and that in maturity the greatest skill of all is the ability to do nothing. So with the greatest show of conviction he can muster he states solemnly, 'This is a serious and despicable attempt to thwart the work of the Commission and is clearly intended to undermine the credibility of the process. I suspect it won't be the last example of this we're going to encounter so we've got to stand up strong. I want you both to prepare a detailed analysis of where you think the file's been tampered with – consult independent experts if you have to – and after you've done that I'm going to contact all the other commissioners. I'll go to the highest office with this if we don't get the right answers.'

He's rewarded by the belief and respect that their faces register and by the end of their discussion he sees the elation in their faces, the sense of a moral stand having been righteously taken. For a little while he bathes in the communal warm glow and then, as he watches them leave his office with a lightness of heart and step, for a second feels a tiny frisson of sympathy for them and what the world still has to teach them.

That night he attends one of the seemingly interminable functions designed to celebrate the new process and honour the commissioners and even if this black-tie do at Hillsborough Castle is the most prestigious so far, Stanfield finds the level of boredom commensurate with his previous experiences. There's a lot of standing around exchanging small talk while black-dress waitresses serve slightly ridiculous canapés and then afterwards the inevitable speeches. He finds his fellow commissioners a stolid bunch; all are slightly older than him and have the cardigan and slipper whiff of the recently retired. He particularly avoids the South African judge who endlessly drones on about their experience and persists in holding it up as a shining template to the backwardness of the present imitation. It feels like colonialism in reverse. Only two things prevent Stanfield slipping quietly away because already he is thinking of Kristal and the pale perfection of her skin seems even more perfect when imagined against this sea of jowelled greyness and faces flushed by the wine – the curiosity of hearing one of the new Prime Minister's first public speeches and the prettiness of the waitresses.

But if the latter continues to please him the former is a source of much disappointment and he chides his naïve anticipation, belatedly realising that the mouth delivering the words may have changed but not the hands of the writers. It's a soft-centred meringue of a speech that leaves Stanfield feeling he has overdosed on sugar as he endures the endless references to healing and closure. He hears the word healing so often that he wants to stand up and shout that perhaps they should have employed doctors instead of representatives of the law. Thankfully there is no attempted knock-out punchline such as the hand of history but only a whimpering petering out with tautological references to momentous moments and rather tired images of building the future. The applause afterwards is polite but restrained. Stanfield looks at his watch and slips away before the subsequent speakers have a chance to take the podium and inflict further tedium on him.

She arrives half an hour after Beckett drops him off. He has decided for better or worse that he will bring her to the apartment rather than meet her in the city-centre hotel, trying to convince himself that it is more prudent to avoid such public spaces but knowing why he wants her here is that he hopes to exorcise the cavernous emptiness of his temporary home. Before she arrives he changes into casual clothes and does a sweep of the rooms removing anything that identifies him, or is too personally revealing, but in truth there is little to do because the residence has never assumed anything other than an austere functionalism.

He is pleased by her punctuality – it allows him to dream that she is keen to see him, a fantasy preserved by the smile with which she greets him and the seemingly affectionate kiss on his cheek. As he brings her into the main living area he keeps a little distance so that he can survey her more easily and once again admire the elegant choice of clothes – this time she wears a woollen three-quarter-length coat with a pale green silk scarf at the neck and when he stands behind her to help her take off the coat, he closes his eyes for a second as he breathes her in, lets his lips linger briefly on the fall of her hair. Underneath she wears a cashmere sweater, dark trousers and the same string of pearls as the first time. He offers her a drink and watches as she walks around the room taking everything in, sometimes lightly touching things with the tips of her fingers. Like a child in a toyshop, he thinks, and then for some unwanted reason remembers the Saturday morning when driven by some temporary surge of guilt for a particular period of neglect he took his daughter to Hamley's. How long the moment of choice took when faced with the magnitude of possibilities, how, too, she touched things with her fingertips as if that light brush might intimately gauge their potential desirability.

'Very nice,' she says, sweeping her arm in a slow half circle.

'It's OK but it's only temporary – it's not my main home,' he answers, embarrassed by his desire to convey the extent of his wealth.

She goes to the window and looks out on the river. He stands behind her as if he, too, wants to share the view.

'Pretty view,' she says.

'Yes, but not the most beautiful river in the world.' And suddenly he has the impulse to take her away from here, take her to Paris and walk along the Seine, and the thought rejuvenates and excites him like champagne bubbling open. He feels the delicious lightness in the recklessness of the thought, drinks from it as deeply as possible before he lets it be subsumed slowly by the leaden weight of reality. He puts his hand lightly on her shoulder and she lays her hand across his without turning round. It is a simple gesture but whatever money she costs he thinks that he has been paid in full in that moment.

Part of him doesn't want to sleep with her because part of him wants to talk to her and hear her talk in return. He sits opposite her and enjoys the burnish of her hair, the blueness of her eyes, the clean ring of her voice. He looks at the way her hand holds the glass, the slight tilt of her head as she drinks. He looks at the paleness of her neck when she removes the scarf. He wants her to feel the way a model feels as she shows herself to a great artist so he's desperate to avoid any crude hint of physical necessity or the selfishness of greed. But perhaps he waits too long because once as they sit

51

listening to some of his favourite music he catches her eyes glancing at her watch and the gesture scatters the consoling weave of his illusion. So in an instinctive defence he assumes a greater sense of detachment, the more formal air of a business transaction. She knows that he is disappointed about something and tries a little too hard to compensate but after a while he is happy to be pampered out of his sulk.

In the morning while she is still sleeping he starts some coffee in the kitchen and in his dressing gown goes to the window. On the river a rowing crew sculls by, the rhythmic pull on the oars slicing the boat through the still grey-coloured water and spurting up little flurries of white. On the other side a jogger moves in a less elegant way with as much up and down movement as forward. Stanfield slightly opens the sliding door to the balcony and lets the morning air hit his face. Already he hears the *thock thock* of tennis being played out on the courts. Unlit by the sun the water below looks cold and skimmed with a misty gauze.

If the sex was largely unsatisfactory he knows, as always, it's a question of diminishing returns and that, after the initial flurry of passion, into the too quickly opening void must pour inevitably the knowledge of other still unfulfilled needs. Stanfield considers it one of life's most bitter little cruelties but decides that perhaps it is the trick that brings the deceived back to the banquet again and again. There was something else as well, something unexpectedly and inescapably ugly in his head when it should've been filled with nothing but release, and that was an image of snow, but snow tainted and stained by his print. He closes the glass and glances at her sleeping. She has one arm thrown back across the pillow above her head. Just as the first time he looked at her like this he is struck by the paleness of her skin, almost subsumed by the whiteness of the pillow. He feels tired, not physically, but by the wearisome predictability of the day ahead, so he goes back to the bed and, trying not to disturb her, snuggles into her penumbral heat. He falls into a soft, comforting sleep but a little while later is wakened by some kind of alarm, then is slowly aware that there's someone else in the apartment and talking to him. For a second he thinks it's Kristal but as he glances towards her she turns on her side and pulls the quilt over her shoulder and anyway, as he blinks and squints at the rising light that fills the room, he knows that it's not her voice. And then he suddenly understands that it's his daughter speaking to him from the other room but as he stumbles myopically towards the voice he senses that there's something not quite right about it and as he slumps back heavily on the bed he realises that it's the answering machine.

'What is it?' Kristal asks, squirming her white shoulders coldly above the snow line of the quilt.

But now he's oblivious to her and abruptly tells her to be quiet as he struggles to hear his daughter's final words. He sits with his back taut and straight, straining to hear the voice he hasn't heard in five years and feeling distant from it, struggling to read its timbre and tone, trying to hear the meaning in the spaces between words, trying in vain to see the expression on her face. He feels Kristal's hand on the small of his back but it means nothing to him as the message clunks dead.

'What is it?' she asks. But he doesn't reply at first because the narrowed focus of his thoughts doesn't allow him to register anything beyond his own confusion and the growing sense of fear he feels spreading in the pit of his stomach. It's the fear that freezes him to the bed, the knowledge that things are swaying in a kind of balance and he's helpless to know what way they might finally come to a halt. She's sitting behind him now and he feels the warmth of her breath on his neck as she presses her hands on his shoulders.

'It's an important message,' he says, still motionless and staring at the open doorway.

'Bad news?'

'I don't know.' For some reason he thinks of all the months when Emma was a child, when she was going through her wake-in-the-middle-of-the-night phase and she would come into their room and somehow manage to tunnel into the space between her sleeping parents, a space that was increasingly wide, then sleep in that neutral sphere, that no man's land in the cold war between two stalled armies.

Without his having to tell her, she knows she has to go and she drifts past him like a pale ghost. He's glad because he knows he can't listen to the message while she's still in the apartment, can't have his daughter and his indiscretion in the same room, and before he listens to it he tries to piece together what he remembers, desperate to read the omens so that he can prepare himself accordingly. He goes to the kitchen and pours two coffees, all the time glancing at the red light on the answering machine. When she joins him her hair is wet, plastered to her head in a way that makes her face thinner. She wears no make-up and her face is primed like a white page, waiting for the story of the day to be written on it.

'Sorry,' he says, without knowing exactly what he's sorry for and confused when she asks him. 'I don't know. For hurrying you, for not making a proper breakfast.'

'That's OK,' she says, using the palms of both hands to push the tails of her hair behind her ears. He knows she senses something's wrong. 'Will I see you again?'

'I hope so,' he says neutrally and then offers to call for a taxi but she tells him that she will walk a little, for the exercise, and then call one. He sits at the kitchen bar as she puts on her coat and knots the silk scarf loosely at her neck but all the time his eyes flick to the red light. She turns to go but then stops and looks at him. 'I didn't please you?'

'You pleased me very much.'

She continues to stare at him, uncertain in her own mind, and unsure whether it's to reassure her, or hurry her on her way, he stands up and coming to her kisses her lightly on both cheeks. He briefly feels the wetness of her hair upon his skin and he can't tell himself whether he will see her again. In the law of diminishing returns there is always a time to cut your losses, a time to move on, and whether it was her stay, or the voice of his daughter on the phone, he doesn't know but it feels as if the apartment is smaller now, not so resonant with its former arching emptiness.

Even after she's gone he doesn't go immediately to the phone but instead sits on the chair opposite it and drains the last warmth from the cup of coffee. Somewhere inside the welter of chips and circuitry rests the voice of his daughter, a voice he wasn't sure he would ever hear again. The red light seems to steadily magnify in brightness until it feels that if he is to stretch out his hand he might get burned. He goes to the window and looks down on the river but there is no answer reflected in the grey dullness of its surface and so he has no option but to turn and walk uncertainly to the phone.

Beckett drops him off outside the café and he tells him he'll phone when he needs him to return. He can tell that his driver is curious as to why he should have chosen such a place to eat, so out of keeping with his normal haunts. By way of explanation he says, 'Meeting an old friend. Their choice.' As he watches Beckett drive further up the main street to park he wonders why she stipulated this place and not her home, which is only five minutes away. His nervousness has made him early and he's unsure whether to go in or wait outside. It's a little country parlour, one down from a restaurant and one up from a café. He can tell just by looking at its prim exterior that it's a solid little place where the menu will not divert from the home-baked, home-cooked, home-spun respectability so beloved by this provincial backwater. He knows already that there will be vegetable soup and wheaten bread, Irish stew and in a slight recognition of the outer world possibly lasagne or quiche.

There's no sign of her and he knows it's a possibility that she'll have changed her mind and won't show but he decides to wait inside and try to stake a claim on somewhere they might be able to talk. What it is they will talk about is unclear to him and although he prepares various scenarios in his head, none of them manages to convince. Inside everything is as he anticipated but even more so and with a hint of a smile he thinks of the London restaurants he frequents. As he sits at one of the white-clothed tables with its doilies and country-cottage chairs, he thinks it's the very worst place for this meeting. He tries to understand why his daughter should choose to live in this forsaken part of the world with which she is linked only through a deceased grandmother, why she should throw away the expensive and cultured start she was given in life to teach in some school he's never heard of and live in a one-street town where at the glass-covered counter they sell tray bakes and homemade shortbread.

He orders a coffee from the waitress and tells her he's waiting for someone, and then reruns the phone message in his head that by now he knows by heart. 'This is Emma,' it began and he knows that no matter how many times he replays it he will never hear her use the word father or any affectionate variation of it. And no matter how many times he tries to analyse it he can find no other tone except a perfunctory neutrality in her speech and her expression of a need to see him. He tries to strip the words of the distortion and awkwardness always involved in speaking to a machine, the sudden gauche expression that inevitably affects the speaker, but is still unable to deconstruct any meaning beyond the literal. She needs to meet him – the word 'needs', however, comes out bereft of any emotional resonance and instead carries the dull inflection of a business request – there are some things she needs to talk about, but no clue as to what these might be and no personal reference to him, no 'hope you are well', or 'looking forward to meeting you'. He wonders for a moment if it's about money but discards this as an unlikely motivation, not just because her mother's will left her financially comfortable but because his daughter some-where along the way has acquired an unhealthy indifference to money.

Feeling a little self-conscious he is aware of the curious stares of the other customers he assumes are regulars and senses their sad interest in the small-town drama of an unfamiliar man in a suit drinking a cup of coffee and waiting for someone. He tries not to meet their eyes and the inap-propriateness of the setting for the meeting begins to irk him. He tells himself that it's confirmation of his belief that there has always been something contrary about his daughter, a wilful disregard for the prerequisites of etiquette, and he feels a sudden resentment that he has come to this, sitting waiting in a tiny cubby-hole that makes him increasingly imagine he's taken residence inside a doll's house. For a moment he wants to think of Kristal but he banishes the images she so readily furnishes because it feels distasteful to place her in proximity to his daughter and he wishes she hadn't been in his bed when Emma's voice echoed in the silence of the apartment. He wonders if a voice, even a disembodied voice, somehow carries the power of intuitive vision and wonders, too, how women always know unfaithfulness. Despite all his best efforts, despite every discretion and without anything ever being said by her in the later years, he always understood that Martine knew every time. How was it done? Lipstick on the collar? A crude cliché that masked the ability to divine the intangible with the springy, willowy rod of her heart however deeply he believed his indiscretion was buried.

She's five minutes late and every time the door opens and its bell rings he feels the beat of his heart. He forces himself to admit that they're not meeting at her home because she doesn't want him to enter her world, that it's still closed to him in the same way that her whole life is. So he counsels himself, advising himself to moderate his expectations, to hold himself in balance, but the coffee tastes bitter – he needs something much stronger. Outside a sudden squall of rain has started to fall and new arrivals take the opportunity to dramatise themselves with shakes of their shoulders and puffed-out cheeks. The audience shake their heads in silent sympathy and postpone their departures for a few more minutes. She isn't coming, he knows she isn't coming, but as he tries to catch the waitress's eyes to pay his bill, the door opens and a young woman enters with her head bowed from the rain and he knows it's his daughter. She looks up and pushes the wetness from the side of her hair with her fingertips and there's none of the uncertainty he'd worried himself with, thinking that her decision to remove herself from his life would somehow change her physically as well. He stands up and raises his hand and for the briefest of moments thinks he must look like he's standing in court promising to tell the truth and he drops it to his side as soon as she sees him. But she's not the same. It's not just the swelling globe of a new world that orbits her old self but there are subtle changes in her face that mark her as older and, in some way he can't quite perceive, not exactly as he remembered. And then with a sharp pierce of sadness he remembers that she's married now and has adopted a different family, so perhaps what is unfamiliar to him is the patina produced by the tight embrace of those she newly loves.

There is a table between them and he doesn't know how best to greet her beyond the conviction that he won't try to impose anything but the problem is solved almost immediately by her simple expression of the word 'Hi' and the quickness of the way she takes her seat. So far she hasn't held his eyes and instead flusters about herself, opening the buttons of her coat and smoothing her hair that still wears a light sheen of damp.

'It's started to rain,' she says as she looks about her. 'Really coming down.'

'Maybe you shouldn't be out in the rain,' he says, placing both hands on his empty cup. He offers it as an expression of concern.

'Why, what do you think's going to happen?' Her voice is quick and sharp-edged.

'Nothing,' he retreats. 'How far pregnant are you?' And every word that comes out of his mouth feels treacherous, liable to betray him by leading in the opposite direction to the one in which he wants to go. He knows his question sounds abrupt, too personal too quickly.

'Eight months,' she says, looking only at the menu she's lifted. 'Have you ordered yet?'

'Just a coffee – I was waiting for you.' It's started badly and once again he silently curses the surroundings and then he understands that she's chosen them deliberately, chosen them to put him on unfavourable ground, to drain away the possibility of dramatics of speech. And so he has to try and speak to his only child within the hopelessly narrow constraints of the mundane. It feels as if she's put him in a straitjacket, that everything's loaded against him.

'Hello, Emma, how're you keeping?' the woman who is obviously the owner asks and it hurts to see the natural, instinctive smile with which his daughter greets a woman who is a stranger to him.

'Not so bad, thanks. Legs are a bit heavy, that's all.'

'Let Alan do all the work – you keep your feet up, girl,' the woman says and then she looks at him but Emma makes no effort to introduce them and he is forced to offer only a brief smile. 'Would you like to order?'

'Just a bowl of soup,' Emma says and then looks at him for his order.

'I'll have the same.' Then after the woman has gone, 'Would it have hurt so much to tell her I'm your father?' He can't help himself, he can't play this game where they are supposed to pretend that what is happening is normal.

'Please don't start,' she says in a whispered voice and looking at him properly for the first time as she leans across the table. 'I don't want any trouble.'

'I'm sorry.' But he feels her words are those of someone trying to placate an attacker. Does she think of him as someone whose purpose is to give her trouble?

'This isn't the place,' she insists.

'So why did we come here?'

'Because I like it here and it'll serve its purpose.'

He knows he has to be more careful or she'll leave and already he sees the signs that she's having second thoughts as her eyes flicker round the other tables and her hands straighten the cutlery on the table. He feels like a climber exposed on the narrowest of ridges where a second's carelessness might send him spinning to disaster so he asks, 'How have you been?'

'Good.'

'Good,' he replies, noticing for the first time in his life that she has her mother's eyes.

'And you?' she asks. There are still little beads of water trembling in the thickness of her hair.

'Not so bad.' For a second he has the crazy idea of inventing some serious illness in the hope of generating the possibility of sympathy but instead he asks about her pregnancy and she tells him that it's been fine and just when for the first fleeting moment it feels as if they're having a conversation, the waitress arrives with the soup and she lapses into silence.

'So you're going to be a mother?' he offers and in that moment how much he would give to hear her say, 'And you're going to be a grandfather,' but instead she merely stares at the bowl of vegetable soup then stirs it slowly with her spoon. 'And Alan, how is he?' It's the first time he has ever spoken the name of her husband and the word sounds inexplicably strange. She tells him he's fine and blows gently on the spoonful of soup. He breaks the brittle freshness of the roll on his side plate and some of the crumbs fritter on to the white tablecloth. 'What does he do?' he asks.

'He's a teacher.'

'In the same school?'

'Yes. He teaches geography.'

Geography. He thinks of cartographers, of maps, tries to see what direction he now should take. The soup is over-heated and overdosed with barley. He stares at her eyes again. Is it his imagination or have the intervening years of absence propelled her to this likeness to her mother, a likeness that he has obtusely failed to recognise in the past? He stares, too, at her wedding ring – a thin, plain band of gold. A functional ring devoid of decoration or the need to proclaim anything other than to herself.

'I'd like to meet him.' She doesn't answer and he has a sudden urge to reach his hand across the table and touch her hair, to express the surge of affection he hadn't expected to feel. But there is no map and he flounders lost and blind in some unknown terrain where even the bright stars of instinct are hidden from sight. 'I suppose he thinks I've got two horns and a tail.'

'He knows about you, if that's what you mean,' she says coldly and without embarrassment.

Her words make him flinch and it feels as if a hand has just unveiled what their circumspect politeness had left discreetly covered and the pain of knowing that nothing has changed collides with the shock of knowing, perhaps for the first time, how much she means to him.

'Emma,' he says, setting the spoon down and resting both hands on the table.

'No, Dad, I don't want to talk about it. That's not why I've asked you to come here.'

She's called him Dad for the first time and it spurs him on. 'Please, Emma; there are things I want to say. I think you have to let me say them and if not here, then somewhere else.'

'And would sorry be one of those things you want to say?'

'Yes, sorry is one of the things I need to say, sorry and many other things.'

'There's just one problem: the person you most need to say sorry to isn't here any more to hear it.'

So this is it, Stanfield thinks, he's to be eternally held to account without the possibility of parole because there's no forgiveness possible from the dead. Like Sisyphus he is to be condemned to ceaselessly push this burden through whatever years lie ahead and at the end be no closer to her forgiveness than when he started. He bridles at the unfairness of it, the moral righteousness of this young woman who sits as his judge.

'The quality of mercy is not strained,' he says, indifferent to whether it sounds portentous or not.

'I don't want a pound of your flesh.'

'What is it you want, Emma?' he asks, exhausted by the vertiginous precariousness he feels, willing to plunge headfirst into the chasm below rather than continue to walk this knife edge. Better to know his fate, receive his sentence and try to let his life continue in whatever ways he himself will choose.

'I want your help,' she says as she straightens her back and looks directly at him. Then she looks away again and asks the waitress if she can have a glass of water.

'Are you all right?' he asks. 'You mustn't get upset in your condition.'

'So you're an expert in pregnancy now?' But there is no bitterness in her words and he's able to reply with a smile and a shake of his head. 'And I'm not upset.'

As the waitress brings the glass, he asks for another coffee, keen to extend their entitlement to the table. She wants his help and that cheers him but he knows it won't be the beautiful simplicity of money that she'll request and he knows so little about the circumstances of her present life that he can't even begin to anticipate what she's going to ask. What he does know, however, is that a request for help opens up possibilities that formerly seemed closed and so he leans attentively towards her.

'Anything,' he says. 'You only have to ask.'

Perhaps it's something to do with the child that's coming – perhaps she needs him to fulfil some role in relation to that, or even might it be that she's thinking of moving back to London. He has a vision of their lives intertwining again in a better place than this, of the infinite possibilities of a newly found future. But his hopes tumble about him as he hears her say, 'It's not for me; it's for Maria Harper.'

Why has he not seen it coming? Why has he not had the intelligence to understand what lay behind her call? And he feels like a fool who's been suckered in and as he watches her sip from the glass he tastes the bitterness of his disappointment and then anger at his blinkered naïvety.

'Maria Harper?' he asks coolly as if the name means nothing to him.

'Yes, you met her a week ago. Maria is my classroom assistant and a friend. Her brother's Connor Walshe.'

'Connor Walshe?' Already this is a name that he doesn't want to hear.

'She wrote you a letter, told you what happened to him.'

'Emma, I can't discuss the private affairs of the Commission.' Immediately he regrets using the word 'affairs' but takes refuge in a flow of words. 'I'm sure you understand that these are delicate matters and we're bound by very strict codes of confidence. I can't sit here in a . . .' he leaves the description unfinished but gives a little gesture with his hand '. . . and discuss matters that are bound by the protocols of the Commission.'

'I'm not asking you to discuss it,' she insists, putting the glass down on the table with slightly too much force so that the water slurps against the rim, 'I'm asking you to help her.'

He has to resist the momentary temptation to punish her with a cold indifference hidden in some supposed strict adherence to a set of rules but he knows this is perhaps his last opportunity to establish a bridgehead so instead he says, 'Of course I'll help her.'

'She wrote you a letter, didn't she, told you everything that happened? She asked me to read it, to help with the writing.'

'It's very well written,' he stalls.

'And you'll be able to help her?'

'Of course I will. It's my job to help her.'

'And you'll listen to what she has to say, listen to what she says really happened?'

'Emma, I'm going to do my very best to give her the truth about her brother,' he says as he stares at her green eyes and for a second recognises something, something that is more than just a physical resemblance to her mother but in its expression reproduces the striated lines of suspicion that always sought to pierce whatever pretence he offered. Never jealousy in Martine's eyes because that would have meant the continued possibility of love, but only the clouded coldness of whatever emotion had replaced it.

'I promise you,' he says.

'That's good,' she answers and something has broken in her tone of voice and when she speaks the guarded hesitation has been replaced by a quicker flow of words. 'They've had a terrible time, all these years. Never knowing for sure and then when they knew, not knowing where the body is or how to get him back. And Maria started with nothing and somehow despite it all managed to make something of herself. But there's something like a hole or a space that they can't fill until they have a body to bury. She's been good to me, she deserves the truth – the whole family does. What's left of them. Over the years they've drifted apart almost as if being separate might lessen the memory.'

'It's very terrible and very sad,' he says but what he wants to tell her is that the truth can't be deserved, that if it exists at all, it exists outside the constraints of need or personal desire.

That truth rarely makes anything better and often makes it worse.

'They need their lives to move on. They can't move on until they have him home.' And this time when she looks at him there is only a passionate intensity in her eyes and now it is he who is jealous, jealous that what she can't give to him is so freely available to strangers.

'I understand,' he says but he doesn't even for a second comprehend how he has come to this place and this moment when he sits with his daughter and she gives her act of love to someone else. What he does understand is that now he is expected to win something back from her through an act of service, that she has told Maria Harper she will speak to her father and that he will help. It seems like something a small girl would do, in part out of righteous indignation at the injustice of the world and in part out of the secret pride she felt in her father's capacity to right a wrong.

Afterwards she thanks him but resumes some of her original detachment as he pays the bill and they step outside, so when he offers to walk her home or to take her there in the car she refuses politely but firmly and he doesn't try to persuade her. Her goodbye is neutral and after a second mumbled thanks she turns and sets off down the main street. He sees Beckett watching from the car and signals that he's finished his business. As a lighter, finer rain begins to slant down he watches his daughter walk briskly away, from the back revealing no sign of her pregnancy. He feels a sudden shiver of sadness, a glimpse of what their future might be, and blinks his eyes against the rain.

That night in the apartment he sits at the seat by the window and looks down on the river where random smears of neon slip across the surface in frittering glazes of red and gold. Only a small reading light illuminates the table he sits beside and the wine glass squints a bleary echo as his hand moves its emptiness away from the letter. He lifts the envelope and weighs it in his hand – so much weight, he thinks, in so much lightness. Then he carefully opens it and lets his eye flick across the neat black rows of type. He won't bring himself to read it again – there's something profoundly draining about the emotional need that generates it, something that tries to cling to the reader and won't let go until it's fastened like some parasite to the lining of the brain. How can he be tied now to a boy whose photograph he's never seen? How can his desire to see his only child be meshed with some other long-dead boy from a Belfast back street? A car's headlights briefly score the surface of the water with spears of light. For a second he forgets the glass is empty and lifts it to his lips then returns it slowly to the table. It feels cold in his hand. Then she calls to him from the bed and he turns his head and smiles at her. Her face is pale like frost, her shoulders white like snow. It feels like there is a ghost in his bed. She calls gently again and he wonders why she's calling him a different name from his own and then he remembers. A ghost who deserves no truth and asks for none, so in a little while he shall go to her, but first there is something he has to do and, taking the letter and its envelope, he tears them carefully into tiny pieces, then lets them flutter to the ground until they drift round his feet like the first fall of winter.

Francis Gilroy

HE BELIEVES THAT THERE are only good habits and bad habits, and good habits don't die hard. In the old days it was bad habits that got you killed and the worst habit of all was to be in the right place at the right time, leaving yourself freeze-framed, the perfect picture begging to be shot. It could happen in many different ways – sleeping too long in the same bed in the same house, taking the child to school by the same route, obeying the call of your thirst at the favoured time and in the same watering hole, even going to confess your sins and meet too predictably with God could ensure the encounter became face to face.

It's something he never forgets and something he struggles to make the youngsters understand – the need for vigilance, the constant need for caution. Struggles and fails. So as Francis Gilroy, the newly appointed Minister with responsibility for Children and Culture, gets out of his bed and goes to look at the early morning, he doesn't open the middle of the curtains but stands to one side and lightly lifts the cloth and the voile drape his wife considers sophisticated elegance away from the sill. The street is empty of people but filled with a metal-coloured mist that drifts in from the mountain and rasps everything soft and smooth. He turns to look at his still sleeping wife as she stirs in the bed, bunching the pillow under her head as if the restlessness of sleep has flattened too much of the life out of it, and for a moment he's tempted to postpone the start of the day and rejoin her. Join her in the newly bought, canopy-covered, wrought-iron four-poster bed that embarrasses him even to look at and makes him hope it's not the place he has to die with an awkward audience standing at its foot. But instead he goes to the other side of the window and views the opposite end of the street. Only familiar cars, but all rendered cold and lifeless by the grey drape of mist and fossilised into frozen memories of themselves.

Less reason to worry now perhaps, but always cautious, a creature shaped by the enforced habits of a lifetime's struggle, so let the younger ones snigger, puffed up on their own bravado and big talk. It's what makes him a survivor. That and luck. And if there's less obvious reason to worry, there still lingers the permanent possibility of a hit – from some maverick, another Michael Stone perhaps, high as a kite on his own ego; one of the dissidents – the fanatics with hurt in their eyes who stand at the back of meetings and shout at him about sell-outs and betrayals; some unknown relative of a forgotten victim who has never forgotten, the memory eating away like cancer until they have to staunch the pain.

Marie pulls the duvet over her shoulders as if putting on a winter coat and he feels the temptation once again to snuggle into the heat of her back but he knows he has work to do so he sits on the edge of the bed and fumbles with his feet for his slippers. Three visits to the toilet to pee during the night. His bladder feels as if it is about to give out. A sack with a hole. Drink anything at all – even a cup of tea – in the hours before sleep and it wants out again, whining away like a locked-up puppy until its plea cannot be ignored. And as he stands up there is a sudden twinge at the base of his spine as if it, too, is complaining about something. It cannot be his weight because he weighs no more now than ten years ago. Sometimes his whole body feels like a sullen malcontent casting up past failures or years of supposed neglect. He massages the area with his fingers and tries to stretch himself straight then slides his feet into the slippers and pulls on his dressing gown. Maybe he needs an MOT and wonders if medical care is one of the rights of his post. Nothing private of course, just someone who will come to him and give him the once-over with discretion. He's not going to see McCann at the Health Centre again, he knows that; the last time he had to sit and listen to all his doctor's complaints about underfunding and hospital waiting lists. That's the trouble with people – they all start to think he has the keys to heaven in his pocket. And the other thing is that if people see him sitting in a doctor's waiting room, then before the day is out the word spreads round that he's at death's door and wizened old women come up to him on the street and tell him they will say a Hail Mary for him, or press some lucky charm into his hand.

He goes down the stairs, unlocks the security door and switches off the alarm system. He stops to gather the pile of papers and his briefcase from the hall table then goes into the kitchen and fills the kettle. The clock's just turned six and that gives him a good hour to read the papers again and try to absorb as much as possible. It's a draft set of proposals for new child-protection regulations for voluntary and community groups. Forty-six pages of it and every couple of sentences Crockett has added handwritten notes or potential issues in blue ink. Nearly as many words as the type and all of it in the same scrupulously neat writing. He thinks of the fountain pen that Crockett uses with its gold nib and clip, its shimmering pearled blue body, and tells himself that the last

70

time he saw someone use a fountain pen was his father sitting at a kitchen table filling in a job application form about 1960. Did no good then either. The kettle comes to the boil and hisses angrily as if looking for a fight before it switches off its fury.

He has to be prepared, show them all that he knows his stuff. And the bastard Crockett is always looking for a chance to expose his ignorance, just waiting for him to put his foot in it. Even the word Minister curdling on his lips gives the impression that there's a bad taste in his mouth. He's a sharp boy, too – so sharp that one day he will cut himself – and Gilroy hopes he's there to see it. Outwardly there's never anything but a scrupulous display of politeness. Even that, however, is an insolence because it only serves to prevent any form of personal exchange and it signals that he will give what is required by the demands of his job as a top civil servant but not an iota more. If they were to meet in the street outside the normal parameters of work – and he's not sure if Crockett has ever been in a street except by accident – he would probably walk by with an almost imperceptible nod of the head, if any form of recognition at all. He goes to the cupboard then throws a tea bag in the teapot and pours in the water. Perhaps he should invite him and his wife to tea – that would wipe the smugness off his face. Tell them it would be best to come in a black taxi, to leave the Merc at home. A journey into the heart of darkness. A visit to the Third World. See what excuse he produced to escape his worst nightmare.

He reads the document again. It's good to be on guard. Never can be too careful. Bloody paedophiles everywhere. Worming their way in. Waiting in the shadows like vultures. And when in the fullness of time and this thing comes to completion he visualises a major launch, a performance by children in the Waterfront Hall perhaps, lots of media cover-age, children being looked after. Taken care of. Children and Culture – it could have been worse, even if the wags are starting to call him the Lemonade Man after C&C the local company. Better to be the Lemonade Man than wear the thorned crown of Health. Thank goodness they shafted a Unionist with that one in the latest incarnation of the Assembly and its musical chairs of ministries. Waiting lists, rationalisation of acute services, superbugs, shortages of specialists, patients on trolleys – what a nightmare! And if he was at death's door he wouldn't be able to go and see McCann.

He sips the tea and tries to read Crockett's mind from some of his comments, tries to anticipate some question he'll suddenly spin up at him, then takes heart from his natural advantage. At least he understands what a community is and unlike Crockett his experience isn't restricted to a golf club or a cluster of holiday homes in Tuscany or Provence. Still he needs Crockett and his cronies' knowledge about legal issues, about how best to frame the legislation and shape it into a coherent whole, because if there is a flaw or a single weak spot they can be sure that the wolves in the Assembly will fasten their teeth on it and tear and tear until it collapses in ridicule. The one good thing of course is that it will be difficult to flag up opposition when no one wants to appear opposed to protecting children. He'll play that one to the hilt.

The tea is hot and strong the way he likes it and in a decent-sized mug and not one of those china cups they use up at Stormont which don't hold a spit and feel as if they might crack in your hand. He sets the mug down carefully to avoid putting it on the papers then takes a book out of the front of his briefcase. It's a volume of poems by Larkin. Minister with responsibility for Culture. Needs to read some books. On the quiet. Try to crack it. Understand what it's all about. It's a weakness and like all personal weaknesses he's conscious of it and determined to do something about it, except he doesn't know where to start and it feels more daunting than anything he has ever done. Worse, too, because there's no one he can ask or reveal the weakness to. He started with Joyce but gave up after the third page. A secret language, a secret society like the Masons, and he has no one to initiate him or introduce him to the rituals. Hardly better with Yeats, apart from 'An Irish Airman foresees his Death'. The useless buggers at school who failed to teach him anything and helped him out the door at sixteen are the people he blames. The wonderful Catholic education – wonderful for middle-class kids maybe with aspiring mothers and fathers. But if he's fair he has to concede that he was never the best of pupils and almost squirms at the memory of his waywardness. School was why he tried to read Heaney – he remembered that poem 'The Early Purges' and its reference to 'the scraggy wee shits' and how they nearly fell off their seats when it came out of Father Dornan's mouth but the attempt was pretty much a failure. After the early poems it all clouded over like the mist that drifts now against the windows of the kitchen, smearing the glass with the soft dampness of its breath. His eyes flick to the security cameras and their blinking, changing, grainy shots of mottled grey. A good morning to step out of the perfect cover and do what needs to be done. He shivers suddenly and cups the tea in both hands then opens the Larkin. It was the line about books being crap that caught his eye – it still makes him smile. But he feels as if he's gone far beyond that now and if he's not yet arrived at a full under-standing of some of the poems, he thinks that he is moving steadily towards it and he's not going to give up. This is the bridgehead; from here there is no retreat. Sometimes it feels like one of those books that contain optical illusions, secret pictures that emerge only when you stare at them for ages and ages. Stare and stare and then suddenly it's there in total clarity. There are times when it feels as if the meaning will emerge complete and perfect but then it slips away again and everything is blurred and unfocused like the mist outside. But even then lines or phrases stick in his mind and during the day he turns them over in his thoughts like small stones picked off the beach.

'You'd be better getting a decent breakfast into you and leaving the books for later,' Marie says as she slithers into the kitchen on the whispering tongue of her worn slippers.

He throws the book into the briefcase as if he has been caught reading pornography. 'Just something I have to look over for work. You didn't need to get up.'

'You're not going out of here without a proper breakfast in your stomach,' she says, bending down to get the frying pan out of a cupboard.

'I've been thinking, Marie, that maybe I should try to watch my health – cut down on fried food, all that sort of thing,' he says nervously, unsure of her reaction.

'So my cooking isn't good for you any more?' she says. 'You seem to have done all right on it so far.'

'No, I'm not saying that. Just that I'm coming to an age when I have to be careful. That's all.' He's grateful that at least she has not called him Mr High and Mighty as she has done twice before when she felt irritated by him or told him that she knew him when there was a hole in the seat of his pants.

'Listen, Francis, if you knew anything at all, you'd know that the experts say that breakfast is the most important meal of the day so get those papers off the table.'

No one speaks to him like she does. Thirty-five years of

74

marriage and she still has an edge that he has softened but never vanquished. He looks at her face that without its normal heavy mask of make-up appears soaped and crimped. The bacon hisses and spits like a cornered cat as she layers it into the pan.

'If you ever bothered to look you'd see that I'm using olive oil to cook in. All the way from Italy. No grease.'

'Has the Pope blessed it?'

'You're bloody funny. Not so funny when you were back and forward to the bathroom last night. What's the matter with you?'

'Might've got a chill. Not sure. Hope it isn't the old prostate.'

'Maybe you should get a check-up. Do you know how they check it?'

'Yes I know and I'm not letting old McCann do that to me – he's been trying to do it to me for years. Bloody SDLP voter all his life. He'd just love the chance.'

He gathers his papers carefully and slips them into his bag. A slow seep of half-hearted light is beginning to dissipate the mist, gradually giving jagged edges back to the world. The kitchen fills with the smell of sausages and bacon. She's doing eggs and soda bread as well. Thank goodness he hasn't showered and dressed yet or he would be going out smelling like a greasy-spoon café. The buzzer on the front door sounds as she sets the heaped plate in front of him. They both pause and look at the camera and seeing it's Sweeney she says, 'I haven't got my face on yet,' then goes back upstairs as he heads to open the front door. A personal rule – no one but him ever sees her without her face on and sometimes not even him.

'Misty,' Sweeney says as he closes the door and follows into the kitchen. When he sees Gilroy sit down to his breakfast he stands at the end of the table and says, 'Cultured, very cultured.' It's his current favourite joke and for Gilroy it's beginning to wear thin but he says nothing and signals him with the fork to sit down.

'Who's driving?' he asks.

'Micky,' Sweeney says, staring at the plate.

'Where's Marty?'

'Taking his mother to hospital for some tests.'

'Has he had the car somewhere safe all night?'

Sweeney nods and pours himself a cup of tea.

'And did you tell him about his dress? He looked like a bloody gangster last time. And another thing – he drives too fast.'

'Don't worry, I'll tell him.' Sweeney's eyes linger on the plate. 'Franky, do you think that sort of start to a day is good for your cholesterol? Clogs up the old arteries.'

Before he can answer Marie returns and offers Sweeney some breakfast. 'Wouldn't say no now, Marie,' he says, opening his coat.

'You're not worried about your cholesterol then?' Gilroy asks.

'Ignore him, Ricky, he's beginning to sound like an old woman,' Marie says.

'A good breakfast never hurt anyone,' Sweeney asserts, winking at Gilroy. 'When it's your turn, it's your turn – that's what I say. No point being miserable.'

'What about the driver?' she asks. 'I'm sure he could put something in his stomach, give him a shout, Ricky.'

'Who's going to watch the car?' Gilroy asks but feeling already that the tide is flowing against him.

'You can see it on camera,' she says. 'It'll be all right. The lad'll probably spend the rest of his day twiddling his thumbs and half-starving to death.'

Then as Sweeney goes to call him in, Gilroy shouts, 'While you're at it, why don't you invite the rest of West Belfast? Tell them we're starting a breakfast club!' For a second, as he listens to the door being opened, he imagines the mist flooding into the house and snaking through the rooms until everything is swallowed by it.

'Morning,' Micky says as he stands at the kitchen door rubbing his hands together in embarrassment at being so far inside the house. He's wearing a suit with a mandarin collar and a black shirt. Gilroy inspects him and decides that he passes muster apart from the large gold earring in his right ear. Marie tells him to sit down and asks about his family, remembering that he's a wife and young child.

'They're dead on,' he answers as he looks at the food on the table. 'Saw them last week.'

'Thought you could probably do with a bit of breakfast,' Marie says, working the pan again.

'And keep an eye on the car as you eat,' Gilroy says as he mops his plate with the last piece of bread.

'To be honest with you, I don't think anyone would be interested in stealing it,' Micky says, staring at the screen. 'It's a bundle of scrap really. There's no acceleration in it at all. I was talking to Marty and he thinks the same. Be a bit of a problem if we ever had to step on it to get away from something like.' He looks up apologetically as if he's just said something indelicate. 'Know what I mean?'

'We know what you mean,' Sweeney says, glaring at him.

'Marty knows this guy does imports and quality second-hands. We could look around if you want. Maybe something with tinted glass or a four-wheel drive even.'

'There was sand everywhere the last time I was in it,' Gilroy says. 'Half the bloody Buncrana beach by the look of it. If somebody didn't rake the guts out of it every weekend and bothered to clean it out now and then, the thing would probably go at twice the speed. What's the schedule, Ricky?'

Sweeney sets down his knife and fork and takes a black diary and tape recorder out of his inside pocket. 'First you've an hour's worth of constituency appointments – I don't know why you put it in. You're pushed for time. Then at eleven it's Stormont for the meeting about the new legislation and over lunch you're meeting the delegation of Dutch youth workers. After lunch more work on the child-protection business, this time some voluntary groups like Childline and the NSPCC will be represented; at three, twenty minutes with some American guy called Jack Donaghy who wants to talk about doing a portrait – some political series he's doing.' Marie sniggers and rolls her eyes. 'And at five-thirty a fitting for the wedding.'

'That's the most important appointment of your day,' Marie says, pointing at him with the knife, 'so don't be late.'

'I won't. This guy Donaghy – is he the real thing?'

'Don't know much about him really,' Sweeney says, making a note in the diary.

'Find out who he's done. What his reputation is. What his style is. If we decide to do it I don't want looking like I've two heads or a hump.'

'Like the dog's bollocks,' Micky says as he is handed his plate. 'Thanks, Mrs Gilroy.'

Gilroy and Sweeney stare at him as he tucks in with gusto and when Gilroy looks at Sweeney he merely shrugs in reply. Gilroy stands up and girds himself with the dressing gown. 'I'm going to get changed,' he says, pausing to stop behind Micky's back and ask, 'Are you keeping an eye on that car?'

'Haven't taken my eye off it, Boss.'

'Don't call me Boss.'

'What should I call you?' he asks as Sweeney smiles behind his raised cup.

'Francis will do just fine,' he says but when he is halfway up the stairs he hears the words Lemonade Man and three voices joining together in laughter, Marie's a lilting descant over the other two.

He stands in the shower and waits for it to turn warm. It seems to take longer every morning. He cowers out of the way of the cold water and as he squirms to avoid its spray there's a sharp twinge at the bottom of his spine which makes him swear. It feels like payback time for all those nights on the run, sleeping on floorboards, in damp roof spaces, the back of a car or any other temporary shelter. He thinks, too, of the squeaking, brightly polished toe-capped boots of the squaddies as they gave him a leathering, their synchronised footwork inflicted to the score of breathless abuse delivered in sharp shards of accents that sounded strange to his ears – Brummie, Scottish, Geordie – the voices part of the disorientating geography of pain.

He tries cautiously to straighten his spine and stand erect under the water but there is something about his body he no longer fully trusts. He cups his testicles gently and tries to find comfort in the warmth of the water. But before he can stop himself he thinks of Ricky and himself on the blanket in a shit-smeared cell and the moment when the warders used the hoses to wash them down. He closes his eyes as if to blank out the memory and lets the water's full force hit the crown of his head, holding his hand like a visor over his eyes. Shading the water, shading what you do not want to remember. He thinks of the day ahead and it feels measured and cribbed, drained of expectation or joy. Meeting after meeting, a torrent of talk channelled through the rigid sides of procedures and agendas. Why is it not possible any more to just sit down and have a talk, sort things out over a slow drink? He thinks of the china cups, the saucers and the neat little sandwiches that vanish in one bite. Sometimes the only people in the room he recognises as people are the women who serve the tea and sometimes, too, he wants to try and talk to them, tell them he lives in a house much like theirs, that he knows what it's like to bring up kids on not much money. Sometimes he wants to flirt with them, to say that they are more real, more beautiful and more important to him than any of the suits, but even they have their strict codes of conduct and because they come from the Protestant estates up the road, he knows they probably still think of him as the Antichrist.

There's a phrase from Larkin in his head which he struggles to re-form like some half-remembered tune. Something about the emptiness under all we do. He drips out of the shower, leaving a trail of damp prints, decides that they need to install a fan as he looks back at the black mould grouting the bottom row of tiles, then shaves himself carefully with an electric razor. He stands naked at the mirror and it strikes him that his body is beginning to turn into an old woman's with its incipient breasts and protruding little pot of a belly. There's a solar ring of grey hair round his nipples and he tries to shave it off, nervous in case he nips himself. He puts his finger to his cheekbone where a little spider of broken capillaries is starting to spin its web. Then when he has finished shaving he applies the moisturiser Marie has bought him and insists he uses.

He had forgotten about the wedding fitting. If only it were possible to forget about the wedding so easily. Christine, the last of his four children and his only daughter they want him to give away. He supposes it might be a chance to talk to Justin, something he has not really done, and get to know him a bit better. Try harder to like him. He goes to the wardrobe and looks at his three suits, picks one that's slightly greyer than the others and lays it on the bed. Armani? Armani his arse. He would like to meet whoever it was cooked that one up. Nice soundbite – former terrorists in Armani suits – but if their paths ever cross he will be able to tell him that the only suits he has ever owned all came from home-shopping catalogues. And anyway if he wanted to wear an expensive suit is he not entitled to as much as anyone? Does it really mean that he has sold his principles or forgotten what the struggle was about? The title poem in his Larkin is about a wedding but it is one of the longest ones so he's not tried it yet. Will it offer any answers to how he feels, tell him how to cope with the burning loss that is festering in his heart? At twenty-five and hardly out of university is it not too young? And if he was married at eighteen it was because they lived in a narrower world with none of the windows or opportunities that are open to her, so why does she not take her time, look around a bit? This Justin that they hardly know two things about, if he really loves her he would wait a while longer, give her time to breathe in the possibilities of life. She was always his favourite – perhaps that was inevitable with three sons – and now he feels as if someone has come in the darkness of the night and robbed him of the thing closest to his heart. He suddenly feels inexpressively sad, so momentarily unbalanced that he sits on the bed and masks his eyes with his hand.

Something is happening to him. Maybe it's the menopause because he has read that it happens to men as well. He feels increasingly sentimental about things in a way that sometimes makes him feel vulnerable and foolish. A memory of his father coming home after another futile search for work and slumping at the kitchen table with the shame of failure smouldering in his eyes. Yeats's poem about the Irish airman not caring whether he lives or dies. An old song by the Beatles

81

on the radio. He tries to shake the moment away, stares at the wet prints of his feet and wonders what it has been all about. For the people? For Ireland? It is a strange thought but several times during the last few months he has been afflicted by the idea that Ireland does not exist. Like God it's just perhaps some concept that has no meaning apart from the one you construct in your head. He feels the shame of his thoughts, the traitorous serpent of doubt snaking through his lifetime of commitment, trying to undermine all that he has achieved. For a second he finds respite in his anger at himself but then after the first flush passes he thinks of how soon he must walk down the aisle of the church and give away what's most precious. All his life he has given away parts of himself – years which he should have spent with his children, the birth itself of Rory; the right to take his family downtown or anywhere public; the right to live an ordinary life and never having to look over his shoulder. So why does this feel so unfair?

'What's wrong, Francis?' Marie asks. He hasn't even heard her footsteps on the stairs. For a second he almost tells her that he feels sad but instead says that he feels a little dizzy. She takes his temperature with the palm of her hand. When he sees the concern in her eyes he feels ashamed of his weakness and tells her that he's all right. She sits beside him on his bed and suddenly he's aware of his nakedness.

'You're right, I am turning into an old woman.'

'What's the matter with you?' Her tone is soft as if she is speaking to a child and she puts one hand on the back of his neck and kneads the flesh.

'I don't know.'

'I'll ring the surgery and arrange an appointment – it doesn't have to be with McCann. There's a couple of bright young women now. One of them could see you. Do your prostate test if you like.'

'So long as they take their rings off first.'

'You're tired – that's all. Why don't we try and get a weekend away somewhere after the wedding? Maybe go to Dublin or something.'

'Do you think she's doing the right thing? You don't think that she's rushing into it?'

'Only time will answer that but if it's what she wants to do then all we can do is help her get on with it.'

'I'm not keen on a lot of this wedding stuff – feels a bit over the top some of it. A bit too showy. Too flash. Like bloody Posh and Becks.'

'Listen, Francis, you spend half your life worrying about people thinking you've changed or got above yourself. If you had your way she'd get married in the parochial hall with a blind fiddler playing in the corner. Why don't you just turn up in your blanket and be done with it? If it's what she wants she can have it and to hell with what anybody thinks.'

He nods his head half-heartedly, looks around for his socks.

'Do you want me to help you get dressed?' she asks but he knows he has to pull himself together or he will never get through the day so he shakes his head. She goes to the door and pauses, looks back at him and smiles. 'Just as well that painter boy can't see you now – it would make some portrait.'

'I must look like,' he pauses. 'What was it that idiot Micky said? The dog's bollocks.'

She laughs then says, 'You look just fine but hurry up and get changed before these two eat us out of house and home.'

When he comes back down, Micky is wiping his mouth with the back of his hand. His plate is a shiny skim of emptiness. 'Never took my eyes off the car, Francis,' he says.

'How did you get the food in your mouth then?'

'Natural instinct, but not all made it,' Sweeney says, dabbing at the corner of Micky's mouth with a tissue.

'Leave the boy alone, the pair of you,' Marie says. 'And, Ricky, under no circumstances let him miss that suit fitting.'

'On my life.'

Gilroy follows the two men into the hall but then doubles back and kisses his wife lightly on the cheek. She nods and pats him on the back as if sending one of her sons off to school. As he walks to join the other two in the car the mist has vanished, leaving only a dampness in the air that feels like someone's cold breath on the back of his neck. He sits in the back with Sweeney for the short drive to the new party offices and again Sweeney suggests that they don't really have the time for this but he says nothing, too busy asking himself if Marie is right, and all it must be is tiredness, to tell his assistant that the day people think he has no time for them is the day he's dead in the water. Adrift on his own power trip and mandated by nothing except his own ego. They pass the Bobby Sands mural. It has fresh graffiti on it.

'Bloody kids,' Sweeney says.

'There's no respect any more,' Gilroy says. 'Not for anything.'

The waiting room is half empty and he greets everyone with light good humour, joking about the mist and making up a story about a returning all-night reveller unable to find his own door. Sweeney takes charge, checking the fax machine and email, speaking to all of the workers, casting his eye over the security-cleared post but letting it sit unopened. A quiet night in the city – a couple of burglaries against old people, a racist attack against Portuguese migrant workers, some minor flooding in the lower Ormeau Road. He checks the names of the people waiting and establishes the order, ushers the first one in and then sits at the side of Gilroy's desk and takes notes. Problems with housing application and benefits, a school dispute involving possible suspension, complaints about anti-social behaviour by young people, problems about noise at night from neighbours. Gilroy has heard it all before, knows what to say, how to reassure, who to see and what can be done. Sweeney notes it all and in his head is already deciding who must follow things up and who must assume the necessary responsibilities. The constituents are nervous at first then pleased with how they are treated and leave feeling a little honoured to have had a personal audience.

Two women come in, a grandmother and her daughter, bookends separated only by the thickening shape of time. Short, bottle-blonde hair, hooped earrings, ringed fingers, jeans and cheap trainers. It is the grandmother who does the talking while the daughter barely lifts her eyes from the desk in front of her.

'It's about our Gerard, Francis,' she says. 'He's fifteen and gone off the rails a bit recently since his father left – nothing serious, just the usual sort of trouble. We're really worried about him. He's not a bad lad really but he's started to hang round with a bit of a wild crowd and we think there might be drugs involved.'

'You don't know that for certain,' the mother says, barely raising her eyes.

'Well, Kathleen, it was you told me that's what you thought.'

'Yes, but I don't know for sure.'

It rambles slowly on, slowed down occasionally by differences of opinion, but Gilroy doesn't let his impatience show, nodding his head in a way that says he understands.

'And you see, Francis, he got in a bit of bother last week

with some neighbours and they said they were going to get him kneecapped and he's really a sensitive boy and we're worried that he might harm himself if it ever happened. He was a friend of the Meaney boy, the one who did himself in – God rest his soul. And the family's never got over it. We're scared, Francis, scared that Gerard might go the same way. Please, please, could someone speak to him, try to help him before it's too late?'

'I understand what you're saying and you've done the right thing in coming here. And listen, God only knows it's not easy bringing kids up any more and I know that as well as the next man. And I'm going to do my very best to help with Gerard and believe me no one's getting kneecapped or beaten. There's lots of kids out there like Gerard and we need to find better ways to help them, bring them back on board, get them to make something useful of their lives.'

Gilroy soothes them, promises them, calms them down and Sweeney makes his notes. He tells them about the counselling services that will help, about experienced people he knows. When he has finished he stands up behind his desk and when the grandmother steps towards him he thinks she is going to shake his hand so he offers it to her but instead she takes it and kisses it and invokes God's blessing on him. The mother contents herself with a mumbled thanks and uses a shredded ball of tissue to dab her eyes.

After they have gone Gilroy sits down again and says to Sweeney, 'Give this to Theo, get him to see the boy and look after it. Tell him to try and sort it out best as he can.' He shakes his head. 'You know what I think? I think half the mess we see is caused by the breakdown of the family. Too many one-parent families, too many young men walking away from their responsibilities. Look at that guy Micky – though in his case they're probably better off without him.'

Sweeney smiles and shows in the final person from the waiting room. It's an elderly man in an overcoat carrying a dog lead. He sits down on the seat but does not speak, and his eyes flit round the room like restless moths, never settling on anything for more than a few seconds before moving on elsewhere. Gilroy looks at the list of names on his desk.

'So what can we do for you, John?'

'I've lost my dog,' the man says.

'You've lost your dog?'

'Not exactly.'

'No?' Gilroy asks, glancing at Sweeney.

'He's been stolen. He wasn't in the yard this morning and the back door was open. Someone's taken him.'

'So what type of dog is he?'

'A sheepdog. He's called Lassie.'

Gilroy shifts a little on his seat and avoids looking at Sweeney who has lowered his head as if concentrating intensely on his note-taking.

'So Lassie's missing? Have you phoned the council?'

'No point – he's been stolen.'

'And you've no idea who might have taken him?'

'No. But he's a friendly dog so he would go with anybody he took a liking to.'

'And have you had him a long time?'

'Since he was a pup.'

'Does he have a collar?'

'With his name on.'

'And would you have a photograph of Lassie at home?'

'Yes.'

'Well here's what we'll do, John. You bring your photograph in to the office and we'll scan it into the computer and make Wanted posters. Then you can stick them up round the area. There's a good chance someone will see it and get in touch. What do you say, John?'

'Right, Mr Gilroy,' the man says, then without another word stands up and leaves the office, the dog lead trailing behind him like a metal tail.

After he has gone Sweeney closes the door and chuckles. 'Lassie is lost,' he says. 'I think thon boy is half barking mad himself. Lassie is lost. What does he think this is – *101 Dalmatians*? Listen, we need to get a move on, hit the road. I'll get Micky to bring the car round.' He pauses at the office door. 'Listen, Franky, I know who would know where Lassie is.'

'Who?'

'The dogs on the street,' he says and as he walks away Gilroy watches his shoulders heaving at his own joke.

Sweeney tells the joke again as they drive across the city but Gilroy concentrates on reading his draft papers, sometimes squinting at the print.

'I need to get my eyes tested,' he says to Sweeney. 'Think the time has come for glasses.'

'Glasses would be cultured,' Sweeney says. 'Wouldn't they, Micky?'

'Make you look like a brainbox,' Micky says.

'You should get a pair,' Gilroy says as they pass the city airport. 'Are you checking your rear mirror to see that nothing is following us?'

'Yes, Francis.'

They sweep round on to the Upper Newtownards Road and then through the ornate, black metal gates of Stormont, pass under the aggressive defiance of Carson's statue with his outstretched arm which always makes Gilroy think the Unionist icon is giving him the finger and up the long, lawn-flanked driveway.

'Another day, another dollar,' Gilroy says as they get waved through the security check but the nonchalance of his words is designed to hide the tremor of anxiety that hits him, as it does each time at this precise moment, and with it an awareness of how far they have come and the magnitude of what has been achieved. Once inside the building his footsteps clack on the marble floor and announce his arrival and he steps out with his head held high. It's a building designed to make you feel small, that arches too much space over your head, that can smother your voice with its heavy wood and white marble, but he will not be bowed by it or intimidated by its ostentatious show of history. Harder, however, not to allow a sense of pride to fill his steps. Pride for himself, the son of a sign-painter, pride for his people – the second-class citizens – who now through him sit at the very top table. So to scatter the distracting weight of these thoughts he makes a joke about Davy Crockett and the Alamo as they come round a corner to suddenly meet Crockett standing with a file under his arm.

'Good morning,' Crockett says.

'Good morning,' he replies, wondering if they have been overheard. Crockett's face betrays nothing. 'Busy day ahead.'

'Indeed,' Crockett says, glancing at his watch. 'We meet in the committee room in half an hour.'

'That's right,' Gilroy says and then walks on to his office. When the door is shut he says to Sweeney, 'That fella gives off a cold draught every time he opens his mouth. He looks at you like you're something stuck to the sole of his shoe.'

'If he was a lollipop he'd lick himself.'

'Try to find out about him. Ask around. Try Montgomery in the Press Office. And are we sure this office is clean?'

'It's been swept twice now,' Sweeney says, glancing round the room.

'Have it done on a regular basis. Go through it with a fine-tooth comb. And no one is to use the phones for anything that's important, either in or out. Now check with the secretary for what's come in this morning and if there's anything really important that I need to see, otherwise I want to spend the half hour looking over this stuff again. Tell her I'm not available during this time.'

As Sweeney shuts the door Gilroy sinks back in his chair and shuffles through the papers in front of him. His eyes are sore already and the day has only started – he will have to see about glasses. Perhaps they add a little gravitas to your image. Perhaps they just make you look like an old man. He tries to focus on the document before him but it's the image of himself walking his daughter down the aisle that dances before his eyes. The blackness of his suit, the whiteness of her dress. Chess pieces on a board. As a child she was always trying to outmanoeuvre him, exploit his weakness for her, and in her armoury she had a cunning range of moves which showed no mercy until she got what she wanted. So she could work on his guilt about his all-too-frequent absences; about the constant strain of living on the edge of fear, of being a child sitting in her pyjamas at the top of the stairs as the Brits kicked in the door, in her child's imagination their blackened faces like chimney sweeps.

Their relationship has been a continual skirmish and long ago he gave up trying to rein her in and if anything he loves her even more for her independence of spirit. He smiles as he thinks of the school revolt she led against the petty strictures of the nuns, of her early experiments with the extremes of fashion, her holiday work as an au pair where the family stuck her for a week then sent her home. And does this Justin deserve her? Justin who works in London in advertising, who wears rectangular designer glasses and watches cricket.

Justin who calls him Franky when no one calls him that who has not struggled at his side for twenty years. Justin whose shell-shocked parents will fly in the night before the wedding and straight out the next morning. His mouth feels dry at the thought of that walk down the aisle. And what will he say in his speech? What words will he compose for the guests? He remembers the Larkin in his bag and takes it out and starts to read the title poem, 'The Whitsun Weddings'. It's about different, newly married couples getting on the same train and heading for London, travelling into the future. He wonders if she will be happy or if she, too, will slowly fade from his life into the vastness of London. He doesn't know if the poem is a happy or sad one. He doesn't understand the ending and he is reading it slowly, word by word, as if climbing a sheer face where each one is a handhold, when Sweeney enters.

'I have an idea,' Sweeney says, smiling. 'About Lassie.'

'And what's that?' he asks, slipping the book back in his bag.

'We could borrow one of the army's sniffer dogs – they couldn't be doing much this weather. Get it to sniff Lassie out. What do you think?'

'Very funny,' he says flatly as he stands up and smooths his jacket. 'When I'm in this meeting watch how they look at each other when I'm talking. Watch what they say with their eyes.'

Sweeney nods and busies himself with the diary and stub of a pencil that makes him sometimes look like a race-track bookie.

'Do you not think you should go a bit more high tech?' Gilroy asks him. 'A laptop or at least one of those hand-held things.'

'Computers are what they love more than anything else.

They understand them, how to hack into them – everything. Might as well just write it on your face. A computer is like an open book no matter how clever you think you've been. And anyway, who's ever going to be able to make sense of my writing?' he says, holding up a page of hieroglyphic scrawl.

'Like an army of worms wriggled across the page,' Gilroy says, narrowing his eyes to take it in. 'But don't ever let Crockett see it. Now, do I look all right?' he asks, straightening himself for inspection.

'Like the dog's bollocks.'

'Good, so let's go, and remember what I said.'

Slow time all day. A snowstorm of papers, agendas and drafts. White paper cold to the eyes and to the touch. He stumbles snow blind through the rest of the day, always trying hard to find familiar landmarks to guide his way, to bring him to the warmth of some friendly hearth. But sometimes his mind begins to drift no matter how hard he tries to focus and he finds himself thinking of an escape, an adrenalin-fired break-out like that day from the Kesh. The west coast of Ireland, perhaps, where the only sounds in his ears are the throaty break of the surf and the only white is in the jagged-tipped teeth of the waves and the scattering of gulls hovering weightless on the salted currents. Others are planning it, others have stashed away nest eggs, so why not him? Marie is right – perhaps he has spent too long wearing a hair shirt, too intent on escaping any accusation of feathering his own nest or the taint of self-interest. His finances are an open book for anyone to examine and God and the bank manager know it wouldn't take very long. After this wedding is paid for he will almost be cleaned out.

Crockett conducts the meetings, his elegantly moving pen the baton that directs the score to the beat of his PowerPoint and his overheads, his appendices and his statistical analysis.

And it's his voice that takes the solos with his, 'Perhaps the Minister might consider . . .' or 'It might be of advantage to point out . . .' but in this particular game all the advantages reside in one pair of hands and as Gilroy watches the pen start to slowly change tempo and move like a metronome he feels as if he is in danger of being hypnotised and has to blink his trance away.

If he's to make any money it has to be through his own transparent efforts that are purer than the driven snow. As they pause for a tea break he wonders if he could write a book, the story of his life, but knows that he would be damned for the truth and damned for what he left out. He tries to engage the tea lady in a meaningless conversation about the weather but she only simulates a smile and serves him with scrupulous politeness. It's not what he wants from her. Her hair is short, dyed blonde like the mother and daughter he spoke with earlier, and her eyes are a delicate pale blue. It's the only colour in a face where sadness lingers lightly below the surface, disguised by the lined weariness of work. He wants to hear words from the thin-lipped purse of her mouth that recognise him as a person, that allow him to ask about her family, to tell her the terrible news that soon he will give his only daughter away to a man he barely knows and doesn't like. But when he returns the empty cup and saucer to her she almost curtsies as she takes it and her eyes avoid looking into his.

Crockett and his team have not returned yet. Sweeney is studying an oil painting of some obscure servant of the state like a prospective purchaser at an auction. Perhaps there could be access to a lecture circuit. He smiles to himself as he suddenly has the bizarre idea of a partnership with the retired head of the RUC. Doing America together, good cop bad cop, both sides of the coin. A symbol of reconciliation. They must be putting crazy pills in the tea. Not in anyone's wildest dreams. He wanders about the room and loosens his tie – it is always too warm in the building. Pausing before Crockett's place at the table he lifts the pen and lets it rest in his hand. Lighter than he expected. Inexplicably beautiful. For a second he slips into a dream of somewhere else, some place that exists in its own perfection behind a kind of veil. His hand wants to reach out and tear it away, to step fully into this place he's never been, but which he now believes exists, a secret whose revelation has been denied to him. There are footsteps in the corridor and he starts, lets go of the pen and resumes his seat, lowering his head as if poring over the documents in front of him. When he glances up the civil servants are grinning at each other. Perhaps they've just shared a smutty story in the gents' or some piece of juicy office gossip across the sparkling white urinals that you can't use without having to think of the people who have stood in the same place.

The day drags slowly on to its conclusion in an unrelenting sequence of point and counterpoint, of people arguing a case, their voices tightly edged with the conviction of their correctness. He feels the clammy fingers of their self-righteousness clinging to his consciousness, battening itself to his increasingly weary being. He thinks of his conversation with the American painter who in his twenty minutes talked of Che Guevara and the Sandanistas, of September the eleventh and political iconology. Of how he works from photographs so long hours are not wasted in sittings. He asks himself now what he has to lose. But he'll let Sweeney check him out and then make a decision. He looks round the panelled walls with their portraits and thinks that one day his own might join them. His eyes drift to the windows but already outside there is a wash of grey and the bright burn of electric lights. Soon it will be time to go home. The thought spurs him to one last burst of energy and full concentration. He notices how even Crockett looks a little weary, his face greying with the fading light outside, blue dregs of colour pooling under his eyes. It feels like being back in school and sneaking glances at the clock to see how long it is to the final bell. His stomach rumbles and he presses his palm against it to smother the noise. He wants his tea but knows that even that is a long way off and that first he must endure the wedding-suit torment.

When the time finally comes and he climbs into the back of the car dusk has dropped suddenly over the city and the night air pinches at his face. Micky has the windows down and he wonders why until he catches the unmistakable smell of fast food.

'Hell's bells,' he says. 'It smells like a burger bar in here. Have you been at McDonald's again?'

'Sorry, Francis, I got a bit peckish,' Micky says, trying to fan the smell out through the open window. 'I had a cheeseburger with bacon. Did the business like. Filled the hole.'

'I want you to drive us back up there again and I want you to get me one.'

'Very cultured,' Sweeney says.

'So you'll not be wanting one then,' he says. 'And give that joke a rest, will you, it's wearing a bit thin.'

'What about the cholesterol then? Clog your arteries that stuff will,' Sweeney says. 'And if we get caught in traffic we'll be late for the fitting.'

'It'll only take ten minutes and Micky'll nip in for us. If we don't get something to eat now it'll be after seven before we get fed. I can't wait that long. My stomach thinks my throat's been cut.'

As the car drives off the lights in Stormont seem to burn sharper in the gloom. Down below the road is hung in parallel strings of amber beads. They are hitting the rush-hour traffic and they have to wait a while to find a gap. His head is sore and he feels his breathing becoming shallower so he sits back in the seat and shades his eyes with his hand.

'You want me to arrange an appointment with an optician?' Sweeney asks.

'I don't know,' he says. 'Maybe I'll give it a while longer, see how it goes.'

'It's not as if anyone's going to call you Specky or anything,' Micky says, half glancing over his shoulder.

'Shut up, Micky, and just drive the car,' Sweeney tells him and his voice is suddenly sharp-edged. 'And turn on the news.' Then in a whisper he asks Gilroy if he's feeling OK.

'Just a bit tired,' he answers. 'Who would have thought that sitting on your arse all day and listening to people rabbit on could leave you done in?'

'Maybe you need a rest – get away from it all for a week or so. Let some of the younger ones take up the reins for a while.'

'You trying to pension me off?' he asks as he shades his face again, this time to block the gaze of a motorist sitting alongside in slow-moving traffic. 'They'll think I'm not up to it, think I'm too old. They're like a bunch of vultures waiting for the first sign of weakness. What did any of them ever do in the struggle? Nothing to get their hands dirty. Too busy getting their university education and all their fancy degrees. Some of them weren't out of nappies when we were putting everything on the line.'

'I know,' Sweeney says. 'There's no respect for the past any more from anyone. And if you fall over they'll put me out to pasture as well. But maybe you need a rest, maybe it would help.'

They pause and listen to the radio report of the day's session of the new Truth and Reconciliation Commission. A rural killing of an off-duty UDR soldier. They look at each other but there is no recognition of the name or the story. It reports the statement of the volunteer who killed him. Both men chorus the words over the radio's voice. 'I was a soldier fighting in a war. At that time I believed the victim represented a legitimate target in that war. I deeply regret the pain and suffering caused to his family . . .'

'You'd think they could think up some variations just to make it sound spontaneous,' Gilroy says. 'This was always a bloody stupid idea.'

'Don't know why we ever signed up to it,' Sweeney says.

'Because we had to. Because we sang so loud about having the truth on everything they ever did that we stumbled blindly into the net and then it was too late to get ourselves out when they turned round and asked for our truth. Maybe it's time to let the dead stay dead, move on instead of digging them back up every day. It's like having a ghost permanently on your shoulder. You've heard of *Hamlet*, haven't you?' Sweeney nods. 'Well apparently there's this thing in it about being blown up by your own bomb – hoist by your own something. What's that guy looking at?'

'What guy?'

'The one driving the Renault.'

'He just recognises you, that's all. He's on his way home from the office, no worries. Are you sure about this burger?'

He nods, even though the idea already seems a bad one, but increasingly he feels the need to kick back against his day and there is, too, a sudden crazed sense of frustration at having so many limits imposed at the very moment when he should be able to embrace his freedom most fully. They reach the McDonald's opposite the hospital and the car swings into the busy car park. There are people everywhere, family groups, teenagers in football shirts.

'I think we should make this quick,' Sweeney says.

'No probs,' Micky answers, steering the car into the drive-through.

'Where the hell are you going?' Sweeney shouts, pushing himself forward on the seat.

'The drive-through's the quickest,' Micky says, his eyes flitting in and out of the mirror.

'Don't be so bloody stupid!' Sweeney shouts as he places both his hands on the back of the driver's seat. 'Get out of here.'

But it's too late, already a car has entered behind them and so there's no way forward or backwards. Gilroy says nothing at first but slumps back into the seat, then says, 'Funny to be killed over a burger. Especially one you didn't get to eat.' The pinpricks of pain behind his eyes are growing sharper, deeper.

'At least there's not far to go to get to a hospital,' Micky says, drumming his fingers on the wheel while the car in front sits motionless.

'Micky, do me a favour,' Sweeney says, 'let someone with half a brain do the jokes.' Then glancing sideways at Gilroy he adds, 'Tomorrow he can start looking for stolen dogs.'

'It was my fault,' Gilroy answers, 'don't take it out on him. Keep your eyes open, Micky, and as soon as it's clear get us out of here. Forget the burger. Just foot to the floor.'

An arm stretches from the serving window and hands a bag in to the driver. The car moves slowly forward and they follow it bumper to tail until they are out in the car park and then they cut sharply on to the main road.

'Micky, turn up the radio,' Sweeney orders and when the volume has risen asks quietly, 'Francis, are you all right?'

'I don't know,' Gilroy says, pressing his thumb and first finger to his eyes. 'Just a little tired, maybe.'

'You need to see a doc. I'll arrange it if you want. We can find the right person.'

'I'll let you know. Something to eat and a good night's sleep would go a long way to seeing me right.'

Twenty minutes later they're entering the city centre. The car radio has been switched off and a brittle silence has settled, separating each from the other and making them loath to be the one to break the fragility of its hold. Their eyes stare blankly out of the car at the city which has almost drunk the day and finds its final dregs laced with a lingering sadness. It rises through the dusk and haloes the motionless heads of those travelling home on yellow-paned buses; it drifts aimlessly in the blurred slur of neon that skims the pavements and roads and brushes the pale faces of those whose hurried weariness reveals nothing but the imprint of their longing for home. Gilroy tries to look up beyond the frazzling fretwork of neon, past the offices where moon-faced ghosts sit still frozen at computers, and tries to see the sky but the buildings are too close together, too garishly dressed in their own light, like the young women who will link arms and claim these same streets in a matter of hours.

They arrive outside the wedding shop and as soon as he gets out of the car, Gilroy glances up and lets the cold night air splash itself against his face. He stands still, looking at the frosted white light of the windows and the ivory sheaths of dresses. The brightness hurts his eyes and he turns his gaze to the sky where he finds respite in the purple and whorled bruise of darkness that feels strong enough to envelop this sickly glitter of whiteness and smother it in the blackness of its embrace. He doesn't want to enter but Sweeney's hand in the middle of his back gently propels him forward. 'The sooner we get this over, the sooner we get to eat,' he says. Gilroy nods but lets him lead the way. The door is held open for them by one of the shop assistants. Inside there's a group waiting for them. He sees Rory and Michael but not his youngest son Peter. Justin is standing beside someone he doesn't recognise and laughing at some joke his companion has made.

'Where's Peter?' he asks Marie as she comes towards him.

'You're late – we thought you weren't coming,' she says, angling her head and staring at him, her face tightened with accusation. 'Peter's on call and had to go back to the hospital but it doesn't matter, Michael's the same height and size so we can go by him.'

'Hi, Franky,' Justin says, stretching out his hand. 'How you doing? This is Edmund, the best man to be.'

He shakes hands with both of them and resists the urge to pull their arms out of their sockets. Edmund is printed on the same press as Justin, right down to the glasses. He thinks they're standing smiling at him the way they might smile at an animal in the zoo.

'So how's London then?' he asks, loosening the knot of his tie.

'Busy, busy – we've a lot of new big contracts,' Justin says. 'Important clients so the pressure's on to produce.'

'That's good,' Gilroy says, not knowing what he's saying good to. 'First time in Belfast, Edmund?'

'Yes, sir,' Edmund says and Gilroy looks at him to see if he is taking the piss but in his face sees only a polite nervousness. Edmund's head continues to nod slowly in silent affirmation of his answer.

'You in advertising, too?' Gilroy asks.

'No, I'm in property – not sharp enough for advertising.'

'You're a builder?' he asks and over Justin's shoulder sees Rory and Michael smile and squirm a little.

'No, I invest, develop, that sort of thing.'

'Very good and how long have you known Justin?'

'Same school, same uni. Long time. That right, Justin?'

'Too long. Knows all the dark secrets,' Justin says.

He's going to ask another question when Marie pushes in and pulls him by the cuff. 'We need to get on with it,' she says. 'Time for the interrogation later.' Then turning to her prospective son-in-law and his friend she says, 'Ever since he got his job he thinks the whole world owes him an answer.'

'Minister for Children and Culture,' Justin says. 'Very impressive.'

'Keeps me busy.'

'You know what Goebbels said about culture?'

Gilroy looks startled and turns to Sweeney but there's no answer in his face. 'So, remind me, what did Goebbels say about culture?' he asks but before Justin can answer, Rory comes forward and rests an arm on his shoulder.

'He said that whenever he heard anyone talking about culture it made him want to reach for his gun. Now let's try these suits on and get this over with.'

On cue the manager and his assistant produce the suits and start to direct them to the changing area. As he's handed his, Gilroy looks at it, then looks at Sweeney and rolls his eyes.

'It's not so bad,' Sweeney says but as he heads for the changing room, Gilroy pulls his sleeve.

'What was he talking about? Was he calling me a Nazi?'

'No, Franky, he wasn't calling you a Nazi – he was making a joke about culture. And don't make this guy Edmund any more nervous than he already is or he'll be shittin' his pants.'

He turns round to see Marie nodding encouragement at him and shooing him on with her hand. In the changing cubicle he pulls the curtain tightly closed, sits on the stool in the corner and tries not to look at himself in the mirror. There's the sound of zips and shoes being taken off in the other cubicles. When he bends over to loosen his laces there's a pain in his back that makes him wince. He catches the tightened purse of his face in the mirror and tries to steady himself by pressing the splay of his hand against the glass. When he lifts it away there is a momentary print like a cave painting, before it fades into nothing. He removes his jacket and drops his trousers, not bothering to hang them up but kicking them into a corner, then puts on the suit.

'All right, Da?' Rory calls.

'No problems,' he says. 'Who picked this outfit?'

'Who do you think?' Michael answers.

'I suppose we should be grateful we're not wearing kilts,' Gilroy says, slipping on his shoes without tying the laces.

'Everything all right, gentlemen?' the manager asks, his words mixing with the spicy scent of his aftershave.

'Everything's fine,' he answers but feels foolish as he looks at himself and as he straightens it feels as if he's given away his dignity. He sits down on the stool again and lets the side of his head loll against the glass. Give your only daughter away and do it dressed like a clown. Give your daughter away to someone you know nothing about.

'What's keeping you, Francis?' Marie calls. 'Everyone's waiting for you.'

'I'm coming,' he shouts as he stands up. Is it his imagination or does he feel a little dizzy? He's too hot and into his head come images of Atlantic breakers, of the salted freshness of sea air washing over him. When he steps out of the cubicle it is not Marie he sees but Christine and she is standing smiling at him, pleased with the suit and enjoying his discomfort.

'Where did you come from?' he asks. 'I thought you weren't supposed to see this until the wedding day.'

'It's my dress the groom isn't supposed to see. You didn't think I'd leave you to your own devices? Suit looks good; love the waistcoat. But it'd look even better if you could bring yourself to smile a bit.'

'Smile?' Marie says as she moves closer to her daughter. 'A smile would crack his face these days. Must be part of the image.'

Behind her the two assistants are checking cuff lengths and securing buttons, their hands moving silently and quickly like card sharps dealing waxen decks.

'And you're going to have a lovely buttonhole to set off the suit. We chose the flowers earlier today,' Christine says as she comes close to him and touches the waistcoat lightly with the tips of her fingers. His eyes rest on the smallness of her hands, the shiny ostentation of the engagement ring.

'Suppose the flowers are costing an arm and a leg,' he says as she palms his waistcoat flat. 'And that's my stomach. Nothing I can do about it.'

'You could go on a diet for my big day.'

'He will not,' Marie interrupts, 'he's already lost enough weight this past while. If he keeps going he'll be skin and bone before this is over.'

'And don't be talking about money,' Michael chips in. 'Whatever it costs it'll be a bargain to get her off your hands.'

Her hands are small, pink-nailed, perfect – the hands of a child, they push him in the small of his back or tug at his sleeve. Always insistent, never taking no for an answer. Directing him to wherever it is she wants him to go. Bossy, demanding little hands, never accepting procrastination or excuse, desperate to show him her latest hiding place or special den. Always building dens or little rooms – under the kitchen table, under the stairs, or in the corner of the yard roofed with a sheet or tablecloth. And she always loved to furnish them, to equip them with all the necessary comforts. Never one for roughing it or going without. He glances at Justin checking his appearance in one of the full-length mirrors and smoothing one of his lapels. Need to earn a lot of money, Justin, to keep her in the style she expects. Need to know how to keep her happy when some unseen wind blows through her mind and makes her restless.

'You'll look just great in the video,' Christine says, then goes to talk to Justin.

'Video? What video?' Gilroy asks his wife.

'All weddings have a video, Francis,' she says, grimacing at him.

'Nobody said anything about a video,' he protests.

'You can hardly complain when you spend half your life in front of a camera,' she insists as she picks a piece of fluff off his jacket.

'What else do I not know about?' he asks.

'Well, Francis, it's good of you to ask because to date your involvement in the wedding has been limited to not very helpful comments. Do you think you could cheer up a bit, try to look pleased for her? She's already starting to ask me what's wrong with you. What am I supposed to say?'

He feels the slow burn of shame, a sense of selfishness, and doesn't try to stem the flow of her words.

'And another thing – if she wants to leave the reception in a hot-air balloon, that's all right by me. In fact anything she wants on what is supposed to be the most special day of her life, as far as I am concerned, she can have.'

The others are returning to change back into their own clothes. Rory and Michael are joking with Edmund about something he can't quite hear. He thinks the joke is about him.

'She doesn't really want a hot-air balloon, does she?'

'No, she doesn't, not yet anyway, but if she does we'll get her one whether we have to beg, steal or borrow it. Francis, we owe her. Big time! For all the times we couldn't take her places, or even go to see her do things. For all the times you weren't there.'

'I know,' he says, suddenly feeling so weary that he wants to sit down, sit down somewhere he's not confronted by his reflection.

As always she reads him. 'Get changed now. Do you want me to help you?'

Yes he wants her help but shakes his head, unwilling to show his need in front of the others. 'Could we all go out after this for a meal somewhere? All of us, Edmund, everyone.'

'They've already got something arranged. Michael and Rory are taking them somewhere. They don't want old fogies like us getting in the way of their plans. Anyway I think we need to get you home. Have you eaten yet?'

'Not yet,' he says, beginning to open the buttons of his waistcoat, his fingers feeling heavy and clumsy.

'Christine,' he suddenly calls, 'seeing as this wedding is costing me an arm and a leg, you better give your old man a hug to pay for it.'

She skips towards him and puts her arms tightly around him. Over her shoulder he exchanges smiles with Marie.

'Paid with interest,' he says.

When she releases him he goes to say something to her but the words feel as if they are lodged too deep inside himself, too far beyond his reach, and so instead he turns and walks slowly back to the changing cubicle.

'Dad, you never told me you were having your portrait done.' Her voice is light, teasing, full of mischief.

'No secrets round here then. And you'll all get a few laughs out of it, I'm sure.'

'You can take it,' she calls.

He nods and entering the cubicle pulls the curtain tightly closed. Just for a second he feels lighter but then as he faces his reflection in the mirror, the old tiredness returns and he slumps on to the chair. There is a sullen rumble of hunger from his stomach. He hears again his self-accusation of selfishness and in his head begins to construct a rebuttal of the charge but it fails to find any form of words that serves to convince or ward off the accusation, so he resorts to feelings, letting them swirl about his pressing consciousness in the hope that they will wash away the clamouring voices. He takes off the suit carefully and places it on the hanger, making sure the crease of the trousers is preserved. He will need to look his very best on the day. On video, preserved for ever – the thought makes him squirm a little as he puts on his own jacket. Something shiny in the pocket catches his eye. He takes out a pen. A fountain pen. Crockett's. He spins round as footsteps pass outside. His breathing is suddenly hurried, finally staunched only by the swelter of swear words that hiss from his lips. How could he have been so stupid? What was he thinking of? Taking a man's pen, a pen that he will now know is missing and believe that someone has lifted it. What was he trying to do – tell Crockett that he works for some back-street wide-boy who would filch the eyes out of the back of your head? Tell Crockett that everything he ever thought about him was true?

'Hurry up, Dad,' Christine's voice calls. 'We're going on somewhere.'

'I'm coming, I'm coming.'

He places the pen back in his pocket. He'll try to leave it back. Drop it maybe in the room they were using when no

106

one is looking. Drop it where someone will be sure to see it and return it to its owner. He tells himself that it's only a bloody pen. He must have done it in his confusion and forgotten about it. Crockett probably has a drawerful in his office – he might not even notice it's gone.

He's the last to emerge. Rory and Michael have gone to look for a taxi. Justin stands with his arm round Christine. He stares at the arm that rests across his daughter's shoulder. In it he reads different things, affection, the offer of protection, but there is also something proprietorial in it, an assertion of new ownership. His own hand presses the pocket where he knows the pen is.

'You took so long we thought you were writing your memoirs,' Christine says.

'Maybe not such a bad idea,' he says, 'but then again who would want to read what I would have to tell?'

'I know some agents in London who have lots of contacts in publishing,' Edmund says. 'I could get in touch with them on your behalf if you like.'

'Thanks, son, but I'm not ready yet to put pen to paper. Maybe when I retire.'

'A lot of these books are ghosted, all you have to do is talk,' Edmund says.

'You think I can't write?' he asks a little too sharply then tries to soften it with a smile.

'No, of course he doesn't,' Marie says.

'I was just thinking of you not having the time,' Edmund says.

'Dad, we need to go now, we have a table booked,' Christine says, staring at him for a second then giving him a perfunctory peck on the cheek.

He watches her as she follows the others out into the street. He hopes she will turn round and let him smile at her but instead Justin holds the top of the door open and she ducks under it like a child playing a game and vanishes into the night.

The day of the wedding is leaden and blustery with gusts of wind suddenly flaring up as if irritated by their own motion. Gilroy sits at the kitchen table in his hired suit and looks at the notes he's made for his speech while Marie pins the spray to his lapel. Her hair is close to his face and looks shiny and stiff with lacquer. There are squeals of laughter from upstairs and mobile phones seem to be ringing in every corner of the house. In his head they chime out like church bells. He feels nervous, more nervous than he's felt in a long time.

'Are we all right for time?' he asks as Marie stands back to admire her work.

'We're fine,' she says, straightening it slowly and angling her head to assure herself that she has got it right. 'I hope this wind dies down or her dress is liable to end up over her head. Close your eyes.'

'What?'

'Close your eyes when you're told. I'm going to spray your hair, stop you looking like you've been dragged through a hedge backwards.'

Before he can say anything she masks his eyes with her palm and there is the hiss of the spray.

'I'd have thought you knew that speech off by heart, the amount of time you've spent looking at it,' she says. 'You're not nervous, are you, with all the speeches you've made in your life?'

'I've never made a speech at my daughter's wedding before,' he says. 'Don't want to mess up.'

Suddenly she bends forward and kisses him lightly on the forehead. 'I've never seen you mess up so I don't think you're going to start now. But you will mess up really badly if you don't tell me that I'm looking nice.'

'You look great,' he says, 'but you don't look old enough to be the bride's mother.'

'Old enough to be a grandmother?' she asks.

'A grandmother? Plenty of time for kids when she's got her career up and running.'

'She'll be putting her career on hold for a while,' she says, not looking at him.

'What do you mean?' he asks.

'She's pregnant, Francis. Six weeks.'

'Pregnant? She can't be,' he says, thrusting his hand through his hair and finding it clotted and brittle. 'Why didn't she tell us before? Is she sure?'

'She told me a while back, I just couldn't find the right moment to tell you.'

'Why didn't she tell me herself?' he asks, looking at his wife as if somehow he has been betrayed. He feels betrayed but by whom and in what way he struggles to understand.

'She wanted me to tell you. I just wanted the right moment.'

Upstairs there is the scamper of feet, the whirr of a hair-drier and a babble of voices. He stands up and then sits down again. 'And you think this is a good time, the morning of her wedding, five minutes before I'm walking her down the aisle?'

'These things don't matter so much any more. They're doing the right thing now, getting married.'

'You don't think she's just getting married because of the baby?' There is panic in his head, an unravelling. 'She doesn't have to get married – we could help her look after the child. She doesn't have to get married, Marie.'

'Shush, Francis,' she says, placing her hand on his

shoulder. 'Everything's all right; she wants to get married. Everything's all right.'

'Are you sure? Are you really sure?'

She takes his hand and tells him she is really, really sure. He tries to steady himself, holds her hand against his cheek.

'It doesn't show,' he says.

'It's still early.' She cradles his head against her side.

'Who knows?'

'Only the four of us and his parents, no one else.'

'I don't want anyone to know. Not until they need to.'

She eases herself out of the embrace and tells him that it's not the end of the world, that it happens every day, that no one gives it a second thought, but gradually her words drift by him and he can hear only the voices in his head telling him that it's his fault for not having looked after her properly, for not being there for her. And then he feels anger towards her. Why just for once can she not bide her time, do things in the right way, in the right order like everyone else? Why does she not think of others instead of following every impulse that runs through her selfish head?

He looks at the few pages of paper in his hand and suddenly the words he's composed seem meaningless. What does it matter to her now if he gives her a father's blessing or not because he can't think of a single time when she ever came to him and truly sought his approval or permission? How can she be having a child when she's still a child herself? Folding the paper he places it in the side pocket of his jacket and wonders how he's even going to look at her. He watches Marie pinning her hat, that to him seems nothing more than a few wispy feathers, and wonders how she is able to take so many big things in her stride when somehow he has, without realising how it happened, become someone who can be knocked off course by the slightest thing. He wonders if he might really be ill, in the first stages of some serious illness where he is afflicted by unseen chemical changes, by antibodies and viruses invading his nervous system and wreaking havoc in his internal circuitry. He shakes his head as if to clear the confusion and uncertainty that fogs itself round his senses, shakes it again as if to stir everything into sharpness of vision. Marie works at her hat with both hands, the pins held between the tightness of her lips, taking one out at a time until they have all been used. He feels a sudden pain, as if he has swallowed something sharp and it has journeyed through his veins to lodge in his heart.

'Why does she never think of us?' he asks.

'Because she's too busy thinking of herself and that's the way life is, Francis. Please God the rain will keep off. What's it doing now?'

He stands up and goes to the kitchen window. 'It's not raining but it's hard to know what it's going to do.' He pours himself a glass of water and sips it slowly like an expensive wine. Perhaps if he had read more books, understood more of the things that were inside them, then he would know now what to say or do, know now what it was he felt. Suddenly the room floods with people and the first cars are arriving to take bridesmaids and Marie. Then it's time for Christine to make her appearance and she comes down the stairs slowly, flowers in hand and holding her dress as if she is about to go paddling in the sea. This is the moment when he's supposed to be overcome with her beauty and a father's pride but something is failing to register and he looks only at her face before he mumbles the expected phrases. There's chaos all around him with people fussing over her and each other and his head feels garlanded with their squealing voices. He slowly backs into the kitchen and sits again at the table. Marie is talking to him but the words aren't really registering. As he glances up at her animated face he thinks she has too much make-up on. Everything about the day now begins to feel unnatural, made-up, too much of putting on a show, and he's never been a showman no matter what others might say. He tells himself that it's what is expected, that there's no harm in it, but his thoughts are interrupted by Marie's insistent voice reminding him not to 'race her down the aisle', to take his time and let everyone see her. He nods and forces a smile that he knows has not convinced her but she has no time to say anything more as someone's calling her to go and suddenly the house empties and quietens, all the stir drains away and there is only Christine and a girl he doesn't know, who is still pecking at her hair with a steel comb. A sudden squall rattles against the kitchen window and pieces of litter shimmy into the air.

'At least they won't have to brush up all the confetti afterwards,' he says.

'We'll need to get into the car as quickly as we can,' Christine says, 'before I blow away. Hold on to me tight down the path, Dad.'

This is what a father does, he thinks, offers his child the strength of himself, protects her from the winds that blow. The thought galvanises him and for an intense moment he shakes off some of the lingering uncertainties, pushes himself into action. He takes a pen out of his pocket – Crockett's pen – and scribbles some additional thoughts at the end of his speech.

'Have you not got that written yet?' she asks with mock exasperation.

'I'm not used to having to write them myself,' he jokes. 'Usually some bright thing does it. I just mouth the words or read the autocue.'

'Just don't make it too long – it's not a political speech.'

'Easier if it was.'

The girl tending her hair is finally finished and wishes her good luck before looking out the window and telling them that their car has arrived. Then she disappears upstairs to watch from the bedroom window.

'Ready, Dad?' she asks as she checks she is holding her bouquet correctly.

'I'm ready. Just hold on to that dress.'

He follows her down the hall, his eyes fixed on the white frost of her dress that feels cold to look at. Her hand is on the door.

'Christine, you won't let the child grow up with an English accent?' he says lightly.

She stops and turns to him, says nothing but throws her arm around him.

'Careful, sweetheart, you'll crush your flowers.' But she holds on and he tells her everything is all right, that everything is all right, and still she doesn't let go until he gently unwraps her arm. 'For goodness sake don't cry whatever you do or I'll get the blame for ruining your make-up. Everything's all right. I'll try hard to be a great grandfather.'

She nods and rubs the corners of her eyes with her free hand. He knows he has to say the right things now if she is to compose herself.

'They'll probably put me out to grass in a few years and right now I don't give a damn if they do because it'll mean I'll have time to spend with you and my grandson.'

'Who says it's going to be a boy?'

'Best to be a boy.'

'Why?'

'Because boys give you less grief and Justin will be able to teach him all about cricket.'

She's going to say more but he opens the door, tells her that everyone is waiting for her and that she looks beautiful.

Then she turns and lifts her head in that gesture of defiance and self-confidence that he's so familiar with and this morning for the first time understands that he should take pride in it. Even as the wind blows she does not bow her head and there is a spontaneous, ragged burst of applause from the straggle of neighbours clustered on the pavement. He walks close behind her grateful that the dress has no long train to worry about and smiles to the onlookers.

'You never told me it was a white car,' he says as he stares at the large white limousine, its bonnet festooned with pink ribbon. But she does not answer as she concentrates on fending off the wind that worries the hem of her dress and shivers through her hair. She holds herself tightly and slithers into the car.

They hardly speak in the car as if slightly awkward or even embarrassed by the strangeness of where they are and what has passed between them. She concentrates on smoothing wrinkles from her dress while he peers at a familiar landscape that suddenly seems strange when viewed from this new place. Sometimes passing cars sound their horns in greeting and when they stop at traffic lights people on the pavement peer in and wave. The first time he waves back but it makes him feel like some visiting dignitary to a poor country and from then on he merely nods or pretends he doesn't see them. Thankfully the journey is over quickly but when they pull up in front of the church to his surprise more people are waiting at the entrance. This time he acknowledges them with a jaunty wave and a smile as he shepherds Christine up the steps and towards the church doors where Michael greets them and teases his sister about being on time when tradition says that she should be late.

'Never do what is expected of you,' she says. 'You should know that about me by now.'

Inside the doors they take a few seconds to compose themselves and wait for their cue. The church is packed and already heads are turning to catch a glimpse of the bride. He feels nervous in a way that is unfamiliar to him and surprises him when he thinks of the rooms he has entered, the hands he has shaken. The light is flecked with dust and in the aisle ahead coloured by the stained glass. This is the walk he has not wanted to make, the one his imagination has enacted too many times, but now everything seeps away except a focus on what he must do and it suddenly feels like a high wire that he must walk without stumbling or looking down. If he is to look down or turn his head to one side or the other then surely he will fall, hurtle into the darkness below. Her arm snuggles in his, they take the first step and he has to shuffle to synchronise with her, then they are in step and the music is playing. Not too quickly, keep it slow – don't race her is what Marie told him – so he tries to measure their pace to the music.

It feels as if she is leading him, leading him the way she always did when she wanted him to come and admire something she was proud of, and he wonders why it always took that compulsion, the press of her hand in his back or the tug at the cuff of his sleeve. Then the moment comes when he has to give her over and he hesitates for a second and as her arm slips out of his it feels like the untying of a knot and he knows she is gone like some small boat unmooring and setting out to sea. He tries to think of himself as the harbour but cannot hold the momentary comfort the image brings because he knows that he was never the provider of safety but rather the person who put her at risk, the father who always put her needs second to what he saw as the bigger needs of the cause. He punishes himself with the assertion that Justin, even Justin, deserves her more than he does so let him not hesitate now, or be begrudging in his giving, and as he takes his seat in the pew he silently promises himself that he will atone for the past through the love and time he will give to her child.

As Father Hagan begins the ceremony he tells himself that he will do what all the rest have done and buy himself somewhere in the west of Ireland, maybe even in the Gaeltacht, and that Christine and the child will come over every summer and spend a long time with them. So as Father Hagan intones in a voice that sounds even more surly than normal, he lets his mind flood with images of white strands where seas embrace the outstretched arms of the shore and there are castles to be built and kites to be flown. If it comes to it he will even play cricket before the bat gradually gets replaced by a hurley stick. Marie whispers to him that Father Hagan's nose is out because Christine has devised her own order of service and insisted on having her own ideas. So now after one of her friends finishes reading a passage from the Song of Solomon, Hagan greets it by remarking on its beauty but then informs them that Solomon had seven hundred wives and three hundred concubines. Someone sniggers but in the face of the priest's stern gaze it quickly fades into silence. Gilroy focuses again on a child playing on a beach, this time slightly at a distance from him, silhouetted against the sea, and then he calls and the child comes running, his feet splashing up little squirms of sand. So while Father Hagan rambles on about the sanctity of marriage and itemises the responsibilities involved as if to put off anyone else who might be thinking about it, there's a warm smile on his face as if by blowing sparks from the ashes of a fire he's able to flame the images into life.

The ceremony is over. Now another man walks her down the aisle. Walks her away from them so they have to angle their heads to follow their path and all eyes are on the couple and for the first time no one is looking at him. Marie squeezes his hand and dabs her eyes with a paper tissue and he is a little shocked that she should almost cry when she's a woman who never lets the world see her without her face on. He pats her twice on the shoulder and then feels the inadequacy of the gesture, thinks that it's a hopelessly meagre thing to give to a woman who has supported him with everything she possesses and never blamed him, so he touches the nape of her neck but she drops the tissue into her bag and tells him to watch her hat. He lets his hand fall again and then they're standing up and making their way down the aisle and people at the end of the pews reach out to shake his hand or slap him on the back. He begins to think about his speech but when he pats his pocket there's only an emptiness and he realises that he's left it on the kitchen table but the realisation brings no sense of panic. There would be time for Sweeney to call and collect it before he has to deliver it but he decides to leave it where it is. It was no good anyway, it was not what he wanted to say: full of platitudes and clichés, it was someone else's voice. And on this day he should speak in his own voice and he should speak from the heart so let it be different from all the times he rises to present a speech. Let him speak simply and sincerely, let him speak truly without artifice or guile, let him not have to talk with the purpose only of saying nothing that has not been said before. So no codes and no set phrases, no old familiar refrains that get sung by rote. Today he will make a speech that will touch the hearts of all who hear it and it will be a delicate thing that will rise up on the lightest of wings like that child's kite on the beach and it will hover over his only daughter wherever she might go in the world and she will always be able to call it to mind. So as he walks into the sudden bright frieze of light that frames the entrance of the church he blinks at first and then puts all thoughts of the speech out of his mind because he knows that when he needs it, it will come as complete and fresh as the sea-salted air.

The confetti fountains sideways in the wind, mostly landing on the throwers. Some of it flutters skywards above everyone's head before swirling back to land. The couple are caught in a cat's cradle of outstretched hands that rise up to throw the coloured snow across their path and by the laughter that breaks boldly free of the solemnity of the church. The feathers in Marie's hat flutter and threaten to take flight until she grounds them with her hand. Then it's into the cars and on to the reception which is to take place in a hotel on the outskirts of the city and as he sits with Marie she picks flecks of confetti off his jacket, then checks her make-up in a little mirror she carries in her bag.

As they sweep into the grounds of the hotel he's pleased to see that they have people already there, pleased too that Sweeney has succeeded in getting them to blend in and look discreet. Even on this day nothing is to be taken for granted or left to chance. Marty is stationed at the front door of the hotel and even Micky standing at his shoulder looks suitably sober and alert.

'Everything OK?' he asks.

'No problems,' Marty says as he opens the door for them. 'Everything looks good.'

'Come in to the disco later on,' Marie says. 'And there'll be some supper served so you can grab some of that.'

'Disco?' Gilroy asks.

'Disco,' she says. 'After the meal is over all her own-age and casual friends come – it's what happens. We can pass ourselves for a while then disappear into the night. Though I think we should have booked a room in the hotel – it would have made more sense.'

'Too many problems with security,' he says, glad that when it's all over he will sleep in his own bed.

He endures the endless permutations of photographs which seem to put the meal interminably on hold. When finally they are summoned to the table Father Hagan seems determined to assert his authority and treats them as if they are know-nothings about the necessary processes and rituals. However, he lightens his tone and as he stands up to launch proceedings after the meal even digresses into a joke that involves a cowboy and his new bride and which spins on a series of incidents where the cowboy is let down in various ways and responds each time by saying, 'I've warned you once, I've warned you twice,' and then shooting the offender. It culminates in the wife dropping a series of plates and the same punchline left hanging in the air. Everyone laughs but Gilroy winces and thinks it inappropriate. He winces again through the best man's speech which is delivered in an accent that grates against his ears and which he sees provokes embarrassed smiles in the audience. He pretends to laugh at the tales of his prospective son-in-law's career disasters and youthful japes and sits rigid in anticipation of potential slights when Justin's father rises to speak but he's only on his feet a matter of a few minutes and sounds sincere in what he says. The applause is generous and as it fades away he know this is his moment so he pauses a second before he rises.

He greets everyone in Irish and then reverts to English, trying to strike a physical pose that suggests a relaxed confidence but already his hand is nervously patting the pocket of his suit in a final confirmation of the speech's absence. He is conscious, too, of the video camera that is pointed at him so he straightens his back and lifts his head high. Trust his own voice, that is what he must do now, but it feels as if he's standing at the edge of deep water and as he stares at its hidden depths he is uncertain of whether he will sink or swim. But as he looks at the room of upturned faces he knows there can be no further hesitation so he strikes out for the far shore and tries to make bold strokes that will carry him to what he wants to say.

'I'd like to welcome you all here today. It's good to see so many old faces and none getting older more quickly than my own. Good, too, to see new friends and I'd particularly like to welcome Justin's mother and father, Kyle and Elizabeth. I'd like to thank Kyle for his generous welcome into his family of my daughter Christine. I'd also like to thank Justin for finally taking this girl off my hands and I salute his bravery and know that he will take good care of her as they build a new life in London. When Christine first told me that she was going out with someone in advertising my first thought was that she was romantically engaged with someone who posted those giant ads you see all over town. But I've got to know Justin a little bit better – he always calls me Franky as if he's known me all his life and tries to tell me that cricket is the greatest sport in the world. Now, Justin, there are a lot of things you could say about cricket but I don't think you're ever going to convert me; in fact I read somewhere that someone once said cricket was invented to give the English, who are essentially an irreligious people, a sense of eternity. It certainly lasts a long time but it's hardly going to catch on in Ireland if you can't play it when it rains.'

He pauses and takes a sip of water. Everything seems to be going well. They have laughed politely at his jokes and the vibes from Marie beside him are positive.

'Now at this point I should say something about Christine, but where to start? As you know Christine is our youngest

120

child. Maybe she got spoilt because of this or maybe we were just too worn out to look after her properly but whatever the reason I can honestly say that Christine turned out to be entirely unique. Whether this was a good thing or a bad thing I will leave it to others to judge. And I'm just going to pause a moment here to ask Father Hagan to convey the family's apologies for all the heartache she caused the Sisters at school, particularly that unfortunate business about the uniform.' He waits until the laughter subsides. 'She always had a bit of a rebel heart – no idea where she got it from. But when all is said and done Christine has been blessed with the very best of hearts because she has survived everything the world has thrown at her, held her head high and never lost sight of what is important in life. She's always been true to herself and what she believes and she's always championed fair play, always spoken out against injustice. So today I want to tell you, Christine, that your father and mother are very proud of you and know that whatever you choose to do in life you will make a big success of it. I also want to say a genuine sorry for all the times when it was not possible for me to be there for you. I hope in time that you will be able to understand that this was not by choice but by necessity and come to believe that the sacrifices we all made will finally be fully rewarded.'

He wants to say that she will be a great mother but knows he cannot and the thought of the coming child makes him stumble a little so he disguises it by taking another sip of water.

'I'm not a man to stand between people and their entertainment so there are only a few more things I want to say, so I know you'll bear with me just a few moments longer. Marriage has got to be considered an old-fashioned thing in some quarters but I believe it to be the best and most important institution in society and at the very heart of the Irish nation. And if we are to be a great nation in the future we need to find a new respect for the marriage vows. Too many people say their vows and then when the first problems arise they forget that they have taken each other for better or worse. A good marriage has to be worked at and it would be remiss of me now if I was not to pay tribute to Marie who has stood loyal at my side through the good times and the bad, who has never wavered in her support. No man could have a better wife and my hope today for Christine and Justin is that they, too, will find in their marriage some of the same happiness that I have found in mine.'

He glances at Marie who does not return his look but stares at the tablecloth in front of her. At the back of the room waitresses are starting to move about. Light suddenly burnishes in a raised glass.

'We are building a new future for our children and perhaps this marriage which spans two nations is a symbol of this new understanding. So let us raise our glasses now to the bride and groom and drink a toast to them and the future.'

Glasses blossom up like bouquets of white roses and voices join in the toast. He has almost made it to the shore but still there's something he wants to say, something that he doesn't totally understand but which feels that it carries the demands and weight of the profound. It's something to do with beauty, something to do with what he glimpses inside himself but doesn't fully grasp. He knows that he cannot let the moment slip away, that he has to try.

'As you no doubt know I now serve you as Minister for Children and Culture. As, too, you no doubt know, I have been labelled "the Lemonade Man" by local wags.' This gets a raucous, good-humoured laugh that momentarily threatens to knock him off balance. 'I don't know about lemonade but it has meant that I have had the opportunity to read some more books than I've previously been able to. And I've been reading a bit of poetry recently.' He pauses to listen suspiciously for more laughter but none comes and he tries to keep going. 'Now no country has better poets than Ireland but it's been an English poet called Philip Larkin that I've been reading and Larkin wrote a poem called "The Whitsun Weddings" about all these marriages taking place on the same day and by chance they're all on the same train heading towards London. Now unless they've built a tunnel that I don't know about Christine and Justin won't be taking a train to London but it's where they're heading, so it feels appropriate almost that the poem includes them.' God, he's out of his depth, doesn't know where he's going, and as he starts to flounder he berates himself for not stopping when he was ahead of the game and just how does he expect to say something to these listening people when he does not fully know what it is himself. 'Larkin calls it a "travelling coincidence", the fact that all these newly-wed couples are on the same train and they're all heading off to start new lives together.' But he doesn't know any more where he himself is going or how he's going to extricate himself and he pauses to sip nervously at the water, the glass shaking in his hand, and then he remembers something from the end of the poem, something about 'all the power that being changed can give', and as the first rustle of impatience slips from his audience, he feels a sudden surge of relief as just with a second's clarity he glimpses what it is he now must say.

James Fenton

J AMES FENTON SITS IN the car park at the foot of Slieve
Donard and waits for his former colleague to arrive. He
feels a growing impatience – if he had been doing the climb
by himself he would have started by now. Even though this is
the North's highest mountain, climb is hardly the right word
because it demands no more than a slightly arduous walk to
the summit. He has come lately to walking – really since his
retirement from the force – and he prefers to walk alone,
finding a pleasure in the solitude after a lifetime of working
closely with others. He likes the mountains for their cleanness
of air that fills the lungs and they feel purer than anything he's
ever known after thirty years of sitting in offices and interrogation rooms laced with the sweet stench of sweat and fear;
sitting in unmarked cars in clothes worn too long, with the
stale taste of those hours when most of the city sleeps. Too long
in offices hyped with human electricity and sour with the
remnants of snatched food and dreg-filled coffee cups. He
thinks, too, there is honesty in the mountains – they have no
pretensions to prettiness but only a rugged bleakness and he
likes their disdainful indifference to who, or what, he is.

He glances again at his watch and hopes that Alec will
arrive soon. He looks up at the sky that's grey and strewn

with wind-blown clouds streaming like shredded shards of last year's flags. The forecast promised some bright spells and if they're lucky it might clear long enough for them to be rewarded with a view from the top. There was none on his last visit the previous Boxing Day when the shoulders of Donard wore a shawl of white and the wind's bite was sharp-toothed on the skin. On the way up he had met only one other person – a young woman who stopped and wished him good morning, both their breaths streaming between them like smoke, her face flushed with the climb and the pure pleasure of the place. But he remembers the morning for another reason – it was the day he fell and was lucky not to injure himself. It was on the way down when, weary of the treacherous ice that had been a constant companion, he had decided to continue his descent by walking on the great granite slabs that funnelled and shaped the fast-flowing river, white-throated where it tumbled over the rocky out-crops. But they wore an invisible veneer of ice and almost as soon as he stepped on one, his feet had shot from under him and he had fallen flat on his back, banging his head against the stone. After the first wave of shock he had lain perfectly still, listening to the roar of the water that seemed now to pour over him until very slowly and tentatively he had moved the various parts of his body, checking for damage, but miraculously, apart from a dull pain at the base of his spine and a slight swelling at the back of his head, he had survived intact. But still he had lain there, curiously calm, and into his mind had come an image that would repeat itself many times in the future. It was of him drifting into un-consciousness and then slowly slipping from the polished slab into the narrow rush of water where he is carried and cribbed by the stone sides of the grey granite until his body is borne to the sea. Then and now, there's no fear in the image but only a sense of calm, an acceptance of his inability to resist or stop the flow.

Afterwards as he soaked in a salted bath, Miriam had scolded him for his supposed recklessness, for his selfishness in going alone when he could enjoy the safety and company of others. When she saw the yellow belt of bruising she had complained, 'I didn't survive thirty years of being a police-man's wife to be widowed by a mountain.'

'Think of the pension and the insurance policies,' he had tried to joke, 'and sure couldn't you go out and find yourself a younger husband,' but she hadn't responded to his humour so he didn't tell her that he had tried walking with the other recently retired officers but hadn't enjoyed it. There was something too forced in the nostalgia, the constant banter that deprived of its context seemed, to him at least, to be meaningless, and their loud laughter in the sanctity of the mountains in his ears sounded like laughter in church. He has affection and respect for them but the past is the past and he feels a need to strike out alone at this new stage of his life. He looks up again at the mountain. At 2,796 feet it's hardly Everest but he wonders what Alec will make of it, wonders, too, why he has suddenly phoned him up and asked if they could do a walk together and knows already that it will not be merely a social call. He smiles as he thinks of how he will make this young man, who has now acquired his former post on a fraction of the experience, climb a mountain before he's given his chance to reveal the reason for his presence. But there's no particularly strong curiosity about the reason as he carefully ties and knots his laces – probably advice on some aspect of the job, some inside track or information on an unsolved case that someone temporarily deems it politically expedient to reopen. Fenton dislikes the label 'unsolved case' because in his experience there were very few that were unsolved but rather some where the evidence didn't exist or people were not prepared to say in public what they'd told him in private. Whatever it was, he doesn't particularly welcome the intrusion of his former life into his present one.

Like all his generation he has accepted the pension and the pay-off deals that were too generous to be refused, even though it stuck in his throat to have to acknowledge that he was considered part of the corporate embarrassment, part of a past that had to be quietly replaced. At times he feels it as a bitterness to have the service he has given, everything that has been sacrificed, swept away with a quick thank you and a cheque but he could live with it if he was able, as he believed he would be, to put it all behind him. But it's been a failure because despite everything, despite his active days, the involvement with his church and the Romanian orphange, it feels as if nothing has been shed, that nothing has left him. It's there in his dreams, in the snatches of conversation that replay constantly in his head as if on a loop, in the sudden sour taste in his mouth and all of which seem able to clutch his consciousness at will and squeeze out the life of the present and deaden any vision of the future. Sometimes he blames the absence of children in his marriage and believes that it diminishes his ability to move on. After thirty-five years of marriage to Miriam they have reached a kind of plateau where they continue to care for each other but lead self-contained lives, always busy – perhaps as a distraction for the absence that leaves an unresolved and instinctively agreed, inexpressible sense of loss lingering indelibly below the surface.

She had said that she would come with him on the next trip when he will drive a van full of supplies to a small orphanage in the north-west of Romania but he knows now it is unlikely and he doesn't mind. Recently she has spent more of her time looking after her declining father who has become increasingly dependent on her. She's been at her best in this care, generous in her time and giving of herself, and he knows, too, that the journey to the orphanage is exhausting and not the type of roughing it that she finds easy. Anyway, he will be happier on his own with all those thousands of impersonal, anonymous miles opening up before him. He has started to think, also, that next year he needs to go on a private journey, go away somewhere and come back whole and fresh, ready to move on. Sometimes he feels like an old boat, his keel barnacled and coated with the debris of the sea. There are secret brochures in the house – one of them is for a walking holiday in the foothills of the Himalayas. It would be a trip of a lifetime but he's a naturally cautious man with money and everything else and part of him feels it might be selfish to spend so much on himself. Still to breathe in clean air, to fill his lungs and really breathe deep, to look up at distant mountains and see the whiteness of the snowy peaks stretch as far as the eye can see . . . What price on that?

He gets out of the car and lifts his rucksack and the boots he has coated with dubbin the night before. There's a smell of leather as he checks the rucksack to make sure it contains everything it should. Although he likes to walk alone, he's not foolish and sticks to the well-worn paths, always carrying sensible equipment, including provision for an emergency. Two elderly women walk past him, their weatherbeaten faces and classically correct gear testimony to their experience. Only the small dog scampering at their feet seems a frivolity against their textbook austerity. He puts his boots on carefully, checking that his socks are smooth and flat and won't produce a blister, then fastens the buckles on the rucksack.

A red BMW sweeps into the car park. Without seeing the

driver he knows it's Alec and despite his impatience has to admit that in reality he's only a few minutes late. He watches him park and walk towards him. He's put on a little weight, lost a little hair, but he still has that trademark boyish face that has the ability always to appear lightened by good humour and the suggestion of openness. It was this disarming quality that led others, though never himself, to embrace him easily, blissfully unaware that it masked a tough ambition and a desire for the rewards of success. Lucky enough, too, to be in the right place at the right time, the perfect candidate with a good degree, youth and most importantly of all – no baggage. Of all the people Alec had quietly studied, he knew he had been observed the most and behind that bland façade was a mind garnering everything that might be useful in the future. But Fenton bears no grudges, so as he stretches out his hand to the approaching, smiling man, his gesture is sincere.

'Good to see you, James,' Alec says, shaking his hand enthusiastically. 'Retirement looks good on you.'

'I'm staying busy,' he replies, using his set response when the issue is raised.

'Everybody's asking about you, send their best. Specially Briggsy. The retired officers have a great social thing going – walks, talks, special events, you name it. I know they'd love to see you turn up for one of them.'

'How is everybody?' he asks, registering the fine lines spreading at the sides of his eyes. It's the habit of a lifetime, noting faces. The light lines on his pale skin are like sand washed over by water.

'Charlie's got a job advising on bank security – after the Northern job, shutting the stable door. Michael's taken a post with a chain store and Andy's been to the Palace to get his gong. Believe it or not Minty Morris is in Iraq training the police. As if they haven't got enough problems of their own. And get this, I don't know if you heard, but Norman's taken a job with Iceland doing home deliveries. Says it's the best job he's ever had but I think he's talking about all those lonely housewives he delivers to.'

'Could prove more dangerous than his job in the police.'

'Oh and if you're thinking of ever going to Florida, get in touch with Montgomery – he's bought some properties down in Clearwater. Will rent one out to you at a good price.'

He watches Alec turn and then lift his gear out of the boot of his car. Everything looks as if it was in a shop window five minutes earlier. He puts on a fleece and zips it to the throat.

'So we're really going up there?' he asks.

'You've never been to the top of Donard before?' Alec shakes his head. 'Well we're going to the top – you'll like it.' He watches him take an envelope out of his pocket and hand it to him. 'What's this?' he asks.

'It's a cheque. Before I forget. The boys in work had a bit of a whip-round and there was a golf outing brought some in. It's for the orphanage.'

Fenton looks at the cheque and says thanks, tells him it'll be put to good use. It's for a thousand pounds and he hasn't expected it but as he carefully places it in a zip pocket he doesn't let it throw him off guard. Alec asks predictable questions but Fenton feels a shallowness in their exchange and soon after they set off thin stretches of silence settle. He checks the sky and tells himself that he sees an edge of blue trying to sneak into the grey and smiles to himself when he thinks of the high price his companion's feet will pay if, indeed, his boots are brand spanking new.

The Glen River is blocked from their view at the start by trees and shrubbery but the throaty gurgling of the water emphasises their own silence and inevitably Alec seeks to break it with enquiries after Miriam or to share some piece of news he thinks might be of interest. They pass through woodland of pine, fir and larch, and the necessity of walking in single file momentarily precludes the possibility of speech. The path they follow is a rough and stony track affording them glimpses of the white tumble of water until they cross a couple of bridges and on the opposite bank of the river walk alongside the section where it is shepherded and channelled through narrow chicanes by the large slabs of granite. They pass the exact spot where he fell but he says nothing and for the first time he takes pleasure at hearing the younger man's broken breathing.

It's not possible yet to see the mountaintop even when they break out into the open spaces of the glen, which is shadowed on one side by forest. The white path is crumbly and bare underfoot and occasionally they meet walkers coming in the opposite direction. He watches how Alec gives even a passing stranger the benefit of his charm and he remembers the young woman whose face was flushed against the whiteness of the snow, how her breath streamed like smoke, and he wishes that there was always snow on the mountains. After a while they pause and he takes a flask out of his rucksack and offers Alec a cold drink, watches him slug it greedily, then they head on towards the stone-ridged path that will carry them up the rising slope to the dramatic gap that links Donard and its neighbouring mountain, Slieve Commedagh. As they commence their climb, a heathery vista sweeps away below them and Fenton knows that with each step the mountains make you feel smaller, less significant, and he wonders what is spinning round his companion's head. They clamber up across the bare swathes of earth that are pitted with rocky outcrops and head for the stone wall that follows the contours of the Mournes. Alec slumps against it, obviously desperate for the rest as his breathing breaks in shallow rasps.

'How did they get these stones up here?' he asks as his hand traces the boulders in the wall.

'Some job all right. And look how steep it is up there.'

Alec turns his head to the section of wall that leads the way to the summit. 'And that's where we're going?' he asks.

'You up to it?'

'A few minutes' rest and I'll be right as rain,' he says, pulling up the collar of his fleece as he feels the colder air beginning to snake around him.

'You need to watch your health, Alec. It's a hard job to stay healthy in – too much riding round in cars all day or sitting in over-heated offices with computers and fluorescent lights blasting you. Too many snatched meals.'

'Maybe I should sign up for the bicycle squad – have you heard about them? A couple of guys patrol the city centre on bikes – apparently volunteered for it. Can't imagine the stick they must get about it.'

'We'll go to the top when we've had something to eat. It'll only take another half an hour. Have you got anything in that rucksack?'

'A Mars Bar, a packet of crisps and a bottle of Fanta.'

'Just as well I made extra then,' Fenton says, pouring two cups of steaming tea and opening a plastic container of cheese sandwiches.

They huddle tightly against the wall, their backs pressed in whatever niche they can find, their rucksacks pulled like blankets against their knees. Fenton knows now that it's almost time to let the mountain hear what it is has made Alec come all this way. He feels safest hearing it here, hoping that whatever it is will fritter and fragment in the face of the mountain's indifferent magnitude, that whatever it is will seem small and inconsequential, quickly blown away by the rising wind.

'So, Alec, why are you here? You didn't come just to admire the view.'

'Is it so obvious?' he asks, cupping his tea in both hands for warmth.

'I haven't gone senile since I retired.'

'I know. But it's not an easy one.'

'So it's bad then?' Fenton asks.

'It's not good, it's not good.'

'Well, you've had plenty of practice in giving people bad news. Comes with the territory, doesn't it?'

'This is personal. I'm not giving it to a stranger – makes it harder.'

Fenton looks up at the dropping, scouring cloud that he knows will rob them of the view from the top then watches a raven sharpen its wings against the cutting edge of the wind.

'Tell me,' he says quietly and finally.

'In a couple of weeks' time you will be called to appear before the Truth and Reconciliation Commission. It will be the case of Connor Walshe – the boy whose body has never been found.'

'Why are they calling me?' Fenton asks. 'What can I tell them?'

'The family want to know the circumstances surrounding his disappearance. They want to know as much as possible about what led up to it and what happened to him. They want some form of closure.'

'We all know what happened to him,' Fenton says angrily. 'The IRA said he was a tout and shot him, then disposed of his body somewhere. How will that help them find closure?'

133

And what about my closure? When am I allowed to walk away and put it all behind me?'

Fenton stands up and leans against the wall, pushing at the bottom stones with his foot.

'Sit down, James, I have to talk to you.'

'There's more?'

'Yes, there's more,' Alec says but falls silent while a couple of walkers pass them. This time he does not look up or make eye contact with them. 'This is very difficult and you're not going to like it but I've been asked to talk to you by important people.'

'Who?'

'People I don't know and don't want to know. Men in suits, the heavy brigade . . . I don't know.'

'And what do these people want you to tell me?'

His companion hesitates. 'They don't want Gilroy's name mentioned. They want him kept out of the frame.'

'Kept out of the frame? It was Gilroy who killed the boy. He may not be the one who pulled the trigger but he was the one who gave the order, the one who arranged it.' At first there's no answer and Fenton watches him pick up some white pebbles and throw them aimlessly. 'I suppose it wouldn't look too good, even in this crazy country, if the Minister for Children had a child's blood on his suit. Just maybe some people would think that wasn't quite right.'

'I suppose not.'

'Let me get this right,' Fenton insists, his anger bursting open so that his words hammer home like hailstones. 'They took the badge, they took the name, any kind of respect that was owed, and now they want to take the truth and twist it into whatever shape they think suits them best?'

'It's hard to grasp,' Alec says. 'I don't claim to fully understand it but it's got to do with protecting the institutions, safeguarding the future. With bringing people inside the system and making sure they stay there. Trying to build something better than we had in the past.'

'You believe that?'

'I don't know what I believe but listen, James, these are important people and this is important to them. They could make things difficult.'

Fenton stands up again, his face pinched and white in the cold. 'You listen: I've had a lifetime of being threatened by thugs, of looking under my car every day, so I'm not scared of a bunch of public-school boys. Who are they? MI5? MI6?'

'I don't know who they are but they could help you, too. They know about the work you do for the orphanage.'

'They told you to say that?'

'They don't say anything directly – the words just slip out the sides of their mouths and hang in the air. They leave you to piece it all together, work out what they mean.'

Fenton walks from the wall with his face upwards and lets the wind stream against it. His eyes catch the raven drifting and free-falling in a great wheeling arc. He throws the dregs from his cup then walks back to where his companion is now standing.

'I've never asked anything of you, Alec,' he says, 'and there's been times when I've helped you so I'm asking you now – if there's any way of me not appearing before the Commission I want you to find it, do whatever you can to find it. Will you do that?'

'Of course I will, I'll do everything I can. I promise I will.'

Fenton picks up his rucksack. He is going to the top now. His sense of responsibility is too great to tell his companion to make his own way down so he hopes he will wait where he is until he returns but Alec asks if he can finish the climb.

'If you like,' he says, shouldering the rucksack into position, 'but there'll be no view.'

'So you won't throw me off the top then?' Alec asks, scurrying to keep up, but there is no reply as Fenton lowers his head and pushes himself into the steep walk to the top. He hugs the stones close to the wall and soon without looking back he knows he has left the younger man behind. Sometimes he has to pause but only for a matter of seconds before pushing himself on again. A few drops of rain touch his face when finally he reaches the top where on a clear day can be seen the Wicklow Mountains beyond Dublin and the Galloway Hills of Scotland. Then without taking off his rucksack, or pausing to rest, he prowls about the summit looking for a view but everywhere is blinded by mist and cloud and in every direction he looks he sees only the face of a boy, the frightened face of a boy.

The transit van is packed to the gills. There is not a single inch of wasted space. The van itself is donated and regularly serviced by a member of his church who owns a garage and all its contents have been supplied by local businesses or bought from funds raised by the congregation. Piled high are blankets and new clothes; pots, pans and cooking utensils; cleaning materials and anti-bacterial wipes; shampoos and soaps; tinned foodstuffs; writing pads, pens and colouring pencils; children's games; packs of nappies and basic medical items. The final things to be loaded, delicately placed in any space between everything else, are the shoe boxes – one each for the eighty children in the orphanage – supplied by the children of the local primary school and jam-packed with personal gifts.

This will be the first time he will make the long journey on his own – on the three previous occasions he shared the driving with another church member – but if he's honest he prefers this prospect to the awkward shared intimacy of someone else's company and the constant compulsion to make conversation over the thousands of road miles. He has planned the route carefully, opting to combine prearranged hospitality, set up for him through police contacts, with sleeping in the van. He's equipped with a good-quality sleeping bag that's already laid out on top of a pallet of soft clothing. It's not possible to know precisely the duration of the journey and in some parts progress will be determined by the seemingly random whims of border security and customs. On a previous trip they spent eight hours sitting on the Hungarian border before getting an all-clear. The orphanage itself is only a couple of hundred miles inside Romania, buried deep in a remote, heavily wooded region of the country. The first links with it had been established post-Ceauşescu when the media had competed with itself to find and reveal existing conditions.

He carefully checks the *Auotorizatie* and the fat sheaf of required papers, the seemingly endless documentation. He checks he has the requisite certificates for clothing, food and medical hygiene then stores it all in a document wallet which will stay close to his side all through the journey. After staying south of London with an old police contact from the Met, he crosses into mainland Europe via Calais and settles quickly into the rhythm of the road. There is a comfort in driving far away from where he's known and a feeling of unaccustomed lightness, remote from all human contact. Through France, Belgium and into Germany, toll roads and the fierce, unforgiving relentlessness of the Autobahns. A thousand miles and the only connection with the rest of the world is through a passing glance from a fellow traveller or in the eyes of the dark-haired, dark-eyed children whose faces are pressed against the rear glass of ancient beat-up Volkswagen campers which carry Turkish migrant families and what looks like all their worldly possessions. Sometimes one of the children will raise his hand but he doesn't respond. Past the random straggling remnants of cities, like tattered ribbons blown stiff by the wind. Glimpses of suburbs flecked and smeared by light in the consciousness of dawn and through towns and deserted small villages softened by the twilight where the only sign of human life is a momentary flicker in a window or the smouldering embers of a dog's eyes. Heading south across Europe through thickly wooded terrain towards Vienna and south again into Hungary.

The boy rests his head on the pillow of his arm as if its weight is too heavy for him, so only the side of it is visible.

'Sit up now, son, and be a man,' he tells him but the boy doesn't move. It allows him to notice the white squiggle of a small scar on his shaven scalp like a nick in the white of new wood.

'I want to go home,' the boy says, still not moving.

'Well sit up now and we'll try to find a way to let that happen.'

'You can't keep me here – I haven't done nothin'.'

'Maybe you'd like a slap, son,' Briggs says, standing behind the boy and jerking his head up by the hair.

'Get off, ye bastard!' the boy shouts, swinging his arm vaguely in the direction of Briggs in that favoured gesture of aggression that Fenton knows he uses to hide his fear.

'Sit up now, Connor, and we'll talk this through,' he says, patting the boy on the shoulder even though he squirms at the touch. The boy raises his head for the first time. There is a red imprint on his cheek where it was pressed against his arm. His face is pale, thin boned and pinched like a grey-

138

hound's. He has red sores round his mouth, the badge of a glue sniffer. If he were to stand up and take off his shirt Fenton thinks that the full cradle of his ribs would be visible.

'I haven't done nothin',' he repeats, holding both sides of the desk as if it's about to take off.

Briggs suddenly lowers his face level with the boy's and watches his eyes blink out a Morse code of fear. 'Yes, but you have and you have to stop telling lies about it, you little toerag.'

'You broke into that old-age pensioner's bungalow and stole her pension money,' Fenton says. 'You also threatened her with a knife.'

'That's not a very nice thing to do,' Briggs says, standing at the boy's shoulder where he can't be seen. 'And you've done other bad things as well, like stealing cars and thieving off your own.'

Walshe slumps back in the chair, letting go of the desk. His body suddenly looks as if it's been de-boned like a fish and that at any moment it might slither to the floor. He turns to look at Briggs.

'I know where you live. I'm goin' to tell the Ra on you. See if you're a big man then.'

'So you know the Ra then?' Briggs asks. 'Well you must be a real big shot. Tell the Ra on me? I'm scared shitless. I'll have to move house now and I've just put up new wallpaper.'

'Think you're funny,' Walshe says, his voice full of defiance but his eyes blinking again.

Fenton wishes the younger Briggs would refrain from obscenities. He considers it disrespectful to the force, thinks it reduces everything and all of them to the same level, but he says nothing, knowing that younger officers see some things differently.

'Well think of this, Connor, my brave boy,' Briggs says, bending his knees with a loud creak, lowering his face level again with the boy's, 'maybe we'll tell the Ra about you. Tell them how you broke into that old woman's house and assaulted her. Tell them how you held a knife to an old woman of eighty and stole her pension and her rings. Stole the old woman's wedding ring.' He straightens up and walks a circle of the table. 'You know what's going to happen then, don't you, son? They'll shoot your kneecaps off – no, wait, maybe they'll decide not to waste the bullets and use a baseball bat. Bullet's always cleaner, not so many bits. And no doubt because you're such an expert I'm sure you've heard they're starting to use ones with nails in them. Makes a desperate mess, as you might imagine.'

The boy places his arms on the table again then rests his head on them once more. This time his face is completely hidden so only the heave of his shoulders reveals that he's crying. Briggs goes to say something but Fenton silences him by raising his hand and then speaks softly to the boy.

'Maybe there's another way, Connor. Maybe there's a way out of this.'

The road feels increasingly narrow as it winds through the mountains and each side is bordered by dense bands of trees that sweep right down to the edge. A thin mist that seems to drift from between the trees swaddles and blurs the road ahead and, as he slows his speed, he reaches patches where it suddenly thickens. Putting on his wipers and lights he haunches over the wheel, his face close to the glass as increasingly it feels as if some creature's breath is streaming against it. He glances at the deep swathe of pine trees, so densely packed that their branches jostle one another for space, and thinks that it must be permanently dark in the forest's interior. For a second he is confused and wonders if he has taken the right road.

A way out. That's what he offers the boy. A way out of the mess. As Walshe lifts his face towards him he studies it carefully, registering every detail permanently in his memory. He sees right away that he's not been really crying, that like all his demonstrative emotions – the anger, the aggression – the tears have been attempted rather than achieved. The thin, feral face is staring at him now with a sly curiosity. His blue eyes are the only trace of colour but even these are vague and unfocused and there is something in this expression, as well as in his speech, that suggests the narrow limits of his intelligence.

'Do you want a drink or a cigarette?' Fenton asks but the boy shakes his head sullenly and then blinks slowly as if trying to clear his eyes.

Gradually the mist sheds its grey skin and slithers itself somewhere far back through the trees. He passes clearings where felled trees loll against each other haphazardly like giant pencils thrown by an angry child. At the border he waits in a queue that takes four hours to clear. Eventually all his paperwork is deemed to be in order and stamped and he is only a couple of hours' drive now from his destination and half a day ahead of schedule but suddenly he feels nervous, apprehensive, even though unsure of the precise reason.

Already there's the sense of travelling back in time as he sees his first Dacia car and passes a horsedrawn cart, the old man's whip flicking through the air like a fishing line. He passes threadbare villages and farms with orange-tiled roofs and suddenly he feels tired, desperate for sleep. Lowering the window he lets the cold night air wash over him but he knows he has to stop. Always conscious of the need to protect his precious cargo from thieves, he waits until he finds himself far from houses or signs of life, chooses a narrow dirt track that winds behind a screen of trees and parks. He carefully locks the doors of the van before climbing into his sleeping bag and stretching out on the pallet of clothes which gives him only a few feet of space between it and the roof, but which feels comfortingly secure.

In the morning he feels stronger, glad that he's taken the rest, and tells himself that it's better to arrive in the morning than in the middle of the night. He clambers outside into the first light of day and thinks of Miriam sleeping alone in a house many thousands of miles from this place and wonders what she dreams of, before his thoughts change to the young woman's face on the mountain suffused with life. There are sudden memories of when Miriam's face bore the same marks, times when love was that intense. He drinks slowly from a bottle of water and feels the seeding of sadness into the morning. In the distance across deserted fields he sees the shadowy, tantalising outline of mountains whose name he doesn't know, then as a young man on a moped passes on the road, he steps behind the van where he can't be seen and watches until its red tail light vanishes into the distance. He pours the water over his hands and splashes his face. He needs a shower and a proper shave. He feels dirty.

There's dirt under the bitten, ragged nails of the boy and a blue scribble of a self-administered but aborted tattoo on the outside of his wrist. He is undersized for a fifteen-year-old, the runt of a large litter, all born to a single mother. His hair is close shaven, the stubble flecked by the white scar. The gold chain he wears seems to shiver against the paleness of his throat but it's the eyes that Fenton stares at now. They are a light, delicate shade of blue, the only softness in his face, the eyelashes so vaguely defined that they are mostly invisible. The eyes look at him now as he promises him things, offers him a way out of the mess, and as Fenton talks to him, he keeps his own gaze locked on them, knowing that this is where he must direct his words.

In the van he takes a towel that smells of home and dries his face then splashes it again and repeats the process. He knows the job's to blame, tells himself that it's not possible to spend over thirty years rubbing up against dirt and not be stained by it. Like a smoker's fingers rusted with nicotine. He has witnessed it over the years in his colleagues, the experiences that gradually coarsen and degrade. He hears it in their language, sees it in the one-too-many drinks, the way they disrespect then deceive their wives. He tries to show through his life rather than his words that they need a higher code to live by, otherwise things get blurred, harder to know where the difference is between right and wrong. He knows, too, for some, that difference has so shrunk that it's hardly visible any more, replaced by what they can get away with and what they can't.

He brushes his teeth, using what is left of the water, wishing it were colder. Wishing he could have a shower before he arrives at the orphanage. But what if the government was right after all? Perhaps too many of them were too damaged to be part of a future supposed to be cleaner. No longer to be called a force but a service as if they hadn't served before and as he thinks of it he can't assuage the familiar anger, the sense of his own shame at taking the money and walking away cap in hand. He spits angrily out of the window then gazes at his reflection in the mirror. He looks rough, his eyes blue-bagged and red-rimmed; his skin like it needs the fresh scour of the mountains; the grey that started at his temples then spread up and consumed most of his hair colour now seems as if it has infiltrated the surface of the skin itself. A tiny cluster of red pinheads peppers his cheekbones and when he inspects his teeth he sees two incisors on opposite sides of his mouth are yellowing in perfect synchronicity. He blinks then looks again as if he hopes to see something different in the glass but nothing has changed. Taking the battery shaver he tries to shave some of the greyness out of his skin then puts on a change of clothes and starts on the final leg of his journey.

He passes a tractor pulling a trailer filled with logs, an axe embedded in its crest. In a short while he sees distant figures working in the fields that look like stick men silhouetted in the morning light. An old man who works the slow swing of a scythe on a stretch of bedraggled grass briefly raises his hand in salute before turning again to the rhythm of his task. In a couple of hours he passes through the closest town to his destination but is unable to detect any obvious changes from his previous visit and then he begins the descent into the wooded valley where the orphanage sits at the meeting of two rivers. The road takes him across narrow bridges where there's not room for two vehicles to cross together and then it spirals down in increasingly tight circles that require him to stay in a lower gear and keep his foot almost permanently on the brake pedal. Sometimes he catches a glimpse of water far below as it streams across stone-pocked gravel beds like white hair lifted and braided by a comb, then eventually he reaches the bottom of the valley where the road straightens to run parallel with the river and the willow trees that lean out and weep over it. A strange hidden place.

Like the places he met the boy. Far from prying eyes. Sometimes on the edge of the city, sometimes in a car park in the empty wastes of closed shopping complexes. Sometimes in a beauty spot or a place where lovers meet. At times he had him picked up in an unmarked car on his way, usually late, to school or after he had travelled to a neutral area. The first time they took him to the country park at Crawfordsburn, walked him along the seashore, his pale eyes wary of the sea. Delicately at first, nothing much more than talk about nothing much, and then the first of the money in his pocket and home again. And taking the money that first time is the hook he will hang on like a caught fish. Sometimes he takes him to places where he can eat and then he would sit with a coffee and watch him devour whatever was on the plate, the fired urgency of the eating facilitated by his tight-fisted grasp of the knife and fork. He gives the boy a contact phone number where he can be reached by day or night and so he becomes part of the electric grid that courses across the city whose currency is information. The bugs and the devices, the cameras, the infra-red toys, the secret recordings – he doesn't put his faith in any of them. It's the human touch he puts his trust in – eyes and ears, tongues loosened by money or, even more reliable and more endurable, by personal hatreds. Sometimes unimportant people like the boy on small retainers, sometimes important people on the inside, and the more important, the less likely he was to know of their existence, their invisible nameless handlers, disdainful of anyone's need to know except themselves. But the boy is his, a little acorn planted in the face of an uncertain future.

It's a Saturday morning and as he drives between the wooden posts that mark the entrance to the orphanage he's seen first by two girls whom he recognises even though they look older. They stare at him blankly and then their faces animated by recognition they jump up and down, running alongside the van as they wave their arms and shout with excitement. It's the first human contact he's had in days and it startles him. He looks at himself in the mirror again. Other children, drawn by the sound of the van and the shouts, begin to rush out of the central building and the dormitories. He slows right down, anxious not to hit anyone as they press on all sides, and finally he comes to a halt in front of the main stone building with its still broken wooden shutters. The grass in front of it is blistered with bare scabs of sandy-coloured soil. Then taking a deep breath he gets out of the van, locking it behind him while the children throng about him, calling his name and pulling at his shirt. He can hardly move through the press and he touches as many as he can on the head and uses as many of their names as he can remember, but it's almost impossible to walk more than a few steps at a time and when he sees one small girl in danger of getting knocked over he plucks her from the crowd and carries her in his arms. As he looks up he sees Estina standing at the top of the steps and at her shoulder Natlia. Behind them is a young woman with long brown hair almost to her waist and whose clothes suggest she is from somewhere else. He acknowledges their presence by raising his hand and then shrugs as if to apologise for his slowness in coming to greet them. Estina smiles back and claps her hands loudly, does a little shouting until gradually the children step back and allow him to reach the steps.

'Welcome, James, welcome back. We've been expecting you,' Estina says as she offers him both her cheeks and he kisses her self-consciously before repeating the greeting with Natlia. Then as they see him looking at the young woman behind them, they introduce her as Melissa. Later she will tell him all about herself and how she has graduated in child psychology from an American college and is spending a year doing voluntary work before returning to do a master's degree, but now she too greets him as if she is really pleased to see him. 'You must be really tired,' Estina says. 'Please come inside.'

'Not too bad,' he says, suddenly embarrassed to be the focus of so much attention. 'It's a long drive all right but it's good to be back again.'

They lead him into the main building and sit at the long table close to the open kitchen. Estina makes him a cup of coffee that smells and tastes better than anything he's had in days and they ask him about his journey. At first there's a certain awkwardness and he's reluctant to discuss the contents of the van too soon as if it would be rude to flaunt the charity he brings, but he knows everyone is thinking about it and he tries to find a way to itemise it that he hopes is undramatic and sounds unexpectant of displays of gratitude. So first he tells them about the shoe boxes, checks the number he has brought against the current number of children to be certain that no one will go without. He is careful to give responsibility to Estina as to when the children will receive them and after she confers with Natlia she decides that they can be given that evening, after the concert that's been arranged in his honour.

While they talk children are watching from the doorway, furtively glancing in at them from the hallway or walking past the windows as if engaged in some unrelated business. Estina gives him an update on the recent improvements that have been made to the main dormitories and tells him about changes in government funding that he doesn't fully understand but he nods his head and when she's finished he presents her with a detailed list of what has been brought. He watches the two women pore over it, their heads close together and talking rapidly in their own language. He senses that sometimes they are helping each other with translation and as they do so he notices that Melissa is looking at him and for a second as he returns her gaze they feel connected through their mutual separation from the animated preoccupation of the two women.

The boy will not talk to Briggs under any circumstances, will hardly lift his head to look at him, so when they meet Briggs has to make himself scarce, sometimes getting out of the car to stand in a doorway or between trees, the red arc of his cigarette in the darkness the only marker of his presence. Sometimes in a wordless protest against the cold, or the injury to his feelings, Briggs obstinately stays in the car and then they get out and walk. The boy's nervousness has gradually diminished and he talks more freely but little of what he says is of any value. He grows a little cocky, talking up his importance, overestimating his potential worth. Occasionally he will phone when he has nothing to tell them and then Fenton is aware of how hard he has to work to enrich the paucity of what he's offering. Once or twice he looks at the money with something approaching disdain, as if it's a poor recompense for what is being given, but he says nothing and always pockets it quickly as if nothing has passed between them except words. But above all things Fenton is patient – the time and money are an investment and he never lets the boy see any sign of frustration or irritation. He understands that sometimes he likes to talk, to have someone to listen to him, and he gives praise and dangles the possibility of a better future in front of him. He tells him that they will take care of him, that they will look after him.

A few of the younger children have been placed with adoptive families; some have been reclaimed by their natural parents. 'We have one new child – a boy called Florian,' Estina says. 'He's fourteen years of age, was being cared for by his grandmother after his parents moved to the city to look for work. When she died the authorities were unable to find his parents and so they brought him here.'

'And what's he like?' he asks.

'He's a strange boy,' she says with a scowl. 'He doesn't get on with the other children and wants always to be by himself. He never speaks of his mother or father or shows any interest in where they are. When his grandmother became ill he had to care for her and try to keep their place together.'

'Sounds like he's had a hard time.'

'Lots of children have hard times,' she says and drains her coffee.

After the van is unpacked Fenton notices him standing at the tree line to the side of the main buildings. He has a compact build though is quite tall for his age, has untidy black hair and an alert face that seems to be constantly weighing everything up. The boy watches him approaching, taking in every step, and then he slips back behind a tree.

'Hello, Florian, my name is James,' he says, knowing the boy speaks good English.

The boy shuffles slowly from behind the tree, both hands hitched by their thumbs to the corners of his pockets, his eyes seemingly focused on something over Fenton's shoulder.

'We've never met before so we should shake hands.' Florian looks at his outstretched hand for a few seconds before deciding reluctantly to shake it. 'Would you like some chewing gum?' The boy hesitates again and Fenton has to encourage him by actively proffering the packet before he pockets it quickly and says thanks with a nod. 'I hear you speak good English, is that right?' The boy shrugs indiffer-

149

ently but it's obvious that he has understood the question. 'Where did you learn it? At school?'

'My father taught me.'

'Your father? Where did he learn it?'

'His father,' the boy says but he does not elaborate. There is defiance in his voice as if he thinks Fenton might not believe him.

'That's good,' Fenton says. 'Wish I could speak more languages. I'm a bit too old to learn now.'

'You're not too old,' the boy asserts as he lets one of his hands trace the bark of a birch tree, his sallow skin darker against the tree's papery whiteness.

Fenton changes his position and stands beside the boy, looking in the same direction as he does. The wind blows strongly off the Lough and engulfs them with the sour-breathed smell of the sea and the sulphurous odour of the landfill sites. A white woven crown of gulls garlands the bulldozer and then fragments as they swoop to scavenge. Their cries are sharp pinpricks pressed into the stillness of the morning.

'That's what we produce in this city, Connor – rubbish, mountains of rubbish. Great mountains of it.'

'My brother had a job on the bins once,' the boy says. 'Said it was all right. Sometimes he brought stuff home. Not junk or anything but brand new.'

'You ever think of what job you'd like to do?'

'Don't know. Wouldn't mind working with cars. I like cars,' he says, looking round him, unsure as always of where he is, and plumping out his arms and cheeks against the cold like some windblown bird.

'You need qualifications to get jobs. How are you going to get qualifications if half the time you're on the beak?'

'I don't like school,' he says, blinking his eyes and angling his head away from Fenton.

Fenton is glad they are outside, that the wind is blowing. They watch the slow work of the bulldozer on the other shore. Bits of paper and white plastic bags inflated by the wind billow into the rawness of the air before lurching drunkenly again to earth. The boy is beginning to smell. Fenton isn't sure if it's real or the product of his imagination. It's not the familiar sickly tang of sweat, or the smell of unchanged clothes, or even feet too long encased in the same trainers, but something else, something that seems to seep from his pores and infect the air around him. He's grown tired now, tired of the boy's whining self-pity, tired of his counterfeit of cunning, tired of the meagreness of his information. A dredger slugs its slow way up the thick waters of the Lough. Perhaps it's time to move on, to cut the losses. No point in good money after bad.

'We're going to have to let you go, Connor,' he says on impulse as he pulls up the collar of his coat.

'Because I beak off school?' the boy asks, panic and the jostle of the wind blanching his face and narrowing his eyes with confusion.

'No, not because of school,' Fenton says, still looking across the water. 'Because what you're giving us isn't any good. There's no point telling us things we know already – that's just a waste of time. If Briggs had his way, you'd have been on your bike a long time ago.'

Walshe turns and stares at the car where in the driver's seat Briggs's head is hidden behind a newspaper. For a second it looks as if the wind has slipped inside the boy's tracksuit, pumping and primping him into temporary bulk, but when he speaks his voice is thin and the whispered words so light it feels as if they might blow away.

'I'll do better for you,' he says. 'I'll do good for you, get you whatever you want, I swear!'

'You know what we want, the names we're interested in, the houses, the cars,' he says, feeling the wind shiver his scalp. Suddenly in his imagination he thinks that it is a contaminated wind carrying malignant spores from the coagulated sprawl of human detritus being patiently untangled and spread across the foreshore. 'I have to go,' he says, deliberately digging his hands deep into his pockets, knowing this will be the first time he's left the boy without handing over money.

'I'll get stuff, I swear to God I will,' Walshe says, his right hand printing the air in a melodramatic gesture meant to authenticate his words, but as Fenton walks back to the car all he hears is the screech of the gulls.

A sliver of white bark peels off under the plane of the boy's hand.

'You like it up here among the trees?' The boy nods but says nothing. 'At home I like walking in woods and mountains.' There's a moment of silence during which the boy shreds the white filigree of bark. 'Tonight, Florian, I want you to help me. Will you help me?' Then without any answer he tells him that he wants him to help with giving out the shoe boxes and with a little act that he's prepared for the children. He tries to explain it to the boy but the meaning gets lost. 'I'll show you later what to do. So you'll help me then?'

'I will help you but I do not understand,' Florian says before planing more bark off the tree then turning and walking deeper into the woods.

Fenton stands watching him go until he finally disappears as if swallowed by the trees.

That night the children stage their concert and while

Fenton recognises the format and some of the content from his previous visits, it doesn't lessen his enjoyment as he listens to their singing and watches their folk dances. The last one is a complex routine involving long streamers in which the eight girls weave increasingly intricate patterns to a cassette of traditional music and when the tape is paused one of the girls comes to him and leads him by the hand to perform. He pretends to protest but goes with them, doing his best to copy their movements, and as soon as he stumbles into a tangled confusion of streamers the children laugh and clap delightedly. He hams it up a little, kicking up his heels and then clasping a hand to his brow in exaggerated exasperation at the complexity of the routine. At the end he takes an elaborate bow and the children stamp their feet and giggle.

This part of the evening's entertainment ends with two songs. The first is performed unaccompanied by a girl of about ten or eleven years of age and when she starts to sing the children fall silent. The girl fastens her eyes on the back of the room and as she sings her voice fills it, dipping and rising in a cadence of sadness that seems to link each child with the song. A large, pale moth trembles above her head and adds to the fragility of the moment and Fenton feels the swell of something inside him, pushing at the edges of his normally sturdy restraint, and he shuffles in his seat and tries to blink his eyes clear. The girl's voice rings out and though the words are lost to him he feels able to grasp something of their meaning.

Then Melissa changes the mood by playing a guitar and leading the children in a rendition of some songs in English. The children pronounce the words deliberately so it sounds as if it is being sung in someone's very best voice. She smiles at them in encouragement and nodding at the start of each verse as if worried that they will suddenly forget the words.

When she finishes Estina settles the children then he understands that she's telling them there is one more item and already he's feeling nervous, frightened of making a fool of himself, but tells himself that if he concentrates he can get it right, so as the children look on in confusion, he goes to the front and with Florian's help rigs up the white sheet over a line of string and sets up the table behind it and positions the light. Then going behind it he slips on the white coat and puts the stethoscope round his neck. When everything is ready Florian walks slowly in, holding his stomach in a dramatic display of pain. Fenton goes through an elaborate examination, checking his pulse, taking his temperature, then produces a torch from his pocket, shines it in the boy's ear, gasps in amazement and slowly appears to pull a long line of knotted handkerchiefs from it. The children laugh and clap and growing in confidence he does the same from the other ear, feigning more amazement at how long the line is. Then he gets Florian to open his mouth wide and conjures a hard-boiled egg from it, holding it up to the audience between his finger and thumb so that they can see it is real. Florian continues to hold his stomach and rub the pain so he listens carefully to it through the stethoscope, shaking his head to reveal the seriousness of the condition.

'I shall have to operate immediately,' he announces, waiting for Estina to translate, then switches on the light that shines up at the sheet, signals for the room lights to be switched off and goes behind the sheet where Florian is already lying on the table. With slow, exaggerated movements he produces a mallet and pretends to knock out the patient by banging him twice on the head. The audience watching the scene in silhouette laugh and clap loudly, groaning in mock horror when he takes out a saw and appears to saw the boy's stomach, all the time accompanying his actions with appropriate sound effects. Then from the boy's supposedly open stomach he slowly removes the causes of the patient's pain, so first there is a chain of linked plastic sausages that he throws over his shoulder, then a Wellington boot, a teapot, a teddy bear, a small kite with a long tail and finally a small doll. Florian is finally restored to consciousness and helped off the table and coming from opposite ends of the sheet they meet in front of it and bow to the audience. Just as the applause is about to end Florian taps him on the shoulder and exactly as he has shown him appears to produce an egg from his ear. The children renew their clapping and Florian smiles. He puts a congratulatory arm on the boy's shoulder and then they give their final bow.

Before supper the children are given their shoe boxes and soon afterwards Fenton slips away into the cool of the evening, wanting the moment to be theirs alone and a little apprehensive in case some are disappointed by the contents. He walks to the line of trees and stands looking down at the lighted windows and wonders what it would be like to have a child of his own, to be a father. He remembers the young woman on the snow-covered slope of the mountain who could have been his daughter, could have been his daughter walking to the top with him instead of a stranger briefly pausing to exchange a few words before heading in the opposite direction. At the start he secretly thought they might adopt one of these children but he knows that they are too old to be considered and that now it's not permitted so even that dream is undermined.

The woods feel still, intensely silent: he wonders how far they stretch, how far the children venture into them. The only sounds are the occasional voice of one of the children calling to someone and somewhere beyond the building the light lisp of the river. The stars are a fierce shock of brightness and then he remembers the day he fell and the rush of the water that seemed to flow over him, the river that might have carried him to the sea. But now in the laughter of the children, the voice of the girl who sang, the goodness he has in this place, there is perhaps something that might yet clutch him from that inexorable torrent. Perhaps after all he doesn't need to go on some distant journey, perhaps this place is enough for him to shrug off whatever it is that clings to him, and part of him doesn't want to go back and step inside the round of his life again. He's pleased with how the performance went, knows that he will have to learn new tricks if he's to come back, and he reminds himself how well Florian had done – an intelligent boy who absorbed everything he was shown in the shortest of times.

The night air grows colder. Out on the road a car's headlights spear the trees. Briggs is nervous tonight. He shuffles in his seat and glances over his shoulder at regular intervals.

'I don't like this,' he says. 'How do we know he hasn't set us up?'

'He hasn't set us up. He wants to talk,' Fenton says.

'He always wants to talk – that's the trouble, isn't it? Talk and nothing but talk. Nothing worth a spit in the wind. I don't like it here – we've been sitting too long.'

'Learn a little patience, man. Sometimes you have to wait.' A pockmarked moon scowls sourly over the darkness of the playing fields.

'I should keep the engine running,' Briggs says, quietly taking his gun out of his holster and holding it in his lap.

'Put that away,' Fenton tells him. 'I don't want him scared off.'

'He's not coming,' Briggs insists, putting his face close to the windscreen and scanning slowly round. When he turns to look over his shoulder the whole seat creaks. 'He's not coming and we've been here too long. He was never any good right from the start – we should have done him for the burglary and the assault. Still could. I knew soon as I laid eyes on him that he wasn't any good.'

'He'll be here,' Fenton says quietly but looking at his watch. And then he sees him coming across the pitches, his pale face growing whiter as he approaches. His face is intensely white like an owl coming out of the darkness.

'Don't bring him in the car, please!' Briggs says, putting his gun back in his holster and slouching lower in the seat.

Fenton gets out and walks towards the boy. Briggs watches them talk, sees the boy's restless movements, the stillness of Fenton as he listens. He lowers the window to try to catch some of what's being said but they are too far away and then after a few minutes Fenton turns and walks towards the car with the boy hovering at his shoulder. Before he starts the engine he hears Walshe say, 'I did good, didn't I?' Then Fenton gets into the passenger seat, lowers his window and answers, 'Yes, you did good.' The car moves slowly forward as Briggs carefully negotiates the worst of the rain-filled potholes that shiver with the cold glimmer of the moon.

He can only stay two days at the most because to remain longer is to impose too many burdens on their limited resources and get in the way of the daily running of the home. He talks to Estina and enquires about what they need most in the future and makes a list but they never talk about how much the home has improved since the first contacts. Some were the result of improved government funding and changes to the administration system but many of the most striking and practical improvements have been the result of outside intervention, especially early on when a team of Irish builders spent three weeks working on the interior of the buildings. He knows that Estina does not like to talk about those times – he assumes it's embarrassing or even painful to be reminded of how things were and she is a proud woman, her natural independence and pride making things all the harder for her.

They sit talking on a long seat carved from felled trees. The bark feels sticky under his fingers and a sweet scent of sap still lingers about it even though the wood looks dried and sun bleached.

'You are no longer a policeman?' she asks.

'No, I'm too old now,' he says, smiling.

'You're not too old,' she says in the slightly abrasive way that sometimes characterises her speech. 'When my grand-father was eighty he still worked in the fields.'

'I still find plenty of things to do – I don't sit at home in an armchair.'

'Everyone must have a purpose,' she says, her eyes scanning the children as they play. The light falling across her hair reveals thin lines of grey filtering through the thick swathe of black. She asks him questions about life back home, about how the education system works, about how much things cost and how much different jobs pay. One of the smaller boys falls and lets out a wail as he sees his knee is cut and his friends cluster round and attempt to administer comfort. Fenton goes to rise but thinks it's not his place and glances at Estina who sits still, staring at the children.

'Is he all right?' Fenton asks.

'He's all right,' she answers as the children steer the casualty in her direction. 'Always someone falling, always someone needs help.' When the wounded child arrives in front of her she bends forward in her seat and inspects the cut, making a clucking noise, and then she says something to them and they usher the still crying child towards the main building. Fenton turns to see Melissa appear in the doorway and take the child by the hand. The voices of the children and sharp little cries of pain continue to echo from the shadowy interior.

'How is Melissa getting on?' he asks. 'Is she a big help?' There's a moment's pause and then Estina drags her feet across the bare, grainy soil. 'Sometimes,' she answers but lets the word hang in the air, her thoughts unexpanded, unexplained.

'What do you mean?'

Estina turns and looks at him, her eyes dark like her hair, and as she pushes a stray strand behind her ear says, 'She is only a girl but already she thinks she knows everything.'

'That's what a little education can do sometimes to people,' he offers.

Perhaps assuming encouragement in his words she goes on, continuing to fix her gaze on the side of his face. 'She knows nothing. She does not understand how things are, what is possible.' Fenton says nothing, not wanting to turn his face towards the intensity of her feeling. 'This is not America,' Estina says with a flush of bitterness. 'We are not to blame for what we have not got.'

They sit in silence for a few moments and Fenton thinks it better to say nothing than say the wrong thing. Then after a while he says, 'It's not easy,' but Estina makes no response and now her eyes are focused somewhere in the distance. He lets his fingers trace the crusted crenulations of the bark. Estina flaps an insect away from her face.

'You have a friend now,' she says, pointing to the tree line with her bare toes that she has slipped free from her sandals. 'Florian.'

He narrows his eyes and peers towards the broken line of trees but it takes a while before he finds him standing motionless under the branches of a tree that lurches at a crazy angle.

'Sometimes I think he lives in the woods,' she says. 'He has a place where he sleeps.'

'He's a good boy,' Fenton says.

'A boy who needs a father. He's been with women too long – his grandmother, us. Here is no good for him.'

'Is there no chance of him being adopted or placed with a family?'

'The only chance is that someone will come and think he is a strong healthy boy who can do work for them on their farm. But Florian is too clever a boy to work in the fields. He should study, go to university.'

'Maybe we could help with money, sponsor him,' Fenton suggests but she shrugs her shoulders unenthusiastically.

'It's not always about money,' she says and he feels clumsy, heavy-handed. 'He likes you. Maybe you could spend some time with him before you have to leave.' She stands up and slips her foot back inside her sandal. 'I must go now.' But after taking a few steps she turns and says, 'Thanks, James, for everything you brought.' He raises his hand in a vague, dismissive way that says it was nothing then watches as she walks away.

As soon as she has gone Florian approaches then stops about ten feet from him and looks about as if he's suddenly arrived at the spot by chance. The boy doesn't look directly at him and Fenton realises that in fact he has never made eye contact.

'So, Florian, how are you?'

'I want to show you something,' he says, staring at his own shuffling feet. 'You come with me but it is secret.'

'I'm good at keeping secrets,' Fenton says, standing up and brushing the seat of his trousers.

He follows the boy towards the trees unsure of whether to walk beside or behind him but Florian does not look round or speak to him as they go. They breach the tree line and at first tread well-worn paths until eventually they fade away and the boy heads into unmarked areas. A light breeze shuffles the top of the trees and sometimes passes right down the branches as if in a sudden shiver. The boy's footsteps are soundless and on the way they step over felled trees that are almost smothered by moss and fern-like plants. Sometimes they pass under arched branches and above them the light lessens and the sky is glimpsed only in shallow pockets. Leaves brush against Fenton's face and his senses are filled with the pungent scent of pine. He shrugs a branch aside and feels something sticky on his fingers.

The boy moves languidly but with purpose, in a dipping, fluent rhythm as he leads deeper into the forest. When Fenton asks if there is much further to go the words sound too loud in the silence. Florian doesn't reply but signals him forward with his hand and almost immediately they are breaking into a clearing, circular in shape, and at first Fenton is aware of nothing except the boy turning to smile and then he sees it. There is a tall tree, green and verdant on each side but hollowed out in its centre with three levels inside it created by floors of cut branches lashed together with rope. Improvised ladders connect each of the floors and there are various pieces of wooden furniture – chairs, a small table and in the top narrowest level what appears to be a small bed.

Fenton walks closer, stepping through the sunlit braids that create a lattice of light in the clearing, and stands with his hands on his hips admiring the building. Then he breaks into a burst of applause and turns to see Florian smiling broadly.

'Can I go in?' he asks and Florian nods and gestures an

invitation. Fenton steps gingerly up to the first level but it feels secure and he sees that both nails and rope have been used to create a solid base. 'How long did it take you to make?' he asks, examining everything in close detail. Seeing Florian holding up four fingers, he says, 'Four months?' but the boy smiles and tells him that it took four weeks. Fenton shakes his head in a pretence of disbelief that makes the boy laugh and nod a rapid affirmation of his claim.

'You should be an architect when you grow up,' Fenton says, slowly lowering himself into a chair, but the boy doesn't understand the word and he has to explain.

'I want to be an engineer,' Florian says. 'I want to build bridges. Big bridges.' And he holds his hands far apart to suggest the scale.

Fenton looks at the sudden passion in the boy's eyes and already he is thinking of what he might be able to bring him on future visits – drawing books, pens, pencils, whatever sort of modern equivalent of Meccano is on the market. Maybe a book of photographs of bridges. The idea of Florian sitting in his tree house studying a book that he's brought gives him pleasure and a good reason for returning. Despite what Estina said maybe there is some way he could create a sponsorship plan for the boy, help him get a good education, help him not to have to spend the rest of his life working in the fields.

'How did you learn magic?' the boy asks.

'I only know a few tricks, just what you saw. I taught myself from a book. You want to know a secret? I've never done it in front of an audience before. I was really nervous, worried in case I'd make a fool of myself.'

'You did good,' he says, holding one of the outer branches of the tree and leaning out from it at a forty-degree angle.

'You know what I'd really like to be able to do, Florian?'

The boy pulls himself vertical again and listens carefully. 'I'd like to be able to do that trick where you make somebody disappear. They go inside a box or cabinet, you do whatever you do and they disappear.'

'That trick is good,' Florian says encouragingly.

Suddenly Fenton wants to ask the boy about his parents, whether he thinks about them, whether he hopes that one day they will come back for him, but he sees a momentary happiness in the boy's eyes which he does not want to take from him so instead he asks if there's someone he would like to make disappear if he was able. He asks it as a joke but sees the boy's face become serious as he ponders the answer.

'I would make myself disappear,' he says quietly.

'Why, Florian?' But the boy does not answer and instead he peers up into the apex of the tree as if looking for something. 'Are you unhappy here?' The boy merely shrugs his shoulders and stares out into the forest before he eventually breaks the silence by saying that some nights in summer he sleeps here. 'You're not frightened?' Fenton asks. 'Not frightened to be out here on your own?'

For the first time the boy looks at him directly, holds his gaze and says, 'I am not frightened.'

'That's good, that's good,' Fenton says.

Later as they walk back he thinks of the boy's lack of fear and can't stop himself thinking of all those moments he has felt it. As the branches brush against him it feels as if he wears the traces on his skin like a tattoo. Stepping into the bar after it was sprayed. Hearing the news coming in that a colleague has been shot. Sometimes just turning on the ignition of the car. Afterwards when he told himself that he was alive, that it was someone else who hadn't survived, it brought no sense of relief but only a sense of fragility, of things hanging by a thread. The randomness of fate. Then as he looks round at

163

the endless stretch of trees he turns his eyes to the boy he's following and thinks it is a good thing to find a place where there is no fear.

When he eventually breaks out of the trees the light hits his eyes and he shades them with his hand then turns to speak to Florian who dropped behind him when they reached the well-worn paths but he's gone, silently vanished, probably returned to his own house. Suddenly he thinks of Walshe's white face swooping out of the shadows of the playing fields and then tries to rid himself of it by walking quickly towards the main building. As he walks, children run up to him or tag along beside him showing him various objects that they have received in their shoe boxes. Their pleasure in these things reminds him only of the inadequacy of what they've been given and that the cost of the shoes that were once in the boxes would probably sustain them for many months. And then nothing feels enough, nothing feels solved or complete. It's as if he has done his best and given his best offering but it's not enough. He wants to be on his own to stop taking part in what suddenly feels like a fraud but the children seem to be everywhere, scampering and running pell-mell in games of chase, flooding round him and conveying by gesture that they want him to do tricks but he has no more to show them. It's Melissa who rescues him, shooing the children away.

'They get so excited,' she says.

'It's a little sad they get so excited over so little,' he answers as she signals him over to one of the rough benches that have been yellowed by the sun. 'How long are you here for?' he asks.

'I go home next month.'

'Looking forward to it?'

'Can't wait, can't wait to see my family and friends, to eat proper food, sleep in a comfortable bed. All that stuff.'

'But you've enjoyed your time here?' he asks as he watches her stir her hair from her face with a slight shake of the head.

'Some of it,' she says, turning to look at him. She looks slightly younger than her age, her brown eyes light with life and her face pretty and seemingly open as if she has no secrets. Taking out a band she pulls her hair back in a rough ponytail, using both her hands to smooth it. 'I won't miss head lice,' she says, shivering her shoulders. 'Check yours when you get home.'

'Not as many places for them to hide in mine,' he says but already imagining he feels an itch.

'There are other things I won't miss,' she says, looking at him more intently, and he knows that if he encourages her at all she will tell him but he is unsure of whether or not he wants to hear and so at first he stares ahead. 'Things you should know,' she insists and then he knows she's going to tell him whether he wants to know or not. He glances over his shoulder but they are on their own. 'Don't worry, no one can hear and it doesn't matter if they do. You have a right to know.'

'A right to know what?'

'About some of the things that are wrong with this place.'

'And what are those things, Melissa?'

'Well take Estina for a start. I don't think she is a fit person to be in charge of a place like this. I don't think she's educated – once I tried to talk of her qualifications and she pretended she didn't understand. I don't think she has any training in child care or child psychology or child any-thing.'

He is surprised by the sudden anger that shows in her voice and surfaces in her face. 'But she seems to care for the children, seems to run the place as well as she can.'

'Sometimes she's cross with the children, sometimes she

shouts at them – you should never shout at a child, James, especially ones who are already emotionally vulnerable, and there are children here who obviously have special needs, who need to be assessed but who just get lumped in with all the rest.'

His concern at her words is tempered at first by the tone of her voice and the impression it gives that it's imparting wisdom to the needy. He listens to her talk and the flow of her words is evangelical, so self-assured that he can't but be struck by the discrepancy between her age and her insistence on knowledge. Perhaps Estina is right about her, perhaps she is a young woman whose education has given her an inflated sense of her own importance, so he says little but his silence only seems to prompt her to renewed efforts to persuade him.

'Sometimes her friends and family come up here at weekends and drink, eat big meals and get drunk.'

'You've seen this?'

'Yes, of course.'

'But you've said nothing?'

'Not directly because whenever I try to say anything at all about the way things are, she gets angry and things get heavy. Sometimes I think I should have left earlier.' She fingers the silver cross at her neck and then pulls it tight to her lips. 'Not all the stuff your church sends goes to the children. There's a room in the basement where she keeps stuff and I think she sells some of it in town.'

Fenton stands up and expels a nervous rush of air. He rubs his hand up and down his throat feeling the tufts of bristles left behind after a week of hurried, inadequate shaves. He stares up at the tree line and wonders if Florian is in his secret place at this very moment. Into his mind comes the memory of a time shortly after he had taken up walking when he was following a path up the Annalong Valley, bounded on one side by a wood and on the other by the mountains when the sky had filled with mist in a thickening tumble of grey. He had kept walking, feeling it feather his face like a clinging web, telling himself that it would lift, but with each step visibility reducing until he stopped and let it engulf him. He felt no need to be frightened because he was on a well-used path, a mile from where he had left the car, the climb into the mountains not yet reached. All he had to do was wait and stay warm or hug the edge of the wood and follow it back. Now as Melissa talks on he thinks only of the feeling of being softly cradled, removed from the hard edges of the world and held in the arms of the sweetest kind of letting go.

'I think you had a right to know,' she says.

He turns and looks at her. Now her face no longer seems open but tight and riven with shades of secrecy that he can no longer gauge or calculate.

'Where is this room?' he asks.

'I'll show you,' she says, standing up, almost excited.

'No, just tell me where it is.'

'It's the last room in the corridor that runs past the kitchen.'

In that second she appears to Fenton like a child, eager to persuade him, eager to impress him. He stares into her eyes but all he sees is that grey swirl of mist separating himself from a world where he has to make decisions, where he has to pick a course. And now there are no landmarks or maps, no way to pick a route except through instinct. She starts to apologise for having to tell him these things but he knows she's glad she has and that part of her motivation is to see him do and say things that she felt unable to do herself.

'What will you do?' she asks.

'I don't know,' he answers even though part of him

believes that he will do nothing, that he will get in his van in the morning and drive, and the thought of the anonymity of the journey, the endless unravelling of the landscape, brings some relief. So he excuses himself, telling her that he has to check the van before it gets dark, and leaves her sitting playing with the rope of her hair.

Getting into the van he locks the door and grips the wheel with both hands but fights off the impulse to start the engine and drive. He tries to force himself into the world where actions have consequences and where everything has to be balanced in ledger columns but at first these thoughts fly asunder like startled birds and nothing can stop their scattering wing-clacking confusion. Turning, he stares at the cardboard boxes and packaging that will go back with him, the empty pallets and the blankets that protected fragile items, and suddenly he feels weary, knows he has to build up his strength before attempting the long homeward drive. He is tempted to sleep but knows he must put it off a little while longer and knows, too, that without some sense of stillness it would be impossible, so he begins with what he knows is certain. The conditions and facilities in the orphanage have improved significantly since it was first revealed to the world. Estina and Natlia, the two full-time workers, were appointed after the worst features of the past had been largely addressed and, under their care and that of the other team of helpers, the children seem well and, as far as he can judge, reasonably happy. He sees nothing that speaks of the former abject physical neglect or the catatonic paralysis of the emotionally abandoned that originally formed the most disturbing images. Even if some of what Melissa claimed was true and even if occasionally a small proportion was creamed off for personal use perhaps it was a small price to pay for these improvements. And if he were to say anything to Estina how could she respond but to deny it and he thinks of the damage it would do to those who have contributed faithfully and sincerely to what they believed had made a difference to the lives of these children.

That night the sleep he felt so much in need of refuses to come. He constantly changes position in his narrow bed in an effort to find one that will allow him to drift into sleep but it eludes him the harder he tries. Moonlight silts like silver through the thin gauze of curtain and the night is speckled with sound. Insects ping against the glass and at intervals the bang of a dormitory door or the cry of a child are sharp pinpricks in the unsettled silence. Sometimes as he listens he thinks he hears the rush of the river but then tells himself that it's too far away and what he hears must be the hum of electricity. He thinks of Florian's house in the trees and for a second is almost tempted to try and find his way there and sleep amidst the sheltering canopy of leaf. Rising he goes to the window and peers at the blanched moonscape which is layered with shadows and where the transit van sits like a beached boat washed round by incoming tides of an opaque wavering light.

He gets dressed but then sits on the edge of the bed unsure for a moment about what he's going to do. Then opening the door he stands listening and as an uneasy silence settles he walks along the corridor towards the stairs. He switches on the torch he has brought from the van and it smears thin slips of white across the green skin of paint coating the stairwell. His steps are light, muffled by the coldness of the bare floor. Sometimes a moth rushes to dance in the fleeting spotlight he offers and as he slowly descends the stairs he pauses at intervals to listen carefully but the whole building seems to have slipped into some fitful slumber that is broken only by the bark of a cough or a whimper perhaps prompted by some dream.

He makes his way through the central rooms, each step still a debate about whether he should return to his room or go on. Somehow not finding out gets linked in his head with Florian's future and simply to walk away feels like it will condemn him to something less than he deserves. Suddenly there's a scurry of feet and two young children, hand in hand, hurry across the corridor in their nightdresses and disappear again into another room. He switches on the torch again as he passes the kitchen area and momentarily it brightens against the shiny surfaces of pots and pans, then he steps into the corridor that ends with the room he seeks. It feels smaller than the other corridors and the floor is bare concrete, cold to the eyes. When he reaches the last room he rests his hand on the handle and hesitates for a final second but when he tries to turn it, he finds it locked and the discovery brings no sense of failure but rather a rush of relief. But before he can take comfort in it a light that hurts his eyes suddenly illuminates the corridor.

'What are you doing, James?' Estina asks, her face hardened into anger, her stare unrelenting even in the face of his blinking.

'I was going to look in your store. See what you have, what you don't.'

'In the middle of the night?'

'I couldn't sleep,' he says, feeling foolish, unused to and embarrassed at being in the position of the accused.

'So you've been talking to Melissa?' she says as she walks towards him.

Now there seems no point trying to sidestep and he feels the unflinching fix of her eyes that are grey like flint under the harshness of the light.

'She told me some stuff,' he says, still hiding in vagueness, 'and I wanted to see for myself.'

'Let me guess. She told you that we are all thieves who steal everything, who starve the children while we get fat. That what she told you?'

'No, she didn't say that, Estina.'

'And you want to see in here?' she asks, pulling a bunch of keys out of her trouser pocket. 'Here, James, here is the key.'

There is no escape from his humiliation as he stares at her outstretched hand.

'I don't think I should,' he says, desperate to find some way out of the situation.

'Take it!'

And this time he obeys her order and turns the key in the lock. She pushes the door open with a gesture of contempt and switches on the light. She has to lean across him to reach it and he feels her breath on his cheek. He doesn't want to go further but has little choice as she presses her hand in the small of his back.

'Please look as much as you want,' she says, standing in the doorway with her hands on her hips. But now he knows that there will be no respite in half-hearted apologies and that it would be better to grasp the nettle so he merely thanks her and shrugs off any sign of hesitation or further embarrassment.

The room has boxes piled high along three walls. Most are shut, some are already opened, and a quick examination shows that most contain tinned foods. In others are kitchen and bathroom consumables. The only time he turns to look at her is when he finds several boxes of children's toys but she returns his gaze defiantly. He sees nothing to confirm or deny what Melissa has told him but knows that his efforts have succeeded in damaging things. He nods curtly to tell her that he's finished and after he leaves the room she locks the door once more. He doesn't know what to say and they walk back down the corridor in silence.

'I think we should talk,' she says, ushering him into the kitchen with an outstretched hand. She gestures him to sit at the table and rummages in one of the high cupboards for an already opened bottle of wine, then sets two small wine glasses on the table and pours each of them a drink. She leaves hers untouched as he sips his cautiously, trying not to grimace at the splurge of sourness that hits his throat.

'What we store is what we don't use, what will be needed in the future.'

'The children's toys?'

'We keep them for when we need them – birthdays, holidays. We need to have these things at different times. You understand?'

'I understand.' He sips the wine again and then asks, 'And you've never sold things you've been given?'

'Never,' she insists. 'But sometimes if we have too much of one thing and not enough of something else then we . . .' She searches for the right word, screwing up her face in momentary frustration.

'Trade?' he offers.

'Yes, trade. We give something, we get something. You understand?'

He nods and splays his hands on the table like a pianist about to play then asks, 'Why do you think Melissa said those things?' The words hang in the air unanswered for a few moments then she shrugs her shoulders and holds her arms outstretched wide.

'The girl sees what she wants to see. Sometimes I think she is a little sick in the head,' she says, tapping the side of her own. 'Did she tell you that she spends half her time telling the children that they must love Jesus? Or that she takes them into the woods and makes them pray?'

Fenton shakes his head and narrows his eyes as he forces himself to sip more of the wine.

'I go back in the morning,' he says, telling her what she already knows.

'Will you tell your people about what she said?'

'No, I won't, Estina.'

'And you will come back?'

'Yes, I will. Thanks for the wine,' he says, standing up. 'I should get some sleep now.'

'But you haven't finished it yet,' she says, smiling for the first time.

'I'm not really a wine drinker. But thanks anyway.'

As he walks away she holds up her glass in salute but as he slowly climbs the stairs to his room he tastes the lingering bitterness of the wine on his lips and the bed he gets into feels cold and solitary.

In the morning everyone has assembled to see him leave and when he says farewell to Estina and Natlia they both offer him a quick handshake but not their cheeks. Melissa stands a little way off and waves while the children bounce around the van excitedly like buoys in a choppy sea. He looks around for Florian but there's no sign of him and he assumes he's still somewhere up in the trees. One of the children hands him a small posy of wild flowers wrapped in silver paper, and he slots it into the dashboard before starting the engine, then as he slowly and carefully sets off, they stream on either side of him waving and shouting. But gradually he pulls away and finds the road that will curve his route back up the valley. The corkscrew of a road feels like the slow unravelling of the last few days and there's a stillness in the van that he welcomes at first but which gradually becomes edged with an unexpected sense of loneliness.

Everything presses in on him through the windscreen – the frayed and ragged encroachment of trees to the road's edge; the grey snakeskin of the river that is spotted by black stones; the remote foreignness of the sky that seems to arch a heavy indifference over his journey. But he tells himself that some day he will return and when he does he'll bring books and materials for Florian that will help him achieve his ambition.

He passes through the same small villages and the town where nothing seems to happen and everything seems smothered under a layer of dust and lethargy and the thought of what he might be able to do for the boy restricts the slow seep of emptiness that threatens now to engulf him. He tells himself that Alec will pull through for him, that it's the younger man's opportunity to pay back what is owed to him, and there are others who owe him, too, and they will not let him be hung out to dry. There's too much respect for that to be allowed to happen. He tells himself that when he returns he'll plan his big journey. It's not the time to go on it now – he knows he'll need a long rest after this trip is over – but at least he should start to make plans and decisions for the future. In the intervening time he will build up his stamina and experience, getting into the mountains as much as he can, and there is a cancer charity walk up Ben Nevis that he could do in October.

The return journey feels like the rewinding of a tape as sometimes he passes places and even people that seem frozen in situ from the outward journey. Occasionally his mind plays tricks on him and he projects the homeward sequence incorrectly but there's really only one road to the border and so he rarely feels the need to refer to the map and is able to slip into automatic pilot. Perhaps that is what takes him so long to realise, or is it just so long to admit to himself what he knew right from the outset? His knowledge springs less from the evidence of the slightest movement, or the sound of breathing, but rather from an instinctive sense that someone else now shares this space that has been exclusively his for so many miles. But he continues to drive, playing it over in his head, desperately trying to think it through and only occasionally glancing fleetingly in the mirror that he has quietly adjusted. Without ever seeing him he knows it's Florian and he feels a welter of confusion as if he has arranged for the boy to be hidden here, but only now is reluctantly admitting the truth to himself. Several times he goes to call out to him but stifles the words because he's unsure of what words he wants to use. He knows the boy must be taken back, knows it, knows it, but there's something else he hears in his head and it's telling him that this is the son he never had, the child that will make sense of his and Miriam's life, pull together all the frayed edges of their existence. His mind races, flooding with the kind of images that only the childless secretly store, and with each one his heart beats a little faster. He thinks of the boy's rightful future life stifled and taken from him if he's imprisoned in a world of narrowed horizons and drudgery. He itemises what they could give that life and all the ways they could open it up to something infinitely better so the appeal to altruism is only partly undermined by the selfish motives he is forced to acknowledge.

He goes to speak again but knows that a single word will signify complicity with the boy's presence. Different options shower up inside his head, each one passionately and momentarily bright like some meteor before burning out and falling to earth. Border guards are only likely to take the most cursory interest in a van returning empty of its delivery – there's just a chance it could be done. But with every optimism comes a subsequent slew of questions to which he has no answer. As he drives he barely registers the world outside – the world itself feels as if it has contracted inside the van, this journey, and if will alone could effect his desire then it would happen regardless of what might stand against it.

More traffic is on the road and every vehicle that passes him seems blind to his secret, intent only on their drivers' own concerns. What would the world really care even if it knew? Who would say it was a bad thing? Up ahead the traffic is beginning to slow. In a short while he will reach the straggle of single-storey buildings that mark the border and soon he will stare into the unsmiling faces of young men in seal-grey uniforms whose eyes will register only a surly indifference even as they mechanically pursue the rituals that justify their own existence. The line of traffic stops. Fumes from the cracked lips of the exhaust of the truck in front spume into a blue gauze of smoke. He closes his window tightly but even then there's the sound of music from a nearby cab – a high-pitched wail of violin and voice. It sounds like music to which there should be frantic dancing, perhaps at the latter stages of a wedding when passions are uncurtailed, dancing where flailing arms propel partners in frenetic, staccato rhythms and the strutting heels of shoes clack like castanets against wooden floors. Never in his life has he danced. Never in his life has he been invited to the wedding feast. He tries to shut his ears against the music, looks at the posy fastened to the dashboard, wants to touch the petals, but his hand shakes when he reaches out and he pulls it back and grips the wheel.

And one night as he sits alone in an office lit only by the screens of computers and the outside ochre sodium lights that try to rebuff the darkness beyond the perimeter, a phone rings. Walshe's phone. But when he speaks to the boy his words fall into a silence opening like an abyss and then there is nothing. He looks at himself in the mirror and thinks of a boy with a white owl face swooping towards him out of the darkness, then turns the van slowly round and follows the road that brought him.

Danny

THE SWELL OFF THE lake pushes through the fringe of reeds and fur-headed rushes forming the shore's inner penumbra and washes against the little wooden jetty. He lights his first cigarette of the day. It's one of only five he's reduced himself to and so every second has to be savoured – even the striking of the match and its sweet flare of sulphur. The best part of the day. Just turned six and the first light already slowly stretching itself a little tighter and sharper. It's the cool he loves best, this time before the sun begins to bake everything dry and crisp and starts to choke the juice out of the day. Ramona tells him he will catch a cold but all he feels is a relief that he's made it through another night and so there is pleasure in everything as he stands at the end of the jetty and stares out at the lake.

A small boat is already far out. Perhaps it's Arnie, eager to catch the fish before they have had a chance to rub the sleep from their eyes, when their stupor summons them to what looks like an easy breakfast. He strains his eyes to recognise the boat but it's still blurred by the softness of the light. Some day he will take up his invitation and join him, even though he knows nothing of fishing and the only thing he has ever caught were smicks in a jamjar when he was a boy. He draws slowly on the cigarette, feels it balance him and clear his head. Only five a day now and this one is the best so it can't be rushed or wasted in any way. He has already promised Ramona that when the child is born he will stop altogether, then as he remembers his words he panics a little and wonders how he will be able to do it, but tells himself it'll be a small price to pay.

Across on the other shore where the big-money houses are, the first lights are starting to appear with housekeepers and cooks stirring things into life, getting things ready. They say some of the owners only come down from up north a couple of months a year and there's always stories about their identity, so sometimes it's big-shot businessmen or movie stars, and sometimes there are even whispers about shady money. The closest you can see the houses is from the lake; he had done the boat tour soon after he had arrived and still remembers his sense of wonder at their magnitude. Great baronial palaces with turrets, mock-Tudor and Gothic extravaganzas – he still remembers some of the descriptive words the tour guide had used – and all with their jetties and boathouses, all with their screened pools and perfect lawns stretching elegantly to the water's edge.

He lets the smoke stream slowly through his lips. No heed to hurry – he has a little longer before it is time to go back up to the house and get the coffee going. Help Ramona waken. Sometimes she will stretch out her arms to him, invite him to join her in the limbo world between wake and sleep, and then he will slip inside the folds of her embrace and she'll say he feels so cold and pull him tighter so that he smothers his face in the splayed black pillow of her hair and buries himself ever deeper in her sleep-stirred warmth. Then after a long while she will break the silence by saying, 'What does a girl have to do round here to get a cup of coffee?' and he will drag himself reluctantly from where he hides and stare into her brown eyes to see if he has dreamed this happiness or if it's some illusion woven by sleep.

It must be some programmed biological clock, whose hands cannot be stopped, which wakes him every morning at the same time. Some legacy of a different time and place, some throwback that cannot be thrown away. At first he had forced himself back into sleep but each time that was when the dreams had come, so now as soon as he wakes, he gets up and goes outside to the lake, the lake where each morning he watches the light strengthen and shape the coming day. As the water breaks in little spurts of white to lap around the wooden posts of jetty, it looks as if he could scoop it up and hold it in the palms of his hands. Because it's still early, the water is not coloured or skimmed by a burning shock of sky and as it seeps and slurps through the reeds and grasses, it lulls his senses, reminds him of where he is. In the condominium, on the other side of the coach house where they rent their apartment, yellow light blinks the windows' eyes awake. Almost all of its inhabitants are old, retirees seeking to warm new or longer life into the tiredness of their limbs. Maybe their biological clocks are still locked in work time because by the time he goes to his own work some of them will have started their early-morning jogs, in their pressed tracksuits and fresh white trainers, their green sun visors shading their eyes but not hiding the serious concentration in their faces. Some will lift a hand in silent salute as they pass him, as if they have no energy to spare for words, and he will say good morning as they pass him with the curious, slow-angled shuffle that they all seem to share.

Gradually the light is beginning to sheen the water, frazzling the sleeping surface into trembling swathes. The cigarette is almost finished and from out on the road there's the growing sound of cars. Already it feels as if the waking day has begun to claim what is rightfully its own, so he takes one slow final drag, then flicks the butt into the water that laps between the rushes. He stands and stretches, breathes some of the clean coolness of the lake and stares one last time at the fretting stretch of light. Every morning its pattern is different, impossible to predict, and that thought is enough now to make him uneasy, to start his day with a sudden shiver, and when he tells himself it's only the cold, he knows it is a poor lie. Then he tries to rekindle a spark of comforting heat by telling himself that the longer things endure, the less chance there is of everything he now thinks as his being snatched away from him. The baby is growing. There is his job to go to every day. There is the lake itself which will soon settle into the fixed frieze of an unchanging and cloudless sky. For some reason he raises his hand. Perhaps it is a wave to Arnie far out in his boat, a greeting to the wakening houses on the opposite shore. His way of saying he belongs here. The syrupy swell ripples through the reeds and rushes. A promise to tell the truth? He spits the sudden sourness into the water and turns his back on the wavering seam of light beginning to stitch sky to water.

As he walks back up the lawn towards the white-painted coach house, the stream of his breath is like lazy smoke and the sky's unfolding itself in a tautening skein of blue. Already he is thinking of Ramona, her eyes still soft with sleep and the possibility of her arms stretched in invitation. It quickens his step and throws the shiver into the shadows of memory. He thinks of the scent of her half-wakened body, the warmth of her honeyed skin that will embrace him and erase afresh whatever it is needs burying. The anticipation warms him and he feels his daily little burst of gratitude to where his life has brought him in the regular, comforting raising of his personal flag, the sincerity of his personal salute. Feels again there's something in this country that makes each morning hold a newness, an opportunity for something more than just the making of a dollar. He tells himself it must be something to do with the light, the certainty of the slow bake of heat, or maybe it's just the knowledge that your neighbour is already at his desk, or has jogged the first of many miles.

In the kitchen he sets the coffee percolator going, starts to stir some breakfast and tries to flap the smell of smoke from his body before going into the bedroom. The white sheet is thrown back like the crumpled and ripped flap of an envelope and the bed is empty. There's the second of panic he always feels when someone or something is not where he expected it to be, before he hears her retching in the bathroom. Knocking on the door even though it's open, he enters to see her kneeling on the floor, her hands holding the sides of the toilet.

'Bad?' he asks and when she does not answer he kneels down behind her and strokes the black shock of her hair which always seems a coursing current of electric life. She points to the paper and he tears some sheets which she uses to wipe her mouth, then she spits several times and he helps her to her feet. Quickly she flushes the toilet as if she doesn't want him to see, then going to the sink splashes her face with cold water. For a few seconds he stands behind her holding the train of her hair before she shakes it loose from his hands.

'Men have it easy,' she says, 'a moment's pleasure and they walk away. It's the woman who has to do all the work.' She holds her face close to the glass and looks at him with her brown eyes momentarily wide. Her face is paler than he has ever seen it, like the lake before the first light touches it. There are beads of water like small tears on her cheeks, on her upper lip and glittering the darkness of her eyebrows.

'I'm sorry,' he says, as if apologising for all his gender, for all the men he knows have treated her badly in her past. For her father who raised his hand to show his love, for Vicente her ex-husband who abused and humiliated her and cheated on her every chance he got.

She half smiles. 'I suppose it's not your fault and I suppose you were only doing what I'd asked.'

He watches her pat her face with the towel, pressing it tightly against her skin and holding it for a while. He rests his hand lightly on the small of her back, feels the heat of her body through the thinness of her nightdress. 'Better if a stork brought them,' he says as she takes the towel away and blinks again.

'I look like shit,' she says, stretching the skin below her left eye with the tips of her fingers.

'You look beautiful,' he answers, slipping both hands round the still faint swell of her belly. She squirms a little then settles back against him and they look at themselves in the mirror. The edge of her hair fans against his cheek. He breathes in the scent of her, takes pleasure from the heat that seems to come from the core of her being. They stand as if waiting for the mirror to preserve the moment in a photograph.

'You're a liar,' she whispers, angling her head against his cheek and pressing the flow of her hair against his skin.

'Would I ever lie to you?' he asks, his face assuming a wide-eyed innocence.

'I don't know, Danny, would you ever lie to me?' she teases and then as she sees his face fall, she presses herself tightly into him and clasps the arms that envelop her.

'Come back to bed,' he says, embarrassed to meet her eyes in the mirror. 'There's still time.'

'I think I'll be sick again if I lie down. I need some fresh air, something cold to drink.'

'So you don't want me to cook you some breakfast?'

'No thanks, just some orange juice and a bit of dry toast maybe.' She pushes gently free from the corral of his arms and reaches for her toothbrush. 'Well was the lake still there? It hadn't evaporated in the night or anything?'

'Still there,' he says, reluctant to give her up to the day, watching as she pulls her hair into a temporary ponytail with one hand.

'And you'll be a good father to this child?' she asks, her attention focused only on placing toothpaste on the brush.

And he doesn't know if she's still teasing him or if she's serious so he hesitates before he answers, looking for clues in her face, but all he can see in the mirror is the top of her head as she bends over the basin. She scrunches her shoulders as she brushes and the sound of the running water suddenly becomes loud in his ears and he tells her yes he will be a good father. Always. And the full force of the future is bright in his mind with truth. Always shining true in the transfigured days that lie ahead. It's of what he can be certain, of what they can both be certain.

He leaves her to prepare the breakfast and set places for them both.

'Do you want to meet up for lunch?' she calls from the bathroom.

'Basketball day, unfortunately,' he says. 'Sorry. You know what the guys are like about it.'

'Yeah, yeah, and the team can't do without Danny, the Irish Michael Jordan. Danny – you're too small to be a basketball player,' she says, standing in the doorway.

'I'm the playmaker, the guy pulling the strings. Playmakers don't have to be big. And anyway you've seen it; some of the guys who play can't see their own feet. Lonnegan, the irrigation man, is so fat it takes about a day to run round

184

him.' She smiles and presses the towel against her face again. 'Once he got whistled out for travelling – his own team cheered, said it was a miracle to see him moving off the spot.'

It's what he does best. Making her laugh. Making her brown eyes spark into smiles. She flaps the towel at him, then disappears into the bedroom. By the time she's dressed he's everything ready on the table. She's wearing the short-sleeved white blouse he likes with a pair of black trousers. The white sets off the brownness of her skin, the black fierceness of her hair. Everything about her strikes him as crisp and fresh, the way she seems able to stay all day, and for a moment he envies her the air conditioning of the college library, the coolness of the alcoves and the silent lairs of books and wooden shelves.

'So you'd rather play basketball than have lunch with the mother of your baby?' she teases.

'We're playing the waste technicians – dirtiest team in the league,' he says and when she smiles, 'No, I'm not joking, they really are. Why don't you come over and watch the game?'

'What you going to do – call time-outs every five minutes so you can share a bite of my sandwiches? Think I'll give it a miss.'

'You could be missing the game of the season,' he says, 'but anyway I'll drop in for a few minutes, mid-afternoon break, soak up the air conditioning. Are you feeling any better?'

She nods her head and sips the orange juice. 'When are we going to get married, Danny?' she asks, setting the glass on the table.

'Soon,' he says. 'Soon.'

'You want to get married? You want me to beg?'

'I want to get married,' he says, looking at where her lips

have blushed and dampened the glass. 'There's no one else I want to marry. There's things I need to sort out first.'

'What are these things you always talk about?'

'Family things, just small things to tidy up.'

'You haven't got a wife already back in Ireland?' she asks, almost smiling.

'No, I haven't. You know I haven't got anything back in Ireland that's important to me.'

'I want it soon, Danny. Before it starts to show and I can't get into anything but maternity wear. They would let us use the college chapel and Father Mulryne would do the ceremony. You could bring your mother over. I'd like to meet her.'

'She's getting on, I don't think she'd be up to the travel,' he answers, glancing at his watch.

'Well in that case, after we get married, we can go over to Belfast, have a blessing ceremony there for all your relatives.'

'You've it all worked out,' he says, his voice neutral and quiet.

'I guess someone has to take the lead because if I wait for you it looks like it might never happen.'

From the apartment above there is the sound of a radio. He tries to think of the calm of the lake, of how he can go to work now without leaving behind the ashes of an argument that will smoulder through the rest of the day and finally slowly flare into unhappiness for both of them.

'It was you, Ramona, who always insisted that we go slow. That everything we did, we did slow. Always you were saying that you never wanted to make the same mistakes as you made before. That you had to be sure in your head.'

'But that's it, Danny, that's what I've been trying to tell you. I'm sure, I am sure. Sure I've got one who's never going to treat me badly, or raise his hand, or any of that shit.'

He reaches his hand across the table and takes hers. 'I want to marry you, I want to marry you soon. And we will. I'll talk to Father Mulryne, see how to go about it.' He squeezes her hand and nods his head at her, and as she smiles quickly back he goes to her, places his hands on her shoulders and kisses her on the top of her head, his lips lingering in the springy tautness of her hair. 'I'll talk to him tonight, I promise. Now I got to go to work, make a dollar for this child that's coming. You be all right?'

She says nothing but pats the back of his right hand with her palm and he tells her he'll see her during the afternoon break and then lifting his cold flask and his cap he opens the door and steps on to the porch. Hesitating he considers going back but he looks at the stars and stripes Ramona draped over the stoop after September the eleventh, at the rising press of light, and knows there's nothing more he can say. The silver flask feels cold against his skin and for a second he holds it against his cheek as if it might soothe away some of the stress beginning to burn in his head.

As always he walks to the college along the lakeside path. By now there's a steady traffic of joggers, some elderly from the condominium, some faculty members and a few serious pursuers of physical perfection. This morning he chooses not to meet any of their eyes and returns any offered greeting with only a nod of his head. On the tennis courts the women's team is having an early-morning training session and the constant thwack of the ball is broken only by the shouted instructions of the white-suited coach, who points with a racket that never seems to hit a ball. Sometimes she does a slow-mo of a particular shot at the same time as her other arm is used to illustrate the angle of the racket head or point to the position of her feet. Through the mesh of the fence it looks as if she is performing a kind of t'ai chi as

187

sometimes the other players copy the rituals of her movements. On a bench a student smokes a cigarette and flicks the pages of a book. He catches the smell of smoke and feels the temptation rising. Just another one, a little before it's time, to ease away the growing worry, but he thinks of the swathe of day he has to get through and fights it off and anyway he doesn't want to be late. In nine years he has never been late or missed a day and so he has come to pride himself on it, hooked on the belief that it's a record worth preserving.

He passes benches where students slump quiet and bleary as if left punch drunk by the early hour, staring miserably at the morning light, their books beside them in slovenly, sliding piles. Outside the canteen a girl on rollerblades is distributing fliers from a yellow bag slung across her shoulder. She is wearing khaki-coloured shorts and her elongated brown legs turn circles of herself like the arms of a compass. Already, knots of students, mostly male, are making their way to the canteen but there's none of the high spirits or goofing about that usually mark these moments. They all wear a kind of uniform, a nondescript downbeat combo of jeans, trainers, open checked shirts over T-shirts, and baseball caps often worn back to front – a camouflage that's carefully constructed to hide all signals of the family wealth and privilege that allow them to study in this exclusive, expensive place where the annual fees are more than he earns in a year. He watches them with no resentment because this is a world where envy is not allowed and he has long since ditched the negative, restricting weight of it. He passes along the front of one of the residential halls where contrary to campus rules brightly coloured towels are draped from open windows to dry. As always his eyes linger on the parked cars outside. In this area at least, ostentation is approved, and Japanese sports cars nestle neatly beside smoked-glass four-wheel drives. He cuts down behind the Health Center and the Marsden Graduate School, before following the narrow path that skirts round the back of the administration building. Down by the services entrance a secretary haloed in a fine gauze of blue is having a furtive smoke and for a second he thinks about joining her but remembers what Ramona said about men having it easy, about her being sick, and finds a new determination to stick to his five. But even that's not enough to assuage his sudden pulse of guilt and he resolves that he will stop completely long before the baby arrives, have his lungs clean and clear before he holds her in his arms, because in his imagination she is always a girl.

In the assembly area at the back of Facilities Management, most of the crew are filtering into place. They all wear the same green overalls but they cluster in teams according to profession. So under the newly planted palms stand the carpenters, plumbers and electricians, united by their belief that they are the skilled élite, while close to the fencing bunch the mechanics and the irrigation specialists. To their right are grouped the custodians, painters and a little way beyond them his fellow groundskeepers. As he passes the waste technicians, one of them slaps him gently on the back.

'Ready for a hiding today, Danny Boy?'

'Dream on, Eamon,' he answers. 'Only in your dreams, boyo.'

'We're up for it,' Eamon says, looking round his colleagues for confirmation. 'Aren't we, boys?'

'It's in the bag, Danny,' one answers. 'You boys should throw in the towel now, save yourselves the embarrassment.'

'Talk on, boys,' he says, smiling, and heads towards his waiting group who open their circle to receive him. He gives a collective nod and they greet him in their familiar and individual ways.

'They try to psyche you out, man,' Raul says. 'Shows they must be worried – that's all.'

'If we can't beat those bozos, we don't deserve to be a team,' Lester offers. 'Last time I saw Eamon play he could just about carry his beer belly round the court.'

Everybody chips in with an opinion, everybody except Edward, the team's best player. Younger than the rest of them, a college dropout and one of the few African-Americans in the workforce, he stands, as always, slightly apart and self-contained. At first Danny had assumed the stance was prompted by arrogance but after a while had come to realise that Edward's shyness was the cause.

'So what you think, Edward?' he asks.

'Ain't no stopping us, man,' Edward answers, then looks away as if he's said more than he meant to.

Josh Thornton, the Facilities Manager, arrives as always flanked by the assistant administrator who hands him the daily copy of the duty roster. 'OK, you guys, listen up!' he calls in his bullhorn of a voice and at the command the disparate groups coalesce and filter towards him. Then he reads out the duty schedules for the day, makes some announcements about charity events that need volunteers and, with his usual go-get-them admonition, dismisses everyone to their assigned tasks.

The first few hours of his morning are spent with Raul and Edward, trawling the picnic areas round the lakeside for litter, pruning back shrubbery that's beginning to encroach on the walkways and removing the detritus that's been washed up against the mesh of the chain-link fence surrounding the sports area. Even though he's thirty-five years of age, this is the first real job he's ever had and although sometimes it aches his body, he likes it and likes how it makes him feel.

Mid-morning they filter back to the administration building and he buys a coffee from the canteen, takes it outside and stands in the shade of a tree while he smokes his second cigarette. During this he likes to be on his own, undistracted from the pleasure by the rattle of conversation. Above him the stretching tree smells fresh and green, impervious to the thin stream of smoke he angles upwards. In the strengthening press of light the leaves tremble, as they are limed and waxed by the sun. The day is warming now, but there is a slight breeze that blunts the edge of its sharpness. He watches two girls cycle past, listens to their laughing voices. Suddenly he feels as if he lives in a big place, that there's room inside his head to construct whatever it is he wants to be his future. It gives him a feeling of lightness as he squints up at the shifting canopy where dappled rays try to flicker through the shade. The leaves are polished and sweetened by the sunlight and he thinks again of Ramona's skin and of her scent in the moments between sleep and wakening. To have her love seems a richer blessing than he could have thought possible and out of gratitude he takes a final drag of the unfinished cigarette and stubs it out in the dirt with his foot.

After break he's asked to help Jolie Peters in the rose garden which has been constructed under the windows of the President's office. There's not much thinking to do, except what his exacting senior instructs as she frets over the roses, moving delicately through them with her secateurs and sprays. He watches her tilt their heavy, blown faces to the severe scrutiny of her gaze, like a mother inspecting the health of her child, and for a second it makes him think of his own mother but there's little nostalgia or meaning in the memory. Sometimes she sends him to the store for another spray or a particular feed. He tries to talk to her, to show his admiration for her skill, tells her that the roses look great.

She lifts her head and glances at him. 'You don't know anything about roses, Danny – that's for sure. If you did you'd know these little bitches are in deep shit.'

'Sorry,' he says.

'Don't worry about it. You got any children, Danny?'

For a second he thinks of telling her about the baby. It's on the very tip of his tongue but at last he swallows the words, frightened that to release them too early might bring it bad luck, so he shakes his head and leans against the hoe which he has been shown how to move delicately round the beds.

'Well these here roses are like a sickly child and if you ever have a sickly child you'll know what I mean. The wind blows a bit too hard, they get a cold. Get their heads splashed, they catch pneumonia.'

He watches her liver-spotted hands cup the black-stippled and blistered head of a rose, then push away a brittle strand of grey hair which has fallen across her face.

'Never had a sickly child gave me as much grief as these. Mildew, spot – you name it, they get it. If I had my way, I'd dig them all out. Spiteful children, too, never let you touch them except they prick you with a thorn.'

'Why don't you get rid of them then? Save yourself all this grief.'

'They're her favourite,' she says, pointing with the secateurs to the President's window. 'Likes nothing better, apparently, than looking out over her roses. Well, let her come and tend them. Then she'd change her tune.'

'Way to go,' he says, uncertain whether it's all right to smile.

Later when he's finished helping and is walking away, she calls to him, 'Danny, never have a child who gives you grief.'

He raises his hoe in acknowledgement and a farewell salute but as he walks away there is a confused and splintered story trying to form in his head of spinning wheels and thumb pricks, of slights and enduring sleeps, of tall towers choked by thickets, and he has to whistle it clear.

At lunchtime he heads over to the Field House where in the changing rooms, the team are already kitting out and joking with each other. Each Friday they get the use of the main court for an hour. The previous year they had to play on one of the outside ones and so are grateful to be spared the midday sun. There is much high-fiving and back slaps – sometimes he thinks the rituals are as important as the game itself. It's as if these help cocoon themselves from the ineptitude of their play. So there's much stretching of muscles and binding of knees and old weaknesses with tape. Raul does his usual quota of ten press-ups followed by the wind-milling-arms routine that threatens to decapitate any collea-gue who stumbles too close, while Cedric uses the mirror to position his headband in precisely the right place on his bald and shining pate. Kenny sips from a lime-coloured sports drink and at intervals puffs out his cheeks. Only Edward sits still and quiet. Someone passes him the ball and he sets it on his thigh for a few seconds before rolling it slowly up and down, using the palm of his hand.

Lester, who is probably the weakest player of them all, gives the team talk, calling them to huddle round. No one jokes any more or fidgets and they link arms and lean into the circle's centre, listening to the words that are delivered in the sombre tone of a homily.

'Mark your man close, stay with him – if he goes off court for a piss stay with him. Let the son of a bitch feel your hot breath on the back of his neck. Be in his face all the time. But, Raul, no fouls, no free throws. Keep it cool, man! And watch out for Eamon O'Sullivan – the bastard's all elbows and wind. Keep it cool, play our game and we can't lose. Danny, let the ball do the work,' he says as both his hands imitate a rapid flow of passes but for a second look like a car's windscreen wipers. 'And keep giving the ball to Edward – ain't that right, son?' Edward nods his head and half smiles. 'In the basket, Edward, every time. In the damn bread bin.'

When they go on court the waste technicians are already there doing a little passing drill. There's a sprinkling of spectators – a few loner students seeking a cool place to sit unobserved and a couple of the college basketball team who train on court next. He always hates to see them there, in his imagination can already hear their laughter and the barely suppressed guffaws at their fumbling mistakes, their ironic cheers when someone scores. And then his eye catches Ramona sitting near the halfway line, her lunch bag on her lap. He goes over to her right away and she tells him she cannot stay the whole game.

'Just long enough to see me make a fool of myself,' he says. She doesn't answer but looks over his shoulder. He wants to please her. 'I'm going to speak to Father Mulryne Saturday morning. I said I'd give him an hour of help with the kids' soccer practice. After it I'll speak to him.'

'Good luck,' she answers and he doesn't know if she's referring to the game or his proposed talk with the priest.

The game plays out to its own soundtrack. There is an underscore of grunts and broken breathing, of names called in sharp-edged insistent voices, and over this is scored the constant stammering bounce of the ball and the heavy slap and sudden high-pitched squeak of shoes. Only occasionally is there the soft trill of the ball cleanly kissing the net. As expected there is, too, the laughter of the waiting college players and their ragged bursts of exaggerated applause at moments of accidental skill. Only Edward is immune to their scorn, as he moves about the court, a thin, languid ghost of a player, evading the clattering bodies of the opposition as if he's spectral, formed only by particles of reflex and instinctive skill.

Conscious of the presence of Ramona, he tries at first to raise his own game, adding a flourish, a decorative elegance, to his movements, but he knows he can't sustain it and so reverts to what he's been told to do and gives the ball as early and as often as possible to Edward. There is a beauty in his play – it's clear that he could have been a college player and in this game he gradually drifts into his own element, moving to his own music, forgetting for a while that he's slumming it and allowing himself to free-flow, giving himself to the memory of other games in other places. The technicians have no answer but after the first time-out, their play hardens and when Edward receives the ball in a corner he's banged so hard in the back by O'Sullivan that he almost hits the first row of seats. O'Sullivan holds up his hands in a simulation of an apology belied by the grin on his face. The college players hoot their derision and he gives them the finger.

'He fell over!' he shouts to no one in particular. 'You only have to look at him and he falls over.'

'Take it easy, man!' shout voices from about the court. Others help Edward to his feet. When open play resumes he calls for the ball, takes it deliberately close to O'Sullivan, dips a shoulder, feints and then darts past him in a seamless flow of speed. O'Sullivan stumbles wrong-footed in his slipstream and reddens before kneeling down as if to tie his lace.

Now the game cuts up rough, rougher than he's ever seen it and with an edge that's new and ugly. Tempers and elbows are raised, every ball is grappled and bumped for and the game collapses into a staccato stopping and starting, a cacophony of disputed calls and fouls. When Edward stretches to receive a short pass in centre court, O'Sullivan clatters him to the floor, then stands over him shouting at him to get up. At first he lies there, not moving or responding, before jumping up and pushing the ball hard into O'Sullivan's stomach, causing him to jack-knife in a winded gasp, and then there's shoving and pushing with players running in from all sides and no one sure if the insurgents are coming to pacify or participate. As O'Sullivan struggles for breath he tries to force his way through to Edward but Danny manages to push himself between the two men.

'For God's sake, Eamon, it's only a game! Let the kid be.'

'Out of the way, Danny, before you get hurt.'

'No one's getting hurt. Cool it for God's sake!'

'He's a showboating son of a bitch! Let's see just how much of a man he is!' he shouts and he tries to push him aside to reach his quarry. Without thinking Danny slaps O'Sullivan hard on the cheek and, in the seconds it slows him down, restraining arms from his own team mates are pulling him away and the referee's whistle is a continuous shrill blast abandoning the game. Suddenly he remembers Ramona and as he looks desperately to the seats he sees her leaving. He calls to her but either she doesn't hear or has chosen to ignore him, hurrying towards the exit without looking back. Now it's O'Sullivan's voice again.

'Never side against your own. You remember that.'

'What the hell you talking about, Eamon? Edward is my own – in case you hadn't noticed we play on the same team. Have you been watching *Gangs of New York* or friggin' something? Get real.' His anger wants to say more but he's thinking of Ramona and so he hurries off to the changing room, with every step remembering her words about a man who never raised his hand, who knew how to treat her properly, and he smarts at the memory of what he's done. Should he go to her now to try to explain? But gradually the thought of trying to talk in the restrictive confines of the library, of trying to say important things in whispers, makes him hesitate before telling himself that it would best be postponed until the evening.

In the changing room the team are claiming a victory, talking it up, making it sound like a battle that's been won, reprising key moments through the distorting lens of their fired-up imaginations. They greet him like a hero, milling round, arms flapping and then hands building a pyramid of high-fives to the fanfare of their hollers. He looks past them to where Edward is changing quickly and slipping into the showers before anyone else. Afterwards he comes across him in the corridor where he is getting a Coke from the machine. As he searches his own pockets for money, Edward drinks slowly from the bottle then uses it to point at him.

'I don't need anyone to fight my battles for me,' he says softly. 'I do it for myself.'

Before he can think of a reply Edward has slung his bag over his shoulder and walked off. When he puts his coins in the machine it swallows them but gives nothing in return and in his frustration he thumps the side with his fist.

'You still fighting, Danny Boy?' Cedric asks as he joins him in the corridor.

'It took my money and gave me nothing back.'

'Must be a woman,' Cedric says before he retrieves the coins by pressing a button. 'Let me try.' There is the soft *thunk* of the bottle dropping and Cedric smiles as he hands it to him, then pats him on the back.

But it is a cigarette he wants. A cigarette more than anything. If he's to have one now, however, it will break his designated schedule so he slugs the Coke instead and tries to tell himself that it's enough.

The afternoon drags out in a sequence of tedious jobs which leaves him frustrated and impatient to see Ramona. He tries to practise and perfect what he wants to say but the words jumble in his head and he decides that it might be best to read the situation before he fixes on an approach. He works with Raul and Edward but there's no reference to what was said in the corridor and he's too preoccupied with his own concerns to build bridges and in truth a little angry that the guy is so contemptuous of his efforts to help, an intervention that has brought him only grief. The heat is high now and everything is framed by a light that seems to pulse against his temples.

When he gets home the temperature has dropped a little and Ramona is already sitting on the stoop with her shoes kicked off and sipping a cup of iced tea. As he walks towards her, her face is shaded, her expression unclear and he feels as if he's stumbling blindly into the force field of her uncertain mood.

'Hi,' she says neutrally as he reaches the bottom of the steps.

'Hi,' he replies as he stares at her face for an answer and then into the awkward stretch of silence, even before he has time to compose them, the words blurt out, 'I'm sorry, Ramona, really sorry. It just got a bit heated.'

'I saw that,' she says, running her hand through the black sweep of her hair.

'It was just boys' stuff. Heat of the moment.' He stumbles into silence and stands watching her sip her tea.

'Boys' stuff? It looked to me like you slapped him pretty hard.'

He stands at the bottom of the steps like a little boy and doesn't know what to say.

'Get your shower,' she tells him, 'the food's almost ready.'

198

In the shower he pushes his palms against the tiles and leans his body forward so the water cascades down his back. The frustration inside him makes him push hard against the wall as if he's trying to throw it over. He thinks of the lake, of what it would be like to swim in it. The water is always cold, Arnie says, even on the hottest day. Maybe some day he will take up his offer to go fishing. Suddenly he likes the idea of being far out in the early morning when the mists cocoon you from the harsh realities of the day to come and the only sound is the press of the swell against the wooden prow of the boat. He puts his head under the water, lets it play against his scalp. But as the water washes away the sweat of the day he feels, too, the erosion of the securities with which it had started. Now everything seems fragile, built on shifting sand, and it frightens him how quickly his secure vision of a future has slipped away. He thinks of foundations, on what he has tried to construct a life, and as always when he thinks like this there is a new surge of unease. The water begins to run cooler but he stays where he is and feels again that he's being followed, that at every moment malevolent and unseen eyes fix their gaze upon him. The thought is shot through with a fierce burn of fear and, as he turns off the water, the droplets on his body drip with ever greater self-torture.

How could he have been so foolish as to raise his hand in front of her? The gnawing memory eats through every other thought and he presses the towel tightly to his eyes as if that might block it out. He thinks of the nights he has heard her whimper in her sleep, remembers the first time he understood what she had never talked about when he stretched out his hand to remove some tiny piece of thread from her hair and saw her flinch and squirm away. In that one moment he understood it all and afterwards when she had cried he had coaxed her to tell him, but even then she revealed only enough, as if recalling it was to feel once again all the pain and the shame. Three years she spent with her former partner and now he's angry again, telling himself that if only he loves her well enough he can make her forget in time, that their future will wipe away the memories that make her whimper in her sleep. And he is angry that he can do something so stupid that makes her remember once more.

They say little to each other over the meal but in the little everything is said. He hesitates to talk of Father Mulryne again because the gambit is too obvious, transparent in its desire to make amends, and so when he speaks, he speaks of nothing except the trivia of the day. Later she tells him she's tired and wants to have an early night but she gives no invitation to follow her and so he sits out on the stoop with a beer and thinks back over the day trying to step back into it in different footprints to rediscover the perfect place he wants to be. But the journey takes him further than he wants to go and so he finds himself wandering once again in a mesh of narrow streets, in windblown housing estates that blister the side of the mountain and squat like gulags above the edges of the city below. He tries to shrug it all away with a deep slug of beer but it tastes bitter on his tongue and he tells himself that he will go to bed now, snuggle into Ramona's heat, slip his hand round the swelling globe of her belly and hope she will not push his hand away, let him embrace a new and better land.

On Saturday morning, as promised, he helps Father Mulryne with the kids' soccer school on the college grounds. As always it strikes him as odd to see the priest out of his normal black and in a blue tracksuit, his unruly swathe of grey hair falling forward when his large body lumbers into a run that with increasing speed always looks as if at any moment he might topple forward like some giant tree felled in the forest. Mulryne compensates for his lack of knowledge about the game by the enthusiasm he generates as he waves his arms in exhortation and salutation of the smallest achievement and the potential scribbling chaos of the session is ordered and punctuated by the authoritative blasts of his whistle. The kids – boys and girls – respond with serious concentration and effort. He likes Mulryne, thinks that he's always been kind to him over the years, taken an interest in him but never asked too many questions, reading accurately his reluctance to talk about his family or the past.

He helps the priest with the practice, organising the passing drills and refereeing some of the small-sided games. As always the session ends with a full-scale game with Mulryne in charge, his weathered face creasing into ever deeper lines as he struggles to keep up with the flow. The players hunt the ball in packs soon oblivious to their designated positions while from the bleachers a handful of parents cheer on their offspring. The ball ricochets from foot to foot as if in a pinball game. After the game is over he will talk to Mulryne, see what can be done about the wedding. Maybe some small, private affair with only a few close friends. No big splash, no photographer. Everything could be all right.

When the final whistle goes he helps collect the bibs from the teams and gathers the balls into a net. He tells himself that Mulryne will understand what is needed. He watches the priest drink from a bottle of water then wipe the broad back of his hand across his mouth. But just as he starts to walk towards him there's the sound of raised and angry voices and two kids come from the side of the bleachers in a dispute that grows increasingly animated.

'Hey, hey!' Mulryne calls. As he hurries towards the two

boys, water sluices out of the bottle in his hand. 'What in the name of fortune is going on here?'

'He's got my shin pads,' the smaller boy blurts out.

'They're mine,' the bigger boy insists.

'No they're not – my dad got me them last week.'

'You calling me a liar?' the boy asks, suddenly turning on his accuser, his skinny frame warping into aggression.

'Hold up, guys, just hold up,' Mulryne says, pushing between them. 'No one's calling anyone anything, Marvin. If everyone stops shouting we can sort this out. Now, Roddy, you tell me what's going on.'

'He's calling me a liar,' Marvin asserts again as if now this is the main issue.

'Let Roddy speak, Marvin – you'll get your chance in a minute.'

Marvin angles himself away from his accuser to show he is indifferent to anything the other boy has to say and concentrates on pressing his foot into the grass as if stubbing out some repellent insect.

'After the game I was gathering up my stuff and I couldn't find my guards. Then I saw Marvin putting them in his bag,' Roddy says. The smaller boy is acting tough, asserting his rights over his possessions, but it's clear he is upset, close to crying.

'What sort of guards are they, Roddy?' Mulryne asks.

'Nike, black and white colour.'

'Show me the guards, Marvin.'

For a second the boy hesitates, then lifts his eyes from the ground and stares into the distance and it looks as if he is considering taking flight. When he hands over the guards it is with a practised gesture of silent disdain, his eyes still not making contact with anyone.

'These look like your guards, Roddy?' Mulryne asks,

holding them in the air in front of the boy while the boy nods his head. 'Are you sure?'

'I got Nike guards,' Marvin suddenly says. 'I got Nike guards, my brother gave me them. You can ask him.'

'There's a grass stain at the top of one of them where I did a slide tackle,' Roddy says.

'Look like this?' Mulryne asks and when the boy says yes he hands them to him, then signals him to go with a nod of his head.

'Bullshit, man!' Marvin says, throwing his bag to the ground theatrically. 'I got a pair exactly like that so if they ain't mine then somebody's taken my pair.'

'Take it easy, son,' Mulryne says. 'Easy mistake to make – they all look the same. Next practice I'll ask if anyone saw yours.' He offers the boy a drink from his bottle of water but it's wordlessly refused. Then Mulryne puts his arm round the boy's shoulder and walks him off across the pitch. He watches them go, the priest dwarfing the boy, and decides that he'll go up to the parish house later in the week and raise the question of the wedding in the privacy of that place. This was the wrong time to talk. Better, too, when he has had more time to consider what he should say and understands how to put it without inviting the questions he doesn't know how to answer. Then before he leaves he turns and stares for a second to the far side of the field where the priest stands with the boy under the shade of the trees.

'How did it go with Father Mulryne?' Ramona asks when he returns home and, seeing the anticipation in her eyes, he says, 'No problem, no problem.'

'What did he say, Danny? What did he say?'

'He'd be happy to do it. I didn't have a chance to talk about dates because something came up – some emergency or something – and he had to go. But he'll do it, no problem.'

'And can we use the college chapel?'

'Yes we can.'

'But you didn't get a chance to fix a date?'

'No, but I'll go back and see him when he's free and fix it up.'

'He'll want to talk to us both, won't he?' she asks.

'Sure, but I just need to fix up some details with him first.'

'We can't wait too long,' she says, patting her stomach. 'I want to be able to fit into a dress. Did you tell him about the baby?'

'No, I thought it was better not to say anything.'

'Why, were you embarrassed?' she asks, smiling at him.

His reply is to hug her, hold her tight but lightly because increasingly he's conscious of the child growing inside her. His child. He wants to tell her everything will be all right, that there is nothing to fear, but as he breathes in her scent and feels the brush of her hair against his cheek, he knows the words are what he himself wants to hear and so instead he kisses her hair and buries himself in her beautiful strangeness. It's the strangeness that he thinks he'll never take for granted if he is to spend every day of the rest of his life with her. It is not just the naked beauty of her body that holds his fascination but everything that goes to make her and which is different to him. So it's in the patina of her skin, the deep pull of her brown eyes that seem to hold an invite to enter some richer world, the timbre of her voice, the smallness of her hands, the way her name sounds when he says it, which exert a constant magnetism.

'Why don't we go to the beach tomorrow?' she says. 'Drive out to the beach – we haven't been in ages. And we'll be able to talk – there's so much we have to plan about the wedding.'

'You don't think we should wait until I've spoken to Father Mulryne, got everything firmed up?'

'No, you said there's no problem and there's so many things to think about. I don't think you have the first idea what's involved in a wedding, Danny.'

He releases her from his embrace and tries to smooth the wiry spring of her hair, tries to calm her excitement. 'The beach would be nice,' he says, then hesitates. 'Listen, Ramona, I want the wedding to be nice but I don't think we should go overboard. We need to keep saving for a bigger place and there'll be a lot of expenses with a baby.'

'You want to give me a cheapskate wedding, Danny?' she asks but there is a lightness in her voice.

'I want it to be nice, really nice, but just quiet, nothing showy.'

'You don't think I'm worth showing off?' But he sees the smile in her eyes and knows that she is teasing him so he plays along.

'No, you're so ugly maybe you should wear a veil or a mask.'

She pushes him in the ribs with her elbow and it feels the closest to happiness he has ever known.

'So you're going to rough me up now, are you?' he says, squeezing her hip. 'This child better have his father's looks or you're in trouble.'

'What should we call it, Danny? If it's a boy what about Ruben?'

'And if it's a girl?'

'I think it's a boy – it feels like a boy. You don't want an Irish name?'

'No, we don't need an Irish name. Ruben sounds pretty good to me.'

He takes her by the hand and they go outside and sit in the shade of the stoop. Across the lawn their neighbour George is washing his four-wheel drive. He has the radio on and the music drifts lazily across the grass in vaguely familiar, soft-etched fragments. He doesn't let go of the smallness of her hand as she sits on the cane chair with her legs curled up below her. George sees them and waves the soap-sudded sponge in the air. His hand accidentally squeezes out little gossamer bubbles which get touched by a sudden lingering kiss of light.

'Having a lazy one?' he calls and they nod their heads in reply. 'Good on you,' he shouts and then goes back to his washing and rinsing, the shiny metal of the car steadily mirroring a polished transfer of the sky.

On the Sunday they take the hour's drive out to Cocoa beach and kick off their shoes as they step off the boardwalk and feel the hot, silver sand press between their toes. The white-crested but soft shift of sea feels cool to look at and there is a gentle breeze that tempers the strain of the heat. He suddenly realises that it's winter and without being able to stop it he thinks of what it must be like back there – the grey slant of rain, the raw-edged wind gnawing through the tight funnel of streets – and he shivers.

'Somebody walk across your grave?' she asks.

He tries to smile and spreads the rug on the sand. She opens the cool box, hands him a Coke and he presses its unopened coldness against his lips. A little way in front of them sits a family with two young children. The father has dug a large hole with a plastic spade and the kids run feverishly to the sea to fill their buckets, then tip in the water, squealing with frustration when it almost immediately soaks away. Ramona watches them intently and he knows what she's thinking because he's thinking it too.

'You better watch,' she says, 'learn how to build sand-castles.'

'I'll build the best sandcastles you ever saw, with towers and turrets, and there'll be little flags on all the towers. And they'll have a moat and a drawbridge. I'll build it closer to the sea so that the incoming tide fills up the moat.'

'So you're an expert on sandcastles then?'

'Every boy is an expert on sandcastles.'

'Did you have seaside holidays when you were a kid?'

'Just the once – I was taken down south on a summer community scheme. We didn't really do holidays.'

'Your mother will want to come to the wedding, won't she? We'll fly her over – there's lots of things I want to ask her about; I hardly know anything about your family.'

'I'm not sure, Ramona,' he says, staring at the label on the Coke bottle as if he's reading it. 'She's getting on, hasn't been keeping too well recently. I think it might be too much for her.'

'Well whether she comes or not, we have to invite her – let her decide. And if she can't make it, then like I said we can have a blessing in Ireland and I'll get a chance to see where you grew up and meet all your relations.'

'Sure,' he says, combing his fingers through the sand. 'You hungry yet?'

'I'm always hungry.'

'You want to go and get something to eat?'

'In a little while. We've so much to get ready for the wedding.'

'We should go get a table before the rush starts,' he says as he lifts a fistful of sand and lets it slowly sift over her foot, then stands up and stretches out his hand to help her up. They walk along the water's edge and she squeals when a wave breaks around her feet and they scamper with high steps to evade its surge. The sun is warm on his face but not oppressive and, as they walk, sometimes their feet sink into the softness of the damp sand, making him feel as if he is suddenly heavier than he is. To live in the moment is what will carry him through, not to have to go back. He looks over his shoulder where almost immediately the tide reclaims their steps and he feels light, safe in the sweet embrace of love.

Out on the piers the restaurants and bars are already busy and there's live music and the sound of people throwing off the working week. They sit at a table outside and have seafood and watch old men hunched over the end railing inspect their fishing lines. Sometimes they throw discarded bait in the air and the gulls swoop then wheel effortlessly away again. The afternoon drifts lazily away and time feels as if it's been rendered powerless, the normal rigidity of the clock's hard hands reduced to vague gestures of indifference. There's only the shuck and rasp of the sea and the high-pitched voices of swimmers shocked by its unexpected coldness which mark the passing of the day. When they drive home early evening Ramona falls asleep after a few miles and he settles into the pleasure of the drive.

The road passes a seemingly disconnected slew of houses and enclaves of shops and restaurants. The only link is the repeated neon logos of fast-food outlets, otherwise it is a rambling line of garages and car showrooms, their forecourts awash with bunting and flags; landscapers and garden suppliers with brightly coloured ceramic pots piled high at their gates; pool installers; convenience stores and a host of cut-price bargain basements. A run-down-looking lawyer's office advertises the price of a divorce across its window. He likes the disconnection, the arbitrary piecemeal nature of it all, the way nothing is pushed tight against its neighbour, the way there's space to breathe between the boundaries and no one has to live inside the pocket of someone else's paranoia. Here there are no interfaces, just ragged-edged sprawls, and if the rich have their lakeside houses and their gated communities with names echoing the promise of a perfect lifestyle then it's only money that's needed to pass through the portal.

He puts the radio on softly and lowers his window to let the night air splash his face. Later that evening he'll go and see Father Mulryne, fix up a date. The sooner the better, less time to let things get complicated. And there is something else on his mind, something that he might try to talk to him about but he's not sure, and it's a big thing so he needs to be sure. Ramona snuggles her head into the pillow of his jumper that she has pushed against the window and wrinkles her nose as if she's going to sneeze. It's been a very long time, maybe twenty years at least, and up to now he has felt no need of it, never crossed the door of a church except for Eamon O'Sullivan's daughter's funeral. But part of him thinks that maybe it's the right thing to do because a wedding is the biggest new start in life and making a confession might carry him across that line clean and ready to build the future. He feels the seep of sweat on his hands and he bites his lip. If only he could be sure that it's the right thing to do. And will he feel cleaner, more deserving of her love, have more right to be the father of their child? He is desperate for a cigarette and in his frustration he blows a thin stream of air against the windscreen.

'What's wrong, Danny?' she asks. 'You tired driving? Want me to take the wheel?'

'No, I'm fine,' he says, watching as she rubs the sleep out of her eyes.

'We'll have an early night when we get home. I'm tired, too; it must be all that fresh air.'

When they reach home the light is fading and most of the windows in the condominium are lit up. As they pass the entrance a doorman is helping an elderly woman laden with bags out of a cab while he tries to hold the lead of her small dog. George's four-wheel drive still sits where it was earlier, but is now a ghostly smudge in the dusk. Within half an hour Ramona is in bed sleeping deeply. He watches her from the doorway for a long time then goes down to the lake and lights a cigarette. The smoke blurs into the grey mist coming off the water as he peers into its depths, tries to see what he must do, but every idea in his head is amorphous and at the very moment when it promises to settle into certainty it swirls away again. Only the sound of the lapping water against the jetty and the reeds remains constant. Normally it calms him but this night it rattles against his senses that even the slow smoke of this final cigarette does not soothe.

There's a rising wind bending and teasing the reeds, brushing through them and tousling their heavy, weary heads. It's not too late, he will go up to Father Mulryne's and try to fix a date, and when he's there he will decide about the confession, try to read what is best in the clarity of the moment. But when he walks the couple of blocks to the parish house a younger priest opens the door and tells him that Father Mulryne isn't there. He doesn't open the door fully and there's no invitation to linger. As the priest closes the door, he hears himself saying, 'No problem, no problem,' and his walk back home is quickened by the thought of slipping into bed beside Ramona. There's no one about apart from a couple of teenagers playing one on one in the yard of their house, a rusted, broken hoop hanging from above the garage door and papery-winged moths teasing the outside light. The slap of the ball accompanies his steps as he hurries on, drawn by the soft warmth he knows awaits him.

In the following week the weather turns cooler and the campus is filled with the complaints of students who have to dig out jumpers and sweatshirts. But it's good weather to work in and the spirits of his workmates are high. A barbecue and softball game are planned for the weekend. They take advantage of the cooler air to do some new planting round the new library extension. Maturing palms and trees are brought in by machines, their root balls cradled in hessian and wire, then lowered into the prepared holes. The beds are covered with weed-suppressing membrane and layered with cocoa shells and bark. There is a sense of achievement when it's finished and the chocolate smell from the shells lingers about their hands and clothes long after they have completed the work. Even Edward jokes around a little, insisting that one of the trees hasn't been planted straight, holding up his hoe parallel to it, one eye closed like a golfer lining up a putt.

'I'm telling you, man, it's out of line. Anybody with an eye can see that,' he insists, smiling like it's a good joke when the others argue with him. Eventually Cedric goes and finds a carpenter and borrows a spirit level but they argue about how to take a reading and by the time they decide it's straight, Edward is laughing to himself and then everyone laughs at hearing him do what sounds so unfamiliar. A group of girl students strolls by, momentarily curious to see what they're laughing about.

'Excuse me, ladies,' Raul says, removing his cap and bowing slightly, 'could you help us here a second? We need a young clear eye to tell us if this here tree is straight or not. What's your opinion?'

The girls giggle and shuffle their books under their arms. One steps forward and says, 'Looks straight to me.'

'Thank you, ma'am,' Raul says, 'we appreciate your help.' And as the students go to walk on, 'May I ask, just for the record, what your subject is?'

'Environmental Science,' she answers as she laughs and joins her friends.

'Environmental Science!' Raul says, turning to them. 'Can't get any more expert than that.'

'She wouldn't know straight if she saw it on her wedding night,' Scott says and they take their caps off and flap them at him as if beating away a disgusting smell.

'It's one of the perks of the job,' says Raul, 'working round so many gorgeous chicks.'

'It's a tightener, a friggin' tease, when you can look but not touch,' Scott suggests. 'It's like that scene in *Cool Hand Luke* where the chain gang are working on the road and they see this babe washing and lathering a car and they're stood there with their tongues hanging out. Oh man, it's a friggin' tease all right. What you say, Danny Boy?'

'Too busy working, bros,' he says.

'Danny only has eyes for one girl – isn't that right?' Cedric says, lightly throwing some of the cocoa shells at him. 'When you gonna make an honest woman of her?'

'Maybe sooner than you think,' he says, unsure of whether he should have said it or not as the guys whoop and kick shells at him.

'Way to go, Danny Boy. And don't you worry we'll give you a send-off you won't forget. We'll drink every Irish pub dry between here and Miami.'

'Talking about drink makes me powerful thirsty,' Raul says. 'What about a quick one after work? We can go to Pat's Bar, start getting into practice.'

But he doesn't have the time or the spare money to fritter away and on the way home from work he calls again at the parish house. It's the same priest as before who answers the door but this time he opens it more fully. He is wearing a green sweatshirt and from the house behind him comes the smell of cooking and the sound of music.

'I'm sorry, Father Mulryne isn't here at the moment,' he says, brushing his hands against his sides as if drying them.

'Do you know when he'll be back?'

'We're not sure – maybe the weekend. Can I help you?'

'No thanks, it's kind of personal.'

'It's what we do – the personal,' the priest says, smiling.

'Yeah, but I think I need to see Father Mulryne.'

'I understand. Maybe you'd like to leave a message?'

He hesitates, fumbles for the words but then shakes his head and starts to turn away. 'Who is it, John?' a voice calls from somewhere in the house, the words filtering through the music, and he can't be sure but it sounds like Mulryne. However, as he turns back the door is being quickly closed, leaving him to stare at it for a few seconds, telling himself that he might have been mistaken. At the end of the drive he stops and stares at the house but its curtained windows are still, imperturbable and indifferent to his questions.

He doesn't want to go straight home and have to report his second failure to Ramona so he drives the short distance to the mall that nestles between the freeway and the hospital. It's a twilight place, a slowly dying centre, the car park largely empty, probably most of the cars belonging to those who still work in it. Sometimes when he wants to think or be invisible he comes here and drifts past the closing-down signs; the shut-up stores still strewn with abandoned debris and their For Rent signs; those open stores where the weary owners stand in the doorways inviting in a miracle. He doesn't know why one such place should decline and one should prosper – perhaps it's the location or the arbitrary whim of fashion, the particular chemistry of the investors – but he's seen it before and when the decay starts there seems no way back, just a slow haemorrhaging of dreams. Some stores have spread their wares outside on trestles as if insisting on their presence, their determination to never give up, but in the end they too will go.

He goes to the second-hand book store and strolls the aisles, lifting out books at random, drawn by the colours of their spines or the illustrations on their covers. There is one on garden design that catches his eye and he flicks the pages slowly taking in the pictures. A couple of times in the last year he has discussed with Cedric the possibility of some day going out on their own, starting up a garden-maintenance business, even maybe a landscaping service. It's only talk but sometimes it's nice to warm themselves at the flame of their dreams and because it remains only in the realm of talk there is no sense of risk or danger. But still all things are possible, he tells himself, and already they've done a few jobs for college staff. The start-up costs would not be so great – a truck, basic equipment – but Cedric says it might be hard to undercut the Cubans who already have cornered a big part of the market. A good cheap job done, dollars in the hand, no questions asked – hard to compete. For a second, however, he thinks of owning a business and working in the gardens of the big houses round the lake, making a success of it for Ramona and their child. Maybe even some day owning one of those very houses. He buys the book and walks slowly back to his car and as always, even after all this time, is surprised by how much heat still smoulders in the day.

When he gets home Ramona is full of talk about choices of hospital and health plans. She's been taking advice from work colleagues who have recently had babies and she has the excited tone of someone who has just been admitted to an exclusive club. Some of them have offered her various necessities and while she is happy to accept she thinks they should buy their own cot. She shows him pictures in a catalogue, each one more elaborate than the last.

'It would be nice to make one,' he says.

'Make one? Out of an orange box? You must be kidding.'

'They don't look too complicated.'

'Danny, you're turning into a bit of a dreamer. There's safety regulations and all. No child of mine is going to sleep in a home-made box.'

'Sorry,' he says sheepishly. 'It was just an idea.'

'You get any more ideas like that, you keep them under your hat. What do you think of this one?' she asks, showing him another picture. 'It's my favourite. You can rock it.'

'Real nice,' he says, looking at the draped canopy and the carved animal shapes. He knows better than to ask about the price but thinks he should try to muster up some more private work. Perhaps he could run off a few advertising fliers, pin them up around the campus where the teaching staff might see them. If he could build up a regular clientele with Cedric it could turn into a nice earner and they're going to need as much money as they can find if they are to give their child everything they desire. He wonders who does the parish house and church grounds but the thought brings back his earlier uncertainty. Watching Ramona turning the pages of the magazine suddenly makes him think he should make the confession. Mulryne has always been good to him, solid, and he knows about Ireland – the real one, not the sickly fantasy of the green-liveried, leprechaun- and shamrock-loving theme pubs. Personally he would rather drink in the backroom of the cheapest juke-joint than wallow in that phoney world of sentimental nostalgia for something that does not exist. A couple of times when too much drink turned his insides bitter he almost stood up and told them so. If anyone can understand, Mulryne will. It's a risk but he will do it for Ramona, do it for the child, take whatever penance brings forgiveness. Start with a clean slate.

When the weekend comes he returns to see Father Mulryne. He turns into the street to see the younger priest cycling off on a mountain bike and as he walks to the door he studies the grounds, the straggling bushes that need to be pruned back hard, the long thin fingers of ivy that are beginning to choke the guttering. When he knocks on the door he can hear the sound of a television but no one comes to answer. Something makes him keep on knocking. Out of the corner of his eye he catches the twitch of a curtain and he knocks again, this time more insistently. There is the sound of a lock being turned and then it is Mulryne's eyes staring at him through the narrow slit in the door. Eyes that are bloodshot and blue-bagged. He has not shaved and there is a thick white stubble lathering his face.

'What you want, Danny?' he asks.

'I need to talk to you.'

'It's not a good time. Is it important?'

'It was kinda. Yeah, pretty important.'

Mulryne hesitates, then opens the door and without inviting him in walks off down the hall towards the kitchen. He is wearing a white vest and baggy beltless trousers. On the kitchen table is a bottle of Jack Daniel's and a single glass. In another room somewhere a television is playing.

'You look a bit rough,' he says and then thinks it's not the type of thing you say to a priest.

'Rough as a bear's arse,' Mulryne says, slumping on a chair at the table, the empty glass directly in front of him. 'You want a drink?' and when he shakes his head, he says, 'For God's sake have a drink, Danny.'

So he sits at the table and watches as Mulryne fills his glass. The priest's bare arms are white-haired, muscular, the blue veins at his wrists raised and dark against the paleness of his skin. They are drinking out of fine-cut glass tumblers, light blushing the contents as they raise them to their mouths.

'You're not well?' he asks, feeling the whisky flame the back of his throat.

'No, I'm not so good,' Mulryne says, tipping his head back slightly to drain the glass quickly, then filling his glass again. 'Been on a bit of a bender.'

'Sometimes a bit of a blow-out does no harm,' he says, trying to work out what are the right things to say.

'That's right, son, it gets things out of your system. Except this time it isn't working very well.' He rubs his stubbled cheeks as if shaving them with the palms of his hands. 'I had a father who liked a drink. Meek and mild he was during the week and then every Saturday night he got bluttered and would have fought the devil. We used to hide when we saw him coming. Once we'd all had enough and after he hit our mother we ganged up on him, got the jump on him and tied him to a chair. He was cussin' and screaming what he'd do to us all when he got free but we paid no heed. And in the morning, Danny, after he'd slept all night tied to the chair, up he gets, washes and changes his clothes and away to early mass. When he comes back he makes us all our breakfast and fries up lashings of bacon in the pan.' There's a moment of silence as he dwells on the memory then says, 'Terrible thing the drink.'

Perhaps out of respect for his observation, the priest sips this glass more slowly, once holding it up to the light as if it is a vintage wine. 'I'm thinking of taking a trip back to Ireland,' he says. 'I still have a sister in Dublin and a couple of cousins in Donegal. She tells me though that you'd hardly recognise the place. Big lot of changes everywhere and apparently you couldn't afford to buy a house for love nor money. Even somewhere you couldn't swing a cat goes for megabucks. I like the idea of Donegal – you ever been there, Danny? I went once as a young man. Had a bit of a sweetheart – before I was a priest of course. Well I think it was,' he says, suddenly bursting into a raucous laugh that seems to shake his whole body. 'Beautiful place, Danny. Beautiful beaches, beautiful deserted beaches.' He rubs his eyes with the tips of his fingers. 'You ever think of going back?'

'No, never.'

'Nothing there for you, Danny?'

'No, nothing there. Everything is here for me now,' he says and thinks that this is perhaps the moment to raise the purpose of his visit but before he can speak Mulryne stands up, runs some water at the sink and splashes his face. He looks around for something to dry it with but seeing nothing pulls up his vest and uses it, then sits down again at the table, seemingly oblivious to the spreading bruises of damp left behind. There are still droplets shining on his cheekbones.

'Have another drink, son,' Mulryne says and before Danny can refuse he is pouring it into his glass. 'You're a bit of a dark horse, Danny – where he comes from, where he goes to, nobody knows. Ask me no secrets and I'll tell you no lies – isn't that right, Danny?' He touches the side of his nose with his finger.

He decides that he should go but when he tries to speak, Mulryne moves his finger to his lips. 'Shush, son, shush. You're a good lad because you're not always jabbering on like some of them do. You keep your own counsel and that's the way it should be with a man. Listen, can you hear that?' The only sound is the chatter of the television. 'You know what that is, Danny? It's the sound of nothing, just an endless jabber that means nothing in this world, filling people's heads with mush so they can't think straight any more.' One of the droplets runs down his cheek and for a second it looks as if he is crying.

'Why don't I put some coffee on?' he says and Mulryne waves his hand vaguely in the air in a slow gesture of indifference. But he goes ahead anyway and brews up some strong black coffee, hands it to the priest.

'You think this will make me feel better, Danny?'

'I don't know, can't make you feel any worse.'

'You know that song by Simon and Garfunkel? "The Sound of Silence" it's called. Good song, Danny; you know it, son?' And when he nods, 'That's what I like to hear more than anything – the sound of silence. Sometimes when the church is empty I go into the confession box, try to hear it. You know what I'm saying, son?'

He nods again and drinks some of the coffee in the hope that the priest will follow his example.

'Do something for me, Danny,' Mulryne suddenly says, stretching out his hand across the table towards him. 'Go and turn that bloody thing off.'

So he goes into the next room and does what the priest has asked and when he returns he finds him sipping from the cup of coffee. Once Mulryne pauses to run a hand through the thick mop of hair that has fallen forward across his brow but then he slips into silence staring intently at the contents of the cup.

'What's wrong, Father?' he asks.

The priest does not lift his eyes away from the cup and for a second he thinks he's not heard the question. Then something makes him say, 'Maybe none of my business, sorry.'

'You've nothing to be sorry about,' Mulryne says, looking at him as if he has suddenly remembered that he is still there. 'Nothing to be sorry about at all – I'm the one who's sorry.'

'You want to talk about it?'

'What's there to say, Danny, except I'm shat upon? Shat upon from a great height.'

'What's happened?'

The priest stares into his face and then cups the coffee in both hands. 'You know how to listen, Danny, don't you? Know how to listen and forget what you've heard,' and when he nods in reply, 'Sure you do, son, sure you do.' Then there is only a drip from the tap and the labour of Mulryne's breathing. 'A child has made an accusation against me.' But then he drops his eyes again and lapses back into silence.

'What sort of accusation?'

'An accusation that I touched them,' and then in a tone of voice as if quoting sarcastically, 'inappropriately – I touched them inappropriately.' He lifts the glass of Jack Daniel's again and drains it. When he has finished he licks his lips, pauses, then says, 'You're too polite a guy to ask so I'm going to tell you now just so that you know, Danny. I never touched that child in any way I shouldn't. Never did. On the Holy Book, I never did.'

'I believe you,' he says instinctively.

'You believe me?'

'I believe you.'

'That's good, son. And why do you believe me?'

'Because I've seen you round kids. Seen how you treat them.'

'Been round kids all my life and never had so much as a whisper. This is the first and the last.'

'Others will believe you.'

'It doesn't really matter who believes me, I'm finished. Shat upon.'

'How are you finished?'

'Because an accusation has been made and even though they know it's a cheap, evil scam for money the Church will pay out and I'll be moved to a desk somewhere out of sight. I'll never get within a mile of kids again.'

'I could speak for you,' he says. 'Maybe they'd listen.'

'You don't understand, Danny. It's open season on priests. I'm dead in the water. It wouldn't matter if the Archangel Gabriel spoke for me. The accusation has been made – a kid's word against mine – and I'm going to pay for all the times we didn't believe kids, brushed it under the carpet.'

'Who was it made the accusation?'

'That little punk Marvin. He's a poisonous little viper.'

'The kid who stole the shin guards. Did he say it happened that day?'

'Yeah, the kid who stole the shin guards. Payback time. They claim it happened a year ago on an overnighter when we travelled to Tampa for the tournament.'

'And he waited to now to make the claim? Still came voluntarily every week to practice?'

Mulryne nods and almost smiles, then pours them both the remains of the bottle. 'We'll have to raid the communion wine next,' he says, pushing the empty bottle to the side of the table. 'You work with his brother.'

'His brother?'

'Yeah, Edward. Now he was a player – could have played big-time basketball at college. I'd have put money on it. Don't know why he dropped out.'

'Marvin is Edward's brother?'

'Yes.'

'I think he's a decent guy. Maybe I could talk to him, sort this thing out.'

'There's no point, Danny – it's a waste of time. They smell a fast buck. Like sharks in the sea they've got the scent of blood money and they're circling for the kill,' Mulryne says, then goes to the sink and splashes his face again, this time cupping some water and pouring it over his head. Without turning he adds, 'I'm sorry you saw me like this. I've taken it hard. But the bottle doesn't help – I should know that.' He shakes his head and shoulders like a dog casting off its wetness. 'You caught me at a bad time.' Then he turns and faces him. 'I think I'd like to go and lie down now, Danny, try to get some sleep.'

'You be all right?' he asks.

'Sure, Danny, I'll be fine. Got it out of my system.'

'You sure?'

'I'm sure and if the worst comes to the worst at least I'll get a chance to go to Donegal and swim in the sea. But what was it you wanted to see me about?'

He hesitates, looks around the kitchen then says, 'I'm thinking of starting up a small landscape business, wondered if you or the church needed some work done.'

'I'll enquire for you. Outside this place could do with a tidy, that's for sure. I'll do my best. Would you mind finding your own way out, Danny? I need to get my head down. It's started to feel so heavy like it might drop off at any moment.'

'No problem,' he says and before he turns to go the priest makes a cradle of his arms on the table and slowly lowers his head so the image he carries out into the night is of Mulryne's hunched shoulders, bulging out from under his vest, and the grey swathe of his doused hair falling forward to hide his face.

Once after a night out when taking a lift home in Scott's car they had dropped Edward off so he knows he lives somewhere in the little enclave that squats behind Fairfields and Alona Avenue. It is predominantly a black area, poorer than the rest of its environs and tucked out of sight. Maybe only a hundred houses, maybe fewer. As he drives over he wonders why he is going. Because he likes Mulryne? Because he wants Mulryne to help him over the wedding? There's a church on the corner of Alona and as he stops in front of it on a red, the doors open and a choir of black women in white gowns cascades down the steps into the dusk of the evening and lingers in conversation. It's like a sudden fall of snow, as if all the city's magnolia buds have burst open at the same moment. The night feels illuminated, spinning in ceaseless clusters of light, and he stares fascinated until the impatient blare of a horn tells him that the lights have changed. He drives on but it is as if the image is burnt on his senses and he cannot blink its intensity away.

He lowers the window and tries to remember where Edward lives, trawling the streets slowly, staring at the faces who stare back at him. He slows down even more to avoid some kids playing on bikes who dart out from between cars like minnows in a shadowy pool. He begins to feel uncomfortable, uncertain of why he has come or what he is going to say. Just when he is going to stop and ask someone for directions he sees Edward sitting on a fence with two other young men. They scrutinise him as he parks and gets out of the car but at first Edward shows no sign of acknowledging him. As he walks towards them he tries to assume a relaxed confidence he does not feel, lifting his hand lightly in greeting.

'What's up, Danny Boy? You got yourself lost?' Edward asks.

'Kinda. Was hoping to have a word.' He hesitates. All three faces stare at him impassively.

'I'll be in work tomorrow – same as always.' He makes no attempt to move from the fence. 'Maybe you've come to learn some hotshot moves.' The other two men smile as Edward slowly pretends to shoot a basket.

'I'm just a water carrier,' he says, smiling. 'Too late for me to try any hotshot moves.'

'Maybe you should take up boxing, bro – you got the

quick hands.' He gets off the fence and, putting his open palms in front of his face, does a little shimmy. 'Danny here did a little boxing in our last game. A real Muhammad Ali – isn't that right, Danny?'

'Sure,' he says. 'I coulda been a contender.'

'What you want, Danny?'

'A quick talk. Could we go somewhere?'

Edward walks off without replying and he follows. Once he turns to look back at his car and Edward sees him. 'Relax, Danny – nobody with any pride would be seen dead driving a pile of junk like that.' He laughs at his own joke and shouts to his two friends, 'Keep a good eye on that sweet machine – Danny thinks it might fill the bros with envy and tempt them to steal it.' Then he turns down a bare earth path running between two houses which leads them into a piece of land that is part cultivated and part scrub. Along a chain-link fence someone has started a vegetable patch and a row of faded sunflowers tiredly lift their still furled faces to the coolness of the night's breeze. At what looks like an old water tank Edward stops and leans against the rust-blistered sides.

'You shouldn't have come here,' he says. 'Everyone is entitled to their own privacy, their own space. I don't go around turning up uninvited on your doorstep.'

'I'm sorry,' he says. 'I didn't mean any disrespect. It's just something I need to talk to you about.'

'I know why you've come.'

'You know?'

'Sure I know. You Irish stick together.'

'I don't think Father Mulryne did what he was supposed to, Edward.'

'And just how would you know that, Danny? You were there or something?'

'No, I wasn't there but I've been around him a long time now – help out with the soccer sometimes – and I've never seen anything to make me think he would do some shit like this.'

'Did he send you here?'

'No, he doesn't know I'm here.'

'Bullshit! He knows you work with me – that's why he told you. And being around him a long time don't mean nothing. You think he does what he does when you're looking over his shoulder? What Marvin said he done, he done and no one's going to tell me otherwise.' He leans off the water tank and his head juts forward. 'We're doing a public service here, doing our duty as citizens, because if he did this to one kid and got away with it then sure as hell he'll do it to some other. That what you want, Danny?'

'If he did it he can rot in hell – deserves everything he gets. I just don't think he did it.'

'You don't think he did it because he's a priest and he's Irish,' Edward says, kicking his heel against the tank and sending a hollow reverberation through the stillness of the night. 'I suppose you think all those other ones with their faces in the paper didn't do it either.' He starts to walk slowly towards the fence.

'I know they did it. This isn't a religious thing – I haven't been inside a church since I was a kid.' He does not know what else to say and instead follows some way behind. At the fence Edward slips through an almost invisible gap and then turns to him again, his face pressed close to the wire, both hands held above his head and clutching the links.

'You know why he picked Marvin instead of one of those rich white boys? Because he was a black kid and he thought he could get away with it. That no one would complain or make a fuss. Now you go back there to that sicko and tell him that we're going to fry his ass.'

There is nothing more to be said. He watches as Edward slips away into the shadows between two buildings then retraces his own steps. At the water tank he pauses and touches the coldness of the metal. He lets his fingers trace the contours of a rust patch and when he looks at them they are stained as if with nicotine. He needs a smoke. Instead he thinks of the choir of women, their white gowns flapping like unfurled flags against the darkness of the night.

At the car the two youths are still sitting on the fence. 'It's still here, Champ,' one says, 'but we had to hold off armies to keep it safe.'

He doesn't answer but gets in the car and turns on the engine. It does not start first time and he sees his two spectators smirking and shaking their heads. Suddenly he feels angry, humiliated, and he wants to roll the window down and say something sassy, something that shows them he is a man and isn't afraid, but the engine starts up and instead he drives off quickly. As he slows for the corner he sees Marvin standing with a soccer ball in his hand. The boy stares at him, proud, indifferent, and as their eyes lock, he takes the ball and spins it on his finger.

As he drives it's not words that fill his head but images – the women on the steps of the church still sharp as the flash of a camera; the spreading patches of rust on the water tank; the scorn in Edward's eyes; Mulryne's head buried in his arms, his grey hair wet and flattened to his skull. But then into the chaos settles another image and it presses all the others to the outer edges of his consciousness and it's that of the priest on the far side of the field standing with his arm round the boy's shoulders under the shadows of the tree. It feels as if it's printed and fixed on the road as he drives and it can't be blinked away even though he tries and now the words he hears are, 'Because he was a black kid and he thought he could get away with it.' Suddenly his certainty is washed away and although he tries to persuade himself once more of his earlier conviction he knows it's gone now, replaced by a confused conflict of clamouring voices insistent on the truth of their assertions. All he knows for sure is that he doesn't want to take the discordant claims and counter-claims of his brain to his home. He tells himself he did his best but then is unsure if it was the best thing to do. He switches on the radio and tries to drown out the voices.

It is Ramona's night to work late so he decides to wait for her, drive her the short distance home. He drives to the mall where there are only about three dozen cars in the car park. He's able to park almost at the door. The single security man leans against an inside wall, the contours of his uniform creased with boredom, his hat pushed back on his head revealing the youthfulness of his face. His languid indifference says that he thinks he should be somewhere else, like cruising in a car with a pretty girl or smoking a joint in some badly lit parking lot. Certainly not here where there's not even the momentary distraction of a shoplifter or a lost child to colour in the time or embroider his uniform with a momentary importance. No breathless thanks from a teary-eyed young mother or the chance to frisk some drugged-up punk. Just the slow passing of time, like watching over an elderly relative who takes too long to die, dragging it out, fighting the inevitable fade into nothingness.

Each time he comes here it feels as if the remaining stores have somehow pulled towards themselves, circling round each other like wagons against the marauding misfortunes that threaten. 'Everything must go', 'closing down sale' – these are the harbingers of another departure. He sits outside the bookshop and watches an old man with a cart push a mop along the tiles. His heavy clacking feet beat against the squeak and slither of the mop. When he comes to empty the trash cans he looks in each one with expectancy, followed by disappointment, and then swiftly consigns the contents to the back of the cart. He watches him trundle the cart towards the next bin, the mop extended in front of him like the sniffing trunk of a baby elephant. Two jobs done at once to the chorused, clacking castanets of his heavy feet. The sound rises up and seeps into the curved ceiling with its painted frescos of blue sky and wispy clouds. For the first time he notices that there are little Zephyrs with blond curls and puffed cheeks blowing the clouds and then his gaze moves to the almost empty second level where a Christmas-all-year shop has draped Christmas lights and tinsel garlands over the railing. It has silver plastic trees at its entrance and a giant model of Santa with a toy-filled sack.

How could he have been so stupid to consider making his confession to Mulryne? What was he thinking of? After all this time to open the closed box of the past and try to unpack what he's been so careful to stow away. The only thing he knows is that it wasn't a religious impulse because he has already stopped believing in one part of his head. It was for Ramona, for the child – to somehow be more worthy of them. To start afresh, step into the future clean and entitled to the happiness that it promises. At Christmas he will drape the front of the house in white icicle lights, light it up like a birthday cake. Do it when she is out with the child so that it's a surprise and she will come home unsuspecting and see the whole house lit up like the biggest smile. So how could he, even for a moment, have thought of letting loose the spores of the past, of casting them to the wind with no way to predict or control where they would land?

He thinks of the anthrax scare, of envelopes seeping with white powder. Of contamination. Of isolation wards and men in white suits like spacemen who cautiously trace the surfaces of unknown and possibly hostile planets like diviners with their outstretched twigs. A young man hands him a leaflet advertising a new car valet service. As one business dies another is born – it's another part of an unending circle of human optimism. So why even in this place should he let these tainted seed heads blow through his mind and infect the future? He was foolish to get involved with Mulryne and try to help, never fully considered what he was getting into. It was nothing to do with him and he was crazy to let himself drift close to the flames of a public dispute that might have spread in all kinds of directions he could not anticipate. Just walk away, let people sort out their own mess in their own ways. Never take risks, never lift your head too high, never draw unnecessary attention to yourself – for a moment he had forgotten the wisdom of his own rules. Keep your eyes only on the future. And so as the tune of 'I'm Dreaming of a White Christmas' slithers slowly like a snake through the sleeping mall, he thinks of the business he could build, of the houses on the lake with the screened pools and perfect lawns, of contracts and franchises.

Ramona is pleased to see him, telling him that she's a little weary and that her ankles are sore. He imagines the smile on her face when he drapes the house in white lights and then asks himself why he should wait for Christmas, deciding that he will do it for her the day she brings their child home from hospital.

'You want to eat Chinese?' she asks as she massages her ankles.

'Sure, save a lot of time and hassle,' he answers and drives the short distance to their favourite restaurant. The manager greets him by name and shakes his hand. He orders their usual to go and while he waits he flicks the pages of a real-estate magazine absorbing the poetry of pool and lakefront homes. That is his only concern now – to make enough bucks to be able to buy into the world displayed in the photographs. He looks at the picture of Barbara Bloemstein – 'She's working ten times smarter to deliver the American dream' – and reads her descriptions of 'lush landscaping', of security systems, of 'small single-entry neighbourhoods' set amid 'greenbelts of mature trees'. Get in a gated community and lock the world outside. Feel safe – it's all he has ever wanted – and he tells himself that it's in reach of his grasp if he works hard enough for it, makes his plans and is bold and brave enough to make them real.

When the owner hands him his order he tells him to call again and holds open the door as he leaves. As he walks towards the car he feels the heat that like some possessive lover refuses to let the day slip out of her embrace. The bright neon of the other shop fronts ignites the dusk with coloured promises of pleasure and issues gaudy invitations that spark the senses. There is a lightness to his step, a new sense of conviction, as he feels the dazzle of light spray across his path. Build the walls high, make the gates strong and everything will be all right. But when he puts his hand to the car door it is locked and he has to knock the glass before Ramona opens it. As he gets in he hands her the bag but as she takes it she turns her head away and stares at the night.

'What's up?' he asks but there is no reply so he asks again.

'I saw him,' she says in a whisper that forces him to lean his head towards her to catch the words.

He knows now that something is wrong. 'Who did you see, Ramona?'

'Vicente. I saw Vicente.'

'Where? Did he try anything?'

'He didn't see me. He was going into the bar. Drive the car, Danny, take me home.'

The sourness of fear smothers the sweet smell of the food. 'Everything's all right,' he says and stretches his hand across to hers as he drives. 'Everything's all right. We'll be home soon.' She doesn't answer but as he glances at her she seems smaller, to have shrunk into herself, and for a moment he gives admission to the anger and frustration beginning to bubble up inside him. Part of him wants to turn the car round and go back and find him, let him feel what fear feels like, but he knows it would be for himself and not for her so instead he goes on telling her everything will be all right. When they reach the house she does not open the car but stays sitting staring ahead.

'I had a bad dream a while back,' she says. He stretches across and puts his arms round her, strokes the back of her hair, but she feels lifeless as if everything that makes her who she is has been drained away. For a second he thinks she's not going to say any more. Now the smell of the food is cloying, oppressive. 'I dreamed he came and hurt the baby.' Suddenly she is crying like he's never seen her do before, breaking free from his embrace to put both hands to her face, perhaps to try to staunch the flow, perhaps to hide what she thinks is the shame of it.

'No one's going to hurt the baby, sweetheart. No one's going to hurt our baby or ever hurt you again. Everything's going to be all right.' He tries to hold her again.

'He can do what he likes to me but not the baby,' she sobs, her words tumbling out in broken, breathless gasps.

'Shush, shush,' he whispers. 'He's not going to do anything to anyone. You're safe now, everything's going to be all right.' He thinks of telling her about the pictures of houses he looked at in the restaurant, of the one they are going to buy when their ship comes in, but he doesn't have the words so instead he holds her and rocks her gently until the tears stop and are replaced by deep breaths, like someone pulled back to shore from a drowning sea.

They get out of the car and she leans against him until they have entered the house, then goes to the bathroom and closes the door. He's unsure of what to do about the food so he lets it sit unopened on the kitchen table but when she comes out she asks him why he's not got it ready and so he smiles and scurries for plates. When he asks her if she's all right she nods and smiles. 'It's the hormones,' she says dismissively. 'They're all over the place. I'm fine now.' But she eats little of the food, mostly pushing it about with her fork, and in a little while she says she feels tired and would like to go to bed. He needs a cigarette and wants to go down to the lake but he knows he won't leave her so he cleans up and joins her on the bed. She is lying on top of it because she is too warm and he stretches out beside her, propping a pillow behind his head. He knows she doesn't want to talk about what happened so he says nothing.

'You know Justine in the library?' she asks. 'Her husband works out at Canaveral and she says she can get us passes next time there's a launch. Says it's really worth seeing. Can we go?'

'Sure,' he says.

'Sometimes it's at night and you have to get there early. It's supposed to be really spectacular.'

'Like to see it. Something to tell our children about.' He watches her slowly rub her stomach with the palm of her hand. 'There were two astronauts on the moon went into a bar but left a few minutes later – you know why?' She shakes her head. 'Because there was no atmosphere.' She pushes her elbow into his thigh and then a short time later she turns on her side and falls asleep. He thinks again of going out to the lake but wants to be there in case she wakens so he curls himself into her back and falls asleep thinking of great fantails of flames as rockets hurtle skyward and lift their heads towards the vast darkness of space.

In the week that follows there is no sign of Mulryne and he doesn't go looking for him. Someone else takes the soccer – two young coaches, male and female, with badges on their tracksuits and T-shirts that say 'Soccer is a kick in the grass'. At work Edward drifts round him as if once more he is out on the court with an opponent to be avoided, sidestepped with silence. As with Mulryne he lets him go, holds tightly to his creed of not sticking his head above the parapet, of not getting involved. He tells himself that it only comes down to doing your job, then going home and looking after your own. The baby is coming, Ramona seems to get bigger by the day and she has started to build a nest, clearing out cupboards and laying in things, telling him where needs painting, getting things ready with an intensity of purpose that galvanises him into action.

He takes some hours off work one afternoon to go with her to the hospital for a check-up where they are told everything is fine and given a copy of the scan and he stares at the swirl of what looks like a satellite weather map and listens to her excitement as he points out the hazy continent of their child slowly emerging from the clouds. She has been given the rest of the day off and he leaves her home and sees her settled before taking the lakeside path back to work. Past the condominium and the empty tennis courts. Only the occasional jogger and a couple of women in shorts, fast-walking, their arms swinging in synchronisation like metro-nomes, their heads pecking at the air as they talk. Two men on a bench with their heads angled towards him. Looking for someone? Waiting for someone? He is struck by the whiteness of one of the men's arms, the slightly awkward sit of his casual clothes as if his body hasn't become fully accustomed to them, as if they are slightly shocked by the sun. A newly arrived perhaps. Maybe on holiday. He nods as he passes.

'Hello, Michael,' the white-armed man says.

He doesn't reply but keeps walking, his heart pressing and pulsing against his chest. A Northern Irish voice. For a second he thinks of running but forces himself to stay calm.

'It's all right, Michael.'

He stops and turns. The white-armed man is standing, looking at him. In his late fifties, thin-faced, gaunt, his eyes narrowing to take him in.

'My name is Danny.'

'That's right, Danny, and mine is Gerry Lynch. I'm from Belfast. I'm a friend, Danny, so you don't need to worry. I can call you Danny if you like or I can call you Michael Madden. It doesn't matter. Why don't you take a seat?'

He watches him stretch out his hand towards the seat but he doesn't take up the invitation.

'Sit down, Danny. This is Sean Manley – he's a friend as well. We need to talk.'

'Not here,' he says, looking back to where he can see the house. Then without saying any more he turns and lets the two men follow him. When they pass someone on the path he lowers his eyes and tries to distance himself from the men behind him. He leads them to a picnic table that sits in a little grove of trees close to the water's edge.

'Don't know how you stick the heat, Danny,' Lynch says, wiping his brow as if the short walk has drained him. There's a sheen of perspiration in the grey hollows of his cheeks like dregs in the bottom of a cup.

234

'You get used to it, don't you, Danny?' Manley says. His accent is Irish American. 'It bakes up a lot hotter than this.'

'Who are you and what do you want?' he asks, trying hard to keep his voice strong and steady.

'I'm going to have to get a cap or I'll be going home with my head the colour of a match,' Lynch says, rubbing his hand through the thin wisps of receding fair hair. He takes out a cigarette and offers him one but he shakes his head. Out on the lake a speedboat is scissoring the water and spuming a wake from the shredded surface. Lynch lights the cigarette and slowly inhales. 'I'm from the Army Council – I've letters of authorisation if you want to see them – and Sean works for the movement here in America. I'm here because I've been instructed to bring you something.' He sets a brown envelope on the table and turns his face to the lake.

He doesn't want to touch it. It feels like the moment he touches it everything will explode in his face. It's addressed to Michael Madden and has his last known Belfast address. To put his hand to it is to retake his name, open the portal to another life, another time, so he stares at it.

'It's all right, Danny,' Lynch says. 'Just open it.'

'Is it about my mother?' he asks.

'No, your mother's fine.'

'Why have you come here? What do you want with me?'

'Everything's cool, Danny. No one wants anything bad for you but you need to read the letter,' Manley says as he slides the envelope across the table.

Still he doesn't touch it. Someone has carved their initials into the wood. The grain on the table has been dried and polished by the sun. There is a black smudge scarring one edge where something has burnt it. Lynch's fingers are heavily stained with nicotine, the same colour as the envelope. The speedboat screams as it passes close to shore and as the two men sitting opposite him turn their heads to look at it, he lifts the letter, takes one last look at the name and address, in the hope that he will see there's been a mistake and that it's for someone else, then opens it. His eyes scan it, reading almost more quickly than he can take it in. The Truth and Reconciliation Commission requires your attendance . . . case number one hundred and seven, the case of Connor Walshe . . . He feels as if he's tumbling downhill and attempts to arrest his free-fall by clutching at the words and trying to hold their meaning in his head. The Commission has the power to compel attendance . . . Where required, legal representation can be provided . . . All political parties, churches and community groups have agreed . . . a necessary part of communal healing and the peace process . . . Closure . . . All participants are indemnified and absolved from any legal or civil repercussions as a result of their testimony . . . Dates and times, more details than he can absorb.

He doesn't speak at first because he's unsure of how his voice will sound, or if words will form at all or merely splinter like glass. The speedboat's wake is a frothing seam of white. There is a tumbling sickness in his stomach. He tries to breathe it away and under the table he grabs hold tightly of the seat's edge.

'I don't know any Connor Walshe,' he says softly.

'It's all right, Danny,' Lynch says, offering him a cigarette for the second time. This time he accepts and tries not to let his hand shake as he reaches for it and the lighter. 'We're friends and the movement always looks after its own. We know exactly what you know and don't know. For better or worse we've signed up to this Truth and Reconciliation thing – if you ask me I'd probably say for the worse but that's just a personal opinion and smarter people than me say we need to do it. So it has to be done.'

'I'm not going back,' he says.

'You don't have a choice, Danny,' Manley says. 'Like Gerry says, we've signed up to it.'

'I do have a choice and I'm not going back. My life is here now and I'm never going back.'

'No, Danny, Sean is right – you don't have a choice. Wrap it up any way you like but the bottom line is it's an order and only a fool disobeys an order.'

'I don't take orders any more – it's over for me,' he says.

'It's never over until you're told it is,' Lynch says. 'You know that as well as I do. And listen it's a ritual, a quick appearance, and you're not on your own, we have people who will prepare you, tell you what to say, how to handle it. It's all over before you know it – it's easy, painless. In and out.'

'Painless? To say what I did.'

'Listen to me, Michael,' Lynch says, angrily stubbing out his cigarette on the wood. 'Don't start talking shit and beating yourself up. We were fighting a war. We all were and we all did the type of things that had to be done in a war. The type of things they did to us and worse. So don't start thinking like that even for a moment. You were a soldier fighting in a war and you're still a soldier but when you do this it's all over. All over for good. The army lets you go, then the army lets itself go, disappears into the pages of history.'

'You don't understand,' he says. 'I'm here illegally. They'll throw me out, never let me back.' He thinks of telling them of Ramona but he will not soil her name by using it in front of them.

'Listen to me, Danny,' Manley says, leaning his arms across the table. 'We'll look after you. We have friends everywhere, important friends, right up to the very door of the Oval Office. The administration played their part in setting this up so we're not going to let you get thrown out. You have to trust us to do right by you. Gerry's already told you – we look after our own. You need to believe that.'

He does not know what to believe so he says again, 'I'm not going back.'

'You don't get this, Michael, so I'm going to have to spell it out,' Lynch says, beads of sweat forming on his upper lip and brow. There are brown freckles on his scalp as if he has run his hand through his hair and tiny flakes of nicotine have rubbed off. 'We want you to come back voluntarily. Do that and we help you all the way, take care of everything, absolutely everything. Don't co-operate with this thing and you're on your own and hung out to dry. You don't turn up and they'll ask the authorities to deport you. You could do time here as well.'

'They don't know I'm here,' he says and Lynch smiles.

'That only takes a phone call, doesn't it?'

'You'd do that?' he asks, already knowing the answer.

'You want to try and live your life knowing that one phone call pulls the plug on it?' Manley asks.

Their voices are hammers in his brain and every word sparks some new fear for the future. He does not know where to turn for respite.

'You'd be away for about two weeks, no more, maybe much less,' Lynch says. 'You'll be back long before it's time for Ramona to have that baby. We have people who will look out for her. We can look after your job as well. There's no other way out of this, believe me, Michael.'

They know about Ramona, they know about everything. Only one thing they do not know because there's no way to know it and that is how he is to tell her. He no longer hears what they say because in his head he's frantically searching for that way, rejecting every conceivable, broken-backed idea that presents itself. There's no artifice, no story that can conceal the fact that he's another man who has deceived her, and deceived her in a way that even she has never experienced before. Then he tries to tell himself that in himself he has been true to her. That a name in itself does not change who he is or what they mean to each other. He thinks of the children on the beach with their father, pouring water into the moat of the castle they have just built. He thinks of sand, of houses, and in his ears he hears the throaty rasp of the sea as it rushes in, taking everything in its path. They're still talking to him and he's nodding his head but all he hears now is the break and tumble of walls. Of things being swept aside. He watches them walk away, Manley's hand raised in a farewell wave, and their walk is purposeful, the walk of men who have done their work. He sits until they have disappeared and then he goes down to the water's edge and is sick amongst the reeds.

The lake is still, with only the gentlest of swells pushing halfheartedly through the reeds. Far out, sky and water like lifelong friends seem inseparable. A little breeze plays with the smoke of his dying cigarette. He wonders if Arnie is somewhere out there on his boat, casting his lines. Sitting waiting patiently for a catch. The sky feels so low he could almost stretch out a hand and touch it. He lights another cigarette – there seems no point any more. Arnie says the water is always cold, cold even in the heat of the day. Soon it will be time. In his broken, shallow sleep, words had slipped like eels through his mind but when he tried to trap the truth of what he must say this morning, and how he must tell her, they slipped into the shadows. A bird skims the surface of the water, a black arrowhead in the slowly strengthening light. He thinks of ever more elaborate lies then blows them away through the purse of his lips with the smoke of the cigarette. He tries to tell himself that there'll be a release in truth, that after all this time the weight of deception will be lifted from his shoulders. He walks to the end of the jetty and throws the cigarette away. It's almost time. He narrows his eyes and stares out into the sleeping heart of the lake. For the next hour or so it is able to wear its own face and does not have the luminous insistence of the sky pressed relentlessly against it. Then he bends down and scoops a handful of water and splashes his face with its coldness.

The walk back to the house is weighted with the words in his head arranged all wrong like the flowers he bought for her birthday and cack-handedly tried to shape in a vase. How many layers of their life will be pulled away by what he has to tell her? And what will be left when he has finished? He thinks of the stillness at the heart of the lake and tries to tell himself that love can endure. Even this. But he's no longer sure of anything he tells himself, of what he can believe and what is just another deception, designed to smooth his way, so it feels as if he knows nothing any more and that everything he wants to hold tightly slips through his fingers like water.

He hesitates at the door then goes in. Maybe she will stretch out her arms to him. Maybe she will tell him that he's cold and enfold him in the embrace of her sleep-stirred warmth. Then after a while she will say, 'What does a girl have to do around here to get a cup of coffee?' and he will slip reluctantly from her side.

She looks at him as he stands in the doorway of the bedroom watching her.

'Well, Danny, is the lake still there?'

He doesn't answer and she sits up in the bed, shaking the black shock of her hair away from her face.

'What's wrong, Danny?'

He looks into her eyes and takes a single step into the room.

'My name isn't Danny.'

She's looking at him and then she starts to smile but stops. No other way. It's the price that must be paid. The water is cold against his skin. He steps further into the room and each slow step is weighted with fear. More fear than he's ever felt and he knows there are no words.

S TANFIELD PRESIDES WEARILY OVER the chamber and glances regularly but surreptitiously at the clock and feels as if he's slowly drowning in words. Day after day, it's as if the dam is breached and out pours a torrent of rising levels of hurt that have been stored over long winters of grief. They come to the chamber to let it finally burst its banks and their breathless flood threatens to engulf him. He lifts his head and tries to draw breath because it always feels as if there's not enough air in the room so he's grateful, at least, for the seemingly straightforward brevity of the case in progress. There's been an admission of responsibility, an apology and even a seemingly sincere little appeal for forgiveness. All that remains is for him to ask Mrs Latimer, or her representative, if she would like to sum up her feelings about her husband who on a summer evening twenty years earlier opened his front door to his killer. He's glad they're reaching the conclusion because it feels as if they're sinking in the hollow of the afternoon where the movement of time has wilted and collapsed into a lethargic slumber.

He glances down at the elderly woman who's not spoken a single word so far. She looks frail, withered, like a desiccated leaf that might blow from the tree in the next wind, but there's also something about her that unsettles him. Is it the fixity of her gaze? Her refusal to look at the man who killed her husband? The way her thin and knobbed hands clutch the Bible that she holds in her lap so tightly?

'Mrs Latimer, would you or your representative like to make your final address?' he asks gently, hoping that it will be mercifully short, then nodding encouragingly as she slowly stands and makes her way to the microphone. She walks more quickly but it's not to the microphone and then as Stanfield blinks his disbelief and time seems suspended, or unfolding in some unpredictable sequence as if in a dream, she has a knife in her hand – Stanfield can't be sure but thinks it's come from inside her Bible – and is lunging towards the killer of her husband. It's the physical change confuses him and takes away what little breath he has. What once seemed withered has hardened into an angular rigidity, her limbs stiff as rods, like a scarecrow suddenly come to life. People are screaming, chairs are toppling over as her intended victim tries to raise an arm to shield himself, but the knife skewers over its top and embeds itself in his shoulder blade. Stanfield stands up but for a second freezes before he shakes himself into action, presses the panic button on his desk and almost immediately police arrive.

She stands perfectly still, the knife dropped to the floor, with the appearance of the catatonic, unseeing, unhearing, unresisting as she's led away. There are medics in green uniforms kneeling over the victim and then the blare and static of radios set in motion. Stanfield slumps back in his chair for a moment before standing again and loudly calling, 'Clear the chamber, clear the chamber!'

The next day Stanfield looks round the table at his gathered team and reads the spreading disillusionment in each of their faces and hears it, too, burrowing into their voices. He would like to be able to take some perverse pleasure in it but is unable to because he worries that if the process continues to slide, then sooner or later some of the slimy mess of failure will stick to him and perhaps damage his future interests. He's already started to compose his letter of resignation but needs to find some point of principle on which to hang it before the whole gimcrack edifice tumbles like a house of cards.

Now his team sit silently and look at him for inspiration. His eyes flit round their faces, lingering lightly on Laura before moving on. He knows it's the moment when he should deliver a rousing call to battle, when like some Roman general he should ride along their line with drawn sword. But at first he can't bring himself to muster anything more than a few unconvincing observations.

'What happened yesterday was terrible and shocking. Thankfully it seems as if the wound isn't life-threatening but if anything was designed to show us the importance of what we're trying to do here it was that moment. There will be people who will seek to use it for their own particular gain but we've got to move on. We've had failures, we've had setbacks, but in a risk-filled process like this these were inevitable. We knew it was never going to be easy. We have to be prepared for early setbacks and cynical attacks on the integrity of the process but we need to remember we're trying to do something in this country that's never been done.' He pauses. Perhaps he might rise to the occasion after all. 'We also need to remember that we're working in a society that's been deeply divided for thousands of years. This is probably the most challenging thing it's ever been asked to do and sometimes it's going to falter and it's going to get frightened but if we can carry this off, then it's the most important step this community can possibly take towards lasting healing.' He can't quite believe he's just used the word 'healing'. But clearly he has underestimated himself: their heads are nodding. Is it just the sun sidling surreptitiously into the room or have Laura's eyes widened? Even Matteo has altered his posture and thrown off his former slump to sit straight backed and alert. 'And don't let anyone for a moment forget that we've also witnessed remarkable things, the coming together of former enemies in ways, perhaps, we could only have imagined. So now let's not falter in our convictions because we've encountered difficulties.' And so he continues until his words ignite some new passionate resolve and there is a babble of voices all offering a contagious and collegiate response.

After they've gone he goes to the window and looks to the other side of the city street where there's a juice bar which each morning sets three small metal tables and chairs on the pavement in an incredibly optimistic belief that passing punters might attempt to brave the slicing wind; a travel agent's desperately trying to fight off the internet and do-it-yourself hols which fills its windows with misspelled special offers and a minimalist optician's where there appears to be nothing inside. How much he would give to be on a plane to somewhere else and whatever destination he imagines he's always accompanied by Kristal and he's always there to observe her pleasure in what he can show her, what he can teach her.

Things indeed have gone more badly than he could ever have anticipated. After an earlier attack they installed a band of protective glass across the witness stand and now they'll have to site a metal detector in the building's entrance. As well as the two incidents of violence there have been regular examples of verbal abuse and threats shouted with an intensity that he's never heard before. Now there is a permanent police presence that he can summon with the press of a button but some days he feels as if he's sitting in an abattoir, where all around him is the raw carcass of human suffering being boned and filleted while the steady drip of human hate coagulates on the floor of the chamber.

The families of the victims have started to reclaim their dead and forgotten loved ones and given this brief moment of public restoration, they parade to the chamber carrying portraits of their murdered relatives and candles that gutter in the wind tunnel of a street. The portraits of children are the most disturbing as they force the viewer to try and project how they now would look and in the imagination construct the life they never knew. But there is no elegy played out in the increasingly elaborate rituals that grief has created, only a fractious, bitter stirring of the water to which people rush with earnest hope of healing. He has presided over some truth but little reconciliation and as each day goes by it becomes increasingly obvious that what the plaintiffs want is truth and the justice that they feel they've been denied. Stanfield has come to recognise it in their eyes, their need for the final assertion of some weighty moral imperative that will sweep the perpetrator to divine justice. Instead they get some formulaic, pre-learned response that expresses a vague regret for the pain caused and then presents the get-out-of-jail card that avoids personal guilt or moral culpability by stating that they believed they were fighting in a war. When it's all over, Stanfield sees, too, the void opening up inside the bereaved, when they understand that this is all they are to be given and they realise it's not enough. Often at the end they have to be helped from the chamber as if they haven't grasped that it's all over, that their time has finished, and then they shuffle towards the exits, their confused, white-salted faces glancing back over their shoulders.

However, it's also true that there are days when something else happens and someone's story rises up like a sad aria that, for all its artlessness, its lack of structure and simple language, sings out and fills the chamber. Some stories – and he can never predict them or see them coming – take on the mysterious power to reach beyond the external world and touch the quick of everyone who hears them. There are even moments when some kind of synergy is created and a fusion of relief or some long-diminished need compels the antagonists briefly towards each other like Priam kneeling to kiss Achilles's hand, before pulling apart again suddenly conscious of their actions.

But an idea, he tells himself, that's come too soon. He has to find some way out – he was wrong to have sneered at the lecture circuit. Perhaps even a visiting professorship in a West Coast university. Each day as he sits in the chamber he feels himself imbibe some more of the toxins that seep from the buried corrosive and carcinogenic emotions that have been given permission to come to the surface. Sometimes he feels a tightness in his chest, senses shallower breathing and he worries about his health. Perhaps he should play that tennis. Perhaps if he could buy out her lease there might be some way that frees Kristal to move in with him.

The killers and their co-conspirators don't look good, whatever side they come from. Even with the cheap suits and their spruce-up jobs, time hasn't been kind to them. Often they come with a well-publicised litany of convictions for petty crime bolstering their CVs, tarnishing whatever claim to idealism they once harboured, and their inarticulacy makes Stanfield squirm with embarrassment. And always the unspoken question hangs over their evidence as to what gave such inferior forms of life the right to take someone else's. Sometimes they arrive with their supporters huddled round them in a tight phalanx, protective arms on their shoulders shepherding them into the building, and they look like punch-drunk fighters being led into the ring by their trainers. Afterwards the cameras show them lighting cigarettes, their heads huddled together to form a windbreak, or else solitary figures hurrying away with pulled-up hoods.

He has his own ritual after each case. It's evolved gradually and serves to throw off what tries to cling to him like a thickly spun web. He makes the debriefing session as short as he can, deflecting as many of the unresolved issues as possible and attempting to appear to be answering Matteo's pertinent questions while at the same time mentally consigning them to the shredder. Then he walks the five minutes to a nearby restaurant where the same table is reserved for him each night and they serve decent food and have waiters who don't say 'cheers' when they're tipped and on to the apartment where he showers and changes his clothes before sitting with a glass of wine at the window overlooking the river. By the second glass and accompanied by the right music he begins to peel away some of the fine filament that fastens to him. He needs music to help reconstruct the equilibrium of his internal life, to reassure himself that he has journeyed to the underworld and safely returned. So although he's devoid of any religious impulse he listens to choral music by Tavener and sometimes Vaughan Williams's 'The Lark Ascending', although the only bird the river seems able to supply as a visual accompaniment is the occasional seagull.

He knows, however, he will never be able to see out this far-flung tour of duty, that if he's to stay, someday he will sit here and not even the music will free him from the spiral of depression; that slowly the welter of words and the ugly raw faces he has to endure each day will insidiously take up permanent residence inside his head. Of course there's Emma but despite their meeting he's started to tell himself that he has to be prepared to let her go, that this hair shirt should finally be discarded. The intensity of feeling he experienced on meeting her again has started to fade and there was no response to the card he sent her with the simple, deliberately understated and unthreatening message that it was lovely to see her and he hoped they might repeat it. He doesn't think that he's ever spent quite so long composing so few words. The card's cover reproduced da Vinci's cartoon of the Virgin and Child with St Anne and its tender beauty reminded him of how long it's been since he's had the pleasure of looking at paintings. For a second as he sips the wine he imagines himself with Kristal in the Louvre or the Hermitage and how lovely she would look against the snow and the golden domes of St Petersburg. When he completes his first cycle of two months of sittings, he has a month's break before resuming the second cycle – perhaps he should try to arrange some reinvigorating trip abroad.

But will he ever see his daughter's child? Will she ever let him be a grandfather or even a father again? He supposes that without the assistance she requested his chances are remote. Stanfield smiles bitterly as he acknowledges the power of Martine's revenge. The closeness she established with their daughter precludes any attempt on his part to discredit her, or even in the gentlest of ways point out some of her flaws and suggest that perhaps she was not an easy woman to live with. But is this what Martine truly wanted? Is this what she envisaged as his punishment? He can't believe that even at the end she hated him so much as to want this.

It's his favourite choral track – 'Love Bade Me Welcome' – and there is something intensely soothing in the ethereal purity of the voices and something also that stirs a pleasurable sense of sadness. Perhaps it's the music, perhaps it's the wine, perhaps even the impeachable emptiness of the apartment arcing over him again, that makes him turn to the memory of what he first felt when his daughter sat in front of him with her hair sprinkled with beads of water and a new life swelling inside her and he knows he doesn't want to let her go just yet.

In the morning he's another interview to do. The world's media have arrived and taken up temporary residence – he's told that the city's running out of hotel rooms. There seems no corner of the globe that hasn't sent a reporting team and, shortly after the first wave, a second wave of circus freaks attracted by what exactly Stanfield isn't sure has blown in. So each morning camped outside the building one might encounter a group of Navaho Indians who do some dance that claims to evoke the spirits of the dead, a Buddhist monk who attempts to give flowers to those who enter or a violin-playing survivor of Kosovo. It's only slightly reassuring to see also the homegrown stalwart Ulster evangelical jostling for his space with a text-covered sandwich board that asks where everyone will spend eternity.

He gives his well-practised little soundbite to a young Japanese reporter and her television crew. Afterwards for some bizarre reason she blurts out that she likes U2 and she wants to see the Giant's Causeway. He smiles and nods encouragingly then extracts himself as quickly as possible. In the afternoon he presides over a session that he finds stultifyingly boring and he has to force himself to concentrate to avoid slipping into a disinterested lethargy. He's moved on, left this case behind, and in his imagination he's already presiding over the case of Connor Walshe and he knows that when he looks down it will be the face of Maria Harper he will see and behind her, if not in the flesh, the face of his daughter.

These people's faces, their guttural voices, are long merged into some soapbox drama that leaves him desperate to reach the end. He looks around the chamber counting off the resident members of the press; the regular attenders in the public seats who in his imagination increasingly resemble caricatures and grotesques that Dickens would have been proud of and have queued for the privilege; the officials and recorders; the medical staff, counsellors and ministers. He feels an increasing immunity to the suffering that is served up for his inspection – by now it is a cold dish, rarely distinguished by an articulacy or differentiation from all that has gone before. Sometimes he has to stifle a yawn and his frequently asked questions as to whether anyone needs a brief adjournment are driven only by self-interest.

That night after everything is over he takes his short walk to the restaurant. It's no more than a couple of hundred yards but he almost looks forward to it. The cold night serves to stir him awake after the stuffy overheated chamber where no matter how low they try to set the heating there is always a flushed and stifling charge that sparks the air. And there is no air – it's as if those who appear before the Commission consume it all in their broken breathing and floundering, painful need as they drown in their own sorrow. Now it's the hour when the city changes shift and those who work in it abandon it to those who use it for pleasure. There are too many people about to feel threatened, but there's still the slight nervousness of the wealthy walking in a city where there are many poor, and he injects his step with a sense of self-confidence and quiet authority to ward off any lurking danger. And there are always pretty women to catch his eye – he's been grudgingly forced to admit that the city has its fair share. Sometimes if one meets his gaze he fantasises about stopping her and persuading her to join him in a restaurant more expensive than she's probably used to and advising her on the menu and explaining to her about wine. But whatever pleasure he momentarily devises for himself is soon vanquished by the imposition of reality and the vision of a solitary meal and afterwards there's not even the prospect of Kristal's company to console him. His last two phone calls have solicited a polite statement that she's not available and his subsequent questions received no further elaboration than the information that she was away at present. And no he doesn't want someone else. Surely he might have expected her to say something if she was going away, even if it was no more than a professional courtesy. He turns the possibilities over in his mind but there's always one more unknown than he's able to assimilate. He's forced to admit, however unlikely and indeed foolishly, that he's grown fond of her and he consoles himself that perhaps her absence will only be a short one.

His sense of irritation is exacerbated when he enters the restaurant and sees two men sitting at his table. They're wearing dark suits and one is perusing the wine list. Stanfield looks round the restaurant and sees other empty tables that might just as easily have accommodated two diners. His unspoken question to the maître d' is answered with an apology and a slightly perplexed hunch of the shoulders but when he leads him to a table it's to his normal one and the same one that now has two other people sitting at it.

Before he can say anything the older of the two men stands up and greets him with a handshake.

'Good evening, Henry,' he says in a voice that Stanfield

immediately associates with a particular kind of breeding, its plummy richness redolent of public schools and public service. 'So sorry to drop in on you like this unannounced but it seemed a good opportunity for us to meet again.'

'We've met before?' Stanfield asks, staring at his face. Out of the corner of his eye he detects a thin sneer on the lips of the younger man whose cropped haircut is curiously out of sync with the expensive cut of his suit.

'I think so. Some time ago. I was working for the Foreign Office at the time of the Balkan trouble. It was only briefly – don't expect you to remember, hardly do myself. Messy business. Please sit down – I'm told the food is rather good here.'

'Not bad at all,' Stanfield says, suddenly conscious that something is happening to him but uncertain what it is and conscious also that he feels a sense of volition that is not entirely under his own control. 'And you are?'

'Sorry: of course. I'm Michael Walters and this is William.'

For the first time he looks at the younger man who stares at him with the same smirk and rudeness of intensity that annoys Stanfield into saying, 'And does William have a second name?'

'Just William I think might be best for the present,' Walters says.

As the waiter arrives and takes a drink order Stanfield thinks of Richmal Crompton books and midnight feasts in the dorm. For a second he thinks Walters might order a ginger beer but he sees something darken in the younger man's eyes. He looks back to Walters's hands with their long effeminate fingers, neatly manicured nails and the two rings he wears. Walters orders a gin and tonic and a beer for his friend who has not yet spoken. Without being asked he also orders Stanfield a bottle of his normal wine.

'So who are you?' Stanfield asks again. 'And what do you want?' Already he has a bad feeling about this.

'I think we've introduced ourselves,' Walters says, smiling thinly at him. 'And we just want to talk some things over.'

'You work for the Foreign Office?' Stanfield asks.

'Not quite, but same firm, if you understand me.'

'I think I'd like to see some identification, be given some explanation as to why we're here talking to each other.'

'Best to keep this purely social, don't you think. No real necessity to worry about the niceties of protocol. But if you want to speak to me you can contact me on this number.' He hands Stanfield what looks like a particularly plain business card containing only his name and a phone number.

'Look, I don't know what this is all about but if you don't mind I'm going to leave now and when I call him, my police driver will be here in a few minutes.'

Stanfield stands up as if to go and fumbles in his pocket for his phone but as he does so the younger man leans across the table and says in a low voice that resonates with threat, 'Sit down, Henry, and don't act the prick.'

'William,' Walters says in a tone that suggests he is gently reprimanding a naughty schoolboy, 'no need for rudeness.' Then he stands up and gestures Stanfield to his seat. 'Please, Henry, I don't think Beckett will mind a little more time in the car, do you?'

Stanfield slumps back into his seat just as the waiter arrives with the drinks. The younger man declines a glass and puts the bottle to his mouth. Walters looks at Stanfield and rolls his eyes. But Stanfield knows already that despite the mock disdain, the older man views the younger with something that approximates affection. A waiter comes to take their order but Walters taps his companion's arm and says, 'Why don't you take a seat at the bar, William? We'll call you if we need you.' William's face assumes a momentary look of hurt but he glowers only at Stanfield before wearily lifting his body slowly from the chair and going to the bar where he immediately lights a cigarette. 'No point wasting good things on William, I'm afraid he doesn't have a very cultivated sense of the finer things of life.'

They know who he is, they know about Beckett, but who they are or what their purpose is remains unclear to Stanfield. He has no recollection of ever having met Walters but now he discusses the menu with the waiter and offers opinions to Stanfield as if they are old friends about to share a meal at their club. He orders only a starter, claiming that he doesn't want to intrude any longer on Stanfield's evening than is absolutely necessary. Stanfield orders quickly and when he's finished he glances up to the bar where in the expanse of mirror he catches the younger man's leering stare. For a second he returns it and then sees William's hand slowly point at him in the glass. It's meant as a gesture of menace and Stanfield feels it as it's intended and for a second it insults him that he should suffer such a third-rate little cliché of a threat. The indignity makes him angry.

'In what zoo did you find him?' he asks Walters, pointing with his wine glass.

'Please don't mind William,' Walters says, 'his enthusiasm sometimes makes him a little bold. Not quite the right type but in these troubled times, sometimes useful, I'm afraid. Please forgive any rudeness – I'm sure it's not intentional.'

'I was appointed personally by the Prime Minister,' Stanfield says and then regrets that he's felt compelled to assert his status so blatantly. He needs to match Walters's self-controlled and apparent casualness of tone, not betray his mounting nervousness so openly.

'Indeed you were and a well-deserved appointment.

You've managed to build up quite an impressive CV in relation to some of the world's troubled spots. So tell me, how do you feel the Commission is going?'

Stanfield feels a sense of relief. Perhaps the purpose of the meeting is simply to gain some insights into his judgement on the process, to unofficially pick his brains about the way forward, but as he glances to the bar again where a wreath of smoke garlands the younger man's head and he thinks of the circumstances of their meeting, this relief wavers. His suspicions are increased by the awareness that Walters isn't really listening and is more intent on exploring the artistic creation that is framed on his white, square-shaped plate. When Stanfield pauses for a second it is to hear Walters say, 'Terribly good, and yours?'

'What is it you want?' Stanfield asks, resolutely setting his knife and fork down on the table.

'A pity business always intrudes in the end,' Walters says, replicating Stanfield's actions. 'It would have been quite nice to enjoy a civilised meal – I haven't had that pleasure recently. It's not quite the culinary capital of Europe, is it?'

'It's not the capital of Europe in any regard,' Stanfield says.

'Perhaps only in creating a sordid little mess and then expecting others to bail it out – it's very good at that. I think we're all a little tired of it: it's time to move on. Except the one problem I find here is that they will give up anything – their wives, their money, their self-respect – before they'll give up their past. And that makes constructing the future a little difficult, as you can imagine. Do you understand, Henry?'

'What is it you want from me?'

Walters pauses as if a student in his class had just asked him a difficult question and he needed time to consider. 'Well, Henry, I suppose, in a nutshell, we need you to help build that future.'

'The Commission is an independent body,' Stanfield asserts. 'It stands free from political bias and pressure from any source. That independence is crucial to the process. I'm not sure we should be having this conversation or where exactly it's leading.'

Walters's smile almost evolves into a snigger but he holds up a hand in a gesture of appeasement. 'Of course, Henry, of course. I understand completely. But sometimes in life you have to see the bigger picture. It's not an attribute we can universally expect but you are a cultured, intelligent man.' He pauses. 'A man who could go on to very great things indeed.' Then he looks at Stanfield and nods slowly.

'I can't be bought,' Stanfield says and then thinks it makes him sound like an actor in a film built on some tedious little tale of a moral dilemma and suspects also that despite its rhetoric they both know it's patently untrue.

'That's a pity, Henry – a real pity – because I always thought of you as a man who might be amenable to seeing the broader picture, who might help achieve what was clearly in everyone's best interests.'

'And what is the broader picture?'

'Well that depends really, doesn't it. You see it's quite liable to change from time to time, even from day to day, in ways that we might not quite expect. There's only one thing that's certain and that is that we're leaving. Not today and perhaps not tomorrow but within a foreseeable future and you see, the problem is, Henry, we can't tip our hats goodbye until the bricks are in place to hold the house together. So as you might also appreciate we need people like you on occasions to understand this broader picture, to have the necessary vision.'

Stanfield smiles briefly – it almost amuses him that Walters should use the word vision when they both know that what he really means is people who will close their eyes at the required time and because he understands now what it is that they want from him. As Walters goes on speaking in his delicate, gossamer riddles Stanfield feels a dislocation from the moment. He thinks of Maria Harper, he thinks of Emma and sees again the naïve earnestness of their faces. What can they ever know of the world's realities? What can they ever guess lies beyond the reach of their simplistic sincerity?

'And this is an official or a personal view that you're giving me?' Stanfield asks.

'Who can know these things? Wheels within wheels – that sort of thing. Pointless to worry about where ideas start. The only thing that's certain is that if it works out, a politician will claim it.'

'So what if I walk away now and ring the politicians or the press and relay this discussion?' Stanfield asks, feeling the first tremble of fear.

'Most unwise and I'm sure when you've had time to reflect you'll see the foolishness of that idea. But I don't want to drone on all evening and distract you from your meal, so I'll let William sort out some details.' He delicately dabs the corners of his mouth then stands up and smooths the front of his jacket before raising his hand lightly in farewell.

Stanfield watches his steady walk through the restaurant and then at his companion's back still hunched over the bar. Their eyes meet once more in the glass but this time Stanfield sees nothing in his watcher's eyes except perhaps a grey glimmer of tiredness. Stanfield is uncertain about what he should do and then after a few minutes he sees him stub his cigarette out with a curious twisting movement of his wrist and come towards him. Now he's close enough for Stanfield to see the light blink of disdain in his eyes and just for a second he thinks of the shiny sleekness of the shark coming alongside the boat and he shivers a little. When he sits down there is a thin smirk on his lips.

'All right, Henry?' he says. 'The old lad's a bit of a tosser, isn't he? Past his sell-by date if you know what I mean.' Stanfield nods non-committally and lifts the wine glass in an attempt to appear nonchalant. 'You like your wine, don't you, Henry? In fact you like a lot of expensive things. I admire your taste.'

'Thank you,' Stanfield says. 'I'm glad it meets your approval.'

'Oh yes it does, Henry. I like a man with good taste. Sometimes in my line of work I have to deal with people who have very poor taste and some who have no taste at all.'

'So what is your line of work?' Stanfield asks.

'Well there's some would say that I'm the monkey and Mr Walters is the organ grinder but if they were to say that directly to me, I'd take offence – know what I mean?' Stanfield nods again – he has a feeling that the less he says to this person the better it might be. 'Now you've heard what Mr Walters had to say, Henry, and he's one of the smartest men I've ever met, even if he is a bit of a tosser sometimes, so my advice is to pay good attention to him.'

'And if I don't?' Stanfield utters the words before he's had a chance to determine whether it was a good thing to say or not. And at first there's no reply as the man leans back on his chair and takes a theatrical little intake of breath. Then he slowly reaches inside his jacket pocket and just for one ludicrous second Stanfield thinks he's going to be shot but what is produced is a brown envelope that is dropped dismissively in the middle of the table.

'This is what happens, Henry. You get screwed. Big time.'

Stanfield lifts the envelope, trying hard not to let his hand shake. Inside are photographs. They're taken in the hotel room that first time with Kristal. As realisation floods in he tries to hold his face impassively and he flicks the photographs with an attempted display of indifference.

'Lovely girl that Kristal. Quality goods. You did all right there, my son.' Then stretching across the table he points to one and says, 'That's my favourite.'

Stanfield feels a sickness welling up in his stomach but tries to hold himself together. It feels like he's on that boat again and the man opposite him is the captain steering him into a dark and deepening sea. He wants to be sick, he wants to go back and place his feet on sure ground. But all he can do now is slide the photographs back in the envelope and wordlessly toss them back on the table.

'No, Henry, you keep them. They're a good reminder and maybe you'll still be able to get a thrill on some dark and lonely night.'

'What is it you want me to do?' he asks, but as he slips the envelope quickly into his inside jacket pocket he already knows the answer.

G ILROY ISN'T SURE WHETHER the tiredness is in his head or his body but after the wedding he feels empty, drained of whatever used to sustain him from one day to the next. Something he took so much for granted that he doesn't even know its name has deserted him. In every speech he makes, every soundbite for the radio or television, he speaks of the future but increasingly he wants to lie down in the comfort of the past; but not his own one, instead it's a past shaped and nurtured by his imagination where his life is divested of all its complications and responsibilities. And in it he's a family man with all his children safely round him. So they sit at a kitchen table and talk about their day and jokes and laughter are passed with the food and holidays are planned. Gilroy isn't a religious man any more but in his dream the meal always begins with him saying a grace and when he's finished the children chorus amen and Marie lifts her head and smiles at him.

Sometimes in his lowest moments he tries to pray but he has no sense of the words going anywhere beyond the tightening confines of his own need and sometimes the words get mixed up with lines and phrases of poetry. He wonders if a poem can be a prayer. 'The Poet Laureate' is what Ricky has started to call him after his wedding speech. He feels a squirm of embarrassed nervousness at the memory – did he make a fool of himself? Or did he say the things that although illusive and only vaguely glimpsed he wanted to say? He shall never know because amidst the congratulations and back-slapping afterwards, he could find no indisputable witness to the truth in anyone's face. He remembers how one old comrade told him how good it was to hear someone quote Larkin again before he slowly realised that he thought the words were from James Larkin, the Labour leader.

Never before has Gilroy felt his life so full of words and so depleted of those that carry meaning. Some days it feels he's wearing a straitjacket or his brain is clamped in a vice. He wants a new way to speak; he wants whatever's still ahead of him to be lived in a different way. As he sits in the armchair and stares at an afternoon quiz show on the television he feels himself slowly slipping into a doze. At first, as his head jerks awake, he tries to fight it but knows that resistance is futile and then he meekly surrenders.

When he wakes, for a few seconds he doesn't quite know where he is and the voices he's gradually aware of seem to come from somewhere inside his head. His mouth is dry as bone and his eyes blink uncertainly as he tries to shrug his mind clear of what sounds like radio static. The voices are layered and then gradually he understands that amidst those coming from the television are those of Marie and Sweeney. He goes to call out but stifles it as their words press a clearer shape in his senses.

'I'm worried about him, Ricky, I've never seen him like this. I think he's depressed.'

'Maybe we need to get him checked over by a doctor. We could go private – find someone sympathetic to the party who knows how to be discreet. If he's depressed maybe we need to get him prescribed some happy pills.'

'I don't think he'll go.'

'Why now? That's what I don't understand. Why now when he's sitting at the table, when we've finally climbed the mountain? He should be singing and dancing.'

'I don't know why any more than you. It's like the bucket went to the well and one day the well was dry. And the wedding – that seemed to really take it out of him. I don't understand because I thought it would bring him out of himself but if anything it made him worse.'

Gilroy blinks his eyes and stares at the screen where celebrity cooks compete to concoct exotic dishes out of mundane and meagre ingredients.

'The wedding?' Sweeney says. 'The icing on the cake as you might say. But listen, Marie, the first thing I think we should try before we start shovelling pills is a holiday – a good old break can work wonders. Blow the cobwebs away. Put a bit of lead in the pencil.'

'So where're we going?' Gilroy says, standing in the kitchen doorway. Marie blushes and Sweeney scratches the back of his neck. 'You could just take me straight to the old people's home, have done with it.'

'We're worried about you, Francis,' Marie says and he can see the concern shaping her face into an expression that causes him shame that he has caused it.

'I'm OK, just a little tired, that's all. I'll be right as rain.'

'Could we not go away, even for a weekend?' Marie asks.

He hesitates, caught on the hooks of her love, unable and unwilling to struggle free from anything that she says. 'Is there a space in the diary?' he asks Sweeney.

'I'll find one,' he says, 'I'll find one.'

'Well that's that then. Any chance of a cup of tea? I've a bake like the bottom of a bird cage.'

'Very poetic,' Sweeney says and Marie smiles as she lifts the kettle.

'But I'm not getting on a plane and I'm not going to Bundoran – it's like you're still in West Belfast.'

'We'll find somewhere,' Marie says. 'Somewhere nice and not too far. I know what you like. You leave it to me.' And then she starts to root round in the tins for a biscuit or a chocolate bar.

What she finds is a weekend in a Donegal hotel that is about to close for the winter. It sits overlooking a bay adjacent to a long dune-backed strand and is about five minutes' drive into the village. They've been here before once and it suits Gilroy that there are few other people staying and there's a quiet, subdued atmosphere. It feels like a house where the owners are packing up to go on a long holiday and as they sit in the lounge in front of a turf fire and have a drink from the bar, there's little to distract them from their mostly silent gaze out to sea. Most of the young staff have returned to university or college and already there's a drowsy sense of rest settling everywhere like dust. They are grateful that the chef has not decamped and although they are required to take their evening meal in the bar, the food is good and the owners attentive. No one intrudes, no one comes up to shake his hand and inform him of his Republican family tradition in which inevitably some relative manned the barricades in 1916. No one shouts abuse or leaves a room when he enters even though most of the cars in the car park have northern registrations.

'Lots of new houses since the last time we were here,' he says to Marie when one of the silences extends slightly too long.

'It's been a long time since we were here.'

'It's northern Prods,' he says, 'buying every house on the market, or building on every plot of land that comes up for sale. The guy in the bar says the prices have gone through the roof in the last five years – the locals can't afford to live here any more.'

'Maybe we should've tried to buy something when things were cheaper – something for our old age, somewhere to retire to.'

'You're right but we never had any money and what we did have went on the kids,' he says without resentment. 'It's hard to beat a real fire. The smell as much as anything.'

'Maybe we could still do it,' she says. 'If we could put a bit of money together.'

'Maybe, but by the time we gathered it up, the prices would be even worse.'

'Could you not ask the boys who did the Northern Bank for a loan?' she says and then laughs at her own joke.

'I wouldn't ask those bastards for the skin of their teeth. It's funny though with Prods – they'd fight to the death to avoid a united Ireland and cut your throat for a holiday home in it.'

When it's not raining they walk along the strand and huddle together like lovers against the squally, fractious wind that forces Marie to hold a hand to her hair to stop it being massacred beyond recognition. The sea, too, is whipped by anger and the waves throw up white-crested running and breaking funnels of foam that sometimes suddenly spume about their feet and make them scurry and scamper further up the beach. Once to their amazement they see a surfer in the sea, a black figure hunched and stiff arms spread as his board dips and pulls through the water like a needle stitching the hem of the waves.

But in bed they aren't lovers. He tries twice but each time it fades like the afternoon light, collapsing into nothing, and even though he refuses to accept it's happening and tries to fire himself into passion there's only the spent rush of his breathing.

'I'm sorry,' he says, the words and his broken breathing whispering in her ear, and she says, 'Shush, shush,' and runs her hand through the back of his hair and tells him it doesn't matter.

But it matters to him and after the second time he stands at the window and looks out at the opaque band of grey. Down in the car park there is a car with its lights and radio on and a young woman he recognises as one of the waitresses is leaning in at the open window and then he sees her kiss her boyfriend before he drives off. Later Gilroy imagines he will return for her and he thinks of them driving somewhere quiet along the coast road and parking the car and as a light spray blows off the sea effortlessly sinking into each other's arms. But he feels no sense of envy or bitterness, only a sadness that the world belongs no more to him but to this young couple and all the others like them who struggle to make their way and search for a love that will sustain them. He thinks of Christine and worries that she'll be happy, worries that London's too big, that he'll lose her in its magnitude.

'Come to bed, Francis,' Marie whispers to him but he stands on staring out at the darkening sky. 'The bed's cold without you.'

'Cold with me,' he says.

'It doesn't matter – you're tired, that's all. No one could have gone through everything that you've gone through and not be tired. It'll be all right. Everything will be all right.'

'I'd like to live here, Marie. You'd like it, too?'

'Yes, I think so. For the first time in our lives away from it all. Maybe, Francis, it's time to think of letting the younger ones do some of the struggling. You've given your whole life to it. Now come back to bed.'

'I'll make you a cup of tea,' he says as some kind of compensation.

'I don't want a cup of tea; I want you to come back to bed and hold me. Do you think you can do that?'

He turns away from the window and stumbles over his shoes then awkwardly climbs into the bed and falls silently and thankfully into the outstretched arms of her tight embrace.

After his return to the city, he tells himself that he carries the freshness of the sea air in his lungs, promises himself that this part of his life will be a finite one and that if he finds the right moment he will launch out in a new direction. It's never too late, no one would have the right to criticise him, but as he calls to mind everything he's endured and what's been achieved, he knows it won't be easy to walk away. And why should he give up these first fruits of victory and resign his place at the table to someone who hasn't shared any of the sacrifices? He needs to stay, even as a figurehead, during this period of transition and he tells himself that when things have finally bedded down there might be a better moment. There are still important things to do before he puts himself out to grass.

So when he meets Sweeney after he gets back he greets him as a man who's found some new sense of resolution and purpose.

'So the break did you good?' Sweeney asks as he stands at the doorway to his office.

'What's wrong?' Gilroy asks as he sets his briefcase on the table, glancing at his colleague's face and then at the pile of papers on his desk. His life has been bound so closely and for so long to Sweeney's that he registers even the slightest changes. There was a time when in the isolation cells they spoke to each other only through the tapped messages on pipes and now, regardless of the jaunty timbre of his words, Gilroy hears something that makes him apprehensive. 'You think I should have stayed away for longer?' He half smiles but then looks quizzically at Sweeney who stares back at him silently and then closes the office door.

'We shouldn't talk here.' Sweeney's voice is expressionless, almost monotone. When Gilroy looks at him he sees the flush of embarrassment in his face.

'Is there a bug?' he asks and sweeps his eyes round the room, then for a few seconds lapses into a wordless speech, asking questions with his face and gesturing with his hand.

'Probably no more than usual. But better to go somewhere else – somewhere we can talk and not be interrupted.'

'I don't like the sound of this,' Gilroy says, glancing again at his desk as if the answer might be found there.

'I'll have Marty bring the car round to the front door. When we go out of this room we'll just say that something's cropped up. If we're needed for anything important we'll tell them they can contact us on the mobile.'

Gilroy nods and feels another stir of apprehension. Sweeney is not given to theatricals so he resists the temptation to ask any further questions and does as he's told. When they get in the car Sweeney tells their driver to take them to Clonard Monastery and Gilroy sinks back in the seat.

'Confession time?' he asks.

'Not quite,' Sweeney says, then they sit in silence during the short journey and when they reach their destination he tells Marty to go back to the offices and he'll ring when he's needed.

'Are we meeting someone?' Gilroy asks.

'No, just you and me. We need to talk. Good place to do it.'

'Only God listening,' Gilroy says as they pass through the outer and inner doors to enter the great arched vault of the church. As always he feels an unwelcome sense of intimidation as he's confronted by the Gothic interior with its side chapels and red granite columns, its imposing high altar and the coldness of marble. He's never liked this place; he feels bullied by it, that he's expected to bow the head and knee without question. 'Could we not do this somewhere else? It's always freezing here. And it looks like that choir is about to start rehearsing.'

'That's good,' Sweeney says, sliding into one of the polished back pews. 'Let them sing their hearts out. There's some concert here at the weekend. The more noise the better. I don't know if you know it or not but I was an altar boy here once.'

'You kept that one a secret,' Gilroy says, slipping in beside him. 'Can't imagine it.'

'They threw me out after a month – I got in a bit of a scrap with a couple of the other boys.'

'So have you got any other secrets you're about to reveal? Hell's bells, Ricky, you're not about to tell me you've been working for the Brits for the last twenty years?' Gilroy asks wide-eyed, but his voice is laughing.

'No, I'm probably the only one who hasn't been. Though I hear there's a good pension scheme goes with it and a one-way ticket to the country of your choice. Maybe I missed out.'

At the front of the church the members of the choir shuffle into their places – there appears to be some confusion as to where everyone should be standing and there's some coughing and clearing of throats. The conductor is speaking to them but his words don't carry fully to the back of the church.

'So what is it you want to tell me, Ricky?'

'Maybe it wasn't a good idea to come here. Maybe we should listen to the music for a while.'

Gilroy goes to swear but stifles it on his lips. The choir breaks into song, their voices suddenly rising and quivering into the great arc of silence that seems shocked by the intrusion. 'Spit it out for God's sake.'

'You remember Connor Walshe?' Gilroy doesn't answer but lightly reaches out his hand and rests it on the pew in front. 'His case is coming up at the Truth and Reconciliation Commission. They've sent out letters. They're calling people.'

'Am I called?'

'No, you've not been called.'

'How long have you known about this?' Gilroy asks, looking up at the ceiling as if he might see the musical notes skirmish in the hidden spaces above them.

'A while, a while. I didn't want to say anything before. You haven't been good, Franky. I didn't want to give you something else to worry about.'

'Does Marie know?'

'No.'

'And should I be worried?' He turns his eyes to Sweeney and sees him shrug.

'I don't know. I hope not. We've people working on this, it could be trouble.'

'Who for, Ricky?'

'For you, for the party. For all of us.'

The conductor stops the music but a few stray voices carry on for some seconds before they falter into silence. Gilroy glances up at the stained glass and the light that seems to bleed colour into the dust motes hovering in the air.

'Connor Walshe. After all this time. Who would have thought it?'

'You remember him, Francis?'

'Of course,' Gilroy says as he rubs a finger across his bottom lip. 'Connor Walshe. I remember him.' He turns his head away from Sweeney for a second and looks to the far side of the church. 'You still practise, don't you, Ricky?'

'Lightly. For my ma, for old time's sake. You know how it is.'

'You go in the box and confess?'

'Once in a blue moon. When I feel the old ticker might be giving out or when I think I've been good. If I was a hypochondriac like you I'd probably never be out of it.'

Gilroy smiles but slumps a little in the pew. The choir starts up again. 'I haven't done it since before I joined up.'

'Must be a good backlog piled up by now. A bit like never emptying your email box. All that junk mail piling up day after day.'

'Nice to be able to press a delete button.'

'You thinking of going now?' Sweeney asks.

'No, I've finished with it. And anyway if you're going to confess something, why not do it direct, cut out the middle man?'

'You're talking like a Prod, Franky.'

They sit back and listen to the music. It sweeps out from the front of the church and then slowly encompasses them in its rising and harmonic power.

'It's beautiful,' Gilroy says, slowly gesturing into the emptiness of the air. He lets his hand linger there for a second, the way a child might hold a hand up to falling snow as if to catch some of its perfection. 'What is it?'

'It's not the Wolfe Tones or Christy Moore – I know that, but beyond that I can't help you.'

'Walshe's family still live local? Has anyone spoken to them?'

'They've been spoken to – respectfully like, nothing heavy – and the brothers don't want it, don't want to know. None of them wants all this dragged up again. But they're not the ones driving it – it's the sister Maria.'

'Anyone spoken to her?' Gilroy asks, trying to listen to the music and Sweeney's words at the same time.

'She's moved away. It's too delicate now to risk anything. We can't take risks with this thing or it'll blow up in our faces.'

Gilroy shades his eyes for a second and in that second he sees his daughter's face and the face he imagines her unborn child will have. But then another face intrudes and he blinks them open again.

'I don't need this, Ricky.' He turns his head and looks directly at him. 'I don't need this. Whatever needs to be done let it be done. You understand what I'm saying?'

'I understand, Francis, believe me I do. There's people working on it, pulling out all the stops, but best we don't talk about that. We need to trust them now.'

'So who has been called?'

'They've found Michael Madden – he's been living in America. He's coming home.'

'He was only a kid, too. He can't be too keen to come back here after all this time.'

'Don't believe he was but things have been explained to him. He had no choice in the end. There's only him left now. Someone has to stand up and say something. We'll make sure that the right things are said. Now I've told you, you need to put all this as far away from you as possible. You need to know as little as possible, we don't need to talk about it again – we shouldn't talk about it again.'

An old woman walks slowly up the aisle and glances at them but their eyes stay staring towards the altar. Two men in overalls come in carrying a ladder and paint-spattered sheets. The music ends.

'Are you all right?' Sweeney asks as his eyes follow the men with the ladder.

'I want to know what the music was called,' Gilroy says.

'The music?'

'Yes, what was that piece of music called? Ask them, Ricky.'

'You serious?' Sweeney says, squirming sideways in his seat and staring at Gilroy. When he sees that he is, he laboriously lifts himself out of the pew and sets off down the aisle, looking back occasionally to check that he's still there, then he excuses himself and asks one of the young women in the choir who's placing her music in a briefcase. Sweeney watches his journey back up the aisle. It looks as if Sweeney is talking to himself as his lips repeat the name so that he won't forget it. ' "Funeral Ikos," ' he says, standing at the end of the pew. 'Maybe we should go before this lot starts to leave.' Gilroy nods but sits on for a second before using his arm to lever himself up and then he follows Sweeney to the entrance where they both blink their eyes like swimmers when they plunge into the glittering coldness of the raw afternoon light. Sweeney turns up his collar as he rummages in his pocket for his mobile. As he stands on the step behind him Gilroy notices how grey his hair has become. He listens while he calls their driver and feels the cold wind brush its lips against his skin. He tries to summon up the Donegal beach and the sound of the surf spending itself furiously on the shore but already the memory has faded into some indistinct and wavering mirage and instead he recalls only the bitterness of his failures.

'You all right?' Sweeney asks.

'Yes,' he says as he turns his head to watch the members of the choir tumbling down the steps in laughing, gossiping clusters. One of their phones rings and her meaningless conversation is shared with everyone in the vicinity. One of the men lights a cigarette and takes deep drags the way Gilroy has often seen both men and women do after mass. It always strikes him as a slightly indiscreet public acknowledgement that the spiritual is never quite enough to satisfy the demands of the flesh. As the choir members filter towards their cars Sweeney turns towards him then steps back to be on an equal footing.

'Franky, you know all that stuff about trusting them, forget I ever said it.'

'What do you mean?'

'I mean I don't know who we trust any more. There's some whispering . . .'

'Spit it out, Ricky, and don't wrap it up in riddles.'

'I've just heard a few things and I don't know where it started, that's all. Just Chinese whispers, that's all.'

'Straight, Ricky; no riddles.'

'There's some saying that if this thing touches you then it would be too big an embarrassment and basically you should be . . .' His voice fades away and he fiddles with his collar.

'Ditched is the word you're looking for.' Some of the cars' horns sound a farewell to each other. Gilroy walks down some of the steps. 'Will Marty be long?'

'He's on his way. Sooner we get out of this cold the better. It's only whisperings from people who don't have the balls to put their names to it.'

'An embarrassment? Fuck them. When they've been through what we've been through then they have the right to judge me. Who are these people?'

'Probably nothing but kids who don't know anything about anything.'

'Except how to talk properly and look good in front of a camera. Who've got degrees coming out of their ears. Who've never had a single night's broken sleep or had to dirty their hands but who know how to write policies and do tricks with computers.'

'Sounds about right,' Sweeney says, looking at his watch impatiently.

'I'll be the one who decides when the time's right for me to go, not them, and I'll not be brought down by this, Ricky, not by this. And I'm owed, you're owed, and everyone like us, who did what we had to do. So let them do their whispering because none of them have what it takes or have the first idea.'

'We'll trust no one, Franky. Come on, let's get out of here – it's starting to give me the creeps,' Sweeney says as he sets off.

'We'll trust no one,' Gilroy calls after him and rubs his hands together as if trying to generate some spark of heat then heads after Sweeney, the heels of his shoes clacking discordantly on the steps.

WHEN FENTON PARKS THE van in the driveway of his house it's already the early hours of the morning and all the internal lights are off. He gets out slowly, feeling as if the automatic, almost somnambulant mechanics of driving and the interior of the van have been absorbed into the very quick of his being, and as he stretches his back there is a twinge of pain and he knows that he's not yet standing fully straight. The grip of the steering wheel is still in his hands like the consciousness of a phantom limb. The security lights have switched themselves on at his arrival and they give the house a clinical starkness that remains unsoftened by the ivy and other climbers that each year spread a little higher up the walls. The night air is mild and the clearest of skies is pinpricked with an intensely bright scatter of stars. A full moon hangs low, its every blue bruise and blemish visible to the eye. He looks up and massages the back of his neck – perhaps in a day or so he should go to a physio, get checked out, have a proper massage that might iron out some of the knotted stiffness of his spine. So many miles, so many roads spooling out endlessly in front of him, and now they've brought him home he struggles to find the feelings that he thinks should be associated with it.

He locks the van and feels no sense of completion but only the slow silt of sadness at the consciousness of its emptiness. Searching for his house keys he tastes the sourness in his mouth and is struck by an overwhelming awareness of his grubbiness and the sweat that beads his pores. It grows into a feeling of physical repugnance and he hesitates for a second, unsure that he wants to bring it inside his home and not wanting to wake his wife or climb into bed the way he is and the way he feels. Then on a slight breeze he catches the scent of the sea, that unmistakable briny tang that is like no other, and he takes the key silently out of the lock and goes back to the van. In that single moment he feels the constraints of his life, that too much of it has been lived according to the codes that he and others have imposed on it, and he tastes the bitterness of that knowledge and a frantic, desperate impulse to break out of its tight corral. His life is finite, there may not be much more time; he has, even at this late hour, to strike out in some new direction, grasp hold of whatever it is he needs.

In his bag he finds a towel and locking the door of the van heads off down the side of the house where another sensor light suddenly blinks angrily at him. His feet feel the damp softness of the grass as he walks the length of the back garden and clambers over the wooden stile into the back lane and then follows the narrow pathway that leads into the dunes. He walks on the wooden boardwalk that has been laid to conserve and protect them from too many feet and the dunes are soft moon-washed mounds feathered by gently swaying, spiky tufts of grass. What was once familiar to him is now contoured and layered with strangeness; it feels as if he's walking in some moonscape and what he wants now is to have the lightness of a world where the deadening grip of gravity is broken. He should have brought the boy, he should have found some way to bring him to a place where he would have all the things that he wanted and needed. He's angry at his own cowardice, at his constant clinging to a correctness that's been nothing more than a spindle-spirited desire for safety. Sometimes, he tells himself, rules have to be broken for good things to come and perhaps his reluctance to break them is not evidence of his loyalty to honesty but the craven scruples of the coward.

Rabbits scurry away at his approach, the white bob of their tails vanishing into the shadowy runnels between the dunes. Already he can hear the dull throb and rasp of the sea and as he lifts his face to its voice he knows he's hearing it in a way that he's never done before. He breaks into the wide-mouthed gap that opens to the beach and the overwhelming force of the sea sweeps over him and its living reality shoots through every one of his senses. At first his feet stumble and shuffle in the sand's softness but he steadies himself and pushes on along the hammered silver of the curving strand. There is the sound of small shells crunching below the heaviness of his feet as he makes his way to where the sand is tide-washed into firmness. Close now to the water he stares at the expanse of dark glass that is lightly engraved with white swirls and shivering streaks of moonlight. If he were smarter, better educated, he might now be able to explain to the boy about the mysterious connection between the moon and tides, or even let the boy explain it to him. And some-where beyond the strand and the sleeping town stand the mountains that have taken him and allowed him to be someone other than who he was and he knows they will accept the boy as well because they come with respect. He has a book of maps and routes and most of them still are new to him and unexplored so there are many more days to walk and expeditions to plan.

Perhaps his journey no longer needs to be to somewhere far away because now the world enters into him in strange and unchartered ways. No longer does it seem differentiated into separate bits, their petty smallness and meanness reconstructing into something less than the whole, because now the night sky, the sea, the shore, are linked and indivisible and he is part of that seamless endless roll of the world. So he holds his face to the breeze that is laden with life and drinks deeply, lets the air fill his lungs and tries to feel the lightness of the moment. But what comes also is an awareness of his tiredness and a need to sleep that is stronger than he's ever known so he makes his way to a narrow little tunnel between two of the dunes and, rolling the towel, uses it for a pillow. The sharply spiked grass fans over his head and he turns on his side and pulls his knees up tightly and when he closes his eyes it feels as if he's hidden from those he doesn't want to see him, those who would never think of looking here for him, and in a matter of seconds he feels himself slipping into the refuge of sleep.

It's the cold that wakes him just before dawn. His body tries to shiver some heat but he has to sit up and hug and beat himself with loud slaps of his hands. The first shards of light are slitting the grey weave of sky and sea and the widening tears are edged with the faint blush of pink and purple as he stands straight backed and instantly awake. Taking off his clothes he walks into the sea, wading into the waves until it's round his waist then douses his hair and face, splashing great palmfuls of the darkness over himself. The cold takes his breath away but he forces himself to stay for a few minutes before he heads back to the dunes, dries himself with the towel and quickly dresses. A steady edge of light is slowly prising the night open as still shivering he takes the journey back to the house. This time he runs until his heart is pumping before the pain stitching his side forces him to stop and he stoops over, his hands on his knees, and gasps for breath. With both hands on his sides he starts to walk, trying to regulate his breathing and ease the pain. The air feels moist and clammy against his skin and he wants the warmth of his bed now, the warmth of his wife.

In the hall he sees the neat pile of mail waiting for him on the table but he pauses only long enough to turn off the alarm, reset it and then drop the van keys in a small red Chinese dish. After the claustrophobia of the van's interior the house feels bigger and more spacious than he remembered it and he is aware of the distinctive smell but unable to identify what its components might be. The bedroom door is open and as soon as he enters he realises that it's empty and for a second he feels a squirm of panic but then guesses that she's staying over at her father's, something that she's done more often recently. He looks at the pristine bed and the insistent tidiness of the room and every other room that is the refuge and consolation of the childless and he sits on the end of the bed and stares around him. He wanted Miriam here, he wanted to slip into the warmth of her bed, he wanted to be welcomed home, but he's glad, too, that he doesn't have to talk and he doesn't know whether he will ever tell her about Florian or not. What would be the point? What purpose would it serve except to tantalise her with the prospect of what they will never have?

Going to the bathroom he stares at himself in the mirror, shaves with the electric razor and brushes his teeth for a long time. Already the objects his hands touch, the things his eyes see, are forming into a familiar consciousness that is gradually distancing him from the world he's left behind. Now everything that happened to him is being slowly shuffled into the store of memory where each time it's retrieved it will emerge a little more vague and indistinct until whatever force it once had will be worn smooth and flat like a stone in the stream. He removes his clothes and places them in the laundry basket then takes a pair of fresh pyjamas from the dresser, feels the familiar comfort of them against his skin and climbs wearily into bed. But it's as if the events of the last few days are fighting against their eventual fate and they weave through his dreams in bright hues that disturb his sleep and leave him constantly turning in an attempt to find some respite.

His fitful sleep is weakened some hours later when he hears a car outside and then the front door opening. Almost immediately and simultaneously, with the ingrained habit of a lifetime of worrying about security, they shout each other's name and he tells her he's in the bedroom. Her car keys rattle in the same dish as his and then there is the sound of her feet on the stairs. He feels nervous and then foolish that he should feel such a thing but when she enters she's just herself and there's only the warm comfort of the familiar and the love that he suddenly knows he feels for her.

'You look tired,' she says, smiling at him and taking off her coat. 'When did you get back?'

'You look tired, too. About five this morning. What time is it now?'

'About nine.'

'Were you at your father's?'

'Yes, I just stayed over.'

'So you haven't been out with another man then?'

'Unfortunately not and that settee doesn't exactly give you a good night's sleep.'

'How is he?' Fenton asks, propping his head with one hand.

'Much the same, no difference really. So did everything go all right?'

'Fine, everything went fine. No problems.'

'Is there any heat in that bed, James?' Her voice is light and playful in a way that pleases him. He pulls the quilt back as an invitation but she starts to hang her coat in the wardrobe.

'Please, Miriam, just leave everything. Before what heat there is gets lost.'

She stands still, a little confused, then walks out of his line of sight and undresses quickly. She lifts a nightdress and he wants to tell her not to, but hesitates and before he can say anything she has it on. In the bed she shivers and teases him that he had lied when he said it was warm so he reaches out to her and holds her in his arms and feels the shock of their embrace as if it's something new.

'This bed's too big without you,' she says, pulling back slightly so she can talk. 'If anything ever happens to you I'd have to get a single one.'

They feel like lovers. He touches her hair, kisses her carefully and without presumption, unsure of what her response might be.

'So you missed me then?' she says, her voice light with enjoyment of the flattery. 'And how did the magic go?'

'Like magic,' he says and laughs a little at his own joke.

'You didn't make a complete fool of yourself then?'

'I don't think so. The kids liked it. I'll have to learn some new tricks.'

'It took long enough to learn the ones you did. You're not exactly Paul Daniels.'

He kisses her again and she relaxes in his arms and closes her eyes and he knows the joy of being truly home and safe in the certainties that it brings and also a fool for all his thoughts of journeys and distant places. Surely this can be enough. He tries to tell her that he loves her but the words slip away and instead he touches her with tenderness as if she is a young girl again. They've never known anyone other than each other and been together such a long time that perhaps it shouldn't have come as a surprise that there've been periods when they've been lost to each other. She tastes the salt on his skin and he tells her that it must have been spray from the crossing but she doesn't question him and afterwards they both fall into a deep sleep that feels free from the boundaries of time or responsibilities.

When they eventually wake they both feel a slight embarrassment and get up quite quickly, trying to slip into more normal rituals as if they have been a little wayward, but he knows she is pleased and glad to have him home. At the breakfast table they exchange fuller accounts about the events of the previous days but he tells her nothing about the boy or about anything other than those things that are simple and easy for both of them to understand. She has made him a cooked breakfast, something they don't usually have, and he eats with pleasure and feels the security of his own world re-forming round him. Perhaps he's got it wrong and what felt like a corral was in fact nothing more, nothing less, than a protective barrier that preserves and protects him from the many who would wish him harm. So even when the phone rings it doesn't set him on edge or press him into alertness as it might normally do as he watches Miriam go to the hall and take the call. He follows her with his eyes, watching the white exclamation marks of her heels below her dressing gown.

The call is for him and as she hands the phone to him she shrugs her shoulders in answer to his silent question. In a habit ingrained by a desire to separate his home and his work he walks off down the hall and into the front room where he stands at the window and looks at the dark overlapping folds of the mountains. It's someone called Ken Young from the

Police Federation and he's offering him things, more things than Fenton can take in or understand at first, so he listens while he speaks of legal advice and counselling, about help in formulating his statement, about support teams and dry runs and video analysis. Fenton struggles to interrupt the flow and stares at the mountains whose tops are swathed in mist so that they look like a child's drawing that's been partially erased. And then he understands and speaks over the voice at the end of the phone. 'Have I been called?'

'Yes, the case of Connor Walshe. Have you not received a letter?'

'I've been away; I haven't checked yet,' he says and then walks back into the hall and shuffles the post until he finds the envelope. 'I'll call you back.' He sets the phone down and stares at the envelope. In the kitchen he can hear Miriam loading the dishwasher and the clink of glass against glass. He takes the envelope to the window as if holding it close to the light might reveal its contents and prevent the irretrievable finality that having to open it will bring. Perhaps Young has made a mistake, perhaps it's some sort of formality that needs to be gone through and will quickly be over. He has to believe that Alec will see him right, that he will recognise what is personally owed and begin his repayment with this. Was it so big a thing to ask? And if there are things they don't want mentioned then surely they can see that it would be best to keep him out of the case altogether. He suddenly feels angry that the letter's come to his home and intruded on his privacy. During his entire career he strove to keep the two worlds separate and now they've thrust this thing into the heart of his home without respect or consideration for everything that he's done. Closing the door he sits down and opens it, scanning its contents before throwing it aside dismissively.

When he makes the phone call it's not to Young but Alec. He rings him several times at work but each time is told he's unavailable and when he rings his mobile he reaches voice-mail. Going back into the kitchen he tells Miriam that he has to go out and when she asks him if everything's all right he smiles and says that he just needs to drop in to see some old colleagues about an idea for fundraising.

'You don't think you should rest up before you start tearing about again?' she asks.

'I won't be long, just an hour or so,' he says, draining his cup of tea and kissing her on the cheek.

'Going away again,' she says, smiling, 'and will it be a repeat of coming back?'

He blushes and looks at her smiling like a girl and then she too colours a little and turns away to the sink.

'Drive safely,' she calls after him, 'and don't forget to drive on the right side of the road.'

He opens the garage and reverses the car out and before he drives off he glances up at the house. It's the fourth of their marriage and the one he likes the best with its proximity to the sea and the mountains. He remembers how much she cried when they had to move out of their first house at twenty-four hours' notice. Twenty-four hours to pack all the hopes and dreams of a first home because their details were in the wrong hands. It felt to her that some part of her had been ripped out and dispersed to the elements and she cried for the first few days in the safe house they found themselves dumped in. That was the first and only time she asked him to find a different job. Years later when she was upset and emotional she let it slip to him that she thought that if they had stayed in that first home they would have had a baby. It makes him angry again that they think they still have control over him and that he can be summoned like a common criminal to appear in a court that he doesn't understand or want to be part of. So who will answer now for his past, for a woman in middle age crying because she thinks somehow she lost her chance to have a child? Who will answer for the things he's had to see?

He drives to Belfast and the slow smoulder of his anger speeds him on. The car at first feels light as a toy after the sluggish heaviness of the van and once he has to brake quickly to avoid driving into the car in front when it stops at traffic lights. He heads to Police Headquarters and is recognised by the security at the gate but when he checks in with reception he's shown a seat by someone he doesn't know and asked to wait. Everything has been revamped and decorated and he tries not to look at the new crest and instead watches the phone call being made and then he's told that Alec is unavailable because he's in a meeting but he says he'll wait and then answers the questioning look with an insistent repetition. A few minutes later his mobile rings and he hears Alec's voice telling him to meet him in ten minutes in the car park of a nearby golf club. His voice is neutral, stripped of its usual coating of affability, and he says nothing beyond the location and time of their meeting.

When Alec arrives he locks his car and gets into the passenger seat of Fenton's and his manner is cool and functional as he asks, 'What can I do for you, James?'

'You can't be seen with me, Alec, that we have to skulk here in a car park?'

'It's not like that.'

'So what is it like then?'

'It's different from what you knew. Everything's different now, James.' A light rain skims across the windscreen and the three women waiting at the first tee put up umbrellas while one starts to search in her bag for waterproofs.

'What can I do for you? So how did your trip go? Hell of a journey.'

'What I want to know is why I've got this,' Fenton says, throwing the letter on the dashboard. 'I asked you, Alec, to keep me out of this, to let me leave everything behind and be finished with all of it. You couldn't do that for me?'

'I tried, James, believe me, I tried, but this thing is bigger than you and bigger than me. Believe me when I say I've got no pull on this. It goes higher and deeper than I can put my hand to.'

'What if I don't turn up?'

'You'll be held in contempt. That would be a bad place to be. There could be unpleasant repercussions. You don't want to go there, James.'

'And what if I send a message to your friends in suits that if they make me go I'll tell the truth. Regardless.'

'I'm not telling you what to say but you need to consider things very carefully. Have the Federation been on to you yet? They've a good support system set up – they could really help you get through it.'

'Will they help me to lie?'

Alec looks out of the side window and doesn't answer. A beer delivery lorry passes behind them and parks at the back of the clubhouse. A few seconds later there is the sound of metal barrels being unloaded and they both stare at the two men in overalls and grey gloves that make their hands seem huge.

'Listen, James, you do what you have to do but do it right and you can walk away. There'll be no more calls – I can guarantee that. Don't make a martyr of yourself. Do whatever it is has to be done and then disappear into your retirement.'

'And you can promise that I won't be back every five minutes for every case I ever put my hand to?'

'That's the one thing I can promise. I've been told this is a one-off and do what's needed and it's all put to bed. You'll have done your bit.'

Fenton stares out at the golf course through the rain-splashed window and after a second turns the wipers on then turns them off again.

'Except one thing, Alec. The moment I tell the first lie they'll have something on me. So how do I know they won't come looking for more?'

'Because they only want this one thing and because they know you're not a man to be pushed around or taken advantage of. Because you only hold the one card they need.'

Fenton's mobile phone vibrates in the pocket of his jacket and suddenly Alec is grabbing him by the arm and patting his coat.

'What in . . .' Fenton shouts.

'Are you wired?' Alec interrupts and his face is contorted into a tight warp of panic.

'It's a mobile phone,' Fenton says, taking it out of his pocket. 'It's a mobile phone. What in God's name is going on, Alec?'

Alec slumps back in his seat and lifts a hand as if to shade his eyes but it's a poor attempt to hide his embarrassment. 'I'm sorry, James, really sorry – I don't know what I was thinking of. I'm the one who's wired – wired to the moon. It's hard to know who to trust sometimes. There's people out there who'd like to see me done down. You always have to watch your back.'

'Times must have really changed for the worst,' Fenton says. 'In my day your colleagues watched your back. I don't know what's going on with you but it's a bad feel about it and maybe you should think of getting out of it before it ends up in a mess.'

288

'I'll be all right. These are difficult days but we'll get through them. I'll be all right in the end.'

Fenton looks at him and believes him because already he's put on his open, friendly face again as if nothing has happened, as if they're sitting in the car waiting for the rain to go off and have a round of golf. And it's obvious that their conversation is over because now he's diverted into small talk and he's trying too hard to be his normal jovial self so when he finally excuses himself by saying he's a meeting he has to go to, Fenton does nothing to delay his departure. He lets him drive off first and then takes the voicemail message from Miriam – it's nothing more than a request for him to bring in milk and bread from the garage on the way home, but her voice is comforting in its familiarity and its utter lack of pretence.

Fenton doesn't take the journey home immediately but instead drives into the city centre and passes where the Commission sits. A fine rain is still slanting down, so fine that it's hardly visible to the eye. He looks curiously at the family groups congregating outside the building in tight supportive huddles. Some of them hold photographs but they're too small for him to see the faces. A little distance apart three women hold up placards where the rain has run the writing but he can still make out the word 'collusion'. As he drives away he blinks his eyes because for a second, just for a second, he sees the boy's white owl face swooping towards him from the darkness of the playing fields. And he blinks again and then there is only the solidifying mass of traffic and the rain bleeding the blur of neon across the windscreen.

THE PLANE FLIES INTO an airport that he doesn't think was there when he left. The journey from London takes under an hour and after the transatlantic flight he's grateful for its shortness. He has endured the company of Lynch for longer than he would choose and although their initial attempts at conversation were soon blocked by the welcome distraction of films and sleep, he felt a physical discomfort in so close a sustained proximity. There's something thin and unhealthy about the older man, in his dried wisp of combed-over hair, the rattle of the smoker's cough in his hollow chest that rings out like a key being turned in the door of a derelict house and in his sunken cheekbones. There is, too, an odour from him that seems to come from his core and envelop him – it's the smell he associates with entering a locked-up, junked-up basement or when he shovels a heaped rain-sodden pile of leaves. Walking out to the plane he thought Lynch resembled a withered stick that a strong wind might snap. He feels a particular repulsion for his nicotine-stained fingers and found himself sneaking glances at them as Lynch tried to compensate his craving for a cigarette with alcohol or a Dan Brown book. It seems almost incomprehensible to Madden that such a man should now exercise power over him and in one meeting is able to control the direction of his life. It also seems incomprehensible that he should be connected with him in any way other than as passing strangers in the street. He tries to stifle his anger and assumes taciturn neutrality as the best defence against Lynch's endless tirades and attempted fatherly advice.

Over and over he hears Lynch repeat like a mantra how different he'll find everything, that he won't recognise the place, that everything's changed. And yet as the plane swoops into the outskirts of the city it feels that he's travelling nowhere but irrevocably and involuntarily into the past and every mile takes him a world away from Ramona and the child that grows inside her. The plane jolts and shudders to a strained landing and he feels one more shock of sickness as he recalls the total incomprehension on her face and his terrible, terrible task of having to persuade her of the truth. She doesn't understand. He tries to explain. She doesn't understand. She cries and speaks in Spanish, only the cadence and timbre of the repeated phrases communicating what it is she feels. He's deliberately locked out of her shock and pain by a different language and all he knows, because he sees it unmistakingly in her broken, glittering eyes, is that now he's another man who's lied to her and abused her love. The next day she doesn't return from work and when he goes to the library he's told she hasn't been there. She's gone and he can't think where to look for her because for the first time he realises that he knows almost as little about her past life as she knew about his. He didn't need or want to hear beyond what she chose to reveal because always he wanted them to live only in a shared future.

'Easy, son,' Lynch says as he's sick into the paper bag. He feels Lynch's nicotine-stained fingers patting his shoulders. 'That's a good welcome home. So you'll not be kneeling to kiss the tarmac then.' They sit in their seats as the passengers start to file off and then Lynch says, 'Come on, kid, I'm busting for a fag.' Then in a change of tone, 'Everything'll be all right. Do the business and we'll have you on a plane out of here before you've time to miss that sun.'

'You'll be able to get me back?' he asks.

'Everything's already sorted. And remember when you walk out of that hearing, you're clean as a whistle – nothing hanging over your head. I've told you, we've lots of important people looking out for you.'

'I've got to get back,' Madden says and then drinks from a bottle of water.

'No sweat,' Lynch says. 'We always look after our own. You believe it, son. Now let's get off this tin bucket, sink a few jars, eat some decent food.'

There's a car waiting for them with a driver and a man sitting in the front passenger seat. 'All right, lads,' Lynch says as he pulls out a cigarette packet. 'This is Michael.' The front passenger turns and shakes his hand, says his name is Micky. The sourness in his mouth is suddenly edged with fear – he's in the back of a car, being taken he doesn't know where. He puts his hand on the car door.

'Relax, Michael. You're in good hands.' Lynch lights the cigarette and inhales slowly and deeply like a drowning man coming up for air.

'Where're we going?' he asks.

'We're taking you somewhere safe, out of the spotlight. If you don't mind we think you should wait until the hearing's over before you meet up with your family. It's best not to get distracted or lose focus until the business's done. And we have work to do, preparation for what has to be said. We don't want you getting up there unprepared. We've good people will sort that out. You understand?'

He nods and looks out of the window and he doesn't know what's changed like Lynch kept saying because everything he sees and everything he feels about this place remains exactly as he remembered it. He pushes back in the seat and tries not to inhale the smoke from Lynch's cigarette then after a few minutes asks if he can have one.

'I thought you didn't smoke, Michael,' Lynch says, offering him the packet.

'I've just started again,' he says and slumps back in the seat and he tells himself that in the light of what he's done one more betrayal won't count for much.

Everywhere he looks seems like it's printed in monochrome, the roads and streets so narrow that after a while they feel as if they're tightening round his throat, the ligature cutting off his breath. In the car, with the smoke and the proximity of Lynch, he feels the choking press of his former world where instead of light and sky there is only an unbroken stretch of grey squeezing out the smallest possibility of colour. He stubs out the cigarette because every drag reminds him of broken promises and if he's to have even the smallest hope of refinding what he's lost then he has to begin with this.

The car journeys along roads he doesn't want to remember and sometimes it feels as if the different shop fronts are laughing at him, so in his head he endures their jeers as they vent their spite and reach out to reclaim him. He wants to say that things are different now, that he's moved on, that he doesn't belong here any more, but there's only the relentless imposition of a trembling, shifting topography that sucks him in like quicksand.

'So, Michael, what's Florida like then?' Micky asks.

'Bloody hot,' Lynch answers, his head swathed in a sulphurous gauze of smoke. 'Like sticking your head in the oven.'

'It's good,' he says.

'Been to Disney and all that?' Micky asks, half turning in his seat.

'Sure, but when you live there you don't really bother with those places. They're more for tourists.'

'It's full of old people,' Lynch says. 'Sometimes you see them driving cars and they must be about ninety years old.'

'People go to Florida to retire,' he says.

'Suppose you thought you had retired, too,' Micky says. 'Bit of a bummer having to come back here to this shit-hole.'

'Yes,' he says and increasingly he's aware that his accent is different from theirs and that more than anything he feels a sense of superiority to all of them and to everything he sees. He asks Lynch again where they're going and this time he tells them it's a place just outside the city, a safe house, and in a short while the city is a molten scoop of yellow light below them. The car's lights are switched to full beam and he sees hedges and the overhanging branches of trees. They turn off the road and then another one and eventually they're in a long potholed lane that brings them to a solid-looking two-storey house whose walls are rendered in a brown pebble-dash. There is light in all the windows and a satellite dish attached to the chimney.

'This is it,' Lynch says, 'you'll be comfortable here.'

'Got a Sky dish,' Micky says. 'You can watch American sport. You like baseball?'

'I prefer basketball,' he says, staring out at the house. He hasn't entirely shaken off the idea that they've brought him here to kill him but he can't think of any reason why they should want to do that. And there's no sense of menace from the two men in the front of the car, nor can he imagine it's ever been Lynch's line of work.

Micky helps him lift his case out of the boot and then tells him he'll be seeing him. The driver doesn't turn off the engine and Lynch doesn't take his own case out of the car but he does go to the door and ring the bell. Almost immediately a young woman opens it and behind her Madden sees a man standing further down the hall.

'Michael, this is Kirsty and her husband John Downey. They're going to look after you until this thing's over,' Lynch says. 'Anything you need they'll get it for you. And Kirsty is the best cook you could get. The only thing you need to worry about is not putting on too many pounds.' The young woman welcomes him shyly and shakes his hand while her husband comes forward and takes his case. 'You get a good rest and get your head clear. I'm going to do the same and tomorrow when we're all fresh we'll go out for a few jars.'

He offers his hand and Madden takes it as briefly and lightly as is polite. While her husband goes to the door to see Lynch off Kirsty invites him into the kitchen. 'There's fresh coffee or would you like a beer?' she says and she's smiling at him in a way that makes him feel welcome and even a little important.

'A coffee would be great,' he says, taking a seat at the large table. There's a heaped bowl of fruit in its centre. The interior of the house is more modern than the outside suggests and he compliments her on it as she sets a cup in front of him and a plate of biscuits.

'It's not ours. We just look after it. Wish it was, though.' She hovers at the sink as if sitting at the table would be too intrusive.

'So you're like caretakers?'

'I suppose so. Lots of people stay here and it's our job to look after them.'

'Are you not having a cup? It's very good.'

'No thanks, I'm not long after one.' She looks away as her husband enters.

'Your bag is in your room, Michael,' he says as he pours himself a cup from the percolator. 'It's the first room at the top of the stairs.' He sits down and leans back on the chair. 'There's beer in the fridge – just help yourself when you want one.'

He thanks him and then studies them as a couple. They're both about thirty years of age and look a little like each other, both being quite tall and dark haired, and, as might be expected, they both seem a little awkward at his sudden presence in their kitchen.

'So you get lots of people staying?' he says, trying to ease the thickening silence.

'Now and again,' Downey says and Madden sees him throw a glance at his wife. 'So how's America then? I have a brother working construction in New Jersey. Never been, though. Kirsty, knock the heating on, it's getting cool.' She momentarily disappears into a utility room and there is a loud rush as it kicks in.

'It's good. Plenty of opportunities for work.'

'He wanted me to go out, for good, but I didn't fancy it. I don't like Americans much – no offence like.'

'None taken,' Madden says, wondering at the stupidity of the statement.

'Too arrogant for my liking. Nine-Eleven was the price they paid for it, for thinking they have a right to rule half the world.'

Madden watches Kirsty take up a position behind her husband. He sees the embarrassment in her eyes and for her sake he humours him with vague and bland answers, letting his inane analysis of world politics wash over him without registering irritation or disagreement. Then at the first opportunity he tells them that he's feeling sleepy and he'd like to turn in.

'The old jet lag kicking in, Michael? Kirsty'll show you your room and the bathroom. Tell you where everything is.'

Madden says his thanks and goodnight and follows Kirsty back along the hall and up the stairs. She is taller than Ramona but thinner and wears her hair shorter and her step on the stairs is light and quick. She opens the bathroom door and tells him that there's lots of hot water if he wants a bath and shows him how the shower works as if he mightn't have used one before. Then she points him to his room and when he open the door he sees neatly folded towels at the bottom of his bed and a black suit laid across it.

'If you wouldn't mind, Michael, could you try on the suit so I can make any alterations need doing?'

'Right,' he says. 'So they've got me a suit for my day in court?'

'I suppose they want you to look your best.'

They want him to go into a court and tell what happened and they think a suit will make him look better. But he says nothing and instead looks round the room with its neat modern furniture and its double bed with cream linen. Everything feels and smells new and how he imagines a superior hotel room to look. He thinks of Ramona and the child that's coming.

'Have you got kids?' he asks as she straightens the closed curtains.

'No kids. John and I aren't married either. I just think Gerry tells people that because he's a bit old-fashioned and thinks it sounds better. Have you got kids?'

'No.' For a second he's going to tell her about the baby but pulls back because he suddenly understands that he doesn't want to bring Ramona into this world, that he doesn't even want to hear her name mentioned in this place.

'Married? Sorry,' she says, starting to walk from the room.

'No, not married.'

'I didn't mean to pry,' she says. 'Come downstairs when you've tried on the suit.'

After she's gone he opens the curtains slightly and looks out but all he sees is his own reflection in the blackness. He turns to the suit. It's plain but expensive and looks to him like the type you might wear to a funeral. He's reluctant at first to try it on. The trousers are several inches too long so he hitches them and goes back downstairs. In the kitchen Downey is still sitting at the table watching the news on a portable television that nestles on a work surface between the microwave and a bread bin. He has a bottle of beer in his hand and each time he drinks from it his mouth makes a slurping noise.

'Trousers are too long,' Madden says and Downey leans round on his chair to look.

'You're a bit of a shortarse, Michael. No offence, mate.'

'I'll pin one up and then shorten them tomorrow,' Kirsty says, lifting a sewing box out of one of the cupboards.

'Better to do it tonight, in case Gerry wants him to wear it tomorrow.'

'Stand over here in the light,' she tells him and then kneels down at his feet and folds one of the legs. 'Does that look the right length, Michael?' she asks as she pulls her head back and measures it with her eye. When he says he thinks so she starts to pin the new length, holding the pins in her mouth and taking one out at a time.

'There you go, Michael, women falling at your feet already.' There's another slurp. Madden looks down as she bends over the hem. Her neck below the blackness of her hair

298

is pale, almost white, and on this whiteness rests a thin silver chain. For a second he feels the impulse to reach down and touch her hair, to say something kind to her, but instead he turns his gaze to the television.

'It's the Commission,' Downey says. 'Every night they put it on and every night it's shoved further back and given even less time. Everybody's sick of it by now and there's no end to it. Another day or so and it's your turn, your fifteen seconds of fame. American television is rubbish, isn't it, Michael?'

He nods and Kirsty tells him that she only needs to do one leg and if he leaves them outside his door she'll have them ready in the morning. Saying goodnight for the second time he returns to his room and after taking off the suit puts the trousers on a hanger on the outside door handle. But he doesn't unpack his bag because he wants to convince himself that his stay is only the most temporary of ones. After using the bathroom he walks back along the landing and pauses for a few seconds to listen to the voices talking in the kitchen but he can't make them out except that John is complaining about something and then it all gets lost in music from the television.

The bed is laundry fresh and part of him wonders who else has slept in it but another part of him wants only to think of nothing and momentarily wipe everything from his memory in the oblivion of sleep. As his head hits the pillow he is suddenly conscious of how utterly exhausted he is and the wave of sleep that overwhelms him seems to have its origin deep inside.

In the morning when he eventually shrugs himself awake, his head feels groggy, unfocused, as if he has a hangover. He thinks of falling back into sleep again but looks at his watch and sees it is almost eleven o'clock. Shaking his head he tries to stir himself, to resist what's threatening to drag him back under, and as he does so he hears a car driving away. He sits on the edge of the bed and rubs the back of his neck before going to the window and opening the curtains. Outside there is only a clotted mesh of small fields tacked together by hedgerows and ragged, scrubby trees. No road is visible and he can't see the car that's just left. He goes to the bathroom and showers and shaves but it's her face he sees in the mirror, standing in front of him, the shock of her hair coursing against his cheek, the warmth of her body permeating his. She's just been sick, her face is sprinkled with water and pale like the lake before the first light has touched it. Men have it easy she says and he says he's sorry. He holds the razor frozen a few inches from his cheek and tries to tell her he's sorry, so utterly and completely sorry, that he will do any-thing to keep her love, but she tells him that she has given her love to someone other than who he is, that he can't be two people, that she loved someone who never existed. And then everything collapses and everything is lost inside a language he doesn't understand. The words are a torrent, a flash flood that carries her far beyond his reach. His hand shakes a little as he tries to finish shaving. But he does exist, he tries to tell her that he does exist and the man she loves is no one other than him, but then she is borne further from him in the tumbling cascade of her words that rush through a canyon created by the sharp-edged gestures of her hands. He tries to calm her by his touch but she throws it off and there is nothing he can do to stem the flow, nothing he can conjure to staunch her pain. Now he holds the sink with both hands to steady himself and then splashes his skin. He presses the towel tightly against his face and holds it there as if the longer he does so, the greater the chance that when it's removed he might see that something has changed.

When he goes downstairs there's some post on the hall

floor and picking it up he looks at the address before carrying it into the kitchen. Only Kirsty is there, standing as if she's been waiting for him in front of the table that's set for breakfast. She tells him that John's gone to the shops and won't be long. He hands her the post and without looking at it she sets it on a shelf where it adds to the pile of unopened mail.

'That was some sleep,' she says as she starts to busy herself about the cupboards. 'Would you like a cooked breakfast? It's all ready to go.'

'I guess I was pretty tired. But if you don't mind I'll just have some coffee and a bit of toast.'

'Are you sure you wouldn't like some eggs, bacon, the traditional fry-up?' And when he says no thanks, 'Your suit's ready – you can take it back up with you when you're going.'

'I'm sorry to put you to all this trouble,' he says, pouring himself some orange juice from a carton.

'Not freshly squeezed, I'm afraid. And this is my job so you don't need to worry.'

'It's fine,' he says, saluting her with the glass.

'I never understand when Americans say all that stuff about eggs over easy in films. What's it mean?'

He explains to her while she pours him a cup of fresh coffee. For a tall woman she has small hands. Her fingers are ringless with nails that are a little ragged and white flecked as if lacking in calcium. In the morning light she looks a little washed out, the blue of her eyes diluted by tiredness.

'What day is it?' he asks, suddenly uncertain.

'Saturday. They're coming to take you out later this afternoon. It'll be good to get out and see some things.'

'Gerry Lynch?' he asks.

'I'm not sure. John said you were to be ready for four. They'll pick you up.'

He wants to ask her if she does everything that John tells her but after his breakfast he thanks her and says that he's going to get some air and take a walk. Immediately he sees that she's nervous about the idea and tries to put him off by telling him that there's a cold wind and it might rain. When he persists she tells him that she'll come with him and he understands that she's not allowed to let him out of her sight but he says nothing and waits for her to clear the breakfast dishes. Once as he helps her they bump into each other and she reddens and apologises. Then she lifts a coat out of the utility room and after she's carefully locked the front door they step into the sharp morning light. She's right about the wind and he shivers as the first cold breath whispers against his face.

'I told you,' she says, 'it's very deceiving.'

'In the college I work in the kids complain about the cold in winter if it means they have to wear a jumper for more than two days in a row.'

'You teach in a college?'

'No, I work in maintenance – for the ground staff. Looking after the campus.'

'Sounds good.'

'I'm thinking of starting up my own landscaping business,' he says instinctively and then understands that what was once a realisable dream has disintegrated with everything else. The knowledge silences him and they walk along the lane on opposite sides of the potholes that punctuate the central passage. At a gate they pause and look at two horses silhouetted nose to tail on the brow of a hill. The horses stir and lift their heads curiously then one begins a slow amble towards them.

'They think we've come to feed them,' she says, plucking at grass growing on the verge. When the horse lifts its head over the top bar of the gate she holds the grass out to it and the horse sniffs it disinterestedly then turns away. 'Suit yourself,' she says, dropping the grass and drying her hands on the sides of her coat.

'It's cold,' he says. 'Let's go back.' They walk back along the lane again, skirting the pools of trapped sky. Everything around him – the hedges, the tussocky fields, the sky itself – feels ragged and damp. He longs for the slow burn of the sun, knows that if he's ever to feel its heat again he won't complain or take it for granted.

When they get back to the house he asks if there's anything he can help with but she tells him that there's nothing so he goes into the living room and flicks the television channels. After a while he feels sleepy again but resists the temptation to doze. John returns and looks in on him, offers him a beer again but thankfully doesn't hang around. He watches an old black-and-white movie but doesn't get to see the ending as Lynch arrives to take him out.

'Marty and Micky are coming with us,' he says. 'Micky's always good for a laugh. We're going to get something to eat first and then we'll have a few jars and a bit of Irish craic.'

Madden gathers his coat unenthusiastically as he imagines the type of evening he associates with Irish theme pubs and fears that authenticity will only make it even worse. But the meal is in a city-centre Pizza Express and then they have a few drinks in a downtown bar that has coffee tables and leather suites and where the barman tries to get them to sample cocktails. Afterwards they go to a club in West Belfast and when Lynch introduces him to people they shake his hand but no one knows him or has any interest in him. There is a group of teenagers in one of the corners playing noisy drinking games and Lynch rolls his eyes as he studies them. A giant television screen is showing live soccer. When Madden goes to the gents' one of the teenagers follows him and offers to sell him coke.

Afterwards he tells his companions and Lynch says, 'The whole bloody world's gone to the dogs. All they're interested in is getting smashed out of their heads. No interest in anything else.'

Madden thinks they're settled for the night so he's surprised when Lynch takes a phone call and then tells him they're due back at the house. 'Work to do now, Michael.' On the return journey there's little conversation and Lynch mostly keeps his face angled to the window. When they reach the house no one moves and they tell him they'll see him in the morning so he gets out and as he does so he sees two cars parked in the yard. He feels apprehensive but when he knocks on the front door Kirsty greets him with her normal smile. She invites him in as if it's the first time she's seen him then leads him into the living room. As he looks at the three people sitting there he hears the door close behind him. The older man stands up and comes towards him with a smile and an outstretched hand.

'Good to see you, Michael, I'm Sean Rollins and this is Ricky and Mairead. Have a seat.' They nod and smile at him as Rollins gestures to a chair that has been positioned in the middle of the room. 'How does it feel to be back home again?'

He wants to tell him that he doesn't think of this as his home but tells them that he's keen to get back as quickly as he can. With a sweeping glance he tries to take them in. Rollins is the oldest but broad shouldered and with a strong head of white hair that doesn't appear to have retreated a single inch on his forehead. He wears a neat herringbone sports jacket and grey trousers. There is something dapper about him unlike the man who sits beside him and who despite the suit looks untidy and uncomfortable in his chosen clothes. His shirt collar is grubby, his tie loosened and askew and there is a fine sprinkling of dandruff on his shoulders. The woman is the youngest – Madden estimates that she's in her late thirties – and she's wearing a dark trouser suit that advertises sober and serious efficiency.

'We understand, Michael, we understand that you've built a new life. And good luck to you in that. We'll be doing everything that we can to get you there as soon as possible but there are things we need to sort out before Monday.'

'Monday?'

'You're called on Monday. We always think it best to do things this way – fast, the way you want it, and no time to get nervous or worried about what's coming. Just let us guide you through this and it'll be done and dusted before you even know. All right, Michael?' He nods in reply and shifts uneasily on the seat. 'But we need to tell you that we understand that for you and for all of us things have moved on but there are some things that are still the same even though sometimes they get called by a different name. This is a new phase of the struggle, Michael, and even though some people might think it's a bit unfashionable to call it that, it's still a struggle.' He pauses as there is a knock on the door and when he gives the OK, Kirsty enters with a tea tray and pours carefully for the three of them. When she offers him a cup he declines. 'You want something stronger, Michael?' Rollins asks but he declines that too. As Kirsty walks past him to leave again she smiles at him and he nods quickly. 'So, Michael, where were we?'

'A different phase of the struggle,' he offers.

'That's right, that's right. We're all volunteers in that same struggle and we'll all be volunteers until we live in an Ireland that's finally free.' He raises his cup as if he's toasting that prospect. Madden turns his gaze to the man beside him who sits staring at him and sometimes angling his head as if he's about to draw him or measure him for a suit. 'Isn't that right, Ricky?'

'It's right, Sean. Just another phase of a long struggle. Michael, you've already played a part in that struggle and we're all grateful for that and mindful of what it's cost you. And now we need you to do one last thing and when you've done it your war is over. It's all over and you can go back to your life.'

'Mairead is going to leave us now,' says Rollins. 'She'll come in later and help with things, the words to use, how to present yourself – that sort of stuff. She's a bit of an expert in court appearances and the law. She'll be with you tomorrow.' At this she places her cup on the tray and lifting her briefcase leaves the room and as she passes him she pats him on the shoulder in a gesture of reassurance. He sits as the two men finish their tea and no one seems to be in a rush to speak but eventually Rollins puts his cup down and dries his mouth with one of the paper napkins.

'OK, Michael, let's give this a go,' Rollins says, crumpling the paper into a misshapen ball and dropping it on to the tray. 'What I want you to do now is think very carefully and remember very clearly and I want you to tell us everything about Connor Walshe. Everything, Michael. Leaving nothing out because this is very important. You understand? And whatever you say you can rest assured that none of your words ever leave this room. Now let's give it a go. Right from the very start, Michael.'

There is a relief in the telling. The thing that has pressed so tightly for so long against his inability to tell is being slowly released. Bit by bit. It feels like a magician's trick, an endless piece of string that slips out from where it couldn't possibly be. He's hesitant at first, stammers sometimes into a dead end, but they look at him with open faces and nod their understanding and he knows he shall never have this opportunity again, be able to tell this thing to someone who will listen to his words without judgement. There is a sense of freedom in it, a frantic relief that the secret stored for so long has finally been given its release. However as he gets to the end he hesitates again because he can't recall it without reliving the inseparable feelings that were bound up with it but he knows they don't want feelings, only the facts, the things that actually happened, and everything that did happen is lodged inside the crevices and hidden places of himself. His hands are shaking – he slips them under his thighs. He hears the quavering tremor in his voice and tries to steady himself. They will despise him if he shows himself weak, if he's less of a soldier, less of a man than them. And so he tells them it all, lets it pour out until there's nothing left except shock at his own words and a slowly unwinding wake of silence that gradually fills the room.

Rollins gets up and pats him on the back. 'You did well, Michael. Very well. He did well, Ricky, didn't he?'

'He did very well, Sean. No two ways about it.'

Rollins goes and sits down again. The two men look at each other and then stare at him. He waits for something to happen but no one speaks. There is the indistinct yammer of the television in the kitchen.

'Except, Michael, there are two ways about it after all,' Rollins says, leaning towards him on the chair. 'And that's not the right way, son.'

He doesn't understand. He goes to speak but his mouth is dry and inside he feels a barren void opening up. He mouths something but no words come out.

'It's all right, Michael,' Rollins says, 'it's all right, son.'

S TANFIELD WAKES EARLY AND after the lightest of break-
fasts takes his coffee to the small table and chair that look
out over the river. The river is a slow, almost motionless flow
of grey and everything appears monochrome and imprecise
like an old out-of-focus photograph. On the table sit two
letters, both sealed and stamped. He will post them as soon
as the hearing is over. One is his resignation and one a letter
to Emma. The resignation was the easier and the quicker to
write and in it he gave up any thought of disguising his
decision with a spurious claim to moral principle and instead
explained it by citing personal circumstances and implying
that health issues had arisen. It's possible they will know the
true reason but it's also possible that the photographs exist in
some underworld that never permeates the higher strata
unless needs must. He also feels a curious moral indifference
to the photographs themselves, the absence of any sense of
shame, and has looked at them only once before destroying
them. Despite it all, despite everything that has happened, he
felt only a strong curiosity about the girl and so she was the
one he focused on. She must have known, been part of it right
from the start, and yet when he studies those eyes he tells
himself that he can see nothing except what he hopes to see.

As he shredded them he wanted to hold to that belief and so he told himself that they used each other and there is nothing more to be said and no blame to attribute. Even now if there was a way he would take her with him when he leaves.

And perhaps he really is ill, perhaps he has imbibed too many of the poisonous spores that filter through the airways of this place. But soon he will be somewhere he can fill his lungs and breathe again. He thinks of his going as a period of convalescence, a time when he can refind his old vigour before entering some new round of his life that will provide him with better nourishment than this. Where he'll go he isn't sure but he imagines a flight to Geneva and a hired car to the French Alps – perhaps somewhere like Chamonix and a good small hotel or an apartment and some skiing. Perhaps even some late sun in Morocco and a riad in Marrakesh complete with courtyard and orange trees. He tries to find some consoling images that will fuel the day ahead but as he looks out on the water below he sees no spark of colour or sheen of morning light that might ignite his imagination. And he does feel unwell. His head is heavy and there's a gently rising swell of stress as he thinks of what stretches ahead. Once more he has to become a ringmaster in a three-ring circus and this is the day when he must perform better than any other day. He's probably ill and then he knows that what he feels, if such a thing can exist, is the withering of his heart and he's angry and bitter that he should suffer such a thing, that such a thing should be visited on him. He has no belief in punishment for sin, which he thinks of as only a convenient excuse for those too frightened to live, but this morning he feels diminished and irrevocably less than himself.

There are two swans on the river, their drifting whiteness bright badges in the lour of grey. After watching them for a moment he lifts the letter written to Emma. In it is the elegantly expressed lie that he did everything he could to help Maria Harper followed by the truth that he wishes his daughter and her unborn child everything good in the world. He tells her that he's resigning from the Commission and that he's going away for a while – it's a letter of farewell, a final letting go, and he rewrote it many times late into the night to try and get it right but even now is unsure if it's what he wants to say. Sometimes truth indeed has to be faced and he believes that there's only future grief if he doesn't accept that what Martine came to feel for him has been transfused into their daughter's bloodstream and silts her veins with a bitterness for him that no passing of time can assuage or ameliorate.

Stanfield stands and looks out for one last moment and then drains the last of his coffee before going to the bedroom and laying out his dark suit on the bed.

Fenton has slept badly, breaking in and out of a shallow, dream-filled sleep. Even Miriam's restraining arm stretched protectively over him had failed to calm him or restrain his constant search for respite. So in the morning he feels groggy and leaden in thought and movement. Miriam has collected his Sunday suit from the drycleaner's and it hangs from the top of the wardrobe door still in the polythene wrap. He hopes the shower will wake him and he takes longer than usual, turning slow circles of himself. When he comes out Miriam is already downstairs and preparing breakfast. The previous night when she asked if she could go with him he was almost angry that she should have even suggested it and told her that he's never let his job affect his home life and he's not going to start now. He'll go and do whatever's required of him and then he'll come home and it'll all be over for good. But as he sits at his breakfast he wishes it were the mountains he was going into where sometimes he can walk for hours and not see another living thing except a raven or a distant windblown sheep.

Just before he's due to leave Miriam kisses him and tells him everything will be all right but as he starts his journey he wants only to steer the car in the opposite direction or to be following Florian along the maze of trails towards his secret hiding place in the woods. What will become of the boy? How could he let him go? He punishes himself by insisting that there must be some way he could be brought out if only he had the ability to think of it. Once he finds himself looking in his mirror because for a second, just for a second, he thinks the boy is behind him in the car. A boy who wants to build bridges that span the widest rivers, a boy who can build what his imagination decrees, who learns things quickly. How can such a boy work in the fields, ploughing and hoeing every last one of his dreams away? He feels the bitter frustration of it rising up before him and darkening the days ahead. He tells himself he has to go back, that he has to find a way. And then he looks in the mirror again and this time it's not Florian but the blue eyes of Connor Walshe he sees. The eyes are more delicate than any other part of him. A light shade of blue, cleaner and lighter than all the things that cling sourly to him. The face and body are thin boned and thin ribbed. Even in the car he shivers against the wind that always seems able to stab through the skimpy layers of sportswear he dresses in and once more there's the smell that slowly permeates from him as if he's climbed his way into existence from some underworld. The memory of the boy courses through his consciousness even after he looks in the mirror and blinks his physical presence out of the car. He thinks of the final phone call – the spreading, thickening silence so tangible that he could feel it on his skin. Somewhere far beyond the reach of sight, beyond the reach of love, lies the boy's pale moon face. He thinks he hears him whimper like the way he did that first time. There's nothing he can do – it's too late now and part of everything that's too late to change with no way to alter the course of a trajectory that feels like a shooting star bursting through from another time, another universe, before it burns up and extinguishes itself in the hidden folds of memory. His phone rings and his heart kicks against his chest but he doesn't answer it and instead tries to shrug himself back to the moment by switching on the distraction of the radio.

When he reaches Police Headquarters he shows the pass that's been given to him and parks in the allocated space, then as arranged he meets his Federation adviser and his legal representative, George Anderson. Part of him thinks them unnecessary and if it weren't for the promise he made to Miriam he would dispense with them because he just wants to say his piece and be gone, let those who took the boy face the spotlight and acknowledge their guilt. When they greet him he's polite but restrained and after some last-minute detail about procedure they go to the unmarked car that waits with its driver and personal protection officer who's been allocated to him for the duration of the hearing and start the drive to the city centre. No one speaks and without knowing why he feels embarrassed to be in the car. The driver and the personal protection officer are both unknown to him and despite their quiet respect he knows he means nothing to them and they have no knowledge of the service he has given or the reputation he has. Once he tries to make a joke, say something that shows he knows what it's like on the inside, but in his own ears it only sounds like an embarrassment and so he sits in silence for the rest of the journey. As they reach the city centre Young turns to him and says, 'Don't get out of the car until Ross opens the door and stay close to him on the way in. Don't speak to anyone on the way in, especially anyone from the press, but if there's photographers or a camera crew, keep your head up and look straight ahead. Don't talk to anyone on the way out either – keep everything for the Commission.' The traffic has slowed now as they find themselves not far from their destination. 'At the start of the hearing George will make a request for your evidence to be heard in private. The Commissioner will have already consulted with the family and most likely they'll insist on it being public. It's a waste of time but it's important we keep making the point that we should be entitled to the protection of a private hearing. Isn't that right, George?'

George looks up from his papers, places them in his briefcase and nods, then says, 'And, James, try to stick to the outline we've gone over. Try to avoid wandering off the agreed outline. Least said is usually best. Cool, direct, factual. Sympathetic is good, of course. Don't splash names around or be led into offering opinions on things you don't need to have an opinion on. Everything has to be answered but sometimes the answer is you don't know or you don't have that information.' He drums his fingers on the hard surface of his briefcase. Fenton glances at it and sees it has a combination lock as if it contains valuables. 'It'll be over before you know it. A bit like the dentist's.'

'I've given evidence in courts before,' Fenton says.

'Of course you have,' Young says. 'And it'll not be a problem for you. Like falling off a log.'

'Except this isn't a court and that doesn't make things simpler but more difficult,' George says. 'No one has to be proved guilty. People have to admit their own guilt, put the truth in their own words, and when you're up there we don't have the normal protection of the law to fall back on. It can be an exposed place, James.'

313

'But we're here for you,' Young insists, shooting his colleague a critical glance. 'Shoulder to shoulder.'

Fenton turns his gaze away and watches the crowds on the pavements and for a moment envies their preoccupation with daily journeys and mundane rituals that he thinks now he would gladly exchange for the day that awaits him.

'Shoulder to shoulder,' Young says again, as if he believes that through their repetition the words might suddenly solidify in the air and form a protective shield around them.

Michael Madden looks at the dark suit on the bed. It makes him think of funerals and as he touches the material it feels as if on this coming day he must bury something. Just maybe that can be done but he knows the words he has to use will bury the future as well so he can't bring himself to put it on. Pulling his hand away he goes to the window and looks out on the morning. In the field the horses move languidly towards the furthest hedge, the flick of their tails the only sign of animation. When they get there they graze and then one lays its head across the other's neck. Why must he do this thing? Why does he have to pronounce judgment on himself? They'll listen and think he's walked away, clutching his amnesty, and not one of them can know the price he'll pay or the sentence he'll have invoked on his future. He thinks of Connor Walshe and the members of his family who'll be there staring at him and he hears a voice say that this is the price that has to be paid and that because they've had to wait so long to hear the truth they're entitled to interest. The payment of that interest they'll never know, never receive in their hands, but it'll be real enough.

He looks at his watch and sees that time's passing so he goes again to the suit. It feels, too, that if he's to put it on he'll immediately become someone else and it's followed by a

314

surge of self-pity which begins with him saying that he's not a bad person, that what he did was done in a different time and in a different world that's a far-off one he stumbled into accidentally, pulled into its orbit by forces beyond his power to resist. If there was any way to change what happened he would grasp it with both hands, whatever it cost him, but he can't bring himself to accept that what now seems like something that happened in a dream, or in a remote and distant land, should have the ability to destroy what he's built for himself. He thinks of parallel universes, of miscarriages of justice and cases of mistaken identity, because whoever he was back then bears no connection to who he is now. Nothing remains, not even the name, so let them do this thing to who he was then, but let who he is now walk away.

He thinks, too, of Arnie out on the lake in the early morning, almost hidden in the soft mist-laden wrap of light. He thinks of the big houses on its shore as they slowly burnish into life and their staff stoke the fires of the day ahead; the gardens that sweep down to the reed-ringed shore and from where their jetties reach out into the still sleeping water. Gardens that need men to manicure them. He knows he could make a success of it if only he's given the chance and that he'll work all the hours of daylight to make a go of it, break his back in the heat of the day. But he thinks, too, of the dying shopping mall and remembers the sad fragility of its dreams, the echoing emptiness of its stores and walkways. Perhaps all he's ever been is a dreamer and now it's time for dreams to fade into the inescapable examination of the reality this day will bring.

It's almost time. They'll be coming for him soon. They'll expect him to be ready. Downstairs he can hear the television in the kitchen and the sound of cupboards opening and closing. He goes to the window but the horses have vanished. The morning light has brightened and for the first time since he arrived there are traces of blue in the sky. He puts on the suit and then he sits on the edge of the bed and cries.

Stanfield takes his seat at the top table and looks down at the rows of people looking back at him. The public seats are not entirely full and the press benches have started to thin out, their initial interest in the proceedings having faded away after the first flurry of saturation coverage. He sees Maria Harper and her mother with their advocate but as far as he can tell, the other members of her family appear to have stayed away. Across the aisle sits the man he assumes to be James Fenton with the people he recognises as members of the police team. Matteo and Laura sit with other members of the secretariat. Outwardly everything appears as normal and he tries to reassure himself that in this, the final case he'll preside over, everything will go according to the script and it can be brought to a speedy and satisfactory conclusion. Then waiting until the clock signals the hour and after his nod to the ushers, the doors are closed and he rises to his feet.

'This morning we have come together to hear case number one hundred and seven, the case of Connor Walshe, and as with all hearings of the Commission I shall begin by asking everyone to stand in silent memory of all those who lost their lives in the conflict. This is an opportunity to show communal respect and in the short silence to prepare ourselves for what we are about to hear.' In the minute of silence he stares at the bowed heads and then sees one lift and look at him and it's Maria Harper and what's in her gaze he can't gauge and he bows his own head to avoid the steady fix of her eyes. 'Thank you. Please be seated. As always, too, I shall open these proceedings by briefly reminding you of their purpose. Firstly, we meet to give a voice to the victims of the violence, to remember those who have died or suffered and to try to help those who grieve to take the difficult and painful steps towards healing. Without this individual healing there can be no societal healing and without confronting our past in a spirit of reconciliation and understanding society can never build a better future. Secondly, we meet to try to initiate a process of healing through the establishment of truth and openness. Truth is vital if this society is to open itself to the possibility of communal atonement and bring closure to those whose suffering has been compounded by uncertainty and unanswered questions.' Stanfield glances briefly at his autocue but the words are lodged in his memory. 'Finally, in this search for truth we offer amnesty to those who appear before the Commission but I remind you that this amnesty is dependent on full disclosure and a full and truthful account of the incident for which they are seeking amnesty.' He finishes his required preamble by reminding everyone of the solemnity and dignity required by the occasion, asks that all mobile phones are switched off and informs them that it's an offence to make any visual or auditory recording of any part of the proceedings, but in accordance with the wishes of the Walshe family there are no reporting restrictions in place.

'I declare this hearing now in session and, as is customary, I begin by asking a member of the Walshe family or their chosen advocate to speak to us about their relative.'

Maria Harper stands and walks to the microphone at the front of the court. Her advocate, a young woman in a grey trouser suit and shiny black shoes, comes with her and stands at her shoulder.

'I am Maria, Connor's sister, and this morning I want to tell you about him.' Fenton stares at her – he doesn't remember ever seeing her before, finds it hard to connect her with the boy. 'When Connor disappeared he was fifteen years, four months and ten days old. Connor could always tell you exactly how old he was. Sometimes he sounded like a prisoner who could tell you exactly how long was left in his sentence but the reason Connor knew was because he couldn't wait to leave school. He didn't like school and, if I'm honest, school didn't like him much. He couldn't see the point of it and all he wanted to do was leave and get a job that earned some money. You see, there wasn't very much money in our family. Our father died just after Connor was born and things were never easy but my mother did her best to see we all got by.' She pauses and looks down at the bit of paper from which she's reading. Fenton shifts in his seat. He always thinks of the boy as solitary, detached from any family or social framework. He knew, of course, he had a family but until this moment it was always anonymous and irrelevant, part of his world about which he'd no need to consider.

'Connor was not an angel. In the year before he disappeared he had many problems in his life and he lost his way quite badly. He did some bad things, got involved in petty crime and ran a bit wild. I often think that the absence of his father was a big factor in this. We tried our best to keep him on the straight and narrow but it wasn't easy and maybe if he'd had a father to look out for him, things could have been different.' Her voice breaks a little and she pauses, gulping the air. The advocate puts a supporting hand on her shoulder. 'But Connor was capable of being a good boy – he could be kind to his mother, he could be considerate. Sometimes when the notion took him he could be funny. And what I want to say is that the people who took Connor, took away his chance to maybe find a better way in life, a chance to make something of himself.' She pauses again and sips some water. When she speaks her voice is wavering and higher in pitch. 'Whatever he did, or was supposed to do, he was only a boy, only a child, and this shouldn't have happened to him.'

She's crying now and the advocate is talking quietly to her. Stanfield asks if she'd like a short recess but she shakes her head and instead takes another drink of water. Fenton stares up at the stained-glass windows and feels his breathing becoming slowly shallower. He opens his jacket and sees a small purple ticket pinned to the lining. Without drawing attention to it he carefully unfastens the pin and slips both into his pocket.

'Would you tell us, Mrs Harper, about the events leading up to Connor's disappearance,' Stanfield says. 'In your own time, just when you're ready.'

She half turns towards him and then faces the front again. 'Connor disappeared on the tenth of May. It was a Thursday night. He had gone out about an hour after tea, said he was going down to the boxing club. We used to joke with him, tell him that he could be the next Muhammad Ali, but none of us really believed he did any boxing because he was skinny as a rake and his brothers used to tease him, tell him that the wind could blow him over. Afterwards one of the men who ran the club told us that he just sat and watched, liked to hang around, but despite trying to persuade him, he wasn't keen to give it a go. Always made excuses, said he'd no kit or he'd broken his arm a while back and wasn't allowed to until it properly healed – that sort of thing. But he did go there that night, messed around a bit with a punch-bag, acted the lig and then he was asked to leave. That was the last Connor was ever seen. He didn't come home.

'Connor often stayed out late and no one waited up for him, or paid much attention. Sometimes he ran the streets very late until he got bored or too cold and then he'd drift home. It was in the morning we realised he hadn't come in, that his bed wasn't slept in. But we weren't really worried because he'd stayed out a few times before and when Mother started to fret we told her not to worry, that she'd see him as soon as his stomach was empty or he'd run out of money.' Stanfield sees her glance at her mother for the first time and he follows her gaze. Her mother's face is wizened, worn old and pinched by each word she listens to. He looks at the back of Maria Harper's head. There are thin threads of grey veining the black and yet she can't be much older than Emma. He thinks of the letter for his daughter that nestles in his inside pocket and wonders how it will feel if he never sees her again.

'But he didn't come back. Another day passed and then we started to look for him. We went round the streets and places he might be hanging out, asked everyone we met if they'd seen him but nobody had. It was as if he'd vanished into thin air and then we checked the hospital and when another day passed we went to the police. Some of the family didn't want to involve them but my mother insisted and went to the police station herself. They took his details and a description but no one came to the house and we didn't hear anything from them for about three days. Then on the Wednesday two of them came to the house and told us that they believed he'd been abducted by the IRA.'

Michael Madden sits at the back of the hall and watches her pause and drink again. His companion plays with her rings, sometimes putting them on different fingers. She seems detached from what she's hearing and he wants to shake her out of the studied calm that mocks his own nervousness and the sickness starting to swirl round his stomach. For a second as Maria Harper pauses to compose herself he thinks of making a run for it but is stopped only by the knowledge that it would be a run with no destination and without any end and that's no good to him, because what he wants more than anything is to return to one place and never have to leave it or look over his shoulder again.

'It didn't make any sense to us. One of my brothers even laughed – that's how ridiculous we thought it was – and the police didn't say much or answer any of our questions so when they left we were more confused than anything. And then we thought that if it was true Connor must have done something bad that had got him into trouble and we were really worried that he'd get a beating or even worse they'd kneecap him. And my older brother, Brendan, went to some people he knew were involved but they wouldn't tell him anything and when he came back he didn't say much but we knew it wasn't good. And then that's when the whispering started and we had the word "tout" painted on the side of the house. My brothers got into fights in the street and after a while they wouldn't go out, as if they were ashamed to show their faces. We got a couple of letters that were disgusting and used the same word. Then we were told through a third party that Connor was touting for the police and that he'd confessed it all, that it was all on tape. We went to the Church and they intervened for us. The priest was told that because he was young he wasn't going to be harmed but that he wasn't allowed to come home, not for a while anyway, but that we'd get a letter from him saying he was OK and where we could get in touch with him. But it never came and then there was like this curtain of silence that fell round it and no matter how hard we tried we couldn't get anyone to admit they knew anything. My mother went to the police station every week and they treated her like she was reporting a lost dog, said they'd no further news but their enquiries were continuing and no one would say whether it was true that he was working for the police. How could Connor work for the police? What did he know about anything?'

For the first time her words are edged with anger and she's lifting her head high, throwing a challenge to the room.

'We didn't know how to use the media, didn't know how to get the right sort of help or the publicity that others have got, and the family split into different camps and things became very difficult. Time passed and we knew, even though we never said it, that he wasn't coming back but even though we knew it in our heads there was always part of you thought you'd hear the back door open and you'd look up and see him standing there. But it never happened and the years went by and still nobody was able or willing to tell us anything. But gradually we knew that we had to get him back, to give him a burial and try to move on with our lives, but even after the ceasefire no one claimed to know anything about Connor or where he was. It was almost as if he never existed but he did exist and he was my mother's son and our brother and we have a right to know, a right to have him back. A right to have him back with his family, back where he belongs.'

She folds her notes carefully and with the advocate patting her on the shoulders she walks back to her seat. Stanfield sees the straightening of pride in her walk, as well as her suffering, but he knows there's more still to come for her and, as he watches her resume her place and take her mother's hand, thinks that when it's all over she, too, will look back into the chamber with a white salted face, frozen in disbelief that truth has been both partial and incomplete.

Madden sits at the end of a row and as she returns to her

place he leans slightly into the aisle and looks at her, tries to remember her face, but there's no recognition and he wonders if it's because so much time has passed and then he's conscious of how long these people have stayed waiting for something that never came. His eyes flicker to the stained-glass windows and they make him think of church and suddenly he sees again the choir of black women pouring down the steps of the church in their white dresses, blossoming in the darkness like magnolias. He wants the warmth of those nights when the baked heat of the day lingers long after the light has faded. He wants to feel the burn of the sun on his back, to sit in the morning on the shore of the lake. There's a boat in the glass, the waves spuming up round its hull, but soon he knows it will be time for him to stand at the front and have the eyes of Connor Walshe's mother and his sister fixed on him and he doesn't know if he should try to look at them when he speaks or if he should try to stare ahead. He rehearses his words in his head, the words he's been given, and tries to calm himself, to bring his focus exclusively on what it is he has to say.

When Fenton is called, his name stripped of its former rank seems to hang naked in the air. However, as instructed, he remains in his seat and instead Anderson rises and approaches the bench where he makes a request that Fenton's testimony should be given in closed court because there is the possibility of state security being compromised and that Fenton deserves the protection of the court.

'As has already been established by the authority of the Commission,' Stanfield says wearily, 'only the defendants have the right to request a closed court and it is the expressed wish of the Walshe family that these proceedings remain open. In relation to the question of state security no public-interest immunity certificates have been presented and so your request is denied. Thank you, Mr Anderson. Now let Mr Fenton take the stand.'

As Fenton passes him Anderson gives him a smile of encouragement, then Stanfield begins by asking him to introduce himself and his connection with the case. He gives them his name and former rank, where he was stationed, the broad outline of his former duties and experience.

'And when did you first encounter Connor Walshe?' Stanfield asks when he's finished.

'I first came across Connor in January of that year. I can't remember the exact date but it was towards the end of January.' He glances involuntarily at the two women staring at him then continues, 'Connor was suspected of being involved in some incidents of petty crime – vandalism, making a nuisance of himself, that sort of thing. There were also some break-ins and his name was mentioned to us as a possible suspect.' He spares them the details – it's one of the few kindnesses he can give them. 'A boy fitting his description had been seen leaving one of the premises in question. We picked him up and informally asked him what he knew about it. Connor denied any knowledge of any wrongdoing and we let him go again. There wasn't enough evidence to charge him with anything so we gave him a word of warning and sent him on his way.'

'When did you hear he was missing?'

'The thirteenth of May. His mother reported Connor missing at the station.'

'And what were the results of your inquiry?'

'No trace of Connor was found. There were apparently no witnesses to what had happened or where he had gone. We did over two hundred interviews and did door-to-door but nothing to assist us was produced. At that particular time it was difficult to get people to talk openly or come forward

324

and that undoubtedly hampered the inquiry.' He glances down at Young and Anderson and they nod in encouragement. 'Some time later, certain sources supplied us with information that he had been abducted by the IRA and taken to a different location.'

'And did these sources say what had happened to him?'

'No, no one appeared to know. We conducted searches locally and further afield but without success. The police on the southern side of the border also conducted enquiries but equally without success.'

'And do you know the identity of those who abducted Connor?'

'I might surmise it was the work of the local unit of the Provisional IRA but I wouldn't be able to identify the actual people involved.' He stares at the back wall of the chamber. 'We had no specific information or intelligence as to who these people might be.'

'And what do you think happened to Connor?'

'Again I can't say but there must be a significant possibility that it was something serious.'

'Thank you, Mr Fenton,' Stanfield says but as he sees Fenton about to leave the stand, 'I think Mrs Walshe's advocate, Ms Clarke, would like to ask you some questions.'

Fenton stares at the young woman coming towards him and thinks she hardly looks old enough to be a lawyer. She stares back at him and he sees that in her hand she's carrying a cassette player. He doesn't understand and looks at Anderson and Young whose angled heads are almost touching and when they finish speaking to each other Young shrugs his shoulders at him then Anderson rises and says that it's expressly forbidden under the remit of the Commission to make recordings and he wishes to lodge the strongest objection to this breach of procedure.

'The purpose of this equipment,' she says, 'is not to make a recording that as Mr Anderson quite rightly points out would be a serious breach of procedure, but to play a tape relevant to the case.'

'I object,' Anderson says, still on his feet and looking flushed in the face and angry. 'We had no prior knowledge of this tape nor were we given an opportunity to listen to its contents.'

'Please come forward Mr Anderson and Ms Clarke,' Stanfield says in an obviously weary tone. Fenton half turns to listen to what he has to say. 'Mr Anderson,' Stanfield continues, 'can I just remind you that this is not a court and that it would be in everyone's interest if you could switch out of adversarial mode and concentrate on giving your best services to the establishment of a communal truth. Your client is not on trial. And, Ms Clarke, can you assure me that this tape is of legitimate concern to this hearing and relevant to our purposes?'

'I can, Commissioner, and believe it's an important part of the story of Connor Walshe.'

Stanfield glances to where Matteo and Laura are sitting. Matteo is nodding his head as if he needs encouragement to approve the playing of the tape. He looks at Ms Clarke who seems preposterously young, hardly older than the students he used to lecture, and tells her to proceed.

'This tape has been authenticated by Mrs Walshe and Connor's sister as being his voice.' She hands a piece of paper to Stanfield. 'Independent experts have also verified that the tape has not been tampered with in any way so with the Commission's permission.' She sets the player on the front desk and Fenton watches her press the play button. He grips the lectern a little tighter and tries to think of being in the van and anonymous miles of roads spooling endlessly in front of him. Of towns and cities glimpsed at dawn and still asleep. Of roads climbing over the mountains where thick swathes of trees border the broken and fraying edges of his journey. He thinks of sleeping on the pallet of clothes, his face close to the roof of the van, of Florian's house in the woods. And then into his futile attempts to fashion an escape from the terrible openness of the moment where he feels as if he's standing on an exposed plain devoid of any feature that might shelter, he hears the voice of Connor Walshe. And then he's transported once again, despite the resistance of his will, to all the places he heard that voice, the voice that is instantly recognisable, and there's the same pleading, the familiar edge of desperation that he heard in it the very first time, but this time there's no pretence of bravery, no attempt at bravado or aggression. The voice fills the chamber with its whimpering, broken stammer of words and it flows down through the rows of seats and laps round Michael Madden like the water laps and slurps round the jetty at the lake. He wants to walk away, return to the house and find Ramona sleeping in the bed, have her look up and then offer him the warmth of her embrace. Instead all he can do is fidget until Mairead rests her hand on his arm in a gesture that's meant to calm him and then she tells him to sit outside in the foyer and she'll get him when he's called.

Fenton leans his forearms on the lectern and keeps his eyes focused on the back of the chamber. 'And they said that they'd get me shot if I didn't tout for them. Said they'd put me in a car and drop me off where people'd be waiting for me to give me a head job.' The voice is high pitched and rising on a wave of breathless insistence, the fear its own lilting descant. On and on it tumbles from the player in a frantic scramble to find some exoneration, some hope of absolution. 'They give me money but hardly anything and I didn't do it for the

327

money but because I was scared and they kept saying what would happen if I didn't help them.' The voice beats against the walls of the chamber like some moth trapped in a tremble of confusion and looking for release. Stanfield looks down on the listeners and sees their eyes drop to the floor as a kind of collective embarrassed shame settles on the room because they know they're listening to the voice of a boy who's about to die and they know that their presence intrudes even all these years later and that their places should be taken by a priest or his family, someone, anyone, who will put a hand on his shoulder and tell him that everything will be all right. They want the tape to stop. They don't want to hear the rest about how Fenton gave him money to supply information, of the places they met. They want the tape to finish, to be able to loosen the coiling ligature of words that constricts and chokes their own sense of who they are and replaces it with a helplessness that pulls everything away from them like some sucking tide going out. And then it does. But the silence that follows the whispering final slither of words lasts only for a second and then there's the voice of a boy asking, 'Can I go home now?' And again when there's no answer, 'Can I go home now?'

The waiting area forbids smoking so Madden goes to the toilets and lights a cigarette. His hand is shaking and he stumbles over striking the match. He leans against the white-tiled wall and inhales deeply.

The clunk of the player being switched off is what everyone wanted but now to Fenton the silence is even more terrible than the words. Stanfield, however, feels a flicker of admiration for her sense of theatrics as Clarke pauses for maximum effect, resisting the temptation to speak while the voice still echoes in the four corners of the room. Fenton glances at Young and Anderson but for the first time they're not looking at him and he knows they've cut him loose, that no one's standing shoulder to shoulder.

'Isn't it true that Connor was working for you?' Clarke asks after a few moments have passed. 'Just as he claimed.'

'I didn't say any of those things to Connor.'

'With respect, Mr Fenton, I asked you if it was true that Connor Walshe was working for you, working for the police?'

'He didn't work for us. We didn't employ him in that sense of the word.'

'In what sense did you employ him then?'

Fenton considers before answering. He has no capacity for lying and no skill in choosing evasive words and he tells himself that if he's to try, it will mean throwing away some part of himself that's important to him, that it will damage the little legacy he has left from all the years of service he gave.

'In the fight against terrorism it was of crucial importance to gather intelligence. We needed that intelligence to try to protect life. People were dying – we had to enlist as much information as possible.'

'So you enlisted Connor?'

'We met him from time to time in the same way we met many people.'

'How many times did you meet him?'

'I don't have a record or an exact number.'

'Five or six? A dozen? About how many, Mr Fenton?'

'Perhaps half a dozen. I don't remember exactly.'

'And you paid him?'

'Small amounts of money. Not very much.'

'So what are we talking about? Five or ten pounds? More?'

'I think mostly about ten pounds.'

'Each time?'

329

'No, not always. Sometimes no money was paid.'

'And in return, Connor gave you information?'

'There wasn't much information. Sometimes I think he just wanted to talk as much as anything.'

She pauses and touches the cassette player with her hand. 'Connor said he was threatened, forced to supply information.'

'No one said those things to him. No one threatened him or said he was going to get shot.'

'So why do you think he said those things?'

'I would guess because he was frightened and because in the situation he later found himself in, he'd little choice about what to say.' Fenton stares at her. She looks no older than her twenties; about the same age as the young woman he met on the mountain that morning when the slopes of Donard were shawled in snow. That same day he fell on his descent. And what does she know except books and examinations that take place on paper? He feels a growing sense of anger and wants to tell her that every day he was examined by what he had to see and do and maybe that sometimes it was hard to know what the right answer was.

'Mr Fenton, you are aware of Connor's age?'

'Yes.'

'So you knew he was a child?'

It feels like he's falling now, powerless to stop himself, carried by a cold rush of water. 'Yes,' he says as he stares at her but sees neither fear nor hate in her face, only a calm resolution, smooth like the slabs of granite, but he can't let it take him and so he struggles against it, determined to break his fall. 'I don't think you understand what we were dealing with . . .'

'I understand that you were dealing with a child,' she interrupts, her voice flecked with the first trace of an impatient insistence.

'Ms Clarke, please let Mr Fenton finish what it is he wants to say,' Stanfield says.

'Unless you were there, unless you lived through it, you can't understand what it was like,' Fenton says. He wants to tell her what it was like to enter the bar after it had been sprayed, about the smells, the sounds, what he had to see. He wants to tell her about what fear feels like when it takes up residence in your stomach, about the heave and churn that accompanied the worst moments, but he doesn't have the words. He stares out at the gathered audience and tries even though he knows the attempt is doomed to failure. 'Things were falling apart, society was falling apart. When you reported on duty you never knew what was going to happen, what you might have to deal with. People were dying. Men, women,' he pauses, 'and children, too. We were in a war, things change in a war. Things happen that shouldn't happen.'

She lets him finish and her face is impassive but when she speaks her voice is calm and measured again. 'Forgive me, Mr Fenton, for interrupting you. Have you finished now?' There's no sarcasm in her voice, no condescension, nothing to help him hate her. But now there is one final thing that he wants to say. For the first time he looks at the boy's mother and sister. 'I want to say that I regret deeply what happened. I'm very, very sorry.' But their faces are closed to him and give no response or recognition to his words. He feels intensely cold now and desperate to return to his seat, to try and wrap some protective coat about himself.

'Thank you for that but I have a few more questions the family would like to ask.' He watches her walk back to her desk and look at a piece of paper then turn again towards him.

'Am I correct in saying that you, a senior officer in the RUC, induced a boy to engage in an activity, a relationship, that exposed him to the greatest danger?'

'Yes,' he says and his own voice is strange to him.

'And you would have been well aware of the fate of so-called informers?'

'Yes.'

'But you disregarded that knowledge.'

'Perhaps I thought . . .' He doesn't know what he thought and the words trail into silence.

'And, Mr Fenton, in the time you had this arrangement with Connor, did he supply you with any information that was of importance or helped you in your fight against terrorism?'

For a second he wants to knock the whole thing over and he hesitates, thinks of the last time he met the boy when his pale face came swooping out of the darkness. 'No.'

'So a boy lost his life for supplying no meaningful information to you in exchange for petty cash?'

'Yes.'

'The family doesn't have any further questions,' she says, then starts to walk back to her seat.

'I didn't kill Connor!' Fenton shouts at her back as something breaks inside him. 'I'm not the person who killed him.'

She stops in her tracks and looks at him for a few seconds but says nothing, then turns away and resumes her seat. Fenton stands on, trying to find a sense of balance, wishing he could reclaim his words. He stands until Stanfield tells him he can go and then he walks down the aisle and when he passes where Anderson and Young are rising to receive him he stares straight ahead before striding towards the doors of the chamber. There are too many people in the waiting area and he follows the signs for the toilets. Going to a washbasin he splashes his face with warm water then as he dries it with paper towels he catches Madden's reflection in the glass. Their eyes meet then both look away. The door opens and Young comes in.

'The car's coming to the front, let's get out of here,' Young says, shooting a glance at Madden.

'Give me a second,' Fenton says. 'I'll be straight out.'

'You all right?' Young asks, patting him on the back. 'It's over now.'

'Give me a second,' he says again and then after he sees him leave he goes into a cubicle to be sick, retching even when there's nothing left. When he comes back out there's no one there and only the slow drift of smoke indicates the former presence. He splashes his face again and knows that what he feels is the old unravelling of fear. Grasping the sides of the basin he steadies himself, carefully checks his reflection in the glass and then goes quickly outside.

Madden stands at the lectern and silently rehearses what it is he has to say. Perhaps being an actor delivering someone else's lines allows him to believe that they have no true connection with him. Perhaps he can speed them to their conclusion and be gone far from this place so he begins with a little pulse of confidence and he hears his voice grow stronger as it says, 'I joined the IRA when I was eighteen. Our home in Bombay Street had been burned by Loyalists in collusion with the security forces and I felt it was my duty to protect my area from such attacks. I was very young and inexperienced and I didn't think of all the consequences of that decision but I believed we were fighting in a war and I was fighting for civil rights and to free Ireland from foreign occupation. I had only been in the IRA a matter of six months when I became involved with Connor Walshe. I had never done anything other than drive a car on recon-naissance exercises and once as ordered I stole a car. That sort of thing. Small stuff. But then one night we were told that Connor was passing information about Republicans to the RUC and that he was to be lifted for questioning. This was a time when people were being lifted by Special Branch and abused in Castlereagh and other holding centres. It was also the time of non-jury trials and so anyone who assisted the security forces in targeting Republicans was considered a serious threat to their community and the movement as a whole.

'We were told Connor had been seen with a known Special Branch member of the RUC and that he had flashed money around that he'd been given so he was to be lifted and questioned about it. I drove the car for two other volunteers who are both now dead and I will not give their names because they can't come to speak for themselves but this is the only information I intend not to supply. Everything else I intend to tell as it happened.

'We picked Connor up after he left the boxing club. I kind of knew him to see and when he came out I asked him would he be interested in making some easy money and after he followed me to the car he was bundled into the back seat by the other two volunteers. I drove him the short distance to a house in Ardoyne and he was taken inside. A couple of hours later I was told that he had to be moved because there was a chance of police raids who we knew would be looking for him. I drove the car in which he was taken to a farmhouse in South Armagh near the border – I now know the name of the place but I didn't then and just took directions from a volunteer who we picked up in Newry.

'When we got there the volunteers questioned Connor but no one hurt him or abused him in any way. He was just a kid and he was scared. I was in the kitchen when most of it was happening. I had to make everybody something to eat. But he told them everything – the times, the places, what was passed on. And then they made the tape. He told everything on the tape that you heard. Afterwards there was a discussion about what was to happen next and the orders came through that in a couple of days he was to be returned to Belfast and there was to be a press conference and Connor would describe how he had been recruited by the RUC. After that he was to be allowed back to his family but advised to leave the area for his own safety. That's how it was and that's all that was intended to happen.'

The next bit is harder. He pauses and gathers his thoughts, tries to remember. 'We had to keep him in the farmhouse for a couple of days until arrangements were made in Belfast. We had to wait until we got a phone call saying that we were to bring him. Connor wanted to go home that night and got very agitated. We tried to calm him and tell him that everything was going to be all right, that he'd nothing to fear. But he worked himself into a bit of a state, crying and that, saying he wanted to go home. I got the job of looking after him most of the time. But I wasn't much older than him and it wasn't easy. I made him something to eat and he was sitting in the kitchen when one of the other men called me from the other room and in that second I was distracted Connor was out the back door and away. I went after him and I had a gun. I was frightened, frightened of screwing up on what was my first real piece of active service. Frightened of getting the blame for him making a run for it. I couldn't see him but I ran into the yard and headed towards the sheds. I went in the one with the open door – it was a kind of metal barn – and as soon as I was inside he jumped on me and we struggled. He tried to get the gun out of my hand and that's when it happened. The gun went off and the next thing Connor's body went limp and he fell back and collapsed. The other two arrived then but it was too late – he was dead. We panicked and didn't know what to do – it wasn't supposed to happen like this. I am truly sorry for what happened to Connor – it wasn't supposed to happen, it was never meant to end like that. It was a terrible thing, a terrible accident, and I feel deep regret for what happened. I wasn't much older than he was and I'd never hurt anyone or anything in my life. We tried to help him but it was no use – I think he died instantly. I'm truly sorry.'

This is what he's supposed to say and as Michael Madden stands at the lectern he knows that while he'll walk away with an amnesty, the self-admitted guilt of his words will be printed on records for ever and he knows, too, that when he releases the words they'll fly in directions that he's no power to control. He thinks of the look on Ramona's face when she saw him strike Eamon in the basketball game; he remembers that first time she squirmed instinctively away from his innocent touch; the way sometimes she whimpered in her sleep. And he knows as much as it's possible to know anything, that if he says these words he's finished without a single hope and that whatever piece of absolving paper they give him, he's destroyed for certain whatever future they might still have. He stands silent at the lectern and the faces are looking at him impatient for him to start. Then into the bitterness of his knowledge surges a sudden spin of anger and he's angry that they've brought him to this place, not just who he is now, but the eighteen-year-old who didn't know anything about anything and who could have maybe made something better of his life. He's angry that they used him and he's angry that they're still using him now. He looks at Connor's mother and sister, sees their sad scrutiny of him

336

and feels the intensity of their gaze, and he thinks of how long they've waited for the truth. Then he glances round the room at all the other faces staring at him and knows this is finally and inescapably the time and the place.

'My name is Michael Madden. I joined the IRA when I was eighteen. I joined because it was a good thing to do and because I thought it was the best way to defend my area from attack. My home in Bombay Street had been burnt out and there was nobody to defend us and that day had a big impact on me. So I joined the Provisional IRA and I thought it made me into somebody, I suppose it made me feel big. I didn't do anything big, however – I wasn't much more than a message boy. I did some driving and collected people and packages a couple of times. That's all. Small-time stuff. Then one night I was told that Connor had touted to the RUC, that he had been seen with a Special Branch man and was taking money from them. We were told to pick him up. I knew who he was but I'd never spoken to him or anything. We were told he was in the boxing club and when he came out I was told to approach him and ask him if he wanted to make some easy money. I did this and two other volunteers bundled him into the car. He was taken to a safe house in Ardoyne but after an hour or so a senior member of the brigade said he had to be moved because there would be police and army raids in the area. So I drove Connor and two volunteers to Newry where a man I believed to be a senior member of the IRA got into the car and with him directing we drove to a farm in South Armagh.

'There was no one else there except us and after Connor was taken inside I was told to park the car in one of the outhouses. When I came in Connor was crying and the man we picked up in Newry was shouting at him, calling him a tout and other things I don't need to repeat. When I came in the room I was told to get out and go in the kitchen and make some food. Connor was sitting on a chair and he was crying and shouting. So I went into the kitchen and as this was going on I tried to make a meal and all I could think of rustling up was toast and cheese and while I was getting this ready I could hear the voices shouting and shouting in the other room. There was a lot of screaming and then it went quiet. I was scared and wanted to be anywhere other than there but it was too late. Too late for all of us. The senior man came in and had his food and drank a cup of tea. Just like nothing had happened. And then he smoked a cigarette. Hardly acknowledged that I was even there. I was scared of him – there was something about him made you nervous to be around him. Then I remember that phone calls were made and at one point I was given the job of sitting guard on him and I was given a gun – it was the first time I had even held one. Connor was very quiet, his nose was bleeding and he had bruising on his temple and round his eye. He asked me what was going to happen to him and I told him I didn't know and I really didn't. Later one of the volunteers told me that they were going to make a tape of him admitting what he'd done. And he was told that when he'd made the tape he'd be taken back home and all he had to do was appear at a press conference and it would all be over. I was in the room when he was told that and I believed that's what would happen.'

Madden pauses and drinks from the glass of water. His hand shakes a little as he lifts it to his mouth and a droplet splashes on his suit. Suddenly he's aware that his voice and the words he's using sound intensely strange, as if he has reverted to an older language that has rusted unused and almost forgotten. He thinks of the rust that lined Lynch's fingers on the day he handed him the letter that brought him here.

'A couple of hours later a senior man from our own district arrived from Belfast. When he saw Connor there was a real bust-up with the guy we'd picked up in Newry. He was angry about the state that Connor was in and how he couldn't be put in front of the press looking like that. They went in the front room and there was a lot of raised voices and the one thing I heard was the Newry guy shouting that we were all fucking soft in Belfast and too interested in looking good to get our hands dirty, that we were users and not worth a spit in the wind. It went on like this for a while and there was obviously bad blood between them. The upshot was that Connor was to be kept there for a couple of days or so until he mended up and then he was supposed to go back and make his public appearance. Someone else – a woman – arrived and left in supplies and then left again. I didn't know much about cooking but somebody thought I did and I got the job of making cups of tea and bacon sandwiches. Endless cups of tea and sandwiches.

'Sometime around midnight and I'm not sure how Connor broke a small window and squeezed out of a space it didn't look possible to get through. He dropped down into the yard and when we came bursting out of the house he had disappeared in the darkness. There was a big moon and torches were brought from the house. After a while your eyes began to see better. So we split up and tried to find him. I went round the shed but there was no sign of him and then I heard shouting from the back of the house so I headed up there where there was a big orchard. I tripped and fell, cut my hand and then when I got near the back of the house there was one shot rang out. There were torches and I walked towards them and the two senior men were standing there and one held a gun in his hand and the light from one of their torches was shining on Connor and he was lying on the grass under a tree and I could see right away that he was dead. I'd never seen a dead person before but I knew he was dead. He'd been shot.'

He's told it and he isn't sure if he really has, or if he's only imagined the words coming out of his mouth, but it's no longer his voice he hears but the sobbing of Connor Walshe's mother and sister. He looks down to where Mairead is sitting and she's shaking her head very slowly at him and he looks away again.

'I'm deeply sorry for Connor's death and deeply sorry for the part I played in it. Soon after this I ran away and tried to make a new life in America but I've never forgotten what happened that night. It was a terrible thing and I regret more than you can ever know that I was involved in it.' He lifts the glass of water but his hand is shaking too much and he puts it down again. For a second the light coming through the stained glass seems to colour the water.

Francis Gilroy sits in the audience of the small studio theatre and watches the children perform. It's the showcasing of a cross-community creative-arts project involving three different schools coming together to produce a performance of dance, music and drama. It's the part of the job he likes best – going out and actually meeting people and children, seeing how funding decisions have been translated into creative results. The theme of the performance is 'Outsiders' and he sits with some of the teaching staff and the usual crowd of Department of Education inspectors, representatives of the Department of Culture and Learning, and arts practitioners and advisers. There are also parents present and the performance is going well. He watches intently as a group acts out a little drama involving migrant workers and racial prejudice, then a group of young teenagers performs a dance that involves papier-mâché masks and beating drums. He thinks it's all very clever and imaginative and it makes him feel better, as if there's value in what he's been doing, as if all the endless meetings and welter of paper actually have some connection with the real world. The children are full of energy, animated by the experience of public performance, and they come close to the edge of the stage and Gilroy is able to see the painted artwork of the masks while behind the dancers the drums pound out an insistent beat.

Gilroy shifts in his seat. Perhaps the performance has gone on slightly too long. He's finding it harder to keep focused and increasingly, although he tries to stop them, his thoughts turn to the hearing that he knows is going on at this very moment. Ricky and the others have come good for him. He knew that when it came right down to it they'd look after their own. It's what they do, it's what they're good at. That's why they've never fractured, never split into civil war even though, God knows, there were times when they came close. Despite this, he still wonders what's happening in the chamber and if Michael Madden has done his bit yet. On the stage a boy stands alone in a white light while behind him are arrayed frozen scenes from his life, so there's a family tableau, a bit from school, a group of his friends and each in turn is acted out before freezing again. It's a play about teenage suicide, about people not ever really knowing what's going on inside someone else's head. So they think he's all right, that he's a real laugh, and all the time he's crying inside.

Connor Walshe cried a lot. He cried so much that it drove Rafferty mad and he'd want to hit him again. He'd already hit him too much and they'd have to wait until his face healed up. Rafferty had had a younger brother killed six months earlier and he was raw as hell, hard to work with, hard to talk to. But he keeps trying. You can't kill him because he's too young and it would be a complete own goal, a complete fuck-up, and even you should be able to see that. You have to see the bigger picture, play with the head. But no, no, so it was, That's all you boys do now – talk complete shite – and you've gone soft, Gilroy, too keen to get yourself into a suit and out of the field. And on and on and Rafferty looking down his nose because he thought that the border brigade were the real men, the ones who held their ground and didn't compromise, didn't go behind backs and look for deals, because they'd marked out their terrain, claimed the land back so that the only way the Brits could move was in fucking helicopters, and if they'd only get them land-to-air missiles they wouldn't even be able to do that. And if they let this worthless piece of shit go who'd touted and squealed like a pig then they were finished because every bit of scum would think they could do the same and walk away and his brother, what about his brother? There were people in the struggle giving everything and there were others begging like dogs for crumbs off the table and if Gilroy didn't want to get his hands dirty then he should get out of the way. Listen, Rafferty, he'd said, you follow orders like we all do but it was fuck the Belfast orders and this is a war not some kind of picnic. On the stage the boy walks into the white spotlight and looks around him and all the groups come slowly to life and wave to him as if they're calling him to join them but he turns away and it looks as if he's in a dream or a trance and he stretches out his own hands but it's as if there's something separating him from all the others who care about him and then the lights go slowly down. Dark night sky and cold so that when they ran their breath streamed in front of them and Rafferty calling to get torches and splitting up and running in blind circles and pausing to listen and listen and then it's Rafferty's voice and he's in the orchard behind the house and then

342

there's a gunshot, please God no but it's a gunshot, and the torchlight shows the gun in his hand. And the boy is sprawled on the ground with a bullet wound in his head and twigs and rotten apples round it and Rafferty is standing looking down at him and whatever was inside him has drained away and he doesn't say anything and so he gives him the gun without saying anything or resisting and for a second he wants to shoot the bloody fool but as the others arrive he takes control and tells them to get the black plastic out of the barn they use for baling and cord and wrap the boy in it. And then Rafferty walks back to the house and leaves them to get on with it and the torches make the plastic shine like moonlight on thick black water as they parcel him up.

Gilroy starts as the audience breaks into loud applause. He gulps for air, clenches his jaw tightly with his hand. The cast is bowing and the clapping rises into a crescendo. Some of them are standing and as he lumbers to his feet his seat tips up noisily behind him. It's his turn now and as arranged he makes his way to the stage where a microphone has been hastily set up and he waits until the applause fades away before he starts to speak.

'I'm sure you'll agree with me that we've been privileged to see something very special today. So much talent, so much creativity, and I think all the young people who participated today and all the teachers and artists who were involved in putting the project together deserve the highest praise, and let's not forget the parents either who have given so much support to their children and the project. The theme of outsiders was highly relevant and provides us all with a lot to think about. And as we look to the future we want to use the talents of our children to be the foundation of an inclusive society in which there are no outsiders any more but everyone finds an equal and respected place. So once again

I'd ask you to show your appreciation for these wonderful young people who give us all hope for the future.' As he walks off stage there is a new burst of clapping and he stretches out his arm to signify that it's directed to the children.

'There is an important question that now needs to be asked, Mr Madden,' Stanfield says and Madden turns his face sideways to him that's blanched of all colour. 'Are you able and willing to help locate the body of Connor and see it returned to his family?'

'I am and I've already prepared a sworn deposition that gives every detail I can remember as to the location.'

Stanfield looks at the Walshes' advocate who nods to indicate she's finished and so he tells Madden he can resume his seat but as he steps away from the lectern someone calls his name. It's a woman's voice and Maria Harper is on her feet and she calls his name again.

'Michael, will you tell us now who killed Connor?'

Her voice is high and splintering. Madden stops and looks at her. He glances at Mairead who's also getting to her feet and is about to speak but it's not Mairead or even Maria Harper that he wants but Ramona with her womb full of his child and to have a chance of getting them back he can't hold any part of this thing any more. It's been part of him too long and he has to rip its corrosive heart out of where it's lain hidden all these years.

'Francis Gilroy. Francis Gilroy killed Connor Walshe.'

Stanfield blinks his eyes and blows a thin stream of breath. The court has ignited into a flare of noise and already journalists are scampering from their seats, phones in their hands, their momentary pretence of dignity disappearing as they start to shove and push each other aside in their haste to

344

make for the door. He calls for order, reminds everyone of the need for calm. And then he almost smiles. The best-laid schemes. There's nothing he can do now, it's out of his control, and Maria Harper is still on her feet and Matteo's almost bursting out of his seat and the whispers are growing louder so slowly he rises and stands waiting until there's perfect silence and then with a curiously light and pleasing sense of recklessness, of flying close to the sun, he says in a loud and steady voice, 'The Commission for Truth and Reconciliation calls Francis Gilroy.'

S WEENEY'S PHONE RINGS AS they're crossing the foyer of the building and about to leave but it's a phone that's always ringing and Gilroy walks on without him to the exit door. Suddenly he steps into a scrum of people – at first he doesn't know who they are but there are voices calling him and tape recorders pushed close to his face and cameras ricocheting with light and the ambushing voices are shouting about Connor Walshe and because they're all shouting at once he doesn't understand what it is they're asking him and then in the confused babble he finally hears the question and in reply he shakes his head and looks for Sweeney. A van is pulling up at the kerb and he sees it's a television crew and someone is pulling at his sleeve but then at last it's Sweeney's voice in his ear shouting at him to get into the car and say nothing, not a single word, and Marty's opening the door and shoving people aside as he's bundled into the back seat and then they speed off with squealing tyres.

'Where to?' Marty asks and at first Sweeney tells him just to drive but then says to take them straight to Gilroy's home.

'What happened?' Gilroy asks and when there's no immediate answer repeats the question.

'Madden said you pulled the trigger,' Sweeney says as he turns on his seat to see if they're being followed.

'What the hell happened? You told me everything was OK.'

'I thought it was. I don't know what's happened.'

'Why would he do this?' Gilroy asks, staring at Sweeney as if he thinks the answer will be printed in the lined whiteness of his face.

'I don't know, Franky, I really don't know. All I know is it's a total bollocks.'

'It's a total fuck-up. I expected better than this,' Gilroy says then slumps back in the seat and rubs his closed eyes with his finger and thumb. It feels as if the lights from the cameras are inside his eyes and then he opens them and blinks. 'I need to ring Christine and the boys,' he says, searching in his pocket for his mobile phone, but remembers he's left it on the dresser at home. 'Best they hear it first from me.' Sweeney offers him his but then realises he doesn't have the numbers.

'We'll have you home soon,' he tells Gilroy. 'You can phone from there.'

We'll have you home soon. It sounds to Gilroy that the words make him an old man found wandering the streets, or some kind of ill person being conveyed to his final resting place. And then he understands the significance of what's happened.

'Am I called?' he asks, already knowing the answer.

'Yes,' Sweeney tells him as he switches off his mobile.

'It's bad then?'

'It's not good, Franky.'

'How bad?'

'We'll have to wait and see,' Sweeney says, turning his head away to look out at the city streets. 'Someone must have got to him.'

'Ours or theirs?'

'I don't know, I just don't know. He looked sound, there's no way we could have seen this.'

'It's all over when you're not sure if you've been screwed by one of your own or the Brits,' he says, pauses for a moment while he angles himself towards Sweeney then says in a lowered voice, 'For what it's worth, I didn't kill the boy.'

'We all did what we did. We don't need to talk about it.'

'Ricky, I want you to know I didn't kill the boy. I didn't kill him and I didn't want anyone else to kill him.'

'We shouldn't talk about it now, Franky. We shouldn't talk about it now.'

'And I'll have to appear?'

'There's no way round that. We'll work out the right things to say. We'll say it's an attempt by the securocrats, by the remnants of the RUC and those opposed to the process to damage it, we'll say whatever it is we have to say. But it's a bollocks, Franky, no two ways about it. Madden looked sound, like we could depend on him. I don't understand.'

Sweeney goes on talking but Gilroy turns his face away from the flow of his words and stares out as the streets gradually become the ones he thinks of as his own but they bring no sense of security and instead he has to blink away his breath streaming before him as he runs, a boy with his head bruised and damaged like rotting fruit and wreathed by twigs and last season's windfall apples. Whatever happens now he knows it's over. The idea he once played with has come for him and it's no longer dependent on what he wants. They'll stand by him – they never give up their own – he knows that, but whatever happens he's damaged beyond repair. He knows it and the whole world knows it and as soon as a respectable time has elapsed they'll pension him off, find him some new backroom job, or say his health has necessitated his retirement from public life.

Sweeney's still talking, trying to reassure him as much as possible, trying to absolve himself of the blame, but he doesn't blame him. He just wants him to be silent now, to let him finish his journey in quiet. They pass a mural with a picture of a British soldier and the slogan that says it's time to go and for the briefest of seconds he smiles. A time for peace. He closes his eyes and tries to shut out Sweeney's voice and then he thinks about the phone calls that he has to make and bowing his head the car is suddenly filled with his own silence.

M ADDEN HURRIES FROM THE building. He knows he doesn't have much time and he's lucky enough to catch a taxi almost immediately. Luck is what he needs now if he's to get out of this place and where he needs to be. It's a risk going back but as he gives the taxi driver the address he's lodged in his memory, he tells himself that he can make it. What will happen to him if he stays is a confused tangle of possibilities but what he's certain about is that these are people who don't like to be crossed and he puts no confidence in talk of new eras and rusting guns. So he urges the driver to go as quickly as he can and tells him there's a plane that has to be caught and when the driver tries to engage him in conversation he makes it obvious that he's not interested in talking.

He should feel lighter having cast off this thing that's festered inside his head for so long but instead there's only a sense of shame that the world knows what he's held so carefully in secret and as they pass strangers on the pavements and drivers sitting in their cars, it feels as if he's been branded with it for all to recognise. And it suddenly strikes him that there'll be no casting off, no simple putting behind him, that what he said will journey with him wherever he goes, and all he's done is allowed it to emerge whole and completely formed into the light. And when Rafferty comes and sits in the kitchen for his tea like a workman taking a break from some bit of house repair, there's blood on his knuckles. The gun sits on the table beside his plate and it must be his imagination but it's as if there's a cold metal smell from it, perhaps of oil, but something that jars and seems out of place on the table and in a kitchen. When Rafferty holds the big mug of tea his knuckles fastened to the handle are red and broken skinned and when he's finished he smokes a slow cigarette and says almost nothing to him as if he's below his notice, and he smokes it as if he really enjoys each second and has no thoughts other than the satisfactions of the moment.

There's little traffic to slow them and he thinks of driving Ramona back from the beach, of how it felt to be taking her home and see her sleeping at his side trusting him to bring her safely there. And he longs for that unravelling ribbon of houses and businesses, those disconnected places where everything exists in its own space and nothing has to overlap or cramp into lives that endlessly intertwine until they rub each other raw. The world he sees from the taxi is small and bitter like the tight clench of a child's fist and he wants to be gone from its reach and never come back so when they begin to climb out of the city he doesn't look back.

The house looks just as he left it and he tells the taxi driver that he's just collecting his bag and that he'll only be a second but as he rings the doorbell he feels frightened. He hears voices before it's opened and then it's Kirsty holding open the door and her face is how he thinks his must look, and it makes him angry that people have to feel this way.

'You really screwed up, Michael,' Downey says. 'You've really shit in the nest.'

But he doesn't answer and brushes past him and up the

stairs to his room. His bag is already packed and he grabs it and heads back down the stairs.

'Hold it right there,' Downey says as he slams the front door shut and bristles himself into his full height. 'I've been told you're to go nowhere, Michael son. They're on their way and it sounds like you've got a lot of explaining to do. Kirsty, go and tell the taxi to clear off. Pay him and tell him he's not needed now.'

'Don't do that, Kirsty,' he says, 'because I'm out of here.' But as he steps forward he's pushed in the chest. He looks at Kirsty and she's turning from one of them to the other.

'Kirsty, do it now.'

'I need to get the money,' she says and goes into the kitchen.

Madden weighs up his chances but the hall is narrow and the door is blocked by a bigger man who looks securely wedged against it so after a second he says, 'OK, I'll wait,' and he turns and walks slowly into the kitchen but as he's followed he suddenly swings his bag in Downey's face. A raised arm parries it from a full connection but it still catches him on the side of his head and momentarily knocks him off balance but as he tries to rush past him Downey reaches out a long arm and catches him by the shoulder then shoves him back into the room. Against the weight of Downey he stumbles backwards and hits the edge of the table as his opponent sees his opportunity and presses him back until he's bent over its top. He's pinned down and Downey's face creases in a smile as he secures his hold on him and one hand tightens round his neck.

'Going nowhere, Michael. Not until you've faced the music. And then we'll say where you're heading. Kirsty, don't just stand there – for frig's sake get the money and get rid of the taxi.'

Out of the corner of his eye he catches her hurrying past and then as he feels Downey's fingers press into his neck she's there standing behind them and he glimpses her over Downey's shoulder and thinks it's the end. It's not Downey but she who's going to finish him off and he blinks his eyes in fear as the carving knife moves towards him and when he opens them the knife is pushed tight against Downey's windpipe and her other hand is pulling his head back by his hair to meet the knife's sharp caress.

'Let him go, John, let him go.'

'What the fuck . . . Are you off your head?' Downey's eyes roll back white but he holds himself motionless.

'Let him go now or I'll slit your throat from ear to ear, so help me God I will.'

For a moment Downey doesn't move a muscle and then Madden feels the pressure on his neck slowly release and he slides out from under him and going behind him he puts his hand over hers and carefully takes the knife without moving it from its position. Downey goes to speak but he tells him to be quiet and presses the knife tighter against his skin. All his anger now is in his hand and it trembles under the intensity of its surge.

'In the utility room,' she says and at first he doesn't understand but she points with her hand and he starts to sidle Downey slowly forwards, a shuffling step at a time. She goes before them and he hears the rattle of keys in her hand then when Downey tries to speak again he whispers, 'Don't tempt me,' and lets the knife angle a little as if it's feeling for the perfect place. At the doorway he shoves him into the small, narrow room and as Downey stumbles forward she slams the door and turns the key in the lock. Almost immediately there's a rush of curses followed by violent kicks against the door and then they stand looking at each other as if neither of them can fully understand what it is they've done until she says, 'Take me with you.' He hesitates and she says, 'Anywhere,' and he nods as the door thuds and vibrates with Downey's attempts to kick it down then tells her to grab a bag and a passport but to do it very quickly. He hears her frantic footsteps on the stairs, the crashing of drawers, and he stands with the knife in his hand and feels the rush of adrenalin flooding over his fear.

She's back in an almost quicker time than he could imagine possible and as the door begins to slowly buckle they're out of the house and into the taxi. They hold each other's hand in the taxi and when she starts to shiver he puts his arm round her and tells her everything will be all right. That everything will be all right. And as they head for the airport and the first flight out of the place to which he knows he'll never return, he closes his eyes and thinks of the lake, tries to remember how each morning the earliest light begins to shape and burnish the surface of the water into some new shimmer of life.

As FENTON DRIVES UP to his house and parks he's glad that Miriam's car isn't there – he doesn't want to talk, doesn't want to go over what's happened even though he knows that in a short while his words will be in the brightest of spotlights for everyone to read. The taste of his sickness lingers in his mouth and he wants a drink but as he switches off the engine he sits perfectly still and holds the steering wheel with both hands. He wishes that he were about to set off on another journey, drifting once more past sleeping towns at dawn, on motorways in the soft cocoon of dusk, on mountain roads that traverse thick swathes of forest, and all where he's unknown and no more visible than a grain of sand on the world's shore. And what's the greatest trick of them all, the very best bit of magic that he wants to learn, but to make someone disappear? He'll go away; now is the time. He'll go away, disappear, and let it all play out without him – somewhere far away that'll take him but not judge him.

He'll be an embarrassment to those still serving, part of their past that they want to shed like some mottled skin. And how would any of them ever know what they'd do until they'd stood where he had? Do they really think it's possible to sit in civilised comfort and complacency and judge a man who's facing a furnace, who every day feels the flames flicker against his face? He's been used and spat out, pensioned off with every other inconvenient legacy of the past. But even though he tries he can no longer summon the protection of anger and what he feels is something opening up inside him as if all the high places are falling away and he's got nothing stretched out in front of him except a great expanse of open plain where he's exposed to the rising heat of the sun and no matter how far he walks there's no sign of reaching any destination.

He gets out of the car and thinks he's going to be sick again but it passes and then he's inside and his fingers are punching the security code to a house that feels emptier than he's ever known it and its silence is heavy and layered like the thick settle of snow. He goes to the kitchen and takes a drink of water, swirls it round his mouth then spits it out. The phone rings but he ignores it and then after it's fallen silent he goes upstairs to the bedroom. For a second he thinks of trying to fall into sleep but he knows the phone will ring again and that people will want to speak to him, some for good reasons, some for bad ones, and instead he goes to the wardrobe and opens the little safe that sits on the top shelf and takes it out. He hurries out to the car – he doesn't want to meet Miriam returning from her father's. He doesn't want her to see him because he thinks that if she sees him now she will see a change in him because, in some way he doesn't fully understand, he will look different to her. And he doesn't want to have to answer the questions that she will surely ask. He doesn't want to answer anyone's questions ever again.

He drives slowly into the Mourne Mountains as already the light begins to slip away, leaving their contours smudged with a vagueness that gradually smothers their definition even as he draws closer. He follows the main road skirting their edge and then cuts inwards down narrower ones bordered by mountains and forest until they bring him to the car park at one of the reservoirs. There are no other cars and the picnic tables sit forlornly empty as a fine rain starts to spray across the choppy stir of the water. A crow with its wings spread for balance is perched on the edge of a yellow rubbish bin and scavenging its contents. It's a silent place and as the light fades it pulls the mountains closer, their rocky outcrops smeared into the sky's greyness. Occasionally the white specks of sheep stutter across the lower slopes and at intervals dark shafts of birds spear the lowering lour of sky. He flicks on the wipers to keep the windscreen clear – it seems important to see it all, to take in everything that he won't see again – but after a while they beat like a drum in his ears and he has to turn them off. He wonders what it must be like to sleep in a forest, to sleep in a secret place that no one else can find. The gun is cold in his hand as he slides it out of the black leather holster. Never in thirty years has he ever fired one in earnest. Never in thirty years has he even needed to point it. Everything was secret, everything was somewhere else and he arrived at the places where they'd been used only in time to see their results, the human debris discarded and blanket covered. Everything was falling apart, breaking up in front of their eyes, and they were supposed to work some miracle, to hold it all together when it was hard to hold yourself together. It couldn't be done, things got broken and damaged. Things merged into one another the way now the sky and the water are a grey mirror of each other with only the little wind-stirred spurts of white signifying which is which.

This is the way it was when Connor Walshe's white face came swooping out of the gloom, running with his excited little litany of names, of what he'd heard and what he'd seen, bringing his capture home to the nest, full of his own importance. Gilroy's name among them. Now Fenton believes that's why he was never to be a father, because one day he would kill a boy. Not only destroy one boy, but two. Two boys who thought he would look after them and tried to shelter inside his protection. So what does it matter if he meant them no harm? It's right that he's come to this place and it feels now like the bleak and barren heart of the world. His hand tries to caress the handle of the gun but its cold metallic reality resists his attempt. He wants it to be part of his body, for it to snuggle warmly against his skin, even for a second, but as he slips off the safety catch he feels only its scorn. The glass in front of him is steamed with his breath, shutting out the view. He raises the gun and holds it to his temple. He holds it a long time until his hand is perfectly steady and then he sets it on the seat beside him. The car is cold – he switches on the engine and makes the demister blow the windscreen clear. Then as the finest of rains slants in squally flurries across the glass and dimples the water stretching before him, he presses his fingers to the temple where a moment earlier the barrel of the gun had nuzzled and tries to still the spreading tremble of his fear.

S TANFIELD FEELS NERVOUS AS he enters the apartment
block. He glances back to see Beckett driving off but then
shrugs off his sudden squirm of apprehension. What happened was outside all possibilities of his control and certainly
not in the anticipated script. Of course they could destroy
him with the photographs but he knows that this would be
an act of spite and that they are unlikely to waste what power
they think they hold over him out of personal animosity, well
certainly not Walters – he's less sure about William. No, they
will come back again with other requests and to do that they
need to hold their trump card in reserve rather than play it
wastefully. And of course he will tell all parties that he did
everything inside his power to propagate whatever version of
the truth to which they chose to adhere. He was powerless in
the face of the outburst, as shocked as anyone – not by the
claim but by the fact that it found a voice from the same side.
The only thing nobody yet knows is that he has an escape exit
of his own and although he hasn't yet posted his letters he
will do so in the morning and then at the first opportunity
he'll be gone and off the public stage and out of public life for
an appropriate period, then when he decides the time is right
to make a return he'll limit himself to backwater stuff.

Anything will do to keep the wolves from the door. Perhaps even a little lecturing might do the job and he's started to think that he should rationalise his assets in a couple of years, sell his increasingly valuable London home and buy a property abroad. Somewhere in the sun, somewhere it will warm the marrow of his bones and slow his decline into old age. Perhaps it's the heat of the sun he needs to stir the flame of his being, to keep him alive in his body and his mind.

He tells himself that if he were to stay any longer in this midden of a country there would be only a slow death as he dwindled and withered away, starved of all the things he needs to sustain himself. So there's a new resolution in his step as he enters the apartment, as always switching on the secondary lighting that softens the sense of emptiness, and invites human voices to speak to him by playing his music. It's a favourite – Tippett's 'Rose Lake' – and he pours himself a glass of red wine and goes to the seat overlooking the river as the music begins to swell into life. And everything seems better because he knows that there won't be many more nights spent here and that to gather up his possessions and be ready to leave could be done in less than an hour. He won't be leaving empty-handed because as well as the handsome salary he's already accrued he's gathered enough experience to write his book if he so chooses. And in the ledger's credit column is also the fact that he's seen Emma and if he hasn't absolved himself of her blame for what happened to Martine, he did get to see her and a channel of communication, however fragile and faltering, was established.

He sits by the window and watches the amber lamps on the other side of the road shed their yellow light on the dullness of the evening. On the edge of Europe, sometimes he thinks this place gets the dregs of light, the left-over luminosity from brighter worlds. Blue skies are what he needs now, some warmth on the skin. He sips the wine and lets the music wash over him so when the phone rings it's an irritation that he thinks of ignoring but then reluctantly he gets up and answers it, the glass still in his hand. But he doesn't recognise the voice and then he understands it's Alan the son-in-law he's never spoken to who's talking about Emma and he grips the glass more tightly in the fear that this call is going to spill some terrible news about his daughter. He's not listening to what he's about to be told and asking the question, 'Is she all right?'

'She's fine. She's fine and the baby is fine.'

'The baby?'

'She had it this morning at eleven o'clock. A boy. He came a bit earlier than expected but he's fine. Everything went well.'

'And how's Emma?'

'Tired but fine.'

There's a pause and they don't know what to say to each other so he tells the son-in-law he's never met that it's great news and he's delighted and then there's another awkward silence and to break it he asks what hospital she's in. He knows now they're both thinking the same thing so he takes a deep breath and asks.

'I think that would be all right,' he's told.

'Thanks,' and then for the first time he uses his name and says, 'Alan, I really appreciate that.'

'That's OK.'

Then the call's over and he sets the glass of wine down beside the phone and thinks for a moment, trying to work out if the caller was just too embarrassed to say no or if she might really want him there, and he doesn't know any of the answers but it's one last risk he's willing to take. He calls Beckett and apologises profusely for the inconvenience then hears his own voice laden with pride tell him, tell Beckett with whom he's never had more than a second's emotional engagement, that he's just heard his daughter's had her baby and would there be any chance . . .? Beckett congratulates him in a typically non-committal way and says he'll pick him up in twenty minutes. In the background he can hear children's voices and he apologises again.

After he puts the phone down and although he knows he can't be after a single glass of wine, he feels a little giddy as a confusion of thoughts loosens and swirls round his head. He's a grandfather but he immediately jettisons the word with its connotations of grey-haired, rocking-chair senility and instead thinks of the child and suddenly he realises he doesn't know his name or what his birth weight was. But they're both all right and that's all that matters so he hurries to the bathroom and freshens his appearance, changes into new clothes. In less than twenty minutes Beckett has arrived as he rushes to the door then realises that the music's still playing but he leaves it on and as he's going out he remembers the title. Flowers! He needs flowers but can't think where they might be got at this time and after thanking Beckett he tells him what he wants so they stop at a large garage on the way to the hospital. His heart sinks when he sees the garish choice available, where everything's some artificial, lurid colour and every tone separates them from the slightest affinity to what flowers should be. He looks at Beckett and shrugs his shoulders then in desperation picks ten bunches and with his driver's help carries them inside and disregarding the queue forming behind him points out the couple of flowers he wants from each and gets the assistant to make a new bouquet of these, discarding all the rest. It's less than he would have wanted but it's the best he can do under the circumstances and as they drive off he tries to improve the arrangement.

The hospital doesn't please him either. If only it had been possible he would gladly have arranged somewhere private that doesn't look as if it's in need of redecorating and that presents a more aesthetically pleasing environment in which to bring a child into the world. He walks along the cream-coloured corridors with their scuffed floors and plastic swing doors and rubs his coat where the stems have dripped water. But despite it all there's a feeling of pride in his steps that helps control his growing nervousness. But what if her husband's apparent affability is to be replaced at worst by his daughter's refusal to see him or even at best her studied indifference? He has little time to ponder the different possibilities because he quickly reaches the wing where he knows his daughter is and he looks with concern at the flowers again as he starts to tell himself that they look tawdry. But Emma never liked ostentation or what she considered the show of wealth so ironically perhaps he has made the right choice. He asks a nurse where he can find his daughter and she smiles at him as she tells him and then compliments the flowers, saying she'll bring a vase in a little while. He walks past the first two wards where visitors lounge round beds and thinks that for some reason he had assumed she would have a room to herself then sighs as he realises it's to be the same homespun style as their last meeting. There's a smell that reminds him of cabbage or custard and he loosens his collar a little by inserting a finger between it and his neck. His confidence has started to drain away and then it crumbles totally as he thinks that it should be Martine coming to visit, that it's her mother she wants now not him. He hesitates, considers turning and walking away and dumping the flowers in the nearest bin, but then there's a young man standing in front of him and immediately they both know who they are.

'Alan?'

'Yes. Emma's father?'

'Henry Stanfield. Very pleased to meet you.' He offers his hand and it's taken without hesitation. He's slightly younger than he imagined, perhaps a few years younger than Emma, and he's quietly handsome in a boyish way. To Stanfield's relief there's little evidence of his preconceived prejudices about what a secondary-school geography teacher might look like. 'It was good of you to call me – I appreciate it very much.' He gracefully shrugs off the thanks with a smile and slight shake of the head. 'And how are they both?'

'They're both fine, both doing well,' he says, gesturing an invitation with his extended arm.

He wants to tell him it's not quite so simple but instead he hesitates again and as a distraction he lowers his eyes to the flowers that he suddenly realises have no scent, and whose dreamy, vacuous faces leer up at him.

'Nice flowers. I'll go and get a vase.'

'The best I could do at this time of night. No need – the nurse is bringing one.' He feels a pulse of panic and he knows he wants the presence of this son-in-law he's never met but who as far as he can ascertain seems to bear no obvious resentment towards him.

'Well go ahead, Emma's in the first bed just round the corner.'

Then he hears himself say something incredibly clumsy and pompous – 'Do you think she's ready to receive me?' He sounds like some suitor in a Jane Austen novel about to plight his troth to one of Mrs Bennet's daughters. But he needs to know of this young man whether he should actually take those next few steps – no one will know more surely than him.

'I think she's ready,' he says and then as if encouraging a child to take its first independent step he nods his head.

'Thanks, Alan. You're coming, too?'

'In a moment. I just want to see the sister about something. I'll be back in a few minutes. You go on.'

So there's no avoiding it any longer and he straightens his back and, holding the flowers in front of him like a shield, steps into the ward where he sees his daughter sitting up in the bed cradling her son. She's so preoccupied with the baby that she doesn't see him and he can't bring himself to speak because he thinks that if he's to speak the moment will fragment and be lost to him for ever. So instead he stands and watches as her loosened hair curtains the side of her face and she lightly strokes the corner of the baby's mouth with the tip of her finger. Part of him tells himself that he should go now, just step quietly out of her line of vision and be gone, because a thousand times better to walk away and hold this moment forever in his memory than intrude and risk it being tainted with his presence. He takes a single step backwards but she looks up and sees him and he isn't sure but it's possible she understands and he stands frozen to the spot until she smiles at him. It's the slightest, quickest of smiles but it's just enough to invite him forward and he sets the flowers on the bed without comment and goes closer so he can see the child she's holding.

'He's beautiful,' he says and his voice is whispery and uncertain.

'Yes,' she says as if what he's said is a simple statement of fact and not a compliment and she keeps her eyes fixed on the baby's face as if searching it for something undiscovered on which to focus her admiration.

'And you're all right, Emma?'

'I'm fine, just a bit sore and tired.'

In that moment he would give everything he owns in the world just to be able to stretch out his hand and touch her cheek or bend over her and kiss her lightly on the top of her head. He looks at her hand and wants to feel it inside his but he holds himself still and tries to steady the beat of his heart with controlled talk.

'And have you decided on a name yet?' he asks as he looks at her in her simple nightdress and thinks she seems to him like the child she once was, his child lodged in his memory just as her child will lodge in hers.

'We're not sure – we were expecting a girl for some reason. But we're thinking of something simple like Tom.'

'Thomas?'

'No, just Tom.'

'Very good,' he says but in that second he knows that it's unlikely that she'll allow him to give the child material things so there'll be no school fees or allowances accepted, no extravagant presents at Christmas. Whether she will permit him to give him something else remains uncertain and he has no right to expect. 'I met Alan – he's very nice.'

'So you approve?'

'I approve of anything you want for yourself.'

She turns her eyes back to the baby as he wonders if he's said too much.

'Thanks for the flowers.'

'They're not the best. Wasn't much choice, I'm afraid.'

'They're fine. The nurse will put them in water later.' Then lifting her gaze from the child she asks, 'How did today go?'

'I think it went well – if that's the right word. It looks as if Maria and her family will get Connor back. Very soon, very soon.' What can he say? And how can he tell her that he has a letter for her in his pocket?

'That's good, that's really good. Thanks for your help.'

He simply smiles slightly and tries not to think of how he did his best to do nothing, as always to do what was clearly in his best interests. And now he's to be rewarded for the service he didn't give as she lifts her face towards him and asks, 'Would you like to hold him?'

'Very much.'

As she slowly passes him the child their hands briefly skim against each other. She was the last and only child he's ever held in his arms and now he holds the small lightness of her son. He cradles the bundle against the blackness of his coat. It feels more delicately beautiful but more alive than anything he's ever held and he's compelled to sit down on the edge of the bed by the sudden power of it. And then he turns his head away so that she won't see.

Afterwards in the car he sits in silence but the moment still resonates inside him as real as if the child's still in his arms. Beckett as always says nothing, driving with the same steady caution and looking constantly in his mirrors. They're almost home when his mobile phone calls and he answers it to find he's talking to a breathless Matteo on a line that's breaking up so the fragmenting words come in snatches only long enough to understand he's to come immediately to the harbour estate.

The black column of smoke is visible from a distance and as soon as they cross the river they can see the sky turning purple like a slowly spreading bruise and there's the clanging scream of sirens as they pull aside to let fire engines and marked police cars blur past. The gates to the harbour estate are flung open and the security men are frantically waving on all emergency services but stopping press vehicles. They try to turn them away, too, but Beckett shows his authorisation and they're given permission to enter. Even before he gets out of the car Stanfield can see the whole building is almost gone as parts of the roof collapse and angry new eruptions of stuttering flames break through in climbing, skittering, trembling tongues of yellow and blue. Above one breached section is a gaping mouth of red from which loudly explode showering cascades of sparks and a black snow of ash. He stands beside Beckett and recognises the primitive sense of awe that comes in the presence of uncontrolled fire and on his face he can feel the print of its heat.

'Thank God you're here,' Matteo shouts as he runs up to them, his face a bleeding transfer of colour. 'I couldn't get hold of you. Your phone was switched off.'

'I switched it off in the hospital,' Stanfield says, turning his eyes back to the fire, and for a second his own sense of shock is replaced by Matteo's words which are uttered as if he thinks he might have brought with him some miraculous capacity to extinguish infernos.

'They can't save it, they say. They won't send men in – say there's too much risk of the building collapsing. You need to speak to them,' and he pulls Stanfield by the cuff of his coat like a child pulling a parent.

'Listen,' he says, gently removing his arm from the young man's grasp, 'it's too late, it's gone and we can't put men's lives at risk. It's gone.' As if on cue there's a sudden snarl and a throaty rush of fire bursting out from above the front entrance. 'It's too late.' After a moment he asks, 'How did it start?'

'We don't know,' Matteo says. 'We don't know. How could it have happened?'

Stanfield steps a little closer to the fire and, feeling a sudden compassion for his young colleague, momentarily thinks of putting his arm around him. For all his knowledge, how very little he really knows about the world, how little he understands that sometimes the angel troubling the water might only darken the swirling pool of the past. There'll be an inquiry of course and for the rest of their bitter, corrosive history each side will blame the other and each year a new and blossoming conspiracy theory will apportion blame. The securocrats? Walters and his crew? One of the myriad groups of increasingly exposed paramilitaries? A loner somehow on the inside? Who can say for sure? When all is said and done, an act of God? Perhaps even the collective fusion of so much smouldering pain in some kind of spontaneous combustion. Who is to know? Who will ever know the truth?

As Matteo slumps against the front of the car with one hand shading his eyes from the heat Stanfield walks away in a different direction. Out on the Lough the fire dances and shimmers, teasing and painting the black canvas of the water. Away now from the others he pauses and recites the words:

> 'About, about, in reel and rout
> The death-fires danced at night;
> The water, like a witch's oils,
> Burnt green, and blue and white.'

He walks towards the bright tracery of water that is given a momentary, vivid filigree of colour. The fire makes no difference in one sense – all the files have been scanned and their contents now sleep in the hard drives of computers, out there in cyberspace beyond the reach of destruction. They weren't to know. A dark, wind-twisted cloak of mottled smoke shakes loose its inky pleats and folds over the city as he feels in his pocket for the two envelopes and takes them out. He has a daughter in this place and now he has a grandchild, a child he has been allowed to hold in his

369

arms. A black rain of ash falls silently out on the water in this berthing place where journeys started. Then he tightly crumples both envelopes and walks back to the car, a little ash settling on his collar as he goes.

Endings

THE SKY STRETCHES grey-rimmed and closed, still resistant to the first soft-edged smears of light smudging slowly in from the east. A vague, half-hearted mist lingers and drapes itself over the shapeless lattice of heather, moss and deergrass. Clumped pockets of scrawny, bone-fingered trees pleach into each other like the clasp of arthritic hands and everything is silent, trapped in the settled dreams of darkness that press against the remote stretch of bogland. The brackish water gives off no reflections but sleeps on motionless and unstirred by the low frieze of sky. Then slowly a rising breeze begins to stir the bog cotton and tussock grass. A birch tree gives a thin shiver and a complaint from its creaking joints as gradually the first sharpening spears of light begin to pierce the morning.

In an hour the vestiges of mist will have faded and light will shock everywhere into new definition. Now any searching eye might see colour if it has the patience to look – the purple moor grass, the mauve tips of heather, the black bog rush, the white beak-sedge and under the trees where the light pushes through the tangle of branches the simmer of faded foxgloves. But this is not somewhere that humans ever come. Sometimes, too, there are sounds in this place where not even sheep or cattle graze – the lisp and sudden inexplicable suck of water where no foot has trod, the liquid burble of some invisible tongue.

Then as the light slowly levers open the sky there is a new sound as dawn begins its daily skirmish with the water to conjure reedy, windblown reflections and stir the drift of bog myrtle. It's a long way off at first but as a hovering kestrel's wings thrum the air the sound grows steadily louder. And then in the first true light of morning a yellow digger trundles along the pitted track and when it reaches the edge of the bog it stops its engine and waits. Soon others will arrive with their transit vans and equipment, their thermal-imaging cameras and their marking poles. But for the moment the driver sits alone waiting in his cab and as the rising wind snakes around him he shivers against the coldness of the morning and, pressing his hands together as if he's praying, lifts them to his mouth and tries to fill them with the warmth of his breath.

A NOTE ON THE AUTHOR

David Park has written six novels and two
short-story collections and won ... He is the winner of
the Authors' Club First Novel Award, the Bass Ireland
Award for Literature and a major award by the American
Ireland ... and the Literary Fund. He lives in County
Down, Northern Ireland with his wife and three children.

A NOTE ON THE AUTHOR

David Park has written six books, most recently the hugely acclaimed *Swallowing the Sun*. He was the winner of the Authors' Club First Novel Award, the Bass Ireland Arts Award for Literature and a twice winner of the University of Ulster's McCrea Literary Award. He lives in County Down, Northern Ireland with his wife and two children.

A NOTE ON THE TYPE

The text of this book is set in Linotype Sabon, named after the type founder, Jacques Sabon. It was designed by Jan Tschichold and jointly developed by Linotype, Monotype and Stempel, in response to a need for a typeface to be available in identical form for mechanical hot metal composition and hand composition using foundry type.

Tschichold based his design for Sabon roman on a font engraved by Garamond, and Sabon italic on a font by Granjon. It was first used in 1966 and has proved an enduring modern classic.